Paul Carus

The Soul of Man

An investigation of the facts of physiological and experimental psychology

Paul Carus

The Soul of Man
An investigation of the facts of physiological and experimental psychology

ISBN/EAN: 9783337396640

Printed in Europe, USA, Canada, Australia, Japan

Cover: Foto ©Andreas Hilbeck / pixelio.de

More available books at **www.hansebooks.com**

THE SOUL OF MAN

AN

INVESTIGATION OF THE FACTS

OF

PHYSIOLOGICAL AND EXPERIMENTAL PSYCHOLOGY

BY

DR. PAUL CARUS·

———————

WITH 152 ILLUSTRATIONS AND DIAGRAMS

———————

CHICAGO, ILL.:
THE OPEN COURT PUBLISHING CO.
1891

PREFACE.

WE all know the legend of the Sphinx, who on the mountain path stops the wanderer on his way and proposes her riddle. And the riddle which she proposes to you and to me and to all mortal beings, is the same old world-problem, What is man ? Whence does he come and whither does he go ?

What is more interesting to man than his own soul ! And what, at the same time, is so mysterious, so wonderful, so marvellous ! Our pleasures and pains, our loves and hatreds, our hopes and fears, our longings, our aspirations and ideals, what is their meaning and whither do they tend ?

For us the centre of the universe lies in our own mind. Here, if anywhere, must be sought the key to the mysteries of the cosmos. And the problem of the human soul is of most vital importance ; for every practical work, every success in human life, is a part of its solution. All progress, all evolution, all growth means a development, an expanse, and an elevation of the human mind. We cannot think of any improvement of economical, political, social, scientific, or religious conditions that is not at the same time an advance in the psychical life of man.

The psychological problem is the centre of philosophy. No philosophy can evade it ; and vice versa, every presentation of the psychological problem must contain at least *in nuce* a philosophy. We cannot have a conception of the soul which is not, or does not at least suggest, at the same time, a conception of the world. The world-problem means to man the problem of the human soul.

But the importance of the problem of the soul is greater still. It supplies the basis of ethics. The prosperity, the salvation, and the health of the soul are the purpose of life ; they are the goal of all our efforts ; they are the contents of ethics and religion.

*   *   *

In delivering this book to the public I feel urged to express my deep indebtedness to Mr. Edward C. Hegeler, of La Salle, Illinois. All the work I have been doing has become possible in the way it has been done, solely through his assistance. It is not so much that he has furnished the means by which *The Open Court* and *The Monist* are supported, it is mainly the enthusiasm for a great cause, the discriminating intelligence and the strength of conviction that have created the opportunity, the aim, and the purpose for which I have been permitted to work.

Among all the ideas which have inspired Mr. Hegeler to undertake a missionary work which is best characterized as a propaganda for the Religion of Science, the most important one has been his recognition of the soul as form. This idea found a sympathetic echo in my mind ; it well agreed with my conception of form and formal thought. Formal thought furnishes the key to the comprehension of the world, because the forms of things are that element which makes the things what they are ; and the laws of form being the same in the forms of the objective world as well as in the forms of subjective thought, are the bridge which overarches the apparent chasm that opens up between the cognizing subject and the cognized object, between the soul and the universe.

The idea of form is not a mere speculative theory. Like all theories that are correct, it is of eminently practical importance. The practical importance of the conception of the soul as form throws light upon all religious and ethical truths, and most so upon the problem of life after death ;* indeed it yields a scientific

---

* The term "life after death" being a positive expression seems to be preferable to the negative term "immortality." The latter has the advantage of being commonly accepted, but this advantage is intimately interwoven with the disadvantage that the errors of the old view are attached to it.

explanation of the truth contained in the religious idea of immortality which is the most powerful factor in the aspirations of our race.

* * *

It is apparent that the ideal of a Religion of Science cannot be realized before the problem of the human soul in its main features at least has been solved by scientific inquiry on the ground of the exact data of verified and verifiable facts. Many diligent workers have labored and are still laboring in the field of psychology, but the results of their labors have not as yet been compared, critically sifted, and collected in one work.

If a work of this kind had existed, the author would perhaps never have ventured to write the present book. There are innumerable Psychologies, innumerable Physiologies, innumerable Anatomies, and floods of pamphlets discussing the many problems and incidents of experimental psychology. But there is not one book in any language as far as I know, in which all the facts of these various branches of science are gathered and presented in their connection. There is not one book in which the problem of the human soul is treated scientifically in its philosophical, ethical, and religious importance. A book of this kind is a want, which the author has tried to fill.

Although the present book is in a certain sense a review of the present state of investigation, it is not a mere compilation of the labors of others. Not only is the method new in which the subject-matter in its connection with philosophy and ethics is presented, but also several important ideas and interpretations of facts have been added by the author. Some of them will perhaps readily find recognition. Others appear to be in conflict with the most prominent living authorities ; thus, for instance, the explanation of the nature of pleasure and pain (pp. 338–345). Others still are hypotheses the value of which will depend mainly upon the light that may be gained through future investigations. Such are the theory concerning the seat of consciousness (pp. 194–

208) and the problem of sex-formation (pp. 234-237). As not the least important feature of the book I consider its philosophical foundation, which (if the author's views are sound) corroborates the unitary conception of the world, commonly called Monism, or, more exactly expressed, Monistic Positivism.

The field of psychological problems is large, and the difficulties of the subject are great. Yet the author has tried to present the different topics with conciseness and with clearness. No trouble has been spared in collecting and critically sifting the latest results of anatomical and physiological investigations from the highest authorities in this field of inquiry; and pains have been taken to reproduce from the best sources the most instructive illustrations of the various nervous tissues and cerebral organs for the explanation of their action.

It is to be expected that this book will not satisfy the expectations of many, for two reasons. First because if a man possesses prejudices, his prejudices will certainly be strongest with reference to the problem of the human soul. Differences of opinion must be anticipated. Nevertheless, if this book does not present the favorite ideas of some among my readers, they are kindly reminded that it is not my purpose to propound transcendental or metaphysical speculations, but to arrange and systematize facts. Whatever speculations a man may hold he must be aware that speculations must never collide with facts; and so the book will perhaps after all be found to be useful. The second reason why the book will not satisfy the expectations of many might be the insufficiency of the author to do full justice to so great an undertaking, which demands not only extensive reading but also great accuracy and precision of judgment. Wherever I have failed either in the former or in the latter, either by not taking notice of important investigations of others or in judging wrongly concerning the importance of the facts offered, I can only say in excuse that I have endeavored to do my best. *In magnis voluisse sat est.*

THE AUTHOR.

TABLE OF CONTENTS.

LIST OF CUTS AND DIAGRAMS.

FEELING AND MOTION.

In physiological text-books there often occurs the misleading expression "change of consciousness into will" or of "feeling into motion." This appears to suggest the interconvertibility of motion and feeling and has prompted philosophers to propound mechanical explanations of the origin of feeling. All these explanations were failures, for the foundation upon which they rested, namely, the interconvertibility of motion and feeling is an error. Motion and feeling are radically different in their nature. Motion can never be transformed into feeling, nor can feeling be transformed into motion.

Before we proceed let us note that feeling and motion, although quite different in their nature, are not separate realms of existence. There are no feelings that exist by themselves; feelings are states that accompany certain motions. Says Ribot in his "Psychology of Attention" : *

" . . . . The intermission in an apparent continuity alone renders possible any long attention. If we keep one of our eyes fixed upon any single point, after a while our vision becomes confused ; a cloud is formed between the object and ourselves, and finally we see nothing at all. If we lay our hand flat upon a table, motionless, and without pressure (for pressure itself is a movement), by slow degrees the sensation wears off, and finally

---

* English translation published by the Open Court Publishing Company, p. 17.

disappears. *The reason is, that there is no perception without movement, be it ever so weak.* Every sensorial organ is at the same
time both sensitive and motory. As soon as absolute immo-
bility eliminates one of the two elements (motility), the function of
the other after a while is rendered null. In a word, movement is
the condition of the change, which is one of the conditions of consciousness."

For the sake of clearness we shall distinguish between feeling and sensation. By sensation we understand a process of nervous irritation which is perceived.
By feeling we understand the state of awareness only,
that accompanies the nervous commotion of a sensation. Sensation is a certain motion accompanied with
feeling. Feeling is that part of the sensation which is
no motion; the word feeling signifies that intangible
something which, we trust, every animal being knows
from experience. Feeling is entirely different from
motion and can be expressed in terms of neither matter nor motion. Feeling is not material and it is not
mechanical, i. e., it is not motion. It constitutes
something *sui generis.*

By saying that feeling is neither material nor mechanical, we do not maintain that it exists by itself.
Feeling is real as much as are matter and motion. In
contradistinction to the objective reality of material
things, we may call it subjective reality. Its existence
is not proved by external activity but by the internal
state of awareness. Its reality accordingly is most
immediate and direct, so that it would be ridiculous to
doubt it. Indeed there have been philosophers who
doubted the existence of the material universe and its
mechanical action, yet these skeptics did not deny the
existence of feeling.

Professor Clifford in his excellent essay on the 'Na-

ture of Things' in themselves, distinguishes between
object and eject. He says:

> " There is the external or objective order in which the sensa-
> tion of letting go is followed by the sight of a falling object and the
> sound of its fall. The objective order, *qua* order, is treated by
> physical science which investigates the uniform relations of *objects*
> in time and space.
>
> " However remote the inference of physical science, the thing
> inferred is always a part of me, a possible set of changes in any
> consciousness bound up in the objective order with other known
> changes."

The objective order is represented by physical
science as a system of motions that follow one another
according to strict laws. What now is an eject?
Professor Clifford says :

> " There are, however, some inferences which are profoundly
> different from those of physical science. When I come to the con-
> clusion that *you* are conscious and that there are objects in *your*
> consciousness similar to those in mine, I- am not inferring any
> actual or possible feelings of my own, but *your* feelings, which are
> not, and cannot, by any possibility become objects in my conscious-
> ness.
>
> " . . . . These inferred existences are in the very act of infer-
> ence *thrown out* of my consciousness, recognized as outside of it as
> *not* being a part of me. I propose, accordingly, to call these inferred
> existences *ejects*, things thrown out of my consciousness to dis-
> tinguish them from objects, things presented in my consciousness,
> phenomena."

Let us represent the processes observable in the
objective world by Italic letters. What we call things
or occurrences are either simultaneous or successive groups of *A B C*, *R S T*, etc. Among these
groups there is one *I K L* which is called our body ;
and some motions of *I K L* are accompanied with feelings. Now for the sake of distinction let us represent
feelings with Greek letters. We find that certain *I K L*

are accompanied by $\iota \varkappa \lambda$.* A certain motion is accompanied by a corresponding feeling, so that as far as certain activities of our body are concerned, there appears a perfect parallelism. If we consider our body as a mechanism, we find only motions and nothing but motions. The chain $I K L$ is uninterrupted. If we consider ourselves as pure mind and nothing but feeling, we find only states of consciousness and nothing else. We find no motion.

Our fellow-men, and also animals, being endowed, as we believe, with feeling, are, so far as we can observe, other bodies, and their lives represent such chains as $I' K' L'$, $I'' K'' L''$, etc., which, as we suppose, are accompanied by $\iota' \varkappa' \lambda'$, $\iota'' \varkappa'' \lambda''$, etc. These series of $\iota' \varkappa' \lambda'$, $\iota'' \varkappa'' \lambda''$, etc., are not directly observable. They are what Clifford calls "ejects."

If physiologists say that a change of motion into feeling takes place, they can mean only that a certain motion is transferred, which now is and now is not accompanied with feeling. It is, however, a loose way of speaking. Instead of saying :

$$H\ I\ K\ L\ M\ N$$
$$\iota\ \varkappa\ \lambda$$

where H is the motion producing a sensory irritation and M muscular motion, N the movement of an object effected by muscular motion, $I K L$ being accompanied by $\iota \varkappa \lambda$, they say :

$$H\ \iota\ \varkappa\ \lambda\ M\ N.$$

Thus they jump from one series into the other.

* The method of employing a series of Italic letters to express objective realities, and a series of Greek letters to express subjective realities or feelings, ($A B C$, $R S T$, representing objects, $I K L$ our own bodies, $\iota \varkappa \lambda$ states of consciousness) was suggested to me by reading an article of Professor Mach on the Analysis of Sensations. However, Professor Mach's application is different.

The method is incorrect and can be considered pardonable only in so far as $\iota \; \varkappa \; \lambda$ appear to us for certain purposes of much greater consequence than $I \; K \; L$. The group $I \; K \; L$ is called soul or mind only in so far as it is accompanied with $\iota \; \varkappa \; \lambda$.

The question now arises : How can we account for the sudden appearance of feeling. It cannot be explained as a transformation of motion. The interconvertibility of motion and feeling must be rejected, and Clifford, in contradistinction to all philosophers who try to explain everything from matter and motion, most emphatically declares :

"To say : ' Up to this point science can explain,—here the soul* steps in,' is not to say what is untrue, but to talk nonsense."

Clifford adds :

The question, " Is the mind * a force?" is to be condemned by similar considerations. . . . . Force is an abstraction relating to objective facts . . . . and cannot possibly be the same thing as an eject, another man's consciousness.

But the question, " Do the changes in a man's consciousness *run parallel* with the changes of motion, and therefore with the forces of his brain ? " is a real question and not *prima facie* nonsense.

Clifford affirms this question. He maintains that there is a correspondence between body and mind,* as there is between a written and a spoken sentence. There is a correspondence of element to element, each written letter although quite a different thing from a sound, corresponds to a certain sound. The

* Soul and mind are used here as a synonym of the sum total of feeling or of consciousness, i. e., concentrated feeling. They represent the series $\iota \varkappa \lambda$, $\iota' \varkappa' \lambda'$, $\iota'' \varkappa'' \lambda''$, etc.

Some understand by such words as soul, mind, etc., mere states of consciousness $\iota \varkappa \lambda$, some the objective nerve structures and their functions $I K L$, others still groups of facts consisting of both series $I_\iota K_\varkappa L_\lambda$. It is apparent that a difference in the usage of terms without further indication as to their meaning, must be productive of great confusion.

written sentence as well as the spoken sentence " are built up together, in nearly the same way. . . . . The two complex products are as wholly unlike as the elements are, but the manner of their complication is the same."

Now we know that certain motions are accompanied by consciousness, and that others, so far as we can see, are not. How can we account for the appearance and disappearance of consciousness ?

We know that certain dim feelings become conscious by concentration. The mechanical process of nerve activity gives us the key to this explanation, for we have different degrees of feeling corresponding to different degrees of intensity produced through a concentration of nerve activity. Consciousness rises from simple feelings. But whence does feeling come ?

Feelings must be considered as a complex of certain elements, which we call "the elements of feeling." The single letters ι and $\varkappa$ and λ and μ also ρ, σ, τ are elements of feeling. We have no right to assume that they exist by themselves, but must suppose that they accompany the elements of motion I, K, L, M, R, S, T, etc. Certain combinations of the elements of feeling produce actual feelings, just as certain combinations of feelings produce consciousness. If the concentration of consciousness is destroyed or for the time abolished, feelings may and under special conditions (as, for instance, in sleep or in hypnotic states) will continue. If a frog is decapitated the ganglions of the medulla will for a considerable time continue to feel. In like manner, if that combination which produces actual feeling is disturbed or destroyed, feeling will disappear, but the elements of feeling will continue.

Unless we consider every act of feeling a special creation of supernatural powers, a break in the continuity of nature, we are inevitably driven to the conclusion that *all* series *A B C, I K L, R S T,* etc., etc., are accompanied by $\alpha \beta \gamma$, $\iota \varkappa \lambda$, $\rho \sigma \tau$, etc, etc. All elements of objective reality are inseparably united with the corresponding elements of subjective reality, and the latter are those facts which under special conditions and in special combinations unite into feelings.

From the monistic standpoint we must look upon nature as being endowed with the potentialities of feelings. Every natural process we suppose to be animated with the elementary germs of psychic life, with that something of which our very simplest feelings are exceedingly complex combinations.

Nature cannot be considered as a dead machinery; it is alive throughout and every process of objective activity must be supposed to be animated by the elements of that subjective phase of life which in the human brain appears as consciousness.

Feeling, accordingly, is a special form of the elements of feeling, and the problem of the origin of feeling from this standpoint is to be stated as follows :

What is the molecular combination, and what is its mode of action that is accompanied by feeling?

This question has not as yet been answered, and physiology is very far still from solving the problem satisfactorily in all its details. The most important features only of the process are known, at least in coarse outlines.

* * *

The process taking place in the nervous system may briefly be described thus : An impression of the surrounding world affects the skin or one of the sense-organs of an animal organism, and produces a shock upon the sensory nerve-fibres. This shock is transmitted to the ganglion where it causes an action in the gray nerve-cells; this action of the ganglion is further transmitted to the motor nerve and when it reaches the end of the motor nerve a discharge takes place which causes the muscle to contract, thus producing muscular motion. Along the whole line from the impression received to the muscular contractions there is an uninterrupted chain of motions.

Physiological psychology, inaugurated by Fechner and elaborated by many great scientists of all nationalities, is busy at work to measure the subtilest movements of nerve-activity. Says George J. Romanes in his Lecture, "Mind and Body":

"If, by means of a suitable apparatus, a muscle is made to record its own contraction, we find that during all the time it is in contraction, it is undergoing a vibratory movement at the rate of about nine pulsations per second. What is the meaning of this movement? The meaning is that the act of will in the brain, which serves as a stimulus to the contraction of the muscle and is accompanied by a vibratory movement in the muscle, is accompanied by a vibratory movement in the gray matter of the brain; that this movement is going on at the rate of nine pulsations per second; and that the muscle is giving a separate and distinct contraction in response to every one of these nervous pulsations....

A sensory nerve which at the surface of its expansion is able to respond differently to differences of musical pitch, of temperature and even of color, is probably able to vibrate very much more rapidly even than this [viz., one thousand beats per second]. We are not, indeed, entitled to conclude that the nerves of special sense vibrate in actual unison, or synchronize, with these external sources of stimulation; but we are, I think, bound to conclude that they must vibrate in some numerical proportion to them (else we should not perceive objective differences in sound, temperature, or color) .... there is a constant ratio between the amount of agitation produced in a sensory nerve and the intensity of the corresponding sensation . . . ."

So far as we can observe a process of nerve-activity, there is no change of motion into feeling and of feeling back into motion. There is no such break in the chain of mechanical causes and effects. Yet in a certain part of the chain of mechanical causation, the motions are accompanied by feelings; and we have sufficient reasons to believe that the place where motions are accompanied by feelings is the ganglion.

We return once more to Prof. Clifford. We followed his arguments and adopted his conclusions except the very last inference he makes. Prof. Clifford concludes his essay with the following consideration. He says:

"That element of which, as we have seen, even the simplest feeling is a complex, I shall call *mind stuff*."

Clifford solves the question in the following manner :

"*As* the physical configuration of my cerebral image of the object

"*Is to* the physical configuration of the object,

"*So is* my perception of the object (the object regarded as complex of my feelings)

"*To* the thing in itself."

Clifford sums up his doctrine :

"The universe, then, consists entirely of mind-stuff. . . .

"Matter is a mental picture in which mind-stuff is the thing represented.

"Reason, intelligence, and volition, are properties of a complex which is made up of elements themselves not rational, not intelligent, not conscious."

Clifford in speaking of similar views propounded by Kant, Wundt, and Tyndall, says in an adjoined note :

"The question is one in which it is peculiarly difficult to make out precisely what another man means, and even what one means oneself."

*

The conclusion of Clifford's arguments that the universe consists entirely of mind-stuff, I must confess, appears to me very abrupt and I cannot admit it. Although in accord with all the rest, I cannot follow Clifford to the end. It may be that I fail "to make out precisely" what he means, but if allowed to make a conclusion of my own in close connection with his reasoning as above described, I would say :

The thing in itself is the inner, i. e., subjective reality, which appears (so as to become perceptible) as motions or outer, i. e. objective, reality. *

The following may be added by way of explanation : The world is as it is, one indivisible whole. All its objective reality is throughout combined with subjective reality. The objective reality we call matter, and its activity motions. The subjective reality we call elements of feeling ; and the compounds resulting therefrom are actual feelings and consciousness. It is this subjective reality alone which Clifford defined as "mind-stuff,", and when speaking of the universe as it really exists, he improperly limits its reality to mind-stuff, as if the objective reality, which is represented in our brains by what we call motions, were a mere illusion. It is true, as Clifford says, that "matter is a mental picture"; but it is not true that it represents "mind-stuff." Matter is no *mere* mental picture ; it represents a certain feature of reality, viz., all that can affect sensibility. The term 'matter' is the most general abstract of its kind and cannot be expressed in terms of "mind-stuff," for it represents a certain set of experiences which Clifford has purposely excluded from his conception "mind-stuff."

* Clifford uses " thing in itself " in a peculiar yet quite legitimate sense, and here we follow Clifford.

Man's method of understanding the processes of nature is that of abstraction. We confine our attention to that feature alone which is to be investigated and we eliminate in our thought the others. Thus, when enquiring into the laws of mathematics, we confine our attention to the mere form of space, and deal with non-material points, lines, planes, and solids. These non-material points, lines, planes, and solids are not untrue (as Mill imagined), but they represent one abstract feature only which can never be found by itself. The same is true of all our concepts. Every concept is formed for some purpose, and every concept by serving one purpose necessarily becomes one-sided. It leaves out of sight those features of the object represented which do not range within the scope of its purpose. We may invent names intended to cover the whole reality, subjective as well as objective, but these names will become inappropriate as soon as employed for some other purpose.

If I consider an object, I may inquire into the material of which it consists, or into the body's form, or its motions. For instance, a chemist making a spectrum analysis of the sun, leaves out of sight the size of the sun, its shape and motion. He confines his attention to the rays, the undulations of which appear in the spectrum as colors and lines. The Frauenhofer lines indicate the material of the incandescent body which emits the rays. An astronomer, however, investigating its shape,—say, he wants to know whether it is a perfect sphere or flattened at the poles— does not care about the substances of which the sun consists. And supposing he investigates the sun's motion in its relation to the milky way, he disregards entirely substance and form, he treats the sun as if it were a mathematical point. All these treatments have in common the method of abstraction. The astronomer in his calculation of the motion of the sun must not, and certainly he does not, think that the sun is a mathematical point, although this conception fits into his calculation and remains correct so far as the purpose of his abstraction is concerned. Accordingly, for every abstraction we have made, we must bear in mind two things : 1) the purpose it has to serve ; and 2) that the totality of things from which abstractions can be made, is one indivisible whole. In short we must not forget that abstractions are only one-sided views of things.

Not only abstractions but every single word is made for a certain purpose. In reality objects have no separate existence ; they exist in a constant flux, and the full and exhaustive comprehension of one object would include a comprehension of the whole universe. If this be true at all, it is most true of ourselves. The human soul is nothing more nor less than a certain action of the universe upon one part of the universe and the reaction following thereupon.*

There are philosophers who are greatly disappointed about what they consider a deficiency of our intellect ; viz., that we cannot view the whole at once in all its details. The relativity of knowledge has unnecessarily been lamented. There is as little occasion for disappointment in this feature of cognition as in the fact that our vision must always depend upon the stand-

---

* See " Fundamental Problems," p. 147 : " Knowledge becomes possible only when we fix certain percepts and give their relative stability. . . . . . It is as if we sat in an express train and were looking at the landscape flitting by us. The picture taken as a whole swims indistinctly before our eyes. If we wish to get a clear idea of the situation, we must allow the eye to rest on some one object, neglecting the others," etc.; and p. 149 : " In reality the whole world is a part of our being," etc.

point from which we view things, and that if we look at
a thing from one side, we cannot at the same time look
at it from the other. Why, let us be patient and look
at things first from this and then from the other side.
But we must not imagine that the one side only is
true reality, the noumenal part of nature, the *Ding an.
sich*, and the other is a mere illusion. Nor must we
declare that both are illusions, and that true reality is
something unknowable between both. Reality is everything that is or can become object of experience ; both
abstracts accordingly represent something that is real.
Reality is not in the one, if considered alone and by
itself, nor in the other if considered alone and by itself, but in the entire whole. The one as well as the
other is a part of reality.

We can under no circumstances suppress or eliminate either mind (elements of feeling) or matter. Nor
can we express the one in the terms of the other,
for the simple reason, that each concept is an entirely
different abstract containing nothing of the other.
Nevertheless both are parts of, and are abstracted
from, reality. What we call motion represents certain features of our experience. Whatever motions
may be in the conception of beings organized otherwise than we are, our motion experiences remain
marks representative of real processes of some kind;
and feelings are certainly no less actual than motions.

We may represent motion or we may represent
mind as the basis of the world or we may conceive
them as being on equal terms.

(1) On the one hand, motion may be conceived as
the objective realization (a kind of revelation) in
which the activity of the elements of feeling appears.

(2) On the other hand, motion may be conceived

as the substratum which carries the more ethereal elements of feeling.

(3) If neither matter nor motion is to be considered the one as the basis of the other, reality, as it exists in itself, may be conceived as a great interacting something, in which the effects of all the surrounding parts upon one special part, an atom or a monad, in so far as this part is concerned, appear as what we have defined as an element of feeling; while the effects of this special part, of every atom or monad upon the rest, in so far as the totality is concerned, appear as motion.

It is indifferent which view we take. All three conceptions are fundamentally the same, although if worked out they would show a difference in terminology that must let them appear as contradictory systems. Upon the whole I should give preference to the third conception as being least one-sided and most unequivocal in representing the Oneness of all reality.

Matter and mind (the elements of feeling) are to be considered as one—not the same, but one. They are as inseparable as are the two sides of a sheet of paper. If we look at it from the mind side, its activity represents itself as elements of feeling and all kinds and degrees of actual feelings. If we look at it from the matter side, its activity represents itself as motions, or as all kinds of potential and kinetic energy.

*   *   *

There is one point which needs further elucidation at least in a few words. Clifford says:

"Reason, intelligence, and volition are properties of a complex which is made up of elements themselves not rational, not intelligent, not conscious."

This is true; for we arrive at the conclusion that

the not-feeling elements of feeling develop into feeling and the not-rational monad develops into rational man. Yet we must at the same time emphasize that the formal laws according to which these not-feeling, not-rational elements combine into higher structures endowed with feeling and reason, are also a part of reality. The formal laws which are the *raison d'être* of all cosmic order, are omnipresent in every particle that exists ; and we can learn to understand that noth-. ing will stir, or change, or be, unless it be in conformity to the law of causation which is the law of change, and to the laws of form in general.*

The world it is true is not rational in its elements ; but the laws of the world are the prototype of rationality itself. Human reason and all wisdom of any possible rational being develops from these conditions and remains in accordance with the formal laws of the cosmos. Human reason is conformity to, it is an expression of the order of, the All. The order of the All contains the possibility of developing reason. We have perhaps a right to call the elements of reality *not-rational*, but we commit a grave mistake when calling the All *irrational*. For the elements of being contain the origin and condition of all reason. Reason ceases to be reason as soon as it does not agree with reality.

* See the chapter " Form and Formal Thought " in *Fundamental Prob-lems*, p. 26.

IS THE SOUL A MECHANISM?

THE question has often been proposed, Is Man a Machine, and more especially is the Human Soul a Mechanism? If we understand by soul not the feeling that accompanies certain physiological processes of the brain, but the physiological activity of the brain itself, there can be no doubt that every thought represented by the motion of this or that cerebral structure, every wish that irritates these or those ganglionic motor cells, whether the wish be suppressed or not, every act of will which not being suppressed by stronger inhibitory impulses passes into motion—in short all the innumerable motions of brain-activity take place strictly in agreement with mechanical principles. Certain motions are accompanied with feelings, while others are not accompanied with feelings (only with elements of feelings). Feeling, however, is not the product of a force; it is not manufactured out of energy; its appearance does not depend upon the disappearance of a portion of motion; it does not rise in exchange for motion.

Leibnitz says:

" We are constrained to confess that perception and whatever depends upon it, are inexplainable upon mechanical principles; that is by reference to forms and movements. If we could imagine a machine the operations of which would manufacture thoughts, feelings, and perceptions, and could think of it as enlarged in all its proportions, so that we could go into it as into a mill, even then we would find in it nothing but particles jostling each other, and never anything by which perception could be explained."

Locke expresses a similar idea :

" Body, as far as we can conceive, being able only to strike and affect body ; and motion, according to the utmost reach of our ideas, being able to produce nothing but motion, so that when we allow it to produce pleasure or pain, or the idea of color or sound, we are fain to quit our reason, go beyond our ideas, and attribute it wholly to the good pleasure of our maker."

Accordingly, if by soul we understand feelings, perceptions, and states of consciousness, we cannot say that man's soul is a mechanism. But feelings, perceptions, and states of consciousness do not exist of themselves. They represent one certain side of a process only, the other side being a certain physiological activity ; and although there is no sense in speaking of the mechanism of a feeling, there is sense in speaking of the mechanism of the physiological process which subjectively considered appears as a feeling.

*   *   *

The soul has often been compared to a piano, but the simile is inappropriate because it does not explain the most important thing, viz., the mechanism of its functions. Mr. Spencer, accordingly, welcomes the comparison of the soul to a piano as an evidence of the inscrutability of psychical processes. He says:

"Ideas are like the successive chords and cadences brought out from a piano, which successively die away as other ones are sounded. And it would be as proper to say that these passing chords and cadences thereafter exist in the piano, as it is proper to say that passing ideas thereafter exist in the brain. In the one case as in the other, the actual existence is the structure which under like conditions again evolves like combinations. . . . . The existence in the subject of any other ideas than those which are passing, is pure hypothesis absolutely without evidence whatever."

Dr. Henry Maudsley who quotes this passage in his "Physiology of Mind," p. 70, adds :

"This analogy, when we look into it, seems more captivating, than it is complete. What about the performer in the case of the piano and in case of the brain respectively? Is not the performer a not unimportant element, and necessary to the completeness of the analogy? The passing chords and cadences would have small chance of being brought out by the piano if they were not previously in his mind. Where, then, in the brain is the equivalent of the harmonic conceptions in the performer's mind? If Mr. Spencer supposes that the individual's mind, his spiritual entity, is detached from the brain, and plays upon its nervous plexuses, as the performer plays upon the piano, his analogy is complete ; but if not, then he has furnished an analogy which those who do take that view may well thank him for. There is this difference between the passing chords and cadences of the piano and the passing chords and cadences in the brain—and it is of the essence of the matter—that, in the former case, the chords and cadences do pass and leave no trace of themselves behind in the structure of the piano ; while, in the latter case, they do not pass or die away without leaving most important after-effects in the structure of the brain ; whence does arise in due time a considerable difference between a cultivated piano and a cultivated human brain, and whence probably have arisen, in the progress of development through the ages, the differences between the brain of a primeval savage and the brain of Mr. Spencer . . . . With the brain, function makes faculty ; not so with the piano."

If you put to me, the question for instance: How much is five times five? I shall answer Twenty-five. The physiological process which represents in my brain the act of perceiving the question and answering it, is perfectly mechanical. There is a memory structure which when innervated says, "Five times five is twenty-five." If any one asks, "How much is five times five?" it is this question which as soon as it is perceived, innervates the memory structure "five times five is twenty-five"; and possibly it awakens many other memories associated therewith. I may think of the teacher who first taught me arithmetic ; or the picture of my multiplication table may appear before my eyes. The answer "five times five is twenty-five" is under ordinary circumstances accompanied with feeling or consciousness.

Not every instance is so simple. There are of course mental processes that are much more complicated, but there is not one in which the motions that take place in the brain can be thought of as being not strictly in accordance with mechanical laws either molecular or molar. The poet's fictions, no less than the schemes of the inventor, are strictly regulated by the mechanics and statics of mind-activity.

*   .*   *

There is a peculiar feature in soul-life which consists in the limitation of consciousness. Similarly as in vision only one object at a time can be in the central field of vision, viz., in the yellow spot where vision is most intense, so in consciousness one idea only, one combination of ideas, one perception, or a thought concerning a perception, one aim, or one activity can at one time fill this centre of mental life. When several ideas are awakened, that which at the time is strongest will attain a state of consciousness. As soon as it has been attended to, it naturally loses its interest, and another idea, that in the mean time has become the strongest will follow. A combination of both may take place and thus new thoughts, discoveries, inventions, ideals, may grow from such beginnings.

Dr. Montgomery in a criticism of the work done by *The Open Court*,* introduces the term "hypermechanical" in order to explain the selective faculty represented by the piano player. The term is not ad-

* See Nos. 156 and 157 of *The Open Court.*

missible because that "selective faculty" so-called is perfectly mechanical. The chief progress modern psychology has made, is, that it is no more in need of what Dr. Montgomery calls "the selective faculty of hypermechanical impulses."

* * *

The view that motions produce nothing but motion while feelings sometimes accompany certain motions, should not be conceived in any dual sense. Feelings and motions run parallel to each other, and where we do not meet with actual feelings we suppose the presence of the elements of feeling. But this parallelism would be most wonderful indeed if it were a true parallelism consisting of two different and distinct lines. The simplest conception of the case is the monistic view, which considers the parallelism as an identity. Both motion and feeling are abstract conceptions. A motion exists of itself no more than a feeling. The reality from which the ideas motion and feeling have been abstracted is one inseparable whole, which if viewed as an objective process appears as motion, and if viewed from the subjective side appears as feeling. Feelings can only be felt, not seen; but if we *could* see them, we might observe the elements of feeling wherever motion takes place.

Fechner seems to have hit the mark, when he compared feeling and motion to the inside and the outside curves of a circle; they are entirely different and yet the same. The inside curve is concave, the outside curve is convex. If we construct rules relating first to the concave inside and then to the convex outside, we shall notice a parallelism in the formulas; yet this parallelism will appear only in the abstractions which have been made of one and the same thing from a different aspect. It results from making two different abstractions. The abstract conceptions form two parallel systems, but the real thing can be represented as parallel only in the sense that it is parallel to itself; it is the parallelism of identity. There is but one line, and this one line is concave if viewed from the inside, if viewed from the outside convex.

The elements of feeling do not by simple addition make up actual feelings, but by appearing in certain relations. But the intensities as well as the qualities of feelings depend upon special conditions, and the proportions between perceptions and their respective irritations have within certain limits been measured with great exactness.

Weber found that in most cases the quantity of sensation is proportional to the logarithm of the quantity of irritation. Thus an irritation expressed by 10 corresponds to a sensation expressed by 1. The irritation 100 would not give 10 x 1, but only 2; viz., the logarithm of 100. The increase in the quantity of sensation can be represented by a curve, the abscissas of which are the gradually increasing irritations, while the values of the sensations are found in the ordinates. The perceptible increment of sensation depends also upon the relative quantity of the increase of the irritation; and the measurement of this "perceptible increment," as Weber calls it, has been a most fruitful method for the formulation of the laws of psycho-physics.

The value of sensations under certain conditions reaches zero. If the value of the irritation becomes equal to 1, the sensation reaches what Weber calls the threshold of perception. On and below the threshold of perception, sensation ceases, i. e., it is no more noticeable, its value is zero.

Psychophysics was founded by Weber, to whom the idea had been suggested by Herbart's proposition to treat psychological phenomena according to mathematical methods, so that we should acquire the data for comprehending the statics and mechanics of mental operations. Weber's method has been perfected by Fechner, Volkmann, Appel, and many other investigators. While Weber's law that the perceptible increment of sensation is proportional to the quantity of irritation had to be restricted to certain limits, from which the greatest and the smallest intensities are excluded, and while many conclusions derived from psychophysical experiments may have been erroneous, or at least mixed up with errors; the whole science of psychophysics was fully justified in many respects. The very exceptions that offered themselves were in the end found to be the strongest corroborations of the soundness of Weber's law as well as his methods.*

* See *Vorträge über Psychophysik von Dr. E. Mach. Oesterreichische Zeitschrift für praktische Heilkunde.* 1863.

THE ORIGIN OF MIND.

I. WHAT IS MIND?

WE must distinguish between two kinds of facts; viz., given facts or data, and deduced facts or inferences. With regard to the facts of soul-life we recognise that the former class, that of given facts, necessarily consists of states of consciousness only; they are feelings of any description, varying greatly in their nature. They are different in the rhythmical forms of their vibrations, in their intensity, and in their distinctness. The latter class, that of inferences, is deduced from the former, and serves no other purpose than that of explanation. This class is mostly representative of external facts, and knowledge of external facts exists only in so far as external facts are represented in deduced facts. What a thinking being would call external facts is nothing but the contents of certain deduced facts.

Deduced facts, and among them the conception of external facts (wherever they exist), have been produced by the effort of accounting for given facts—viz., the elementary data of consciousness and their relations. Deduced facts are the interpretation of given facts. They are, so to say, conjectures concerning their causes as well as their interconnections.

The organised totality of deduced facts, as it is developed in feeling substance, is called mind. Feel-

•

ings are the condition of mind. From feelings alone
mind can grow. But there is a difference between feelings and mind. Feelings develop into mind, they grow
to be mind by being interpreted, by becoming representative. Representative feelings are mind. Accordingly, we characterise mind as the representativeness of feelings.

Although deduced facts are an interpretation of
given facts, this "interpretation" is not expressly
designed. These inferences from given facts are not
invented with a premeditated purpose; they are not
constructed with foresight or intention. Deduced facts
grow naturally and spontaneously from given facts,
which are the elements of sense-activity. There is
not an agent that oversees their fabrication; there is
not a devising "subject" that surmises the existence
of external facts and thus matures their conception
into deduced facts. Deduced facts are rather the natural product of a certain group of given facts. Deduced facts issue from a co-operation of a number of
feelings. They are the result of an organisation of
certain repeated sense-impressions which produce a
disposition not only to receive sense-impressions of
the same kind, but also to react upon them in a certain
way. Mind is not the factor that organised the given
facts of mere sense-impressions so that they became
representations. There was no mind as long as feelings remained unorganised. Feelings acquire meaning; and as soon as they have acquired meaning they
are what we call "deduced facts," representations—
especially representations of external facts. Deduced
facts are the elements of mind; and mind is not their
root, but their fruit.

II. SUBJECTIVE AND OBJECTIVE EXISTENCE.

The whole domain of mind-activity (i. e., of the representativeness of feelings) is called subjective; while the totality of all facts that are represented in the mind is called objective. Subjective existence consists of feelings and of states of consciousness; objective existence is represented as things that are in motion. Motion and feeling are quite different things, yet in spite of their radical difference experience teaches us that both spheres are intimately interwoven. Subjective existence constantly draws upon objective existence. Not only do states of consciousness exist as they are by virtue merely of the objects represented, but also that group of facts called our body, the action of which appears in a constant connection with and as a condition of our consciousness, is kept in running order only through a constant renewal of its waste products out of the resources of objective existence.

We distinguish between our body and external facts; but the boundary between both provinces is not distinct. There is constantly an exchange of substance taking place, proving that our body is in kind not different from the substance of which external facts consist. It must be regarded as a group of the same kind as external facts, existing in a constant interaction with and among the external facts. In other words, the body of the thinking subject is an object in the objective world.

Concerning the subjective sphere of existence we recognise that consciousness does not act uninterruptedly; there are moments when consciousness is lost. If they are normal, we call them sleep; if they are abnormal, swoons or trances. Former conscious states can be revived; they form a chain of memories which is very limited in comparison with the extension of the objective world. There is a time in the past beyond which our memory does not reach. Moreover we have reason to believe, that there will be a time when the chain of conscious states will be broken forever. This consummation is called death. In short the subjective world is transient; it grows by degrees; its existence is very precarious; it flickers like a candle in the wind and will disappear again. The objective world however is eternal, it is indestructible. Experience teaches that it constantly undergoes changes, but that in its totality it is imperishable.

The objective world is in a certain sense a part of the subject. In another sense, we must say that the subject is a part of the objective world. Indeed these two sentences represent the same truth, only viewed from two standpoints. The subjective world being transient and the objective world being eternal, the question presents itself, "How does the subject originate in or among the objects of the objective world?"

The problem is complicated and we must approach it step by step. First, we are inevitably driven to the conclusion, that the subjective world of feelings forms an inseparable whole together with a special combination of certain facts of the objective world, namely our body. It originates with this combination, and disappears as soon as that combination breaks to pieces. And, secondly, we must assume that the conditions for building up such material dispositions as have the power of developing the subjectivity of consciousness are an intrinsic quality of the objective

world. Subjectivity cannot originate out of nothing;
it must be conceived as the product of a co-operation
of certain elements which are present in the objective
world. In other words, the elements of the subjective
world are features that we must suppose to be inseparably united with the elements of the objective world,
which are represented in our mind as motions. This
leads to the conclusion that feeling has to be considered
not as a simple but as a complex phenomenon. Feelings as explained in the first chapter, originate through
a combination of elements of feeling; and the presence
of the elements of feeling must be supposed to be an
intrinsic property of the objective world. The objective elements, the action of which is accompanied
with the elements of feeling, arrange themselves, we
suppose, into such combinations as display actual feelings, in exact agreement with the laws of molar and
molecular mechanics. This, we must assume, takes
place with the same spontaneity as, for instance, an
acid and a base combine into a salt. To use another
example, it takes place with the same necessity as,
under special conditions, a certain amount of molar
motion is transformed into the molecular motion of
ether-waves, called electricity. Motions are not transformed into feelings, but certain motions (all being
separately accompanied with elements of feeling),
when co-operating in a special form, are accompanied
in that form with actual feelings.

III.   HOW FEELINGS ACQUIRE MEANING.

There is a certain class of philosophers who look
upon feeling as an incidental effect, as a fortuitous by-
play of the interacting elements of matter. This con-

ception has little if anything in its favor. On the contrary, if the elements of feeling are throughout inseparably connected with the elements of objective existence, it must appear natural that wherever the conditions fitted for organised life appear, irritable substance will originate. We may fairly assume that feeling will arise on the cooled surface of a planet with the same necessity as, for instance, a collision between non-luminous celestial bodies will cause them to blaze forth in the brilliant light of a nebula containing all the elements for the production in the course of ages of a planetary system.

Wherever a combination of substances originates that displays the quality of feeling, it will form a basis for given facts of soul-life. Feeling substance having been exposed to a special stimulus, or having performed a certain function, has thereby undergone a rearrangement in its molecular parts. The structure has suffered a change in its configuration, the form of which is preserved in the general flux of matter, and there is thus produced in the feeling substance a disposition to respond more quickly to impressions of the same kind. The feeling accompanying a subsequent impression of the same nature is coincidently felt to be a revival of a former feeling, similar or the same in kind. In other words, feeling substance, preserving the forms of its functions, is possessed with memory.* The preservation of form in a function which is accompanied with feeling makes it possible that the feeling accompanying a special form of function will become a mark of signification. By being felt to be the

* Memory is no mysterious power; it is the preservation of form in feeling organisms. See Ewald Hering's treatise on Memory, English translation in Nos. 6 and 7 of *The Open Court*. Compare also the author's article *Soul-life and the Preservation of Form*, in this book.

same in kind as a former feeling it will come to denote a certain condition of feeling tissues. A feeling that is felt to be the same as or similar in kind to a former feeling, the revival or memory of which it causes, is in this way endowed with meaning ; by which we understand the awareness of the congruence or similarity of two or several feelings. Thus in the lapse of time, by constantly renewed experience, one special feeling, whenever repeated, will naturally become the indicator showing the presence of certain external facts that cause it. An isolated feeling is naturally meaningless ; yet through a preservation of form, viz., through memory, it is by repetition necessarily changed into a symbol of representative value.

Feelings, accordingly, in the course of time, necessarily acquire meaning ; they naturally and spontaneously develop mind. They can as little avoid coordinating into a mental organism, as water at a low temperature can escape congealing into ice ; or as a seed can keep from sprouting when it is exposed, with sufficient moisture, to the light. Mind, accordingly, is the necessary outcome of a combination of feelings. It is as necessary an effect of special causes, as, for example, a triangle is the product of a combination of three lines. The first step in the organisation of feeling, which will throughout remain the determining feature of its development, is the fact that with the help of memory the different sets of feeling acquire meaning, and in this way the mere feelings are transformed from given facts into deduced facts.

IV. SUBJECTIVITY AND OBJECTIVITY.

The nature of given facts is subjectivity, while the character of inferred facts is objectivity. The latter having grown out of the former will nevertheless, so far as they are states of consciousness, always remain subjective; yet they contain representations of that which is delineated by certain given facts.   Thus they contain an element which stamps upon them the nature of objectivity.   They represent objects, the existence of which the feeling subject cannot help assuming, because this is the simplest way of indicating certain changes that are not caused within the realm of its own subjectivity.

Objectivity, accordingly, does not mean absolute objectivity.   Objectivity means subjective states, i. e, given facts or feelings representative of outside facts, i. e., of facts that are not subjective, but objective.

V.   THE PROJECTION OF OBJECTIVE FACTS.

The sense-impression of a white rectangle covered with little black characters is a given fact ; yet the aspect of a sheet of paper is an inferred fact.   The former is a subjective state within; the latter is the representation of an objective thing without.   The process of representing is a function of the subject, but the fact represented is projected as it were into the objective world, where experience has taught us to expect it.   And the practice of projection grows so naturally by inherited adaptation and repeated experience that the thing represented appears to us to be external. We no longer feel a sensation as a state of consciousness but conceive it as an independent reality.

The practice of projecting subjective sensations into the outside world is not an act of careless inference, but the inevitable result of a natural law.   This natural law is that of the ''economy of labor.''   When a blind man has undergone a successful operation, he will first have the consciousness of vague color-sensations taking place in his eye. Experience will teach him the meaning of these color-sensations and his motions will inform him where to find the corresponding outside facts. His consciousness will more and more be concentrated upon the meaning of the sensations. The less difficulty he has in arriving at their proper interpretation, the more unconscious his sense-activity will become and at length consciousness will be habitually attached to the result of the sensation alone, i. e., to its interpretation.

In the same way, every one who learns to play an instrument will first feel that part only which his hand touches. By and by, however, he will acquire a consciousness of the effects produced by the slightest touch. Constant practice forms in the brain of an expert certain living structures which are correspondent to the action of the instrument and represent it with great accuracy. Whenever these structures are stimulated, the action of the instrument is felt to take place. In this way consciousness is projected into the work performed by the instrument. The touch of the hand has become purely automatic, and the operator now feels the full effects of his manipulation although he is not in direct contact with all the parts of his instrument. The instrument becomes as if alive under his treatment, he feels it as a part of himself; for its action stands *en rapport* with his brain-activity.

VI.   THE SUBJECT-SUPERSTITION AND AGNOSTICISM.

States of consciousness, collectively considered, have been termed "subject," and we have also em-

ployed the phrase "subjective world." But we must
not forget the fact, that the adoption of the name
"subject" is based upon a misconception. Subject
means "that which underlies," and the subject was
supposed to be that something which formed the basis
of all the states of consciousness present in any one special case—in you or in me, or in any person like you
and me. The subject was considered as a being that
was in possession of sense-impressions, of feelings, of
thoughts, of intentions, etc.; and the existence of this
subject was proved by Descartes's famous syllogism
Cogito ergo sum. The subject was supposed to produce
the states of consciousness, while in fact (as we have
explained above) it is exactly the opposite. Feelings
change into mind, they produce the subject which
thinks. The subject is nothing underlying but rather
overlying. It is the growth out of and upon feelings.
It is the sum of many feelings in a state of organisation.

The fallacy of Descartes's dictum has been pointed
out by Kant. The existence of states of consciousness,
or the fact *cogito,* does not prove the existence of something that underlies the states of consciousness. It
simply proves the existence of feelings and thoughts.
There are certain sense-impressions, there are perceptions, there are ideas. Ideas develop from perceptions, and perceptions develop from sense-impressions.
States of consciousness are nothing but the awareness
or the feeling that is connected with certain perceptions and ideas.

Descartes's subjectivism is a transitory phase lead-
ing from the authoritative objectivism of the middle
ages to the critical objectivism of modern times. The
authoritative philosophy of the Schoolmen yielded to
the arbitrary philosophy of metaphysical subjectivity,

commencing as a matter of principle with doubt, instead of commencing with positive data, and establishing anarchy through lack of any objective method of arriving at truth. The reaction against the arbitrary authority of scholasticism was indispensable to further progress. But we must not rest satisfied with its negative result. We cannot commence a business without capital and without making a start. So we cannot begin philosophy with nothing. Knowledge is not possible without positive facts to serve as a basis to stand upon.

The negative features of Descartes's philosophy naturally found their ultimate completion in agnosticism. The assumption of the existence of a subject led to the doctrine, that this subject is unknowable. Moreover, the assumption of something that underlies the acts of thought leads to the assumption of something that underlies objective existence, and thus it begets the theory of things in themselves. This theory involves us in innumerable contradictions and thus it ends ultimately in the proposition that things in themselves are unknowable.

There are few who know the historical meaning of agnosticism; but those who can survey philosophical thought in its evolution, its growth, and decay, know that agnosticism means failure in philosophy. The word is a foreign-sounding name for "knownothingism," denoting a half-concealed confession of bankruptcy. The philosophy of the future, in order to escape from the fatal consequences of agnosticism, has to discard the subject-superstition inherited from Descartes. Descartes was a great thinker, a star of first magnitude in the realm of thought, but it is time that, without returning to the authoritative philosophy of the Schoolmen, we should free ourselves from the errors of his one-sided subjectivism.

Let us not forget, that all subjective states contain an objective element. Objectivity is no chimera, and we are very well enabled to establish the truth or untruth of objective facts. The philosophy of the future, accordingly, will be a philosophy of facts, it will be *positivism ;* and in so far as a unitary systematisation of facts is the aim and ideal of all science, it will be MONISM.

From the standpoint of positivism, the subject, in the old sense, does not exist, and things in themselves do not exist either. Their existence is an unwarranted assumption, a superstition of philosophy, and we can retain the word subject only on the condition of a complete change of its meaning. The word subject, accordingly, (which has acquired a place in philosophical language and is for several purposes quite an appropriate expression,) must be corrected so as to mean, not an underlying substratum, nor an agent which does the thinking, but simply a collective term designating a certain group of sense-impressions, perceptions, ideas, and volitions. These sense-impressions, perceptions, ideas, and volitions, which form, simultaneously as well as successively, the elements of soul-life, carrying consciousness upon the waves of many subconscious states, make up the reality of the subject ; they are the facts of its existence, and it is the states of consciousness only, not an underlying something, the existence of which is beyond all doubt. They form the basis of all knowledge.

VII. THE OBJECTIVE ELEMENT IN SUBJECTIVE STATES.

We must bear in mind that states of feeling are not empty feelings, but always feelings of a certain kind. There is no consciousness pure and simple, but only consciousness of a certain state. Let us suppose, for instance, the consciousness of a certain pressure. What is it but a feeling of being pressed in a certain direction and with a certain intensity? If a certain pressure is resisted, the feeling indicates a state of active reaction against pressure, and experience teaches by comparison with other pressures how much counterpressure is necessary to resist or overcome it.

Among the states of consciousness there are accordingly some that represent an awareness of *receiving* impressions, and there are others of *making* impressions. There are some feelings of a passive nature, which are felt to be produced by impacts from a something that is not the subject, and there are other feelings of an active nature, which are felt to produce effects on something that is not the subject. This something that is not the subject is called "object." It is represented as lying outside the subject, although the latter stands in a close and inseparable relation to the object, which, so far as this relation is considered, forms a part of the subject. A given subjective state possesses a definite form ; it exists as it is on account of the object only; for its form has been produced by its relation to the object, and it represents this relation. The object, therefore, is no unimportant part of, and indeed is an essential element in, the constitution of the subjective state.

Idealist philosophers are apt to say that the subject alone is known to us, while the existence of the object must forever remain a vague hypothesis. This, however, is incorrect. It involves an unjustifiable deprecation of the objective element in the given facts of conscious states, and is based on a misconception of the entire state of things. The data of knowledge are not mere subjective states, they are relations between subject and object. Neither the subject is given, nor the object; but an interaction between subject and object. From this interaction we derive by a very complicated process of abstraction both concepts, the subject as well as the object. It is true that the subjective world of feelings and of representative feeling is very different from the objective world of things. Nevertheless they are one. The subject together with all objects forms one inseparable whole of subject-object-ness.

Every special object, accordingly, must be conceived as a part of this inseparable whole—of the All; it is a certain set of facts, represented in a certain group of experiences, and is to be described as that something which in a special way affects the subject and can again in a special way be reacted upon by the subject.

Here we have the clue for the proper meaning of objectivity. What is a piece of lead but something that at a definite distance from the centre of the earth exerts a certain pressure proportionate to its mass; that is seen to become liquid at a certain temperature; etc., etc.? If it is treated in a particular way, it will be observed to suffer certain changes. What lead is has been established by experience; i. e., by systematic observation through sense-impressions.

From this standpoint the differences between the

schools of idealism and realism appear as antiquated. The questions whether matter is real, whether objects exist, and whether there is any reality at all, have lost their meaning. That which produces effects upon the subject and against which the subject does or can re-act, is called object. The sense-effects produced by the object upon the subject, and also the reactions of the subject upon the object, are realities ; and every name of a special object signifies a certain group of such effects and their respective reactions. Thus, for instance, the word lead comprises a certain set of ex-periences that have always been found combined with certain whitish objects.

Some philosophers have denied not only the ex-istence of objects, but also the reality of space. What is space but a certain group of experiences ? The con-ception of space originates by moving and by being moved about. The conception of space is the con-sciousness that by moving, or by being moved, a change is effected ; that is, a certain object serving as a point of reference is either approached or left at a greater distance. The acts of approach or withdrawal are as much realities as are any other acts of the subject. Dis-cussions concerning the reality of space accordingly become mere verbal quibbles as soon as we under-stand by space the condition common to all motion-experiences.

VIII. HALLUCINATIONS AND ERRORS.

The mental state in which through contact with external facts one or several of the senses are affected so as to produce a direct awareness of their pres-ence, is called perception. The effects of external facts upon the sense of touch appear as different forms of resistance. To the other senses they appear as odors, tastes, sounds, and images. All these sensations are so many subjective methods of representing certain objective processes. Perceptions represent immediate reality because the objects perceived, i. e., the objects represented by an image in the eye, a taste on the tongue, etc., are in an immediate contact with our senses. The feeling subject is directly conscious of their existence by their present effects. They are our *Anschauung*, i. e., the living presence of objective reality.

Besides this living presence of objective reality, of which our immediate surroundings consist,—besides our *Anschauung*—, man is in possession of more general representations, which comprise all the memories of a certain class of percepts. We call them concepts. Man alone through the mechanism of word-symbols has been able to form concepts. Abstract reasoning as well as scientific thought will grow with the assistance of concepts in the course of a higher development.

The higher we rise in the evolution of representative feelings, i. e., in the development of mind, the more numerous are the opportunities for going astray. A scientific hypothesis, if erroneous, is more sweeping in its fallacies than a single hallucination, which is a misinterpretation merely of certain feelings. The subjective part of an hallucination, namely the feeling itself, is real ; but the objective part, the representative element of the feeling, is not real; that which it is supposed to mean, does not exist. The interpretation of the feeling is erroneous in an hallucination.

Hallucinations are possible, and in the more abstract domains of mental activity errors are possible also ; and will be ever more frequent. Nevertheless the reality of outside facts in the sense stated above can as little be doubted as the reality of immediate perception ; and all the facts established by science, if they are but true, are as much realities as is the resistance of the table to the pressure of my hand or the perception of the sheet of paper by my eye.

Facts established by science are those observations which are made with all the necessary exactness as well as completeness from certain groups of experiences, and formulated with precision. The theory · of atoms, for instance, is true in so far as all elements combine in certain proportions, which shows that the ultimate particles of which the elements consist are of a definite mass. Atoms, if the word is understood in this sense, are realities. The theory of atoms, however, is not proved in the sense that atoms are $\overset{\text{v}}{\alpha}\tau o$- $\mu o\iota$; or single, isolated, minute bodies of a peculiar individuality—separate, indivisible, and eternal entities. Whether they are concrete things or certain forms of motion in a continuous substance, whether they are vortices or whirls of a certain density and velocity in an ether ocean, or whatever else be their character, is not yet known. If we exclude from the concept "atoms" all hypothetical views and confine their meaning strictly to the formulation of certain experiences, we have to deal with facts that are real. Theories are true in so far as they comprehend in a formula a certain group of facts, and a hypothesis becomes reliable to the extent that it agrees with facts. The slightest actual disagreement with facts is sufficient to overthrow the most ingenious hypothesis.

This leads us to the question, What is meant by
true ?   What is truth ?

IX.   FACTS AND REALITY.   TRUTH AND MIND.

The epitheton "true" has reference to representative states only.   A representation is true, if it con-
forms to, or agrees with, experience ; in other words,
if it is an interpretation of given facts, is free from
contradiction, and nowhere collides with any one of
the given facts and their consistent interpretation.
There is no sense in speaking of mere feelings as
being true.   We can never meet, in our own experience, with given facts that are nothing but meaningless feelings ; for we (as thinking beings) are incapable
of bringing meaningless feelings into the scope of consciousness, since in the very act of thinking we com-
ment upon the given facts of our feelings.   But supposing there are mere given facts, mere meaningless
feelings void of any representative element, the application of the word true to such non-representative
feelings would be improper.   States of consciousness
become true or untrue only by being representative of
objective conditions or things.   There is no trace of
truth in mere feelings, but only in representative feelings.   Truth and error are the privilege of mind.   A
representation is true, if all the various experiences
concerning a certain thing or state of things agree
with the representation ; it is untrue if they do not
agree.

We observe that certain classes of facts, in spite
of all variety, exhibit in one or another respect a
sameness, and science attempts to express the sameness in exact formulas.   These formulas we call natural

laws. If a natural law covers all cases of a class that have come or even that possibly can come within the range of our experience, if it agrees with every one of them, we call it a truth.

"Truth" accordingly is not at all identical with "fact." These two words are often used as synonyms, but properly employed they are quite distinct. Truth is the agreement of a representation with the facts represented. The fall of a stone is a fact; it is an inferred fact deduced from certain sense-impressions. In so far as the inference is made with necessity as the only proper and simplest explanation of a certain given fact or sense-impression, it must be considered as a fact or as real. The law of gravitation, however, is not a fact, but a truth.

Facts are real. There is no sense in speaking of facts as being true. Representations of facts are true or untrue. Reality is the characteristic feature of all facts, but truth is a quality that can reside in mind alone.

Facts are always single, concrete, and individual. Every fact is a *hic* and *nunc*. It is in a special place, and it is as it is, at a certain time. It is definite and of a particular kind. Yet a truth, although representing certain objects or their relations, is never a concrete object, nor is it a *hic* and a *nunc*. It possesses a generality applicable to all instances wherever and whenever the objects in their particular relation appear represented in that truth. Truth accordingly possesses as it were an ubiquity; it is omnipresent and eternal.

Truth in one sense is objective ; it represents objects or their relations conceived in their objectivity, in their independence of the subject. This means that the representation of certain objective states will under like conditions agree with the experiences of all subjects—i. e., of all feeling beings having the same channels of information.

Truth in another sense is subjective. Truth exists in thinking subjects only. Truth affirms that certain subjective representations of the objective world can be relied upon, that they are deduced from facts and agree with facts. Based upon past experience, they can be used as guides for future experience. If there were no subjective beings, no feeling and comprehending minds, there would be no truth. Facts in themselves, whether they are or are not represented in the mind of a feeling and thinking subject, are real, yet representations alone, supposing they agree with facts, are true.

*   *   *

Mind, or the representation of facts in feeling substance, is the creation of a new and a spiritual realm above the facts of material existence. By spiritual we understand feelings that are representative ; and we say that it is a new creation because it does not exist in the isolated facts of the world. It is formed under special conditions. It rises from certain combinations of facts ; being built upon those facts which produce in their co-operation the subjective state of feeling. The activity of mind if methodically disciplined is called science. Science attempts to make the mental representations correct : it is the search for truth. The object of all the sciences and of philosophy is to systematise knowledge, i. e., all the innumerable data of experience, so that we can understand and survey the facts of reality in their harmonious interconnection. The most important problem of philosophy has always been the problem of the origin of mind ; for we are anxious to comprehend how it is possible that feeling can spring up in a universe of not-feeling objects, and that thinking beings can originate in a world of not-thinking elements.

Dualism assumes that the gulf between the two empires, the thinking and feeling on one side and the not-thinking and not-feeling on the other side, is insurmountable ; Monism however maintains that there is no gulf, for there is no reason for such an assumption. Both realms, the feeling and thinking on the one hand, and the unfeeling and unthinking on the other hand, are not at all distinct and separate provinces. The transition from the one to the other takes place by degrees, and there is no boundary line between them. The atoms of oxygen which we inhale at present are not engaged in any action that is accompanied with feeling, but some of them will be very soon active in the generation of our best thought accompanied with most intense consciousness. After that they are thrown aside in the organism and pass out as waste products in the shape of carbonic acid.

X. TELEPATHY.

The spiritual originates from and disappears into the non-spiritual not otherwise than light originates out of, and dissolves again into, darkness. Light is usually considered as the emblem of mind, for light also discloses to our eye those objects which are so far away that we can never expect to touch them with our hands. So mind, the representation of the objective world in feeling substance, unveils the riddles of the universe and shows the secret connections of most distant things and events.

Spiritualists discuss with great enthusiasm the problem of telepathy. Telepathy means "far-feeling." Mental activity exhibits in all its elements instances of telepathy in the literal sense of the word. We do not feel our sense-organs; but in and through our sense-organs objects outside of us are felt. In and through our eyes most distant stars are seen. If telepathy has no other but its natural and proper meaning we must confess that the whole activity of the mind rests upon telepathy.

However, we cannot recognise telepathy in the sense in which the word is often employed by spiritualists. With many it denotes a process of such far-feeling as is not caused in the natural way and as stands in contradiction to the mechanical interconnection of causes and effects in the universe. It is supposed to supersede the order of nature. We recognise telepathy fully in the sense that feelings represent distant events and that mind can thus penetrate into the remotest regions of time and space, but not in any other sense that stands in contradiction with the universal order of mechanical causation.

What is the soul but a telepathic machine! It is an organised totality of representations in feeling substance employed for the purpose of reacting appropriately upon the stimuli of external things. Man is a part of the cosmos, he consists of a certain group of facts, belonging to and being in intimate connection with the whole universe. Man's mind is the cosmos represented in this special group of facts. A correct representation of the cosmos includes a proper adaptation. Accordingly the human soul is a microcosm and its function is the endeavoring to conform to the macrocosm.

XI. MIND AND ETERNITY.

Light is a most wonderful phenomenon; and yet we know that the objective process taking place in luminous bodies and thence transmitted through ether vibrations to our eye where it causes the sensation of light, is a mode of motion that can be produced mechanically by changing simple or mechanical motion (i. e., change of place) through friction into molecular motion. As light originates out of darkness, being a special mode of motion, so feeling originates out of the not-feeling. The not-feeling accordingly contains the conditions of feeling in a similar way as potential energy contains the potentiality of kinetic energy, or as molar motion contains potentially the molecular motion of heat, light, and electricity.

Mind sheds light upon the interconnection of all things and gives meaning to the world. If the world consisted of purely objective facts only, it would remain a meaningless play of forces. Mind and the whole realm of spiritual existence rises from most insignificant beginnings; yet is it so grand and divine because it represents the world in its wonderful harmony and cosmic order.

The function of spiritual activity appears to us as transient; but mind is not as transient as it seems. The continuous light of a flame depends in every instance upon the conditions of the moment. But the continuity of mind shows a preservation of mind-forms, the corresponding spiritual activity of which is called memory. Memory or the mind-form of former states is the most important factor in the determination of the representative value of present states of mind. The continuity thus effected makes it possible for mind to represent not only things and processes distant in space, but also those distant in time.

The continuation of form in feeling substance, not merely in the life of single individuals, but also in the life of the race, produces the growth, the development, and evolution of mind. Thus facts can be represented in their connections, and the necessity of their connection can be understood. To use Spinoza's phrase: The world can be viewed *sub specie æternitatis.*

The fulfilment of mind is truth, or a correct representation of facts, not as they are now and here, but as, according to conditions which constitute a given state of things, they must be here and everywhere. Mind expands in the measure that it contains and reflects the eternity of truth.

The activity of mind is in one respect as transient a process as is the phenomenon of light. Yet in other respects mind is able to grasp eternity within the narrow span of the moment.

VITALISM AND THE CONSERVATION OF ENERGY.

A GREAT difference appears to exist between an animal that moves about and a stone that remains on the spot where it has been placed. It seems as if every child might easily explain it. And yet it required the lapse of centuries before scientists could tell us what were the characteristic features of animal life.

In former centuries people were satisfied to state that the animal was alive, while a stone was not alive. And we may perhaps, even in the present day, accept this explanation. But we refuse to be paid with empty words. We now ask : What is life ?

In past ages it was assumed, that certain things were alive, because they contained vitality or a vital principle. This simple explanation was called Vitalism. The vital principle, it was held, manifested itself through spontaneous motion. Things that contained no vital principle were not alive ; and could therefore be moved by push only, by a *vis a tergo*, as they said ; that is, through a mechanical pressure from without.

The striking feature of living things, of both plants as well as animals, is their organic growth of which inanimate objects are destitute. Thus it became customary to distinguish an organic and an inorganic kingdom ; and when chemistry, the youngest science, was born, a new flood of light was expected to be shed upon the obscure problem of vitality.

Chemists, indeed, discovered, that all living substance of the animal and the vegetable kingdoms consisted chiefly of four elementary substances ; viz., of oxygen, carbon, hydrogen, and nitrogen. There were very slight admixtures only of a few other ingredients, such as phosphorus, sulphur, iron, chloride of sodium (salt), etc. Life, it appeared, must depend upon the interaction of oxygen, carbon, hydrogen, and nitrogen. Accordingly, these four elements were called organic substances. They were supposed to be the substances of life.

But the hope that from a difference of matter the problem of vitality could be solved, was preposterous. In many respects the so-called organic substances do not differ at all from the inorganic substances, and there exist many combinations of the organic substances that are neither of an animal nor of a vegetable nature. We cannot therefore look upon living things as combinations of the organic substances ; they are more than combinations of organic substances ; they are organic substances in a special form which admit of a constant interaction. Substances of such a form are called organized substances—well to be distinguished from organic substances. The idea of a life-substance had to be abandoned, and scientists now tried to explain the problem of vitality from the supposition of a vital energy. This vital energy was considered as different from any other kind of energy, and many very prominent scientists looked upon it as a supernatural quality which lay beyond explanation.

The theory that a vital energy animates living bodies was maintained until half a century ago by our most prominent physiologists. But it received its death-blow, when the law of the conservation of energy was recognized to the full extent of its importance. We now know that all forces in nature are motions of some kind : light and electricity are undulations of ether ; heat is a molecular vibration ; and mechanical motion, change of place or visible movement, can be transformed into any other energy, electricity, light, or heat. *Vice versa,* motion can be reproduced from the other energies.

Energy* certainly often seems to disappear and can apparently be created again. But it can be shown that energy, when it disappears, reappears in another form, and that the energy thus created did exist before, it was only transformed. Energy may be latent ; and latent energy can be set free again. Because latent energy *can* be set free again, it is called *potential* energy (*L. L. potentialis,* from *possum,* I .can).

Suppose my hand exercises a force represented by *A B* upon your hand, and your hand resists the pressure by exercising an equal force in the opposite direction *B A*, there will be no motion. Let the stress between the two hands represent the force of *A B+B A*. This stress is latent energy ; it .is potential and can be converted into an energy of motion, or, as it is termed, into *kinetic* energy.

If it takes a pressure of *A B* to set the spring of a toy gun, the spring will exercise the same amount of force (*B A*) upon the catch that keeps it compressed.

* Leibnitz .called a force that acts as motion of some form "*vis viva*," or "living force." He defined *vis viva* as the product of the mass by the square of the velocity, $M V^2$. But now the term kinetic energy (from κινεῖν, to move), energy of motion, has become customary, and we understand by kinetic energy half the mass times the square of velocity ($\frac{1}{2} M V^2$). See Maxwell, *Theory of Heat*, page 90.

There will be no motion, so long as the catch is strong enough to endure the pressure $B\ A$. But the force $A\ B$ is not annihilated; it still exists as potential energy and can be set free at any moment by the removal of the catch, which is done by pulling the trigger. The pressure $B\ A$, that the spring exerts, was created through the expenditure of the force $A\ B$ during the act of setting the gun. The spring is, so to say, loaded, it is freighted with a certain amount of energy; and if the trigger is pulled, a kind of explosion takes place—i. e., kinetic energy is suddenly set free, which is available for doing work. In a toy gun it is used for throwing pebbles or peas.

A house of cards in the same way represents potential energy. One card keeps the other standing by pressure and counterpressure. If through the interference of some change the pressure of one card ceases to be quite equal to that of the other, the house breaks down, thus changing stress into motion—or, in other terms, thus changing potential energy into kinetic energy.

The building up and breaking down of a house of cards is a process visible in all its details. But there are chemical compositions that are similar to such houses of cards, yet do not show the details of the building up and breaking down. It takes a certain amount of energy to build them, and they thus contain potential energy. Whenever a very small change, a slight concussion, an increase of temperature, or a spark, can cause their breakdown, they are called "unstable." Gunpowder and all other explosives are of this character.

Although kinetic energy may disappear when it is changed into potential energy, yet energy itself cannot be destroyed. Neither can it be produced. Like matter, energy is indestructible.

The question now arises : Is vital force different from both these energies? And the unequivocal answer is, No! The energy which living beings expend in their activity, in their motions, their passions, and in their thought, is the same energy that we meet with everywhere, and which is produced in animal bodies in a·more complicated way, yet in a similar manner as work is done by machines.* As machines are fed by coal and heated by the combustion of coal, so the animal receives food, which through the organs of digestion is assimilated and transformed into highly complicated, unstable combinations. Like gunpowder, or like a drawn spring, these unstable combinations contain potential energy. An unstable combination of high complexity, when breaking down into a more stable combination of less complexity, sets free that quantity of kinetic energy that was necessary to build it up and to keep it in a state of tension. In the animal body, as in the fire-box of a steam-engine, a process of combustion takes place : the exceedingly unstable oxygen of the air combines with carbon and nitrogen compounds, which are also unstable and to which oxygen bears a great affinity, i. e., it easily combines with them into more stable compositions. All the details of this process are not yet fully known and calculated ; but the theory itself can no longer be doubted.

Combustion means oxidation ; and oxidation, converting substances into more stable combinations, sets energy free, which appears either as heat or as work performed. The process of oxidation in the fire-box of a steam-engine is a luminous process, while in the

* See Gavarret, *De la chaleur produite par les êtres vivants.*

body it is not strong enough for developing visible flames. Oxygen, in the process of combustion, unites with carbon into carbonic acid and leaves behind water and other incombustible parts.

Oxygen is conveyed into the body by respiration ; in the lungs the blood is oxidized, which carries the oxygen to the different organs. Through the oxidation of the tissues in the nerves, in the muscles, and in other living substances, potential energy is set free which partly appears as heat, partly as work performed. The heat is called animal heat, the work performed is the movements of the body. The products of the oxidations are carbonic acid, water, and certain nitrogen compounds, which are given off in the secretion of urine, in the air expelled from the lungs in breathing, and through perspiration.

Professor Bunge in Basel has again recently adopted the expression vital energy. Bunge justly maintains, that the forces that appear in a living animal organism are entirely different from all other forces in nature. In this manner he re-admitted the obsolete term vitalism. In Professor Bunge's writings, however, the term vitalism is in so far modified and modernized, that the Professor does not at all contest that this vital energy is just as much energy as any mechanical movement, heat or electricity, and that it originates by way of transformation from other forms of energy. Vital energy is nevertheless entirely different from other forces, even as electricity differs from heat or from visible motion, from friction, or from light.

In the old electric machine friction is transformed into electricity, and we know that electricity as well as friction is a certain mode of motion : still electricity is not friction. Thus, vital energy is likewise quite a special form of energy, which form is different from all the other forms of energy from which it can be produced.

Vitality is an energy just as well as all other energies, but its form is peculiar; it is neither electricity, nor light, nor heat alone, nor any other energy we know of, although it may be more or less similar to the one and to the other. Vitality originates from the same great reservoir of energy as all the other forms of energy, and it stands with them in a constant interaction. Yet the only engine by which, to our knowledge, vital energy can be created, is the animal organism. According to the present state of knowledge, we can, to say the least, hardly expect to be able to produce vital energy in any other manner. This truth is most concisely formulated in the statement that life comes from life only.

ORGANIZED AND NON-ORGANIZED LIFE.

IF by life is to be understood spontaneous motion, we must acknowledge that the whole universe is animated, and that the animal world owes its life, its growth, and its whole existence to the universal life of nature. For a long while, under the influence of materialistic philosophy, it was believed, that we should be able to explain the psychological and physiological action of the animal world from the chemical and purely mechanical processes of nature. The world was considered as a dead machine moved by push from the outside. As a matter of fact, the inverse is true; science has been compelled to explain even the mechanical processes through the facts of physiology and psychology. For there is life and spontaneity everywhere in nature; in the falling stone no less than in the blowing of buds and in the decisions of the human will.

The simplest mechanical movements appeared so self-evident, that scientists believed they might properly be regarded as the most general facts, to which for the sake of explanation all other natural phenomena would have to be reduced. Mechanics, after all, only explains the form of visible motion; it only shows how one form of motion necessarily proceeds from another or how it is transformed from potential energy. The fact of the motion itself remained un-

explained. How a stone falls can be correctly calculated ; the cause that occasions its fall in each single
instance can be stated, but the reason why it falls,
why it is attracted toward the earth, remained an
open question. Repeated attempts were made to
explain gravitation from the pressure of a surrounding
ether, simply because scientists had been accustomed
to regard organic nature as dead. In this, however,
they entirely overlooked the fact, that even if in such
case the descent of a stone could be sufficiently explained through mechanical pressure (we need not
mention here the many contradictions arising from this
hypothesis), the pressure itself, which the ether exerts,
would remain unexplained. By virtue of this explanation the presence of ether must cause all movement,
and ether would be the source of all life, the agency
that produces the spontaneity of nature. But, if
ether itself is not alive, through what push or pressure
could it have attained its energy ? In this manner the
problem is only delayed,—and can be delayed *ad infi-
nitum* without the approach of anything that looks
like an explanation. We therefore regard these ether-
theories as a failure, and rather adopt the simpler
conception, according to which nature as a whole is endowed with spontaneity, i.e., self-motion. A stone is not
pushed toward the earth by a pressure, by a *vis a tergo*,
but it spontaneously moves. The stone (like all bodies)
has a quality, called gravity, which is manifested in
gravitation. One body attracts another body inversely
as the square of their distance. Gravity is not outside of the stone pulling or pushing it ; it is in the
stone itself, it is an inseparable part of it, a quality
being identical with its mass. Accordingly, the falling stone is not acted upon, it is self-acting.

This same principle applies to all more complicated processes, and even to human action itself. A chemical combination is not affected through the pressure of some unknown or unknowable agent outside the substances that pushes them together; but through their own inherent energy, through qualities that are inseparably connected with their very existence—qualities that in their totality constitute their whole being.

The spontaneity of living creatures, which in the form of organized life is called vitality, is accordingly derived from other forms of energy, just as the materials that are constantly building up the body are substances that are found everywhere about us in nature. We drink the water that falls from the clouds or is drawn from a spring. The carbonic acid of the air is transformed in plants into hydrates of carbon, and we consume them in our daily bread. We breathe the oxygen of the air, and through all the complex and peculiar processes which these substances undergo within our body through constant combinations and decompositions, we derive in every second of our life fresh strength from the great store-house of living nature to live, and move, and have our being.

Spontaneous motion is the universal feature of all natural processes. But if spontaneity is not the characteristic feature of animal life, if the self-motion of living men and animals is only a special instance of the universal spontaneity of nature, if they are but a peculiar form, a particular, grand, and wonderful revelation of the same—what then is to be regarded as the essential difference between both these kingdoms? A difference which, despite the intimate connection of both, is so very striking and manifest.

That which particularly distinguishes so called living beings in their contrast to the so-called not-living beings of inorganic nature is their organization. We, therefore, must carefully distinguish between organic substances and organized substance.

Organized substance, or rather organizing substance, is that which displays all the special functions, which exhibits the properties of life in the narrower and in the ordinary sense of the word. Organized substance not only possesses that spontaneity of movement which is common to all substances, and which it shows in a striking manner especially by the transformation of potential into kinetic energy; it also possesses the faculty of continuing without interruption the process of self-organization. It takes from its environment fresh substances, which it assimilates into the higher (that is, unstable) combinations of its own ; whereupon in animal beings these higher and unstable compositions again are decomposed through a process of oxidation.

The process of organization, accordingly, consists in what we usually understand by assimilation of food, resulting in nutrition and growth, accompanied by disassimilation, i. e., a constant expulsion of the used elements. In animals, moreover, the setting free of energy in the form of motion is a further characteristic trait of the most important peculiarities of the higher forms of organizing substance.

We learn from this that every trifling act of vitality, be it ever so insignificant or little, the slightest movement, even the blinking of an eye, and also every thought and every emotion of our soul, is a decay of built-up living substance. How closely, then, are death and life akin ! Nay, they are in this sense iden-

tical, for each act of life is an act of death and the old
hymn is true,

In the midst of life by death we are surrounded.
Media vita nos in morte sumus.

And this idea contains even a deeper truth than
was dreamed of by the poet of those lines, or by the
millions of human souls of past ages, who in their
anxieties and in danger of death repeated the words of
that grand hymn.

Decay is the condition of activity.   Thus the characteristic feature of death is the very nature of life.
Death constantly hovers about us, and out of his hand
we receive—through the decay of the forms which
hoard potential energy, that vitality which warms our ·
hearts and glows through all our being, which we expend for our own necessities as well as for the weal of
future humanity.

The truth, that every vital act is at the same time
an act of death, would find a wrong application if its
influence would drive us to melancholy, if it would
make our lives gloomy and our souls despondent.
On the contrary, it must make us brave and courageous, for indeed it does not show life in a terrible and
death-like shape, but death himself with all his terrors
appears in a milder and nobler aspect.   Death, the
giver of life, will bestow the richer gifts, the better we
learn to appreciate their value.   To both the spend-
thrift who wastes, as well as to the miser who leaves
his powers of life unused, the fountain of life will cease
to flow.   But through wise use we may do both, preserve and even increase its bounties.

Who wishes to preserve his life loses the same ;
but he who loses his life in the service of a higher and
of a more lasting cause than is that of self-hood, will

truly preserve his life. Activity of work not only keeps the fountain of life flowing, but the work performed will live even in the generations to come, and the greater, the purer, and the nobler, the more moral our work is the more lasting will it be, the more will it partake of the grandeur of eternity.

MEMORY AND ORGANIZED SUBSTANCE.

THROUGH the monistic conception the yawning chasm that seems to separate living nature from dead nature, is bridged over. Dead nature only appears to be dead in comparison with the higher manifestations of organized life. Nevertheless, the latter springs from, and is constantly drawing upon the resources of, the former. It is true, it has not hitherto been possible to create organized substance from non-organized substance. So far as we can judge this cannot be done otherwise than by the natural process, with the help of previously extant organisms. All attempts to the end of making the organic elements (O, C, H, N) organize, have utterly failed. This, however, does not disprove, that under certain definite circumstances (which, perhaps, are no longer realizable on this planet of ours) the organic elements do actually organize with the same necessity as under certain given circumstances electric tensions spontaneously arise, which afterwards discharge in thunder-storms.

The spontaneous rise of organized life from the "all-life" of nature cannot be contested, unless indeed we wish to lose ourselves in interminable contradictions or in incomprehensible wonder-theories concerning supernatural powers.

In view of the fact that we must grant even to inorganic nature a certain kind of life, manifested in spontaneous self-motion, the question has been mooted, whether a piece of coal that burns away, and a stone that falls to the earth, are not endowed with a kind of feeling, that is, whether in such substances actually there does not take place something that, on a miniature scale, might correspond to that which in ourselves we perceive as feeling.

The question is perfectly legitimate, and, perhaps, ought to be answered in the affirmative. The non-organized substances must, in fact, possess all the conditions of organized life, and consequently those of feeling also. Still, in admitting this, we ought to bear in mind that the mere conditions of feeling are not as yet feeling itself, even as mere friction does not as yet constitute electricity.

The processes of inorganic nature, as compared with those of organized life, are isolated and instantaneous proceedings. They are not organically linked to previous processes by a chain of memories. An atom of oxygen goes through a thousand different conditions which leave, so far as we are able to judge, no mark, no impression upon it. With equal indifference it will now sustain life and now cause iron to rust. That it did pass through the former process has no influence upon its action in the latter, and although all processes of nature, even those of inorganic nature, are interconnected, the connection is meaningless in such cases. Every process of inorganic nature is an isolated act, limited to the instant at which it takes place. This is one and perhaps the most important reason why inorganic processes can not exhibit feeling—certainly not that which in the life of animal existences we are wont to designate as feeling.

Coal and stones and atoms of oxygen in the air are not sentient beings in the same sense as animals, and not even in the sense in which mimosas are sentient, simply because they are not organized, and according to all appearances are destitute of memory. Only memory can create feeling—that which we commonly understand by feeling, which is a discriminative faculty. The retentive power of memory preserves former impressions, and thus renders a comparison of the present state of things with past experiences possible.

Professor Hering most ably demonstrates in his famous monograph on Memory, that *memory is a universal property of organized substance.* Memory, indeed, is the result of organization and all the superiority of organized substance over inorganic matter, is first of all due to its memory.

Every organized substance that we know, is but the summation of its history from the beginning. Every impression, and every mode in which the organism ever reacted against impressions, are faithfully preserved, in the most delicate and recondite features of the living substance. By the aid of its memories an organism creates a unity with its own past as well as future, which enables it to turn the fruits of former experiences to advantage for experiences to come, and in this manner renders possible a progression to ever higher stages of development, to more varied forms, and to more powerful and nobler types of being.

The rise of organized substance from non-organized elements constitutes the triumph of nature over the blindness of a purely material reality. The elements previously isolated combine and their very union builds up in their forms a higher kind of life. Substance, in becoming organized, peculiarly connects the existence of materiality from molecule to molecule. It produces above or among the molecules a new kind of existence, manifested in ceaselessly interacting structures which, not unlike living fountains, preserve their forms in the constant flux of matter. Material existence has the advantage of being indestructible and eternal, but the life of forms has the greater advantage of being plastic, and while preserving the treasures of its former days, it can, in every moment of its activity, gain new ones. This higher life of nature, deriving its superiority and grandeur not from its material resources, but from its form, may very well be characterized as spiritual.

It is said that the human body every seven years completely renews all its constitutive elements. But the connection with the work done by the lost and disintegrated parts is therefore not broken, after their having performed their respective functions. We still very well remember what we did and thought seven or fourteen years ago, nay even twenty-one, twenty-eight years, and more. The reason of this wonderful fact is, that the forms of organized substance as created under the influences of events and actions amidst all the elementary changes of growth, still remain faithfully preserved.

The preservation of form in living substance is the principle that explains memory. Indeed, both are equivalent terms. By memory we understand nothing more or less than the psychical aspect of the preservation of form in living substance. The skin of my hand, which once, some twenty years ago, was slightly wounded, has been renovated again and again, through the expulsion of all disintegrated parts, but the form of the wound has nevertheless been preserved in the white line of a scar. The brain similarly preserves certain impressions, the forms of which remain, though the nervous substance may change. And if these forms happen to be stimulated or irritated, we experience the same feelings over again, as when we received the impression—only much weaker in its resuscitation than in the moment when they were first experienced. And yet not a single particle is preserved of the matter that, at the time of the impression, performed the function of feeling.

The higher life of nature begins with memory through the preservation of living forms, and in the course of the ever-ascending higher development of the organizing substances, it will reach the consciousness of animal life and ultimately rise to the stage of human intelligence.

This same higher nature, that created spiritual existence, still continues active, and in the depths of human hearts incessantly creates new ideals, which in organic growth sprout forth from past experiences. The memories of both successes and failures live in our brain, and shape themselves into new images of better conditions, under which disappointments can be avoided. Thus they lead humanity onward on the highway of an endless and boundless progress.

The spiritual life of higher existence, which to organized substance imparts its superiority and proper character, we commonly call *soul*. Accordingly, we define soul as *the form of an organism*. This definition may seem exceedingly simple, but like all simple truths it possesses a far-reaching significance.

The development of our soul is the highest task of humanity; to attend to this task constitutes our most sacred religious duty. But the indispensable condition for this is self-knowledge.

The pursuit of self-knowledge being the basis of re-

ligion, the words Γνῶθι σεαυτόν, "know thyself,"
were inscribed above the portals of the most venerable
sanctuary of ancient Greece. Self-knowledge is demanded from those who wish to cross the threshold of
the sanctuary of Apollo, of the divinity of light, and
spirit.

To investigate the nature of the soul, to study the laws
in accordance with which the soul is developed, and preserved in a condition of health, is of greatest importance to every human creature ; for even in our own day,
to the most advanced and radical adept of free thought,
as to all, the grand words of the Gospel apply : "What
shall it profit a man, if he shall gain the whole world
and lose his own soul ?" (MARK VIII. 36.)

SOUL-LIFE OF ANIMALS AND PLANTS.

THE soul of man is the result of the total development of organized substance from its first beginning
and through all its phases of transformation. Man is
the sum of all the memories of his ancestors. In the
man of to-day all the memories of the past continué
to live, as naturally as the child continues to live in
the youth and the youth in the developed man.

Death vanishes, when we thus conceive mankind
as one grand totality, as a huge wave sweeping onward across the ocean of life. The wave in its progress
incessantly lifts other particles of water and leaves
the old ones behind ; yet it remains the same, and ever
must remain the same in its onward career. The wave
is not the water, although it consists of water ; it is a
special form of motion in water. Humanity is not the
matter of which men's bones and muscles consist.
Humanity is a certain form of life—a form of motion
that sweeps over the ocean of matter. The material particles of which humanity now consists, are left behind,
they sink back into the ocean, but humanity continues
to progress ; it continues to live, and remains the same
through all the changes which the material parts of
living substance have to undergo. By humanity we
do not understand the clay of which man is made,
nor even the life which moves the clay, but the form

of life in the clay—his soul; and the soul lives even though the body may die.

From this point of view the life of the individual man is enlarged beyond the narrow limits of the ego. He feels himself a part of a great whole, for which, even in the most modest sphere, he can work and exert himself. And in so far as he represents the soul of humanity, he breathes the atmosphere of immortality. The tidal wave of life, that now bears him along, even after his earthly part has returned to the dust whence it originated, will sweep resistlessly onward toward grand and glorious goals, that now in our ideal aspirations we dimly can presage.

Let us throw a glance upon the beginning of organized life where it separates into two distinctively different kingdoms, *viz.*, into plants and animals.

Living substance, animal as well as vegetable, which has not as yet assumed a perceptibly specialized form, is called protoplasm. Mi-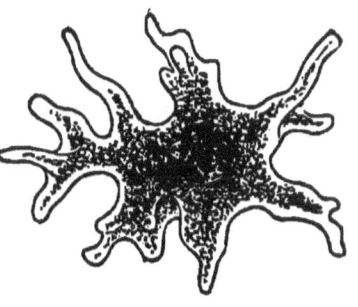nute lumps of animal protoplasm can frequently be found in stagnant water. They are called change-animals, or amœbas. Amœbas do not yet possess a distinct mouth; they take nourishment by absorbing and assimilating all kinds

AN AMŒBA.

of animal and vegetable particles, which they draw into their interior through any point of their surface. They have no distinct members; they move by sending out protuberances and dragging the rest of their mass behind. They multiply by division. Their constant changes of form gave them their name.

Amœbas cannot as yet be characterized as organisms. The simplest organism into which living substance develops, is the cell.

Simple as the cell really is in comparison 'with any higher organism, it still appears extremely complex, when submitted to a careful investigation. Under ordinary conditions it consists :

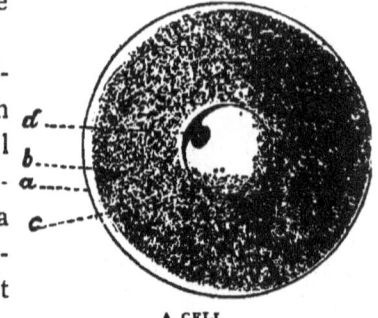

A CELL.

The granulated appearance, according to Fleming, is caused by coagulation due to chemical reaction. In the living cells which he examined, minute particles of fat vibrated in the interfibral matter.

1. Of a membrane or skin, *a*, formed under the influence of its environment.

2. Of the kernel or nucleus, *c*, and

3. The plasma or cell-substance, *b*.

According to Prof. Walther Flemming,* the cell-substance, as well as the nucleus, is made up of special fibral structures and an interfibral matter, which in living cells, we have good reason to infer, is of the nature of a fluid.

The kernel contains a smaller kernel, *d*, called the nucleolus.

In the activity of the cell there subsists a division of labor : the skin acts as the agency of communication with the outside world, the cell-substance assimilates and disassimilates food, the kernel serves for propagation. When the kernel has split, the cell begins to branch off into several filial cells.

The principle of division of labor is carried farther

* *Zellsubstanz, Kern, und Zelltheilung.* By Walther Flemming, Professor of Anatomy at Kiel. Leipzig, 1882. F. C. W. Vogel.

still, when, as in the Hydra or Gastrula, several cells
form one greater whole. Each cell retains its individuality, but it is differentiated through its service upon
the organism, to which it belongs.

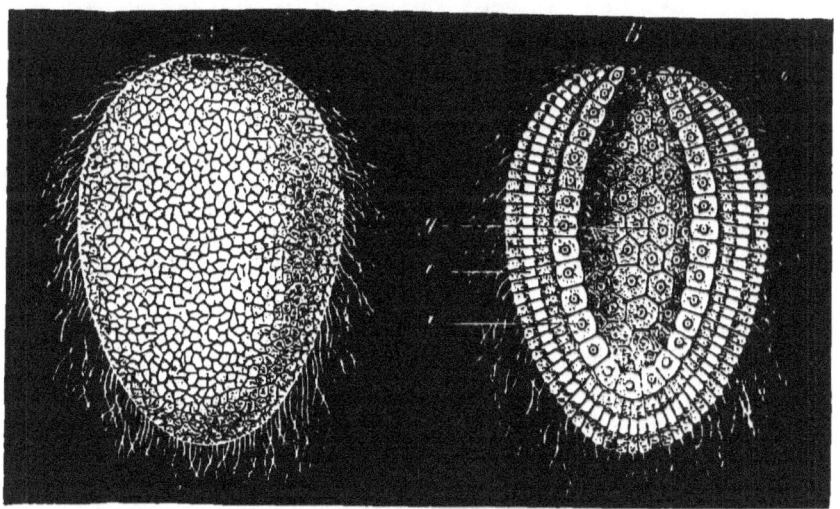

GASTRULA (OLYNTHUS.)

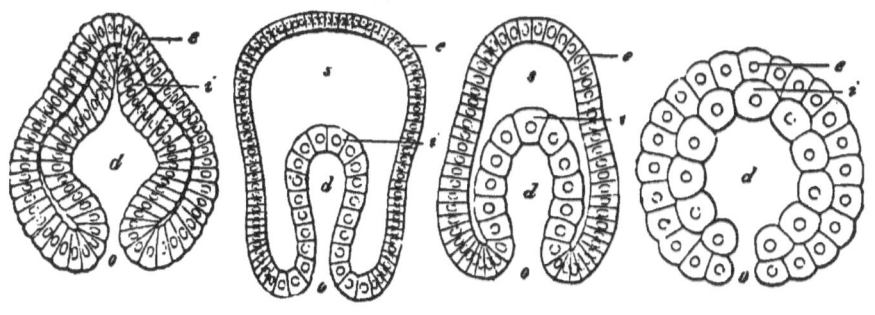

| SAGITTA. | URASTER. | NAUPLIUS. | LINNÆUS. |

FOUR DIAGRAMS OF DIFFERENT HYDRAS, ACCORDING TO HÆCKEL :

i, Inner skin, or entoderm.
e, Outer (exterior) skin or entoderm.
o, Orifice or mouth.

d, Stomach.
s, Reservoir of assimilated food.

The law of specialization which makes the parts
of an organism work with and for each other, is the

fundamental condition of all higher evolution of life. Organized life, therefore, with all the varied spiritual treasures that it has created, ultimately depends upon a moral condition ; it depends upon the condition that the individual earnestly devotes all its life and efforts to the service of the greater whole to which it belongs. Or shall we not rather state the fact in its inverted and more natural order ? Because the devotion of the work of every part to the life of the whole is the condition of all evolution and of all progress, therefore it is ethical. Ethics is no creation of our mind. Being the code of rules for our conduct, it must stand on facts. The facts that have produced man, are the data from which the rules of our conduct must be derived. If ethics were a human invention, it would be a mere fancy of our imagination. It might then be called poetry, or romance, or subjective opinion, but it would never be a science. Ethics, as we conceive it, can be derived from and applied to facts. It is a science and among the sciences it is the science of sciences. It is applied philosophy.

*
* *

The Hydra, or fresh water polyp, being the next step in the progressive development beyond a cell, has the shape of a double-skinned bag. (See Figs. on p. 69.)

The outer skin, or ectoderm, *e,* performs the functions of sensation and motion ; if irritated, its cells contract. The inner skin, or entoderm, *i,* performs the function of food-assimilation. The cells of the ectoderm being connected among themselves by long fibres, are called neuro muscular cells, because they

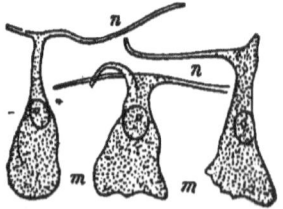

NEURO-MUSCULAR CELLS.

perform in the simplest manner possible at the same time both the functions of nerves as well as those of the muscles in more highly organized animals.

Man, considered from the standpoint of the theory of evolution, must be regarded as a most highly developed Hydra. In man the inner skin, or entoderm, through constant specialization of work, through the perfectionment and increase of the functions, has been developed into lungs, stomach, intestines, heart, liver, and kidneys. The ectoderm, or outer skin, has been transformed into the epithelium, muscles, nerves, bones, and brain. The activity of the soul proper— *i. e.*, of that part of the soul, or the whole form of the organism, which discharges the most important functions,—has been concentrated in the brain.

Professor Hæckel, in one of his lectures, beautifully explains, how each cell, even the plant-cell, is endowed with a peculiar soul of its own ; but in higher animals there are formed through a division of work special soul-cells in the shape of nerve-substance.

The vegetable world could not raise its humble and modest existence to such a height, as to differentiate its soul-life in special soul-cells or nerves. And the reason why plants remain on a much lower level than animals, is mainly due to the fact, that the plant chiefly lives upon inorganic elements, deriving nourishment from its immediate environment, from the earth, the air, and the water. Under the influence of the sun, the plant decomposes water and carbonic acid, setting free their oxygen. It retains the carbon of the carbonic acid, and the hydrogen of the water. At the same time it absorbs nitrogen compounds from its surroundings. The products of these decompositions are then united into those combinations of carbon, nitrogen, and hydrogen, which serve animals as food. The plant, accordingly, (or more correctly expressed, the solar-heat in the plant,) performs the work of decomposing the surrounding elements and building up out of the simple products of decomposition higher combinations that are more complicated and contain potential energy. The functions of the animal body are performed exactly in an inverse order. The plant-cell decomposes in order to build up, the animal-cell builds up in order to decompose.

The higher a combination is, the less stable it is. Like a house of cards, it easily breaks down and sets free the energy stored up in its structure. Animal bodies decompose vegetable combinations in order to transform them into much higher combinations which are extremely unstable, and thus they gather a store of potential energy that, whenever wanted, can be converted into the kinetic energy of living movements.

Animal life is conditioned by plant-life; plant-life must perform the preparatory work; it collects by the aid of sun-beams a treasure of potential energy, whence animal life can derive the strength of its existence.

Since plant-life disengages comparatively little energy and that which it disengages, seems solely devoted to decomposition, plants naturally lack voluntary motion, and therewith all the higher soul-life of the animal world. Exceptions to this rule are mostly illusions. Such motions as those of the sun-flower, turning its head toward the light, and the closing of the morning-glory after sunrise, cannot be considered as voluntary. And such instances as the movements of the Mimosæ and the Venus fly-trap are at best slight indications only of the higher possibilities which are realized in animal life.

Darwin's interesting and well-known researches upon this subject seem to confirm, that the movements which take place in these plants in consequence of an irritation, can partly, at least, be referred to the contraction of certain cells. As soon as the hair-like fibres on the upper edge of the fly-trap are irritated, they transmit the irritation to the cells of the middle-ribs of the side-leaves, whereby such a change is effected in the cells that both halves of the leaf approach each other. The nature of this change in the fly-trap has not as yet been sufficiently established. But, it is highly probable, that the movement in question is caused by some kind of purely mechanical pressure, and not through any disengagement of energy in the plasma of the cell. Yet, even if this were the case, it still differs immensely from the voluntary movement of animal substance, even in so low an organism as is the amœba ; and we can look upon the motions of the Venus fly-traps as upon a faint analogy only to the activity of the animal world, and very rare, indeed, are instances of such motions in the world of plants.

The work of the nerves or soul-cells consists in the transmission of an irritation, caused through an outward impression. The irritation provokes a movement which is called the reflex-motion of the irritation. It is considered as a reaction, and physiologists speak of "a change of irritation into reflex-motion."

Nerves, accordingly, perform two functions :

1. An irritation is received at the periphery (the outer skin) of an organism ; and

2. A reaction takes place in the interior of the nervous substance. It is conducted on another path back to the periphery, causing the contraction of certain fibres beneath the skin, thus resulting in motion.

In this manner two kinds of nerve-fibers are formed, in-going and out-going lines, centripetal or afferent, and centrifugal or efferent nerves, which meet in a knot, the so-called ganglion. The centripetal nerves are called sensory, the centrifugal motory.

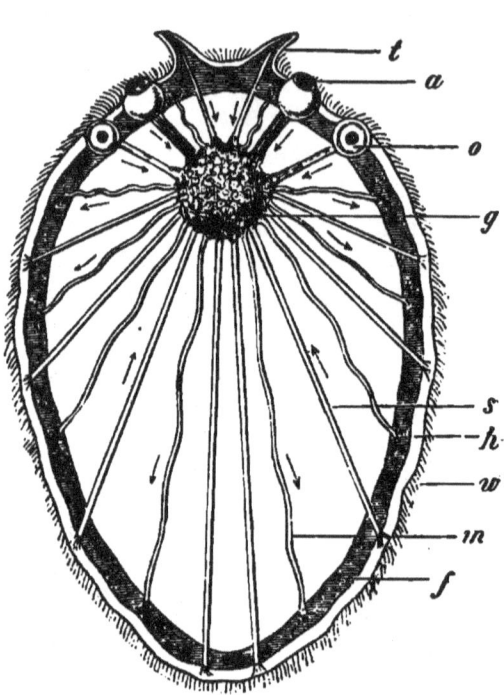

As an instance of an extremely simple nervous system consisting solely of a ganglion with afferent and efferent nerves, we mention the whirl-worm or *Turbellaria.* The skin of this worm is differentiated in two places on each side, in the one as eye in adaptation to the rays of light, and in the other as ear, under the influence of the waves of sound.

TURBELLARIA, ACCORDING TO HÆCKEL.

g, Ganglion.	*o*, Ear.
s, Sensory fibres.	*h*, Skin.
m, Motory fibres.	*f*, A layer of muscles.
t, Tentacles (feelers).	*w*, Cilias covering the
a, Eye.	skin.

What an enormous distance from a worm like this unto man, who in his complicated nervous system contains hundreds and thousands of such minute ganglion-systems, partly coördinated and partly subordinated in a rich and systematic arrangement!

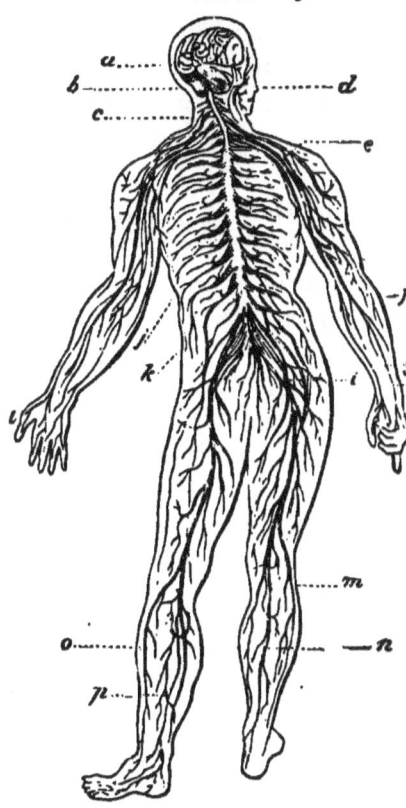

THE NERVOUS SYSTEM OF MAN.

a, Brain.
b, Cerebellum.
c, Spinal cord.
d, Facial nerve.
e, Brachial plexus.
f, Internal cutaneous nerve of the arm.
g, Mesial nerve of the arm.
h, Cubital or ulnar nerve.
i, Sciatic plexus, giving rise to the principle nerves of the lower extremities.
j, Intercostal nerves.
k, Femural plexus.
l, Radial nerve of the arm.
m, o, External peroneal nerve.
n, p, Tibial nerve.
o, External sapheneous nerve.

If comparative physiology has not as yet succeeded in discovering all the many millions of links from the amœba up to man, what does it matter? The evolution of man from a lowly origin can no longer be rejected if we consider that continuity is throughout the characteristic feature of life. Man represents life from the very beginning of life and what he is he is through the history of his race.

That man has risen from a low beginning to that height, is not humiliating to him but elevating; it proves that he may continue to develop his soul even to a greater and nobler future.

FEELING AS A PHYSIOLOGICAL PROCESS.

In the first chapter of this book "Feeling and Motion," the question was proposed: "What is the molecular combination that is accompanied with feeling, and what is its mode of action?"

This question is not as yet answered by physiology. It is a problem still, and we are far from a solution that would be satisfactory in all its details. We know something about the subject, but that something is very little in comparison to what our physiologists would like to know.

The ganglions are for good reasons supposed to be the seat of feeling; yet it must not be understood that feeling is created there alone. It is there alone that feeling is centralized. It appears that the sensory organs with their natural covering, the skin, also belong to the whole feeling apparatus. Every one of them is an indispensable part for the production of normal feelings. If any one of these parts is injured, feeling will either cease altogether or at least be disturbed. If, for instance, the tactile bodies (the Pacinian corpuscles) are not covered with skin, irritations will no longer be felt as tactile impressions, but as pain.

The process of a nervous transmission is extremely complicated, and our observation is limited to its crudest outlines only. We know, however, that the transmission through the ganglions must be even more complicated than the transmission through the fibres, for according to minute measurements by Helmholtz, a nervous shock travels through the human nerve fibre at an average rate of 30–40 metres in a second, but it is much retarded on its passage through the ganglions.

* * *

Du Bois Reymond has proved that every transmission of nervous irritations is accompanied with electrical phenomena. The apparatus connected with the nerve for measuring the electric tension shows a decrease of the strength of the current during a state of nervous activity. This was called by Du Bois Reymond *negative Schwankung*, "negative fluctuation."

The negative fluctuation of the electric tension, it may be incidentally mentioned, is not at all a phenomenon of nervous activity alone. Du Bois Reymond's law holds good for muscular fibres also. In a state of rest, the living muscle, like the nerve, shows in the galvanometer the presence of a low and constant current, which in a state of activity noticeably decreases, proving that that much electricity is being used in other directions.

The nervous system is often, and not without good and obvious reasons, represented as a telegraphic apparatus. The method of transmission also has repeatedly been compared to our modern system of telegraphing through electric currents. The wonderful achievements which man accomplished with the help of electricity, seemed to suggest that nervous transmission might be of an electrical nature. Since the discovery, however, made by Du Bois Reymond, *we know for certain that this is an error.* Nervous transmissions are accompanied by electrical phenomena, yet they cannot be explained as such. This is evident even from the different rate of transmission ; electricity travels, according to Wheatstone, 464,000,ooo metres in one second, while the velocity of nervous irritations, in spite of all the fabulous swiftness of thought, is more than ten million times slower ; and if nerve-activity is to be regarded as electrical action, how can it differ from muscular activity which exhibits the very same electrical phenomena ? Neither can the nerve-fibres be compared to the wires of a telegraph, which are transmitters simply of the electric current ; for every single nerve-cell in a nervous fibre, and also every cell in the muscular fibre, is in itself a small electric battery. The whole process of nervous transmission may rather be compared to a number of small explosions transmitted over a line of grains of powder. An irritation, i. e., an impression received by some contact with the outer world in a sensory organ, being transmitted through the sensory fibre to the ganglion, and from the ganglion through the motor fibre to a muscle, causes along the whole tract of its transmission a continuous discharge of potential energy stored up in the nervous substance. The transmission being accompanied with many other phenomena, ends in an innervation of the muscle which forms the terminus of the motor nerve. This innervation is the nervous discharge that causes the muscle to contract and thus produces mechanical motion.

*　　*　　*

Let us for the sake of illustration represent the nerves as a series of compressed springs, so arranged that if one is released it will at the same time release the next following ; thus any disturbance will travel from one to the other along the whole series. The organism is constantly at work to repair the losses incurred. As soon as potential energy is set free, new structures are built by the circulating fluids freighted with vitalized substances. Thus by the activity of the blood, to return again to our simile, the discharged springs of the nervous system are again and again compressed, and thus they are, unless the exhaustion be carried too far, always ready for action.

If a shock is transmitted, the effects produced depend first upon the shock itself. The more violent a shock is the more sudden will the disturbance be. And if a shock covers a larger field of the skin, it must necessarily irritate a larger number of nerve-fibres, thus producing a greater excitement than if two or three nerve-fibres were disturbed only. Yet the main determining factor of the effect, it appears, is the specific energy (as Johannes Müller called it) of the nervous substance in the nerve as well as in the ganglion. Similarly, if a shock is transmitted through a series of springs, the effect will depend upon the springs chiefly—upon their form and their tension ; form and tension are the ''specific energy ''of the springs. The different nerves became adapted to special irritations. The optic nerve became adapted to the ether waves ; their irritations are transferred to the optic ganglions, and there possibly the disturbance is accompanied with a feeling called light. The auditory nerve became adapted to air waves; this irritation is transmitted to the auditory ganglion, and there possibly it is accompanied with a feeling called sound ; etc. By a constant and exclusive use for their specialized purposes through many thousands of generations, the tissues became so adapted to their special work, that now they cannot otherwise react against

any kind of irritation than as sensations, the one of
light and the other of sound. Any disturbance, a ray
of light as well as an electric current, or a mechanical
concussion, will produce sensations of light on the
optic nerve, and sensations of sound in the auditory
nerve. The same causes will produce sensations of
smell in the olfactory nerve, and sensations of touch
or of temperature in the sensory nerves that terminate
in the skin.*

The feeling which originates in the ganglion, during the transmission of a nervous perturbation, can
depend upon the forms only of the different cells. A
certain shock is received which sets free a series of
tensions ; the liberation of some of these tensions in
the ganglion is a commotion of sensory cells, accompanied by feeling. It is called a sensation. The
course of motions nowhere ceases to consist of motions. We have a continuous transference of motions,
yet some of these motions are accompanied with feeling. These feelings are different among themselves,
and we have sufficient evidence to believe that their
difference exactly corresponds to the different forms
of nervous action which they accompany. We may,
accordingly, without impropriety, speak in this sense
of the different forms of feelings.

Suppose we had before us a line of cards arranged
in pairs leaning one against the other, in such a
manner that a slight shock will upset the whole
series ; a simile often employed to explain the transference of nervous shocks. At a certain point, in
about the middle of the line, let us suppose that a
bell is fixed, the tongue of which strikes the bell upon

---

* Compare E. Hering, "The Specific Energies of the Nervous System,"
Nos. 22 and 23 of *The Open Court.*

the overthrow of the two adjoining cards. At the end of the line, upon the two last pairs of cards, stands a small vessel filled with water. Upon the overthrow of the cards the water is spilt. The striking of the bell represents sensation,* the spilling of the water muscle-innervation. The striking of the bell is not changed into a spilling of water: the former only precedes the latter in time. If a nerve is irritated below the ganglion, a muscle-innervation takes place without sensation, with the same necessity as the water is spilt without any previous sounding of the bell, when the cards below the bell only have been upset. But when the motor nerve is cut, and the sensory nerve is irritated alone, then sensation only occurs, without any reflex muscular motion, just as a perturbation of the upper line of cards will make the bell sound, but if the line below the bell is interrupted, it will not cause the spilling of the water.

The mechanical connection of causes and effects need not be interrupted, if that part of the transmittance of nervous irritations which takes place in the ganglion is so disturbed as to produce no actual feeling.

---

* The simile is in so far inadequate as the striking of the bell and the air vibrations of sound are motions also. Feeling, however, is no motion, and does not originate from a transformation of either potential or kinetic energy.

Some psychologists compare the phenomenon of feeling to the shadow which accompanies the motions of a body. But a shadow is the absence of light and light again is a mode of motion. Feeling is no motion, nor is it the disappearance of motions. Other psychologists have compared consciousness to the sparks that an engine emits with the smoke. Sparks also, being little particles of fire, are modes of motion. Thus these similes are also inadequate.

It will be difficult, if at all possible, to find an appropriate simile, and why? Because, whatever allegory we take from the processes of the objective world, we constantly remain in the province of objectivity. Whatever unspeakable difference there may be between two processes of objective phenomena, they belong to the same domain; while the domain of subjective reality or feeling, in spite of the parallelism between both, is so heterogeneous that it suffers no comparison.

Suppose the bell be covered with a woolen cloth, will not then the phenomenon of sound that accompanies the process cease altogether, although otherwise there is nothing changed in the mechanism of the transmission? And when, through alcoholic poisoning, through medical drugs (anæsthetics), or through any nervous disturbance, consciousness is for a time obliterated, may not a man under certain circumstances act exactly as if he were in full possession of consciousness? Does not often an intoxicated man or a hypnotized subject move about and talk like other people, and yet he knows nothing and afterwards he will remember nothing of all that happened?

The concatenation of circumstances is such that we are easily misled to suppose that when the cards are overthrown the striking of the bell causes the spilling of the water, and that consciousness sets the muscles in motion. On this supposition only, which takes a *post hoc* as a *propter hoc*, i. e., a mere sequence as a causal connection, is based the assumption that consciousness is the motor power, the *primum movens*, of the soul; the cause, the principium, and beginning of man's muscular movements, the origin and source of his activity. However, consciousness does not produce the activity of our body. Consciousness, as M. Ribot says, does not constitute the situation; on the contrary, it is constituted by the situation. Consciousness is an indicator only of a certain condition of our nerve-activity. It is not the cause of a man's will, but it is the expression of a certain state of mind, which, under normal conditions, will be followed by an act of will, be it a real muscular motion, a spoken word, which of course is muscular motion also, or the inhibition of a motion.

Every idea considered not as a mere feeling but as a brain-structure fit to serve as an irritation to action (we call such ideas impulses), will, if not inhibited, pass into an act, whether it be connected with consciousness or not. Consciousness itself is not the motion that causes the transmission of nervous irritations, it is not the agency that discharges the innervation for contracting the muscles. It is a phenomenon that merely accompanies the physiological process of a nervous transmission through the ganglion.

It is not the shadow that makes our body move ; it is the body that moves ; and the shadow accompanies the movement. It is not the ticking of the pendulum that sets the wheels of the clock in motion, but the swinging. The motion of the clock is produced by the pressure of the weight which is transferred to the pendulum in the form of vibrations. The motion of our limbs is caused through the transmission of a nervous perturbation, setting free a part of the potential energy stored up in our motor nerves and in our muscles; but there is, properly speaking, no change of "consciousness" into "will," no change of "feeling" into "motion."

When we compare consciousness to the ticking of a pendulum, we do not wish to maintain that consciousness is as superfluous and indifferent as the ticking of a pendulum. We merely express in this simile that it is destitute of motor power. Although consciousness is destitute of motor power, it is nevertheless of paramount importance. There is nothing redundant in nature ; how can consciousness be a superfluous factor in the constitution of man's mind ?

Consciousness may be compared to a light. It affords in novel and difficult situations the possibility of circumspection. The light in a machine room will enable the attendant engineer properly to regulate the motions of the engine ; but the rays of the lantern have no locomotive power upon the wheels and piston, so as to set the engine into action. If the engineer is a novice, he cannot do his work without light, but the expert knows how to direct the lever even in the dark. The consciousness of mental states is an indispensable condition of the proper direction of will, but it does not possess motor power.

THE NERVOUS SYSTEM OF WORMS, RADIATES, AND ARTICULATES.

THE simplest nervous system consists of a single ganglion with afferent and efferent fibres. Its action is represented in the adjoined diagram. The sensory irritation is transmitted as a primitive reflex motion from the skin, or the sensory organs in the *G* skin (*SI*), through the ganglion (*G*) to the muscles (*MM*), thus starting from and returning to the periphery; and we have reason to suppose that the transmission of this *SI   MM* nervous irritation is accompanied in the ganglion by an extremely vague kind of feeling.

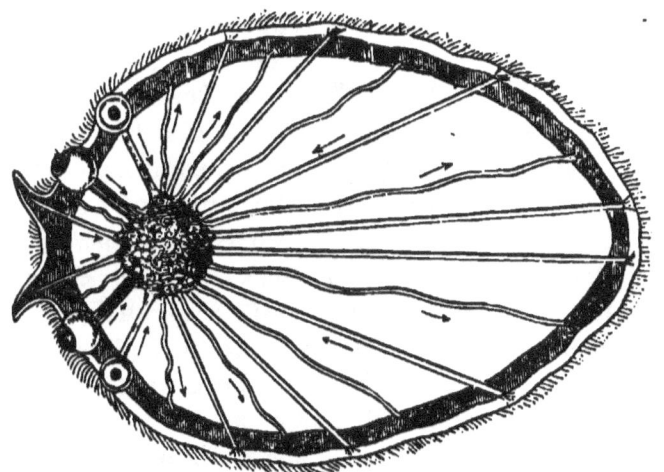

A ganglion constituting the centre of so simple a nervous system as is for instance that of the whirl-worm, is called a primitive brain.

Not much more complicated are the nervous systems of Radiates, whose organs are arranged in a circle like the parts of a flower. The starfishes belong to this class ; they may be regarded as five worms having

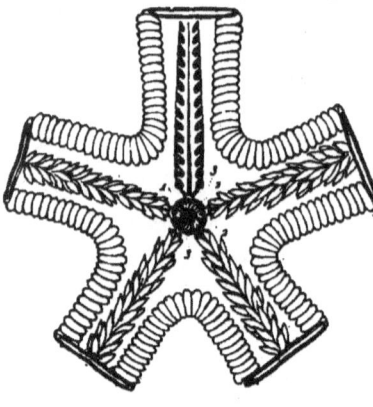

a mouth and a digestive organ in common. Each arm possesses a small ganglion (1) near the mouth. The five ganglions are interconnected by a ring (2) around the mouth ; and a nervous fibre passes along on the lower or ventral side from each ganglion to the end of each of the several arms.

NERVOUS SYSTEM OF A STARFISH.
(The rays are cut off.)

1. Ganglions.

2. Connecting fibres, encircling the mouth and establishing a communication among the five ganglions.

3. Nervous fibres running along lower surface to the ends of the rays

Mollusk life is characterized by a strong development of the vegetative functions. Mollusks are mere bags containing organs of digestion, respiration, circulation, and generation. Ascidians (or pouch-creatures) and Conchs (or shells) have no head whatever ; they lead a mere vegetative life. Conchs are now regarded as degenerated snails. Snails are in possession of a feebly developed head with eyes, tentacles, mouth, jaws, and a tongue. The ventral part of the body, the foot of the snail, is its sole organ of locomotion ; it consists of a contractile layer of muscular fibres. The highest developed mollusks are the Cephalopods, or head-footed creatures, possessing a circle of organs of locomotion (we may call them arms or feet) about their mouth. Such creatures are the cuttle-fish, or Sepia, and the Nautilus.

The most characteristic feature of the nervous system of Mollusks (as represented in the snail) is the œsophagean ring, surrounding the gullet. There are ganglionic knots at the upper and at the lower part of the ring. The upper part is a primitive brain, receiving sensory fibres from the tentacles, etc., while the lower part acts as the centre of the respiratory and locomotive functions. The lower ganglion is often differentiated into two distinct parts, and in that case the œsophagean ring appears double; the anterior ring connecting the brain with the pedal ganglion for locomotion, the posterior with the branchial ganglion for respiration.

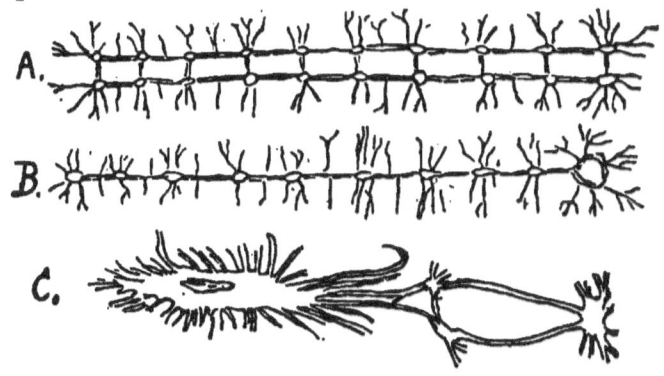

NERVOUS SYSTEMS OF

A. Common Sandhopper. (*Talitrus locusta.*) Showing (on the right side) two separate cerebral ganglia, each about the same size as the other ganglia situated below it on the separate ventral chords. (After Grant.)

B. Cymothoa. (Fish-louse.) Cerebral ganglia (on the right side) almost wholly absent from œsophagean ring.

C. Crab. (*Palinurus vulgaris.*) The cerebral ganglia (on the right side) receiving the optic, tactile, and other nerves, are fused into one. The œsophagean ring elongated; the ventral ganglion strongly developed.

The nervous system of Articulates consists of a series of ganglions, situated below the intestinal canal and interconnected by a nervous fibre. In addition to this series of ganglions the front segment or head possesses an œsophagean ring, similar to that of Mollusks, bearing at its upper part the head-ganglion or primitive brain.

The single ganglions of Articulates, being situated in the various separate segments, are endowed with an extraordinary independence. They act not so much in subordination to as in co-operation with the front ganglion. For instance. If the head of a centipede

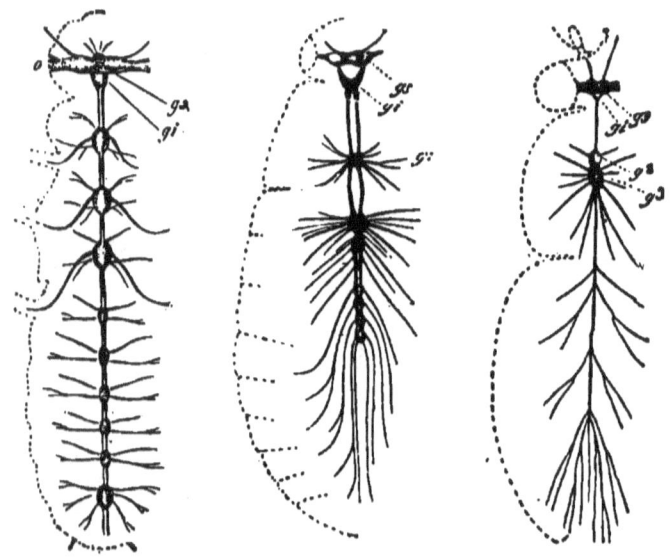

WHITE ANT   (*Termes*).   WATERBEETLE (*Dytiscus*).   FLY (*Musca*).
(From Gegenbauer. After Blanchard.)

gs. Supra-œsophagean ganglion (brain).
gi. Infra-œsophagean ganglion.
gr., *g2*, *g3*. Thoracic ganglions (partly fused).
o. Optic nerves.

be quickly cut off while the creature is in motion, the legs will mechanically continue to run on until they are brought to a stop by some interposed obstacle. The

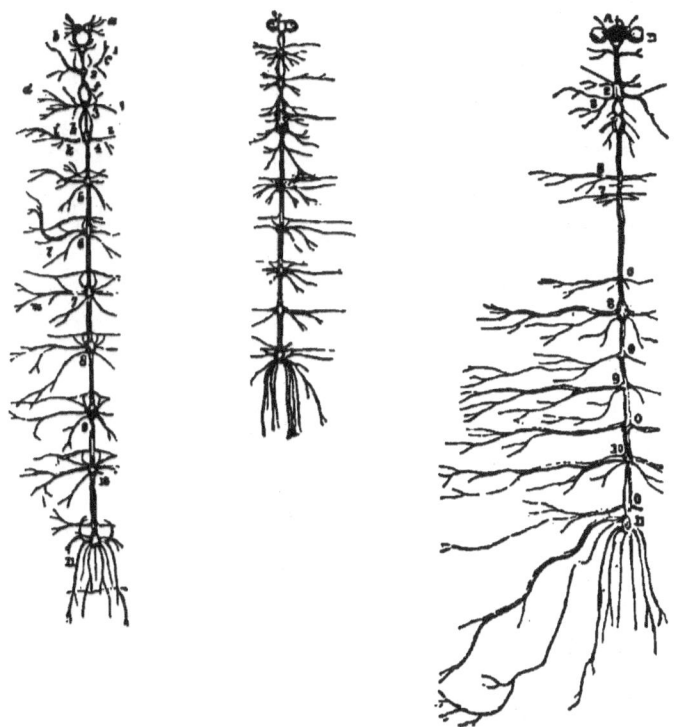

CATERPILLAR, CHRYSALIS, AND PERFECT INSECT OF HAWK-MOTH (*Sphinx igustri*).

The first figure shows the full grown caterpillar about two days before changing to a chrysalis. It resembles much the nervous system of the Centipede. The two cerebral ganglions are small, and the ganglions in the ventral cord (1–10) are almost uniform. The nerves of the head (*ab*) are weakly, those of the other fibres (*c-n*) fairly, developed.

The middle figure represents the chrysalis of the same creature 30 days after the change from a caterpillar. The abdominal chords are much shortened, some of its ganglia fuse.

The third figure shows the perfected insect.

A, Cerebral ganglion.

B. Optic ganglion.

Note the increased size of the cerebral ganglion and of some parts of the ventral cord; while some parts are concentrated or even suppressed.

O. Respiratory nerves.

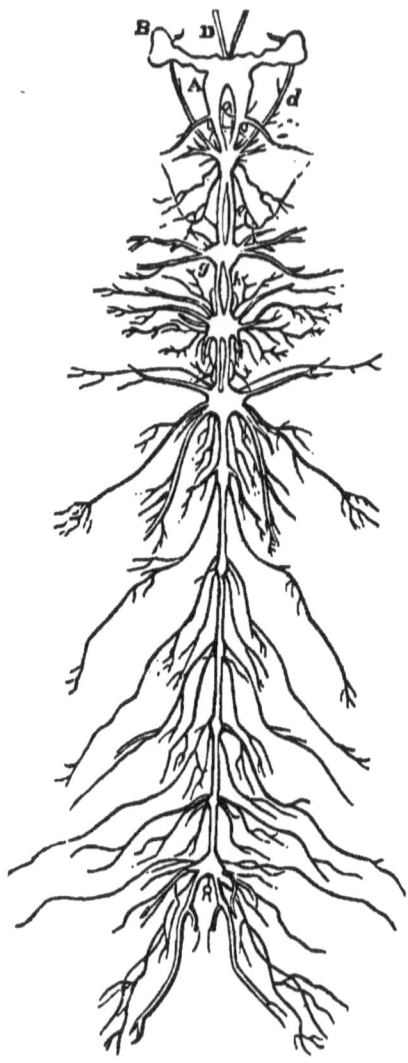

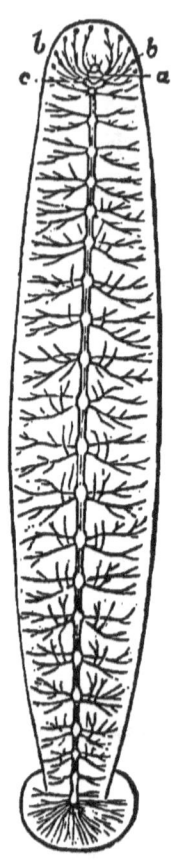

NERVOUS SYSTEM OF THE GREAT GREEN GRAS-
HOPPER.   (After Newport.)

A. Cerebral ganglion.
B. Optic nerves.
D. Antennal nerves.
d. Motor nerves of mandible, from sub-œsophagean ganglion.
e. Fibres connecting the sub-œsophagean
with the first thoracic ganglion.
g. First thoracic ganglion.
h. Commissures connecting thoracic ganglia.

NERVOUS SYSTEM OF MEDICAL
LEECH.   (After Owen.)
a Double supra-œso-
phagean ganglion con-
nected with :
bb nerves ending in rudi-
mentary ocelli ;
c infra - œsophagean
ganglion, continuous with a
double ventral chord bearing at intervals distinct com-
pound ganglia.

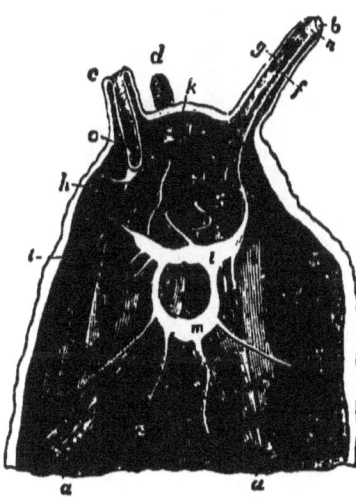

NERVOUS SYSTEM OF THE COMMON
GARDEN SNAIL. (After Owen.)

l. Cerebral ganglion, situated
above the œsophagus, receiving
nerves from the tentacles.

a, Small tentacle withdrawn.

b. Large tentacle with eyes (ocelli).

c. Large tentacle withdrawn.

d. Small tentacle.

f. Nerve fibre of large tentacle.

k. Nerve fibre of small tentacle.

l. Cerebral ganglion situated
above the œsophagus, receiving
nerves from tentacles.

m. Sub-œsophagean ganglion, a
double mass, representing a pair of
pedal and a pair of branchial
ganglia.

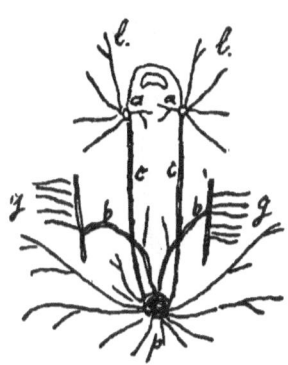

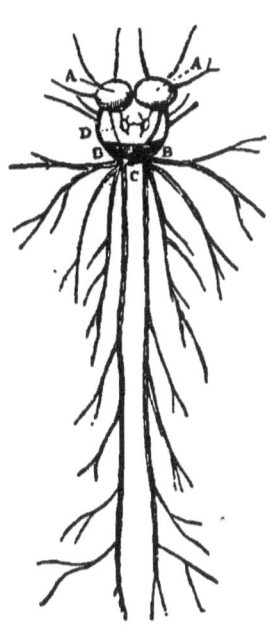

NERVOUS SYSTEM OF AN OYSTER.
(Todd. After Garner.)

aa. Anterior ganglia ; being
situated on each side of the
mouth, interconnected by a fibre
over-arching the mouth.

ll. Labial fibres.

p. Posterior or branchial
ganglion (double, for respiration).

bb. Branchial nerves going to
the gills (*gg.*)

cc. Commissures between labial and branchial ganglia.

NERVOUS SYSTEM OF THE COM-
MON SLUG.

(The naked common garden
snail; one of the nudi-
branch mollusks.)

A, A. Cerebral ganglia.

B, B. Branchial ganglia.

D. Pharyngeal ganglia.

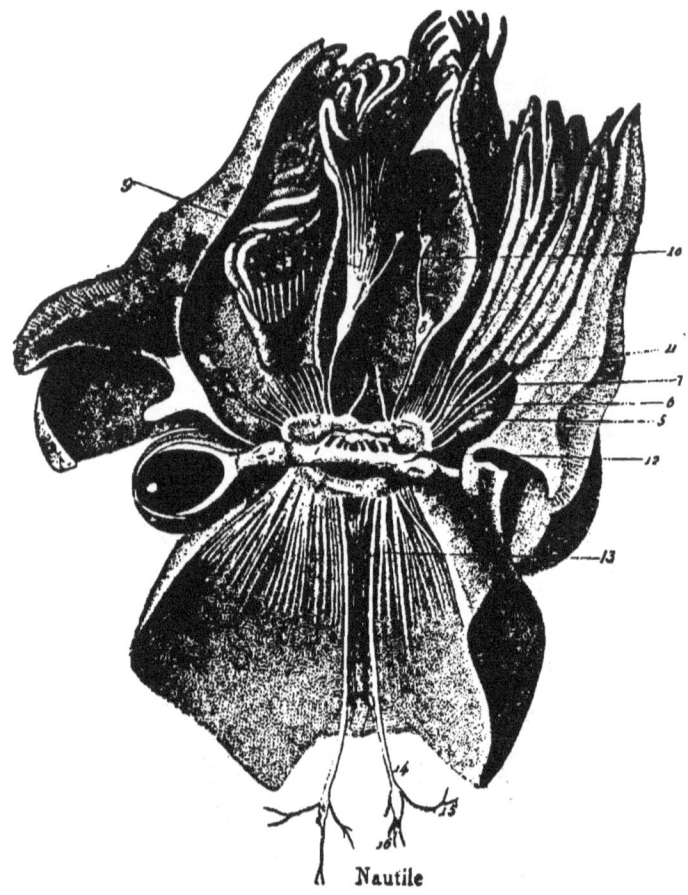

Nautile

PEARLY NAUTILUS.

(After. Owen.   Reproduced from Fr. Leuret and P. Gratiolet.)

1. Cerebral ganglion.
2. Optic nerve.
3. Anterior sub-œsophagean ganglion.
4. Posterior sub-œsophagean ganglion.
5. Digital tentacles.
6. Nerves of external labial tentacles.
7. Commissural fibres between 8 and 3.
8. Labial ganglion.
9. Nerves of internal labial tentacles.
10. Olfactive nerves.
11. Infundibular nerves.
12 Lingual and maxillary nerve.
13. Motor nerves.
14. Visceral nerves.
15. Branchial nerves.
16. Visceral ganglions.

ganglions of the various segments, it appears, have not as yet received information respecting the loss of their leader. Similarly, flies, after decapitation, will fly about and execute all kinds of motions, like their uninjured companions.

The Articulates (according to Haeckel) consist of three classes: (1) *Annellata*, or ringed worms—for instance, earth worms and leeches; (2) *Crustacea*, or crust-animals—for instance, crabs and lobsters; and (3) *Tracheata*, or wind-pipe animals, so called by Haeckel because they breathe through small tubes. The most important Tracheates are the myriapods, or thousand-legs, the spiders, and the insects. The nervous systems of the best known specimens of these three classes may be studied in the prefixed diagrams.

THE CONNECTING LINK BETWEEN THE INVERTEBRATES AND THE VERTEBRATES.

PROFESSOR ERNST HÆCKEL* in explaining the evolution of Vertebrates calls our attention to the importance of *Amphioxus lanceolatus*, a little fish about two inches long, shaped like a lancet, and living, mostly hidden in the sand, in shallow places of the Mediterranean, the Baltic, and the North Sea. It has no head, no cranium, no brain. The front part is distinguishable from the hind part almost solely by the presence of the mouth surrounded by a number of cilia ; and yet the Lanceolate belongs to the aristocratic class of Vertebrates : it possesses a spinal cord. The Lanceolate, accordingly, is the last surviving representative of the lowliest family among the Vertebrates.

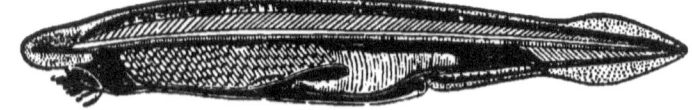

AMPHIOXUS LANCEOLATUS.

Pallas, the first discoverer of the Lanceolate, did not at once recognize the importance of his find. He considered it as a kind of imperfect snail. Yet the presence of a *chorda dorsalis*, i. e. of a cartilaginous string forming the axis of the skeleton, and the *medulla spinalis*

* *Natürliche Schöpfungsgeschichte*, Chap. 24.

(spinal cord), fix the relation of this little fish beyond all doubt. Kowalewsky and Kupffer, moreover, have proved, that to a certain degree the ontogeny of the Lanceolate corresponds in all particulars on the one hand with that of the lower Vertebrates and on the other with that of the Ascidians. Thus we can consider it as an established truth that the Lanceolate is the connecting link between the Invertebrates and the Vertebrates.

Leuckart and Pagenstecher discovered in the front part of the spinal cord of the Amphioxus (see Müller's Archiv, 1858, p. 561) a small vesicle, which represents a primitive brain—if brain it can be called. However, whether this vesicle represents the initial state of all three bulbs that appear in a higher development (as W. Müller says), or whether it represents the third bulb only (as Mihalkovics says), or whether it corresponds (as Huxley says) to the thalamencephalon, i. e., the second bulb, is still an unsettled question. It is not improbable that the Amphioxus which we are acquainted with, is a degenerated form of that creature from which the higher vertebrates have developed.

In the adjoined plates Professor Hæckel compares the development of a mollusk, like the Ascidian (A), with *Amphioxus lanceolatus* (B). How small are the differences in the beginning! And yet they were destined to keep the one creature in its humble condition of a mere vegetative existence, while the other in the course of further evolution was enabled to gain dominion over the whole creation of the earth.

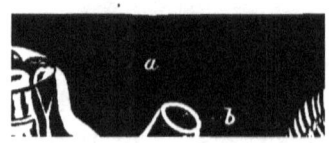

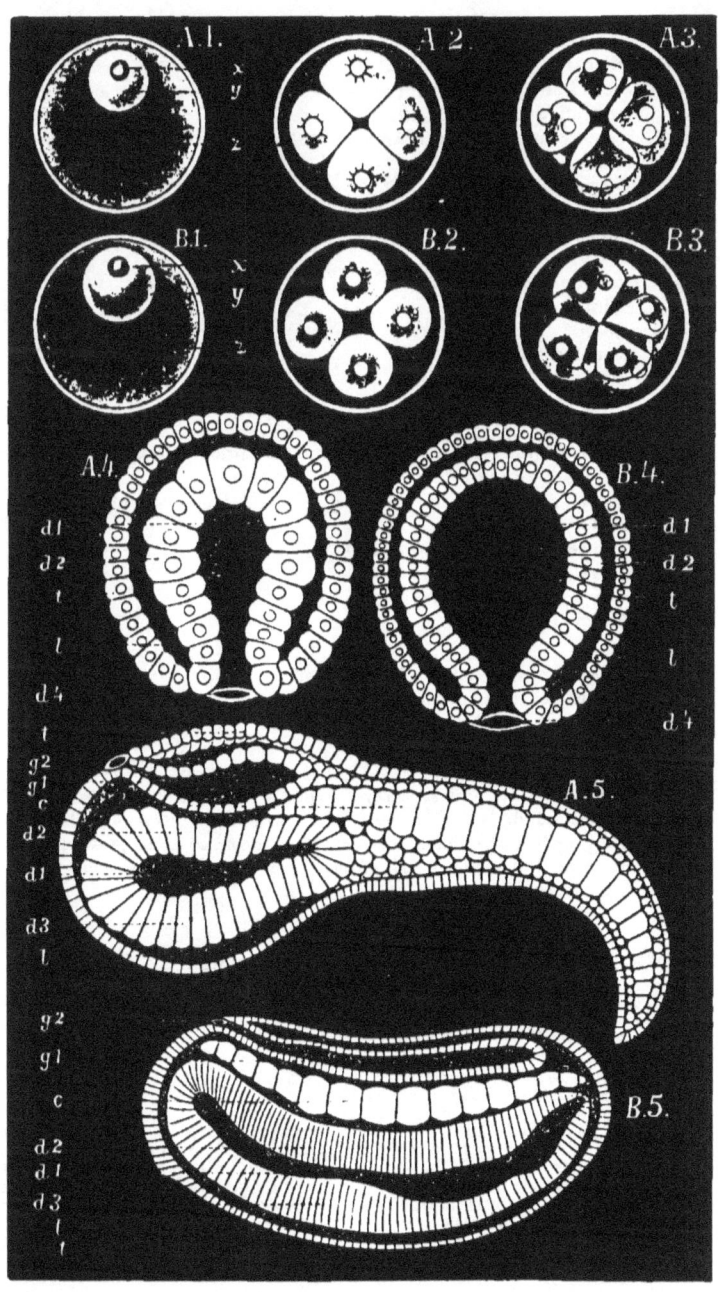

The skin of both creatures being transparent, their inner organization is plainly visible.

The Dot in the front part of the Amphioxus is a rudimentary eye.

The Ascidian A 6 is firmly attached to the soil by root-like processes (w), as if it were a plant. The adult Amphioxus however moves about like a fish

   a. Mouth.

   b. Porus abdominalis.

   c. Chorda dorsalis (appears only in the Lanceolate.)

   d. Intestinal canal.

   e. Ovary   } appears only in the Ascidian.
   f. Ovarean duct

   g. Spinal cord (medulla dorsalis.)

   h. Heart.

   i. Vermiform appendix.

   k. Gills.

   l. Cavity of the body.

   m. Muscles.

   n. Testicles (the Ascidian being hermaphroditic, the testicles combined with the ovary).

   o. Anus.

   p. Sexual aperture.

   q. Mature embryos of the Ascidian.

   r. Dorsal fins.

   s. Tail of the Lanceolate.

   w. Roots of the Ascidian.

   A. The egg of the Ascidian.

   B. The egg of the Lanceolate.

   Z. Protoplasma of the egg.

   V. Nucleus.

   X. Nucleolus.

A2, B2, A3, B3, etc., the successive stages in the development of the eggs After a repeated division, the germ forms a globule of many cells (called *Morula*) the surface of which in one part sinks down so as to present almost the shape of an india-rubber ball from which the air is removed. Thus a gastrula is formed (A4, B4).

   d1. Primitive abdomen.

   d4. Primitive mouth.

   d2. Entoderm, inner membrane or abdominal wall.

   l. Cavity of the germ.

   f. ectoderm, outside skin.

   A5. The Larva of the Ascidian.

   B5. The Larva of the Amphioxus.

     d1. The abdomen is closed.

     d2. The dorsal part is concave.

     d3. The ventral part is convex.

     g1. The medullar cavity (in the Amphioxus the primitive spinal cord).

     g2. The orifice of the medullar cavity, not as yet closed.

     d. Chorda dorsalis, in the Amphioxus the axis of the primitive backbone. In the Larva of the Ascidian the chorda dorsalis forms a tail which is thrown off during its metamorphosis. Those Ascidians which do not become stationary, retain their tails.

NERVOUS SYSTEM OF THE VERTEBRATES.

THERE are several differences of radical importance between *Amphioxus lanceolatus* and the higher Vertebrates ; yet besides that of the absence of brain and cranium in the former, there is no greater disparity than in the arterial system of blood-circulation. The *Acrania* (the Vertebrates without cranium, represented by the Lanceolate) have no proper hearts ; their hearts are mere arterial tubes, while the *Craniata* (the Vertebrates with a cranium) are throughout endowed with a regular heart, which, engine-like, drives the arterial blood through the whole system.

The nervous systems of all the Vertebrates are greatly different from those of the Invertebrates. There is no œsophagean ring encircling the gullet ; and instead of isolated ganglia, we have one continuous column which is no longer below but far above the intestinal canal. This column is protected by bony covers (the vertebræ) which constitute a flexible yet strong backbone. The foremost ganglia together with their vertebral cases are transformed into brain and cranium ; but the hemispheres and their bony cover, the top of the head, are an additional growth, which has developed out of the first vertebra.*

*Gegenbauer, *Untersuchungen zur Vergleichenden Anatomie der Wirbelthiere.* Part. III, *das Kopfskelett der Selachier als Grundlage zur Beu rthei lung der Genese des Kopfskeletts der Wirbelthiere.* Leipzig : 1872.

•

The most prominent divisions of the nervous system in the Vertebrates, i. e., in Fishes, Reptiles, Birds, and Mammals, are :

1. The Spinal Cord ;
2. The Bulb (*Medulla Oblongata*);
3. The Small Brain (*Cerebellum*);
4. The Bridge (*pons Varolii*);
5. The Optic Lobes ; and
6. The Thalami Optici.

(The Optic Lobes are of greater importance in the lower Vertebrates ; they are called in the physiology of man the Four Hills (*corpora quadrigemina*). The Thalamus remains entirely undeveloped in the lower vertebrates. The Optic Lobes not showing in lower vertebrates, as in man, Four Hills, but only two, are sometimes called *Corpora bigemina*, or the Two Hills.)

7. The Striped Body (*Corpus Striatum*).

8. The Hemispheres, or brain proper (*Cerebrum*).

The following chapters will be devoted to the physiology of these divisions in the brain of man.

As the most representative examples of the various Vertebrates we select a number of diagrams of the brains of fishes, amphibians, birds, and mammals.

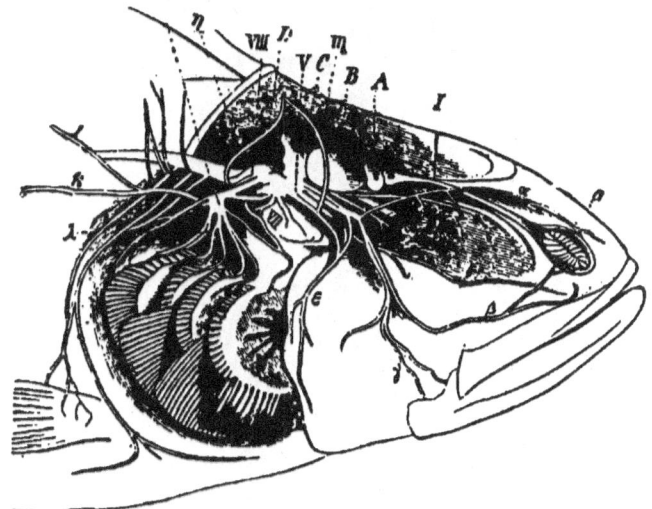

BRAIN OF A PERCH. (Gegenbaur, after Cuvier.)

A. Cranial lobe with olfactory ganglion (*I*).

B. Optic lobe.

C. Cerebellum.

D. Medulla oblongata.

    I. Olfactory nerve.

      a. Nasal sac.

    II. Optic nerve, severed.

    III. Oculo-motor nerve.

    IV. Trochlear nerve.

    V. Trigeminal.

    VII. Auditory.

    VIII. Vagus with its ganglion *g.*

      kl. Branches of vagus.

      m. Dorsal branch of trigeminus in connection with *n.*

      n. Dorsal branch of vagus.

    $a_{,}\beta\gamma.$ The three branches of the trigeminus *V.*

      $\delta\varepsilon.$ Facial nerve.

    $\lambda.$ Branches of the vagus.

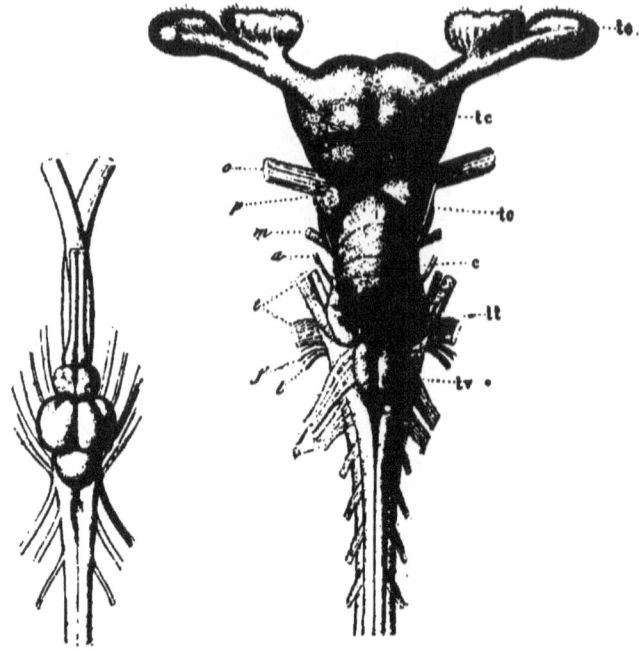

BRAIN OF A PIKE AND OF A SHARK.   (After Leuret and Gratiolet.)

tc. Cerebral tubercles (lobes).

to. Optic tubercles (lobes).

te. Ethmoid or olfactory tubercle.

tv. Vagus tubercle.   The ganglion of the vagus nerve.

c. Cerebellum.

e. Olfactory nerves.

o. Optic nerves.

p. Pathetic nerve.

m. Oculo-motor nerve.

a. Abducent nerve.

t. Trifacial nerve.

f. Facial nerve.

l. Labyrinthic nerve.

v. Vagus or branchial nerve.

NERVOUS SYSTEM OF FROG, VENTRAL SIDE. (After Ecker.)

H. Hemispheres.
Lop. Optic Lobes.
M. Medulla.
M1.-M10. S p i n a l
  nerves.
S. S y m p a t h e t i c
  nerve.
S1.-S10. Ganglia of
  the Sympathetic.
MS. Branches c o n-
  necting spinal cord
  and sympathetic.
No. Femoral nerve.
Ni. Sciatic nerve.
I-X. Cranial nerves.
I. Olfactory.
II. Optic nerve with
  (o) eye.
III. Oculo-motor.
IV. Trochlear.
V. Trigeminal.
VI. Abducent.
VII. and *F.* Facial.
VIII. Auditory.
IX. Glosso p h a r y n-
  geal.
X. Vagus.
Vg. Gasserian Gang-
  lion (of fifth nerve).
V5. Connect i o n o f
  Gasserian ganglion
  with the S y m p a-
  thetic.
F. Facial nerve.
G. Ganglion of t h e
  Vagus.
X1-X4. Branches of
  the Vagus.

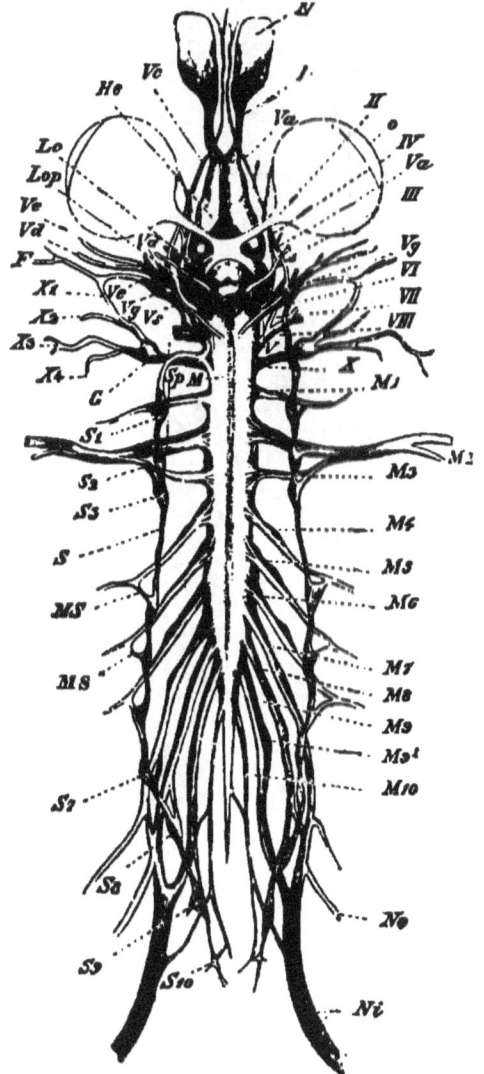

BRAIN OF THE BOA CONSTRICTOR.   (After Swan, reproduced from Bastian.)

a. Cerebral lobes.

b. Optic lobes.

c. Cerebellum.

d. Membrane of the nose.

1. Olfactory nerve.

2. Optic nerve.

3. Third nerve, i. e. main oculo-motor.

4. Fourth nerve or trochlear to the superior oblique muscle of the eye.

5. Fifth nerve.

6. Sixth nerve.

7. Seventh nerve.

8. Eighth nerve.

9. Auditory nerve.

10. Glosso-pharyngeal nerve.

11. Trunk of vagus nerve.

12. Twelfth nerve.

13. A sympathetic ganglion.

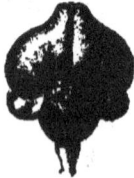

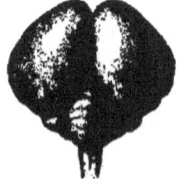

CUCKOO.   OWL.

(After Leuret and Gratiolet.)

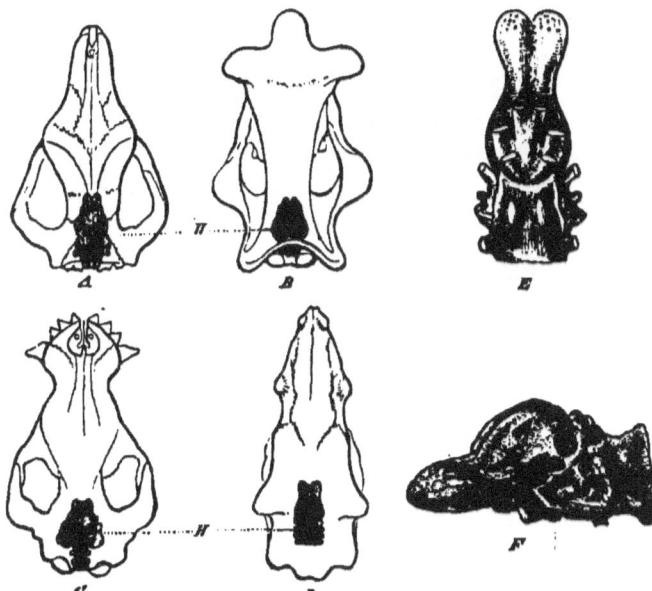

BRAINS OF EOCENE MAMMALS. (From Wiedersheim, after Marsh.)

A. Tillotherium fodiens.
B. Brontotherium ingens.
C. Coryphodon hamatus.
D. Dinoceras mirabile.
E. Ventral ⎫
F. Lateral ⎭ view of the brain of Dinoceras mirabile (from a cast).
H. Hemispheres.
Note the enormous size of the skull in comparison with a relatively small brain. The olfactory lobes are strongly developed.

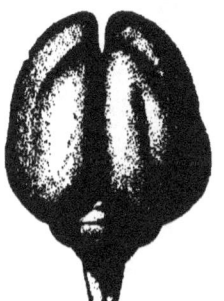

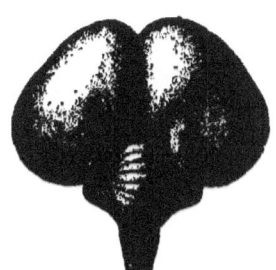

PARROT.   RAVEN.
(After Leuret and Gratiolet.)

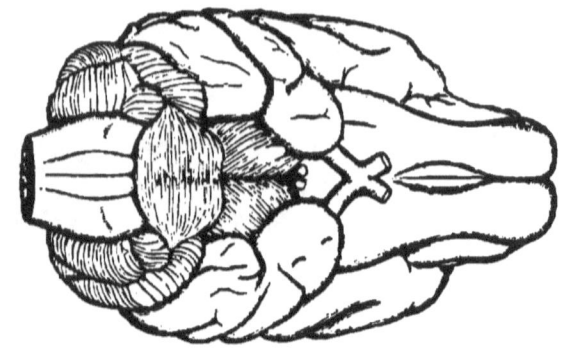

BRAIN OF A BEAR.

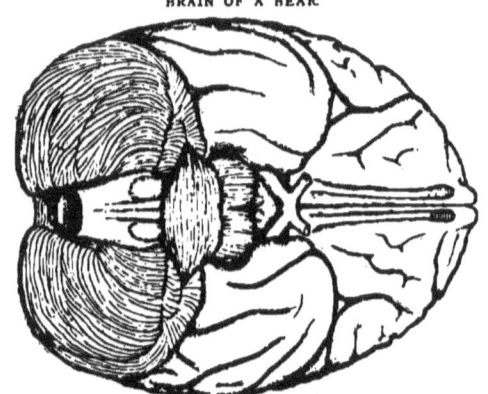

BRAIN OF A GORILLA.

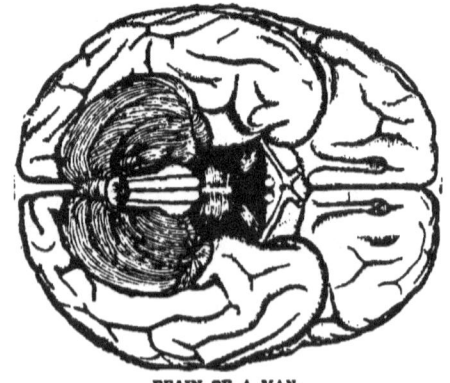

BRAIN OF A MAN.

THE DEVELOPMENT OF THE BRAIN.

The nervous system originates as a hollow tube formed by a very thin film. At an early stage of its development, the upper end (as seen in the adjoined figure) bulges out into three continuous bulbs. The first is to be the fore brain, the second the mid brain, and the third the hind brain.

EARLY STAGE OF THE NERVOUS SYSTEM IN THE DIFFERENTIATION OF THE EMBRYO. (From Wiedersheim.)

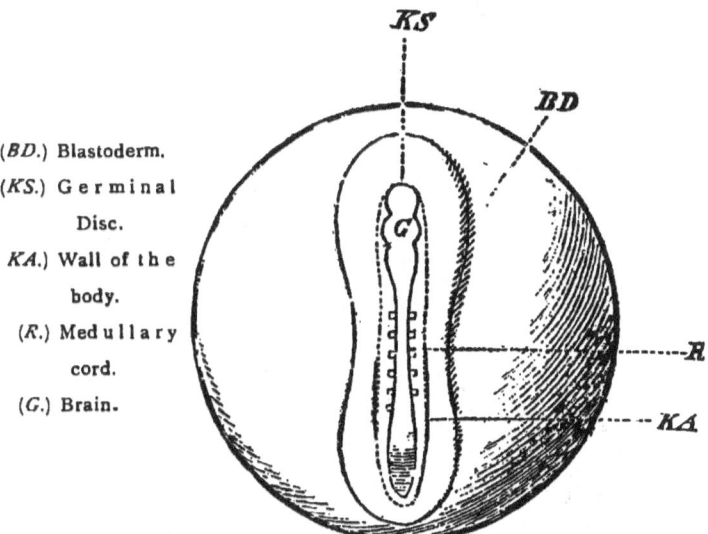

(*BD*.) Blastoderm.

(*KS*.) G e r m i n a l
     Disc.

KA.) Wall of t h e
     body.

(*R*.) Med u l l a r y
     cord.

(*G*.) Brain.

In the further evolution of the embryo we observe excrescences on each side of the fore brain. The pas-

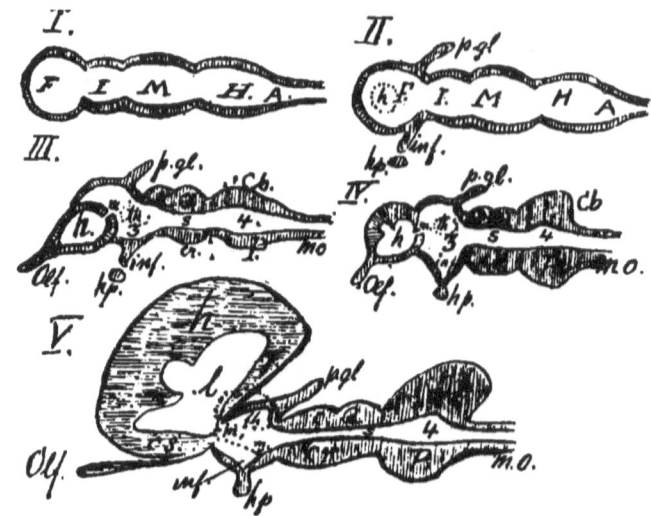

SAGITTAL SECTIONS REPRESENTING FIVE STAGES OF CEREBRAL DEVELOPMENT.

F. Fore brain.
I. Intermediate brain.
M. Mid brain.
H. Hind brain.
A. After brain.
h. Hemispheres.
hp. Hypophysis.
p.gl. Pineal gland or epiphysis.
inf. Infundibulum.
cs. Corpus striatum.
th. Thalamus (represented by a dotted line, because growing out from the side walls it does not appear in a sagittal section).

mo. Medulla oblongata.
P. Pons.   *Cb.* Cerebellum.
CQ. Corpora Quadrigemina.
Cr. Crus Cerebri.
F. (in No. V) Fornix.
m. Foramen Monro.
3. Third ventricle.
4. Fourth ventricle.
l. Lateral ventricle.
s. Aquaductus Sylvii.

In a further development *m* sinks down to *m2*, as indicated by the dotted line *m*, *m2*. Thus the corpus striatum is placed alongside the thalamus and the latter (*th*) is overarched by the Fornix (*F*).

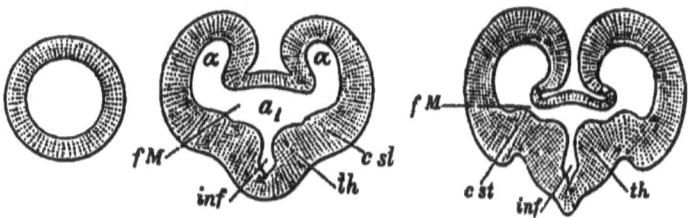

FRONTAL SECTIONS REPRESENTING THREE STAGES OF THE FORE BRAIN.
(After Wernicke.)

a1. Cavity of primitive fore brain; (representing the third ventricle).
aa. Lateral ventricles.
fM. Foramen Monro.
inf. Infundibulum.
cst. Corpus striatum.
th. Thalamus.

sage to the mid brain is elongated and we call it the intermediate brain. The hind brain shows a new division which makes it slope by degrees into the spinal cord. This part is called the after brain.

The excrescences of the fore brain are to become the hemispheres; they constitute the cerebral region of the brain. The fore brain will shrink so as to disappear almost entirely. The intermediate brain will develop the *Thalami.* The mid brain the Four Hills. The hind brain the *Cerebellum* and pons, while the after brain will change into the *Medulla Oblongata.*

The cavities of the tube will remain also, although much modified. The cavities in the hemispheres are called the lateral ventricles. Through the growth of the walls they become straightened into three narrow caves called the anterior, posterior, and lateral horns. The cavity of the original fore brain fuses with the cavity of the intermediate brain into the so-called "third ventricle." The passage from the two lateral ventricles into the third ventricle is very much reduced; it has the shape of a Y, and is called *Foramen Monro.*

The adjoined figures and diagrams show the growth of the different parts of the brain from its simplest beginnings.

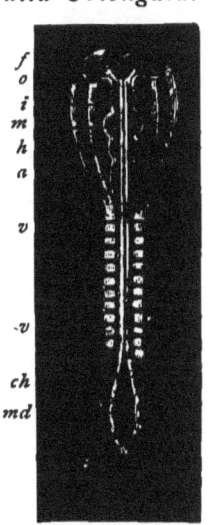

THE EMBRYO OF A MAMMAL OR BIRD. (After Haeckel.)

f. Primitive fore brain.
o. Primitive eye.
i. Intermediate brain.
m. Mid brain.
h. Hind brain.
a. After brain.
vv. Vertebræ.
ch. Chorda dorsalis.
md. Lower part of medulla dorsalis.

CORONAL SECTIONS.

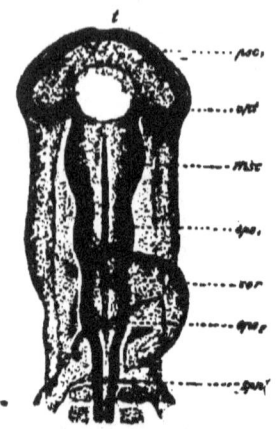

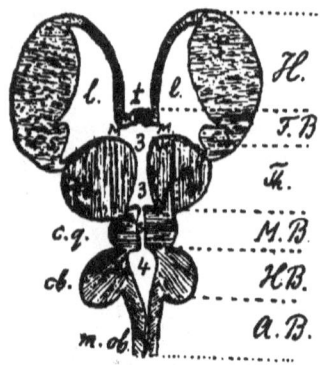

Early stage, representing the fœtal brain of a chick.

(After Mihalkovics.)

psc 1. Primitive fore brain.

opt. Primitive eye.

msc. Mid brain.

epc 1. Hind brain.

epc 2. After brain.

spn. Spinal cord.

cor. Heart.

     t. Lamina terminalis.

Later stage, representing in a diagram the fœtal brain of a mammal. (McAllister.)

    H. Hemispheres (secondary forebrain), representing the excrescences of the primitive fore brain.

    FB. Primitive forebrain.

    Th. Thalamic region or intermediate brain.

    MB = cq. Mid brain = Corpora quadrigemina.

    HB = cb. Hind brain = Cerebellum.

    AB. After brain = Medulla oblongata.

    cs. Corpus striatum.

    ll. Lateral ventricles.

    mm. Foramen Monro.

    3 3. Third ventricle.

    s. Aquaductus silvii.

    4. Fourth Ventricle.

    t. Lamina terminalis.

The similarity of arrangement and the difference of development in the various parts of the brain among fishes, birds, reptiles, and mammals may be studied in the following diagrams, reproduced from Edinger.

SAGITTAL MEDIAN SECTIONS (After Edinger).

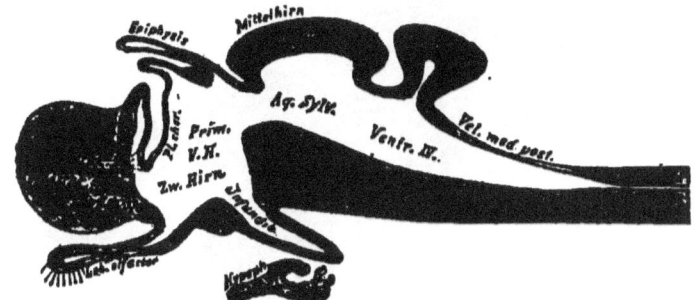

GENERAL PLAN OF VERTEBRATE BRAINS.

GYMNOTE.

TELEOST (OSSEOUS FISH).

AMPHIBIA.

REPTILE.

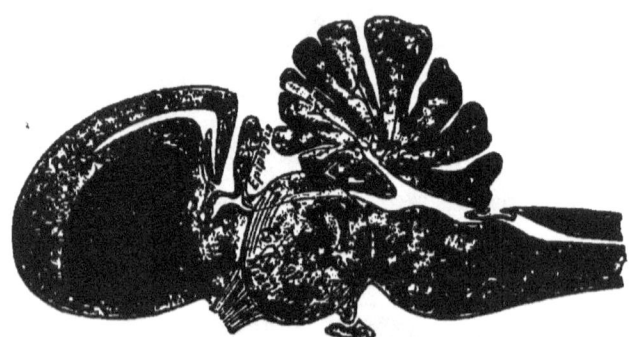

BIRD.

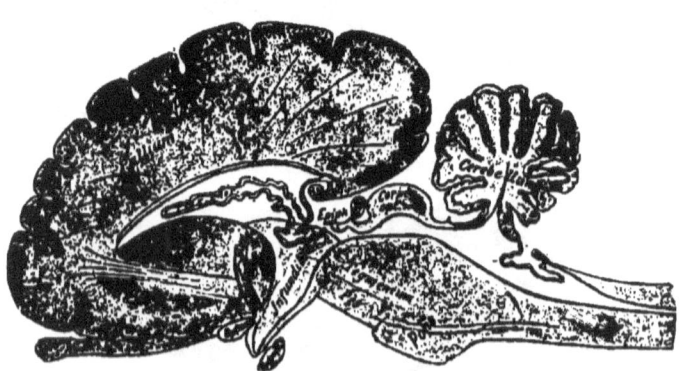

MAMMAL.

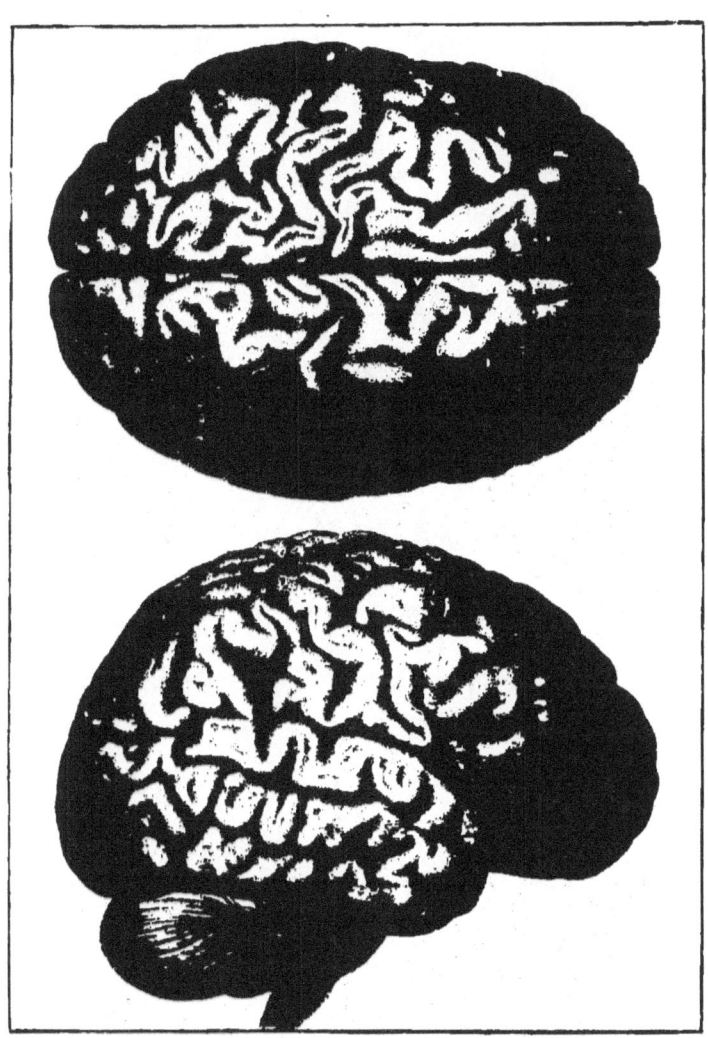

THE HUMAN BRAIN, FULLY DEVELOPED.

SPINAL CORD.

The nervous system is built up of (1) nervous substance and (2) neuroglia. Nervous substance consists
either of ganglionic cells or of nerve-fibres, the latter

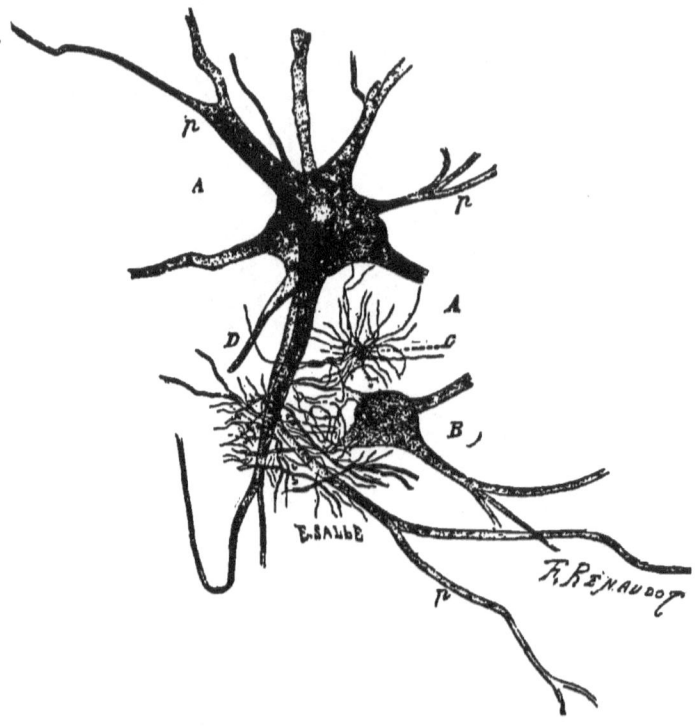

NERVE CELLS FROM SPINAL CORD. (Afer Ranvier.)

A. and B. Ganglionic cells.
C. Neuroglia cells.
D. Axis cylinder.
p. Protoplasmic process.

being processes rising out of ganglionic cells. Neuroglia, the nervous bindweb, is as it were the framework which supports the nervous substance. The membranes which envelop the ganglionic cells and the

Posterior Part.

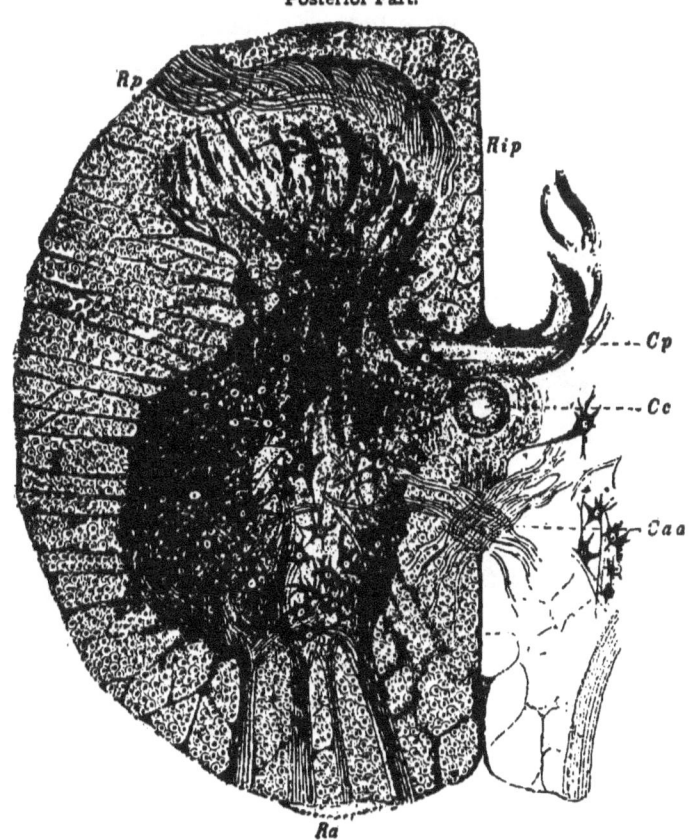

Anterior Part.

SPINAL CORD. (Cross-section after Deiters.)

Ra. Radix anterior.
Rp. Radix posterior.
Rip. Inner part of Radix posterior.
Cp. Commissura posterior (gray substance).
Caa. Commissura anterior.
Cc. Central canal.

sheaths which encase the nerve-fibres and nerve-bundles are neuroglia; and besides these comparatively strong ligaments there are most delicate neuroglia-cells which in outward appearance resemble heaps of burs thickly crowded about the ganglionic cells and nerves, and filling the spaces between them.

The spinal cord is a long tube of nervous substance supported by neuroglia, having comparatively thick

Anterior Part.

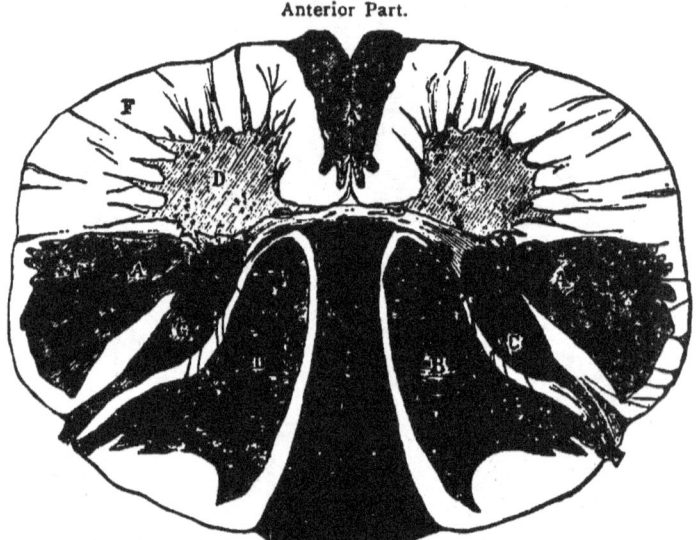

Posterior part.

TRANSVERSE SECTION OF SPINAL CORD.   (Reproduced from Charcot.
   A'. Columns of Türck (direct pyramidal).
   A. A. Crossed pyramidal tracts.
   B. B. Posterior root zone (Burdach's column).
   C. C. Posterior horns.
   D. D. Anterior horns.
      E. Column of Goll.
   F. F. Anterior root zone.

walls.   Its cavity has almost disappeared.   The gray matter of the spinal cord appears when viewed in a horizontal section to be arranged in the shape of two crescents the anterior and posterior horns. These parts contain the ganglionic nerve-cells. The white matter consists of fibres which stand in connection with the gray matter of the horns. These fibres lead up to, and arrive from, the different parts of the brain. The nerve bundles coming out of the spinal cord are called *radices* or roots.

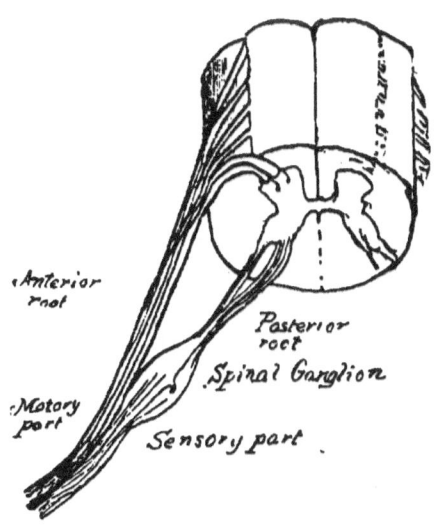

SPINAL CORD.
With anterior and posterior roots. (After Edinger.)

The nutrition of nervous substance takes place in the direction of its functional activity. Accordingly, if we cut a nerve, it will degenerate, in case it be motory, below, in case it be sensory, above the cut. With the aid of this law, named after the English physiologist Waller, experiments have been made (especially on dogs) with a view to tracing the directions of the different nerves. The results of the experiments were then compared with and corroborated by pathological observations.

•

The posterior roots have by this method been proved
to be sensory.   Peripherally they originate in the Pacinian corpuscles which are embedded in the mucous
membrane of the skin.   Shortly before entering the
spinal cord they pass through a ganglion, while the
anterior roots, or motory fibres, terminate directly in
their respective muscles.

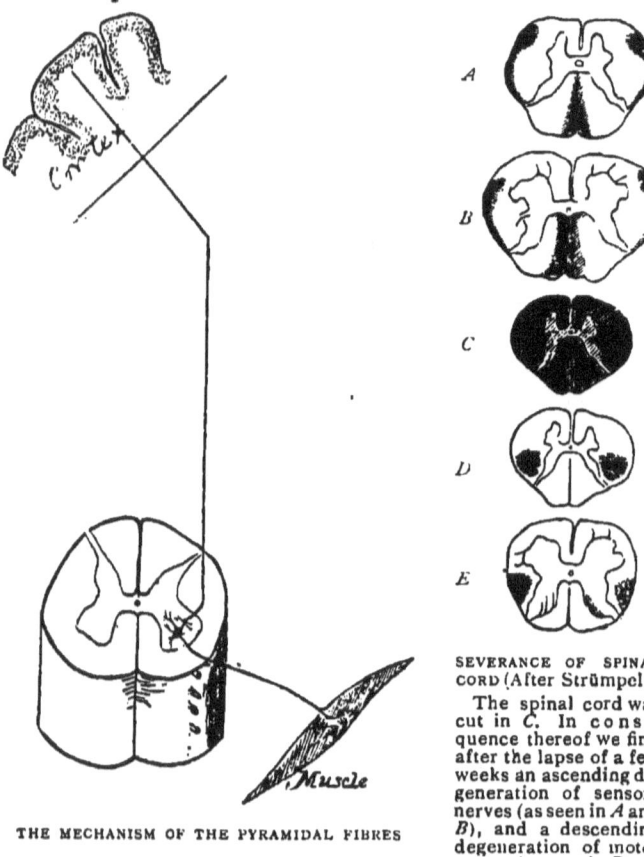

SEVERANCE OF SPINAL
CORD (After Strümpell).
    The spinal cord was
cut in *C.* In conse-
quence thereof we find
after the lapse of a few
weeks an ascending de-
generation of sensory
nerves (as seen in *A* and
B), and a descending
degeneration of motor
nerves (as seen in *D* and
E.)

THE MECHANISM OF THE PYRAMIDAL FIBRES

All further details are best studied by an inspection
of the adjoined diagrams.

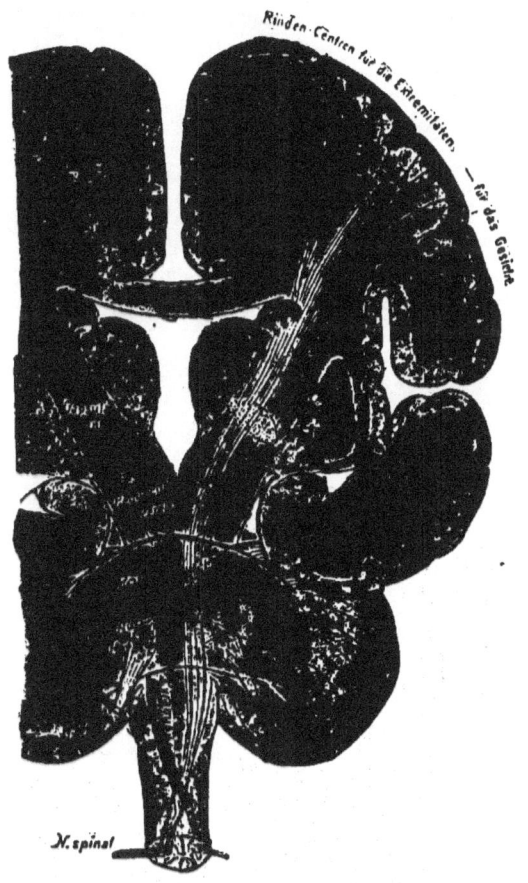

PYRAMIDAL BUNDLES AND FACIAL NERVE (Reproduced from Edinger).

The diagram shows how different situations of diseased portions will produce different effects.

A tumor in the left capsule (*A*) will produce paralysis in the muscles of the right portion of the body. A tumor in *B* will affect the facial nerve of the left side and some of the muscles in the right extremities. A tumor in *C* will affect part of the right facial nerve of the right pyramidal bundles.

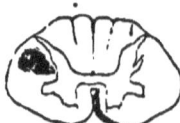

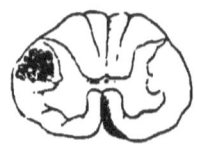

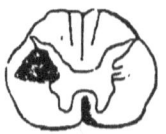

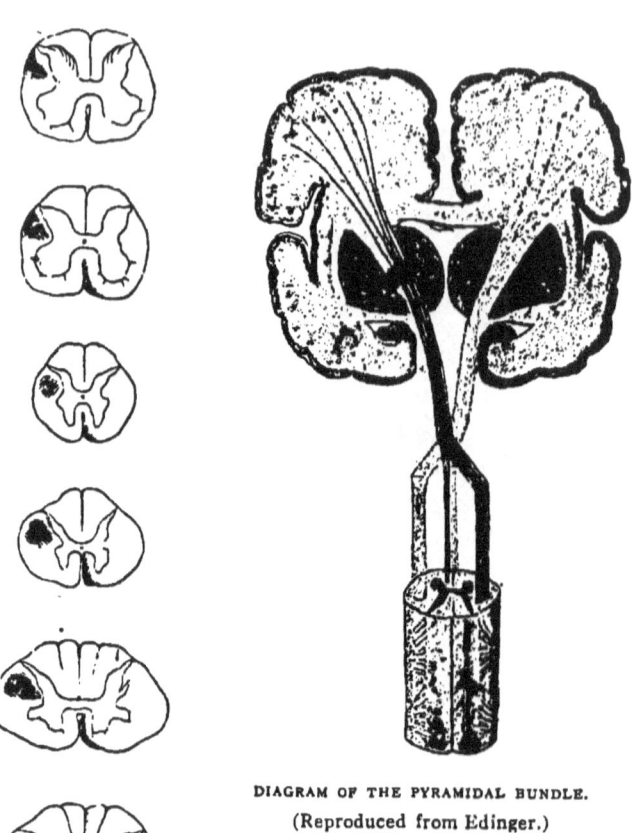

DIAGRAM OF THE PYRAMIDAL BUNDLE.

(Reproduced from Edinger.)

Showing the degeneration of the direct fibres on the left, and of the indirect on the right side, in consequence of a tumor in the left *capsula interna.*

The adjoined sections (After Erb) of the spinal cord show the same process viewed transversely in cervical, dorsal, and lumbar parts. The topmost lies above the place of decussation.

CROSS-SECTION CF

SPINAL CORD.

(After Erb.)

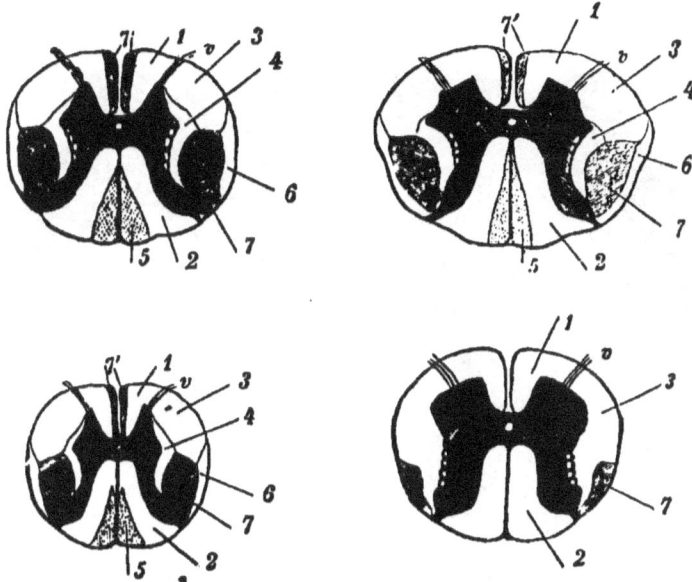

DIAGRAMS REPRESENTING FLECHSIG'S INVESTIGATIONS.

Showing the different bundles of nervous fibres in two cervical sections, a pectoral, and a lumbar section of the spinal cord.

1. Anterior bundle of mixed nerves, paths to and from reflex centres in the medulla oblongata.

2. Burdach's bundles receive fibres from the posterior horns and lead them through the corpus restiforme to the vermis of the cerebellum.

3 and 4. Lateral bundles of mixed nerves being (like 1) paths for centres of reflex motions in the medulla oblongata. 3 and 4 contain some sensory fibres, originating in the posterior horns.

5. Goll's bundle, ascending nerves, which can be traced to the gray nuclei in the funiculus gracilis of the medulla oblongata.

6. Cerebellar fibres, pass through the corpus restiforme and connect the posterior horns with the cerebellum.

7. Pyramidal bundles. Indirect or decussated tract.

7. 1. Direct pyramidal bundles.

v. Anterior roots.

Posterior Part.

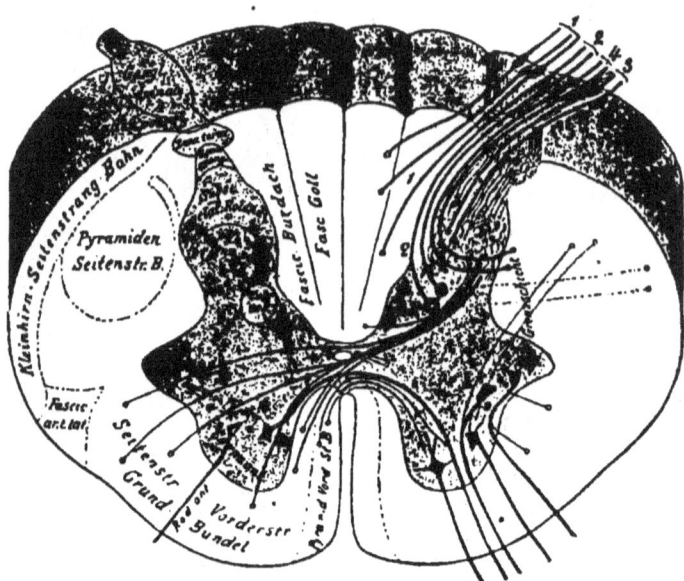

Anterior Part.

Transverse section of the spinal cord. (Reproduced from Edinger).

The diagram represents the course of various fibres: sensory nerves (1, 2, 3, 4) entering the posterior horns; motory nerves passing out from the anterior horns ; and commissural fibres, bringing certain gray centres into relation with one another.

The sensory cells are of globular, the motory cells of pyramidal form. Imbedded in the posterior horns is Clark's Column (*columna vescicularis*) which can be traced from the lumbar region up to the cervical region and reaches most probably into the medulla oblongata.

The mechanism of the sensory or posterior horns is apparently much more complicated than that of the anterior or motory horns. Between the gray cells and the marginal layer, (called by Lissauer *zona terminalis*,) there is a gelatinous substance (*substantia gelatinosa Rolandi*). Moreover all the nervous irritations transmitted through sensory fibres, have to pass through a net-work (*zona spongiosa*) in which the connection between the processes of the gray cells and their respective fibres ceases to be visible. The continuation of fibres to their cells is solely inferred from processes of degeneration.

MEDULLA OBLONGATA.

THE bulb or *medulla oblongata*, the continuation of the spinal cord, is, as the seat of the most vital reflex centres, of extraordinary importance. It is here that, with two exceptions, the most important higher nerves originate. These two exceptions are the First and Second nerves. The First Nerve (the olfactory) stands in close connection with the cerebrum or hemispheric part of the brain; the Second or Optic Nerve with the *thalamus opticus* and the optic lobes (*corpora quadrigemina*). All other nerves that are higher developed and more differentiated than the spinal nerves, have their roots in the *medulla*.

The following reflex centres are situated in the *medulla*, viz.: those that effect—

(1) The closing of the eye-lids;
(2) Sneezing;
(3) Coughing;
(4) Sucking and chewing;
(5) Secretion of saliva;
(6) Swallowing;
(7) Vomiting ; and
(8) Contraction of the iris.

There is in addition to these reflex centres a super-ordinated centre, which combines the different centres among themselves so as to make complicated reflex motions possible without interference of cerebral ac-

tivity.   This superordinated centre is situated in the
rabbit about 6 mm above the *calamus scriptorius*.   Its
presence is proved by experiments on decapitated
frogs, lizards, eels, and also on mammals in which the
medulla has been severed by dissection from the upper parts of the nervous system.   (Proved by the experiments of Sig. Mayer, Luchsinger and Owsjanikow.)

The reflex. centres of breathing seem to be of a
complex nature.   There are two centres in the *medulla*,
one for inspiration, the other for expiration, and both
are automatic.   They continue to work even after the
section of all sensory nerves, and depend upon the blood
circulation ; venous blood operating as an irritation for
breathing.

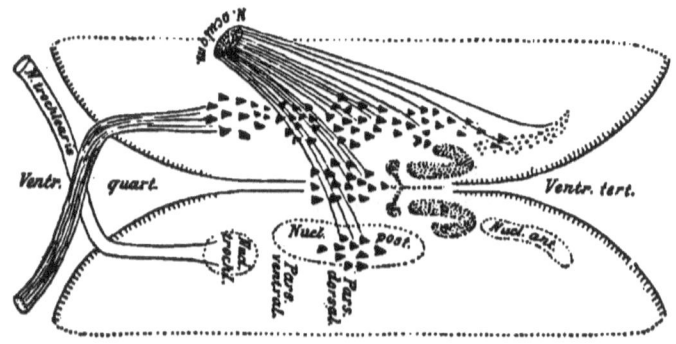

THE NUCLEI OF THE THIRD AND FOURTH OR OCULO-MOTOR AND TROCHLEAR
NERVES. (Half diagrammatic, after Edinger.)
Showing the complexity of the mechanism in the origin of nerves.
a and *b* are two gray hook-shaped nuclei, the connection of which with the
oculo-motor is as yet uncertain.

Flourens has localized the *noeud vital* or centre of
breathing, on both sides between the nuclei of the accessorius and the vagus nerves.   But further researches
have proved that the mechanism of breathing is more
complex still, for there are some subordinated spinal
centres which even after the section of the *medulla*

keep up certain motions in the thorax. (Proved by Bra-
chet, Lautenbach, Langendorff, and Landois.) Besides, some superordinated centres have been discovered in the posterior hill of the *corpora quadrigemina* (by Martin and Booker) and in the *thalamus* on
the bottom of the third ventricle (by Christiani).

The action of the heart is regulated chiefly through
the *nervus vagus* and *nervus sympathicus.* There are
inhibitory as well as accelerating fibres. An irritation
of the vagus produces a decrease of the activity of the
heart, while an irritation of the first pectoral sympathetic ganglion produces an acceleration. This part of
the nerve was accordingly called *Nervus accelerans
cordis.*

The reflex motions of the *medulla ob-*
longata may, but need not be connected
with consciousness ; they are of a higher
and more complex order than the direct
reflex motions of a simple ganglionic mechanism and are represented in the adjoined diagram. Sensory impressions (*SI*)
are received in the Pacinian corpuscles at the peripheral terminus of the sensory nerve. They are transmitted through the spinal ganglion to the gray matter
of the posterior horns (*ISN*) and thence in the ascending spinal fibres to their respective centres in the
medulla oblongata (*S*). The motory reflex action starts
in the medullary reflex centre (in *W*), is transmitted
through descending nerves to the anterior horns
(*IMN*) and thence through the anterior roots to their
respective muscles (*MM*).

The *medulla oblongata* may be considered as the
seat of the vegetative soul ; since a destruction of its

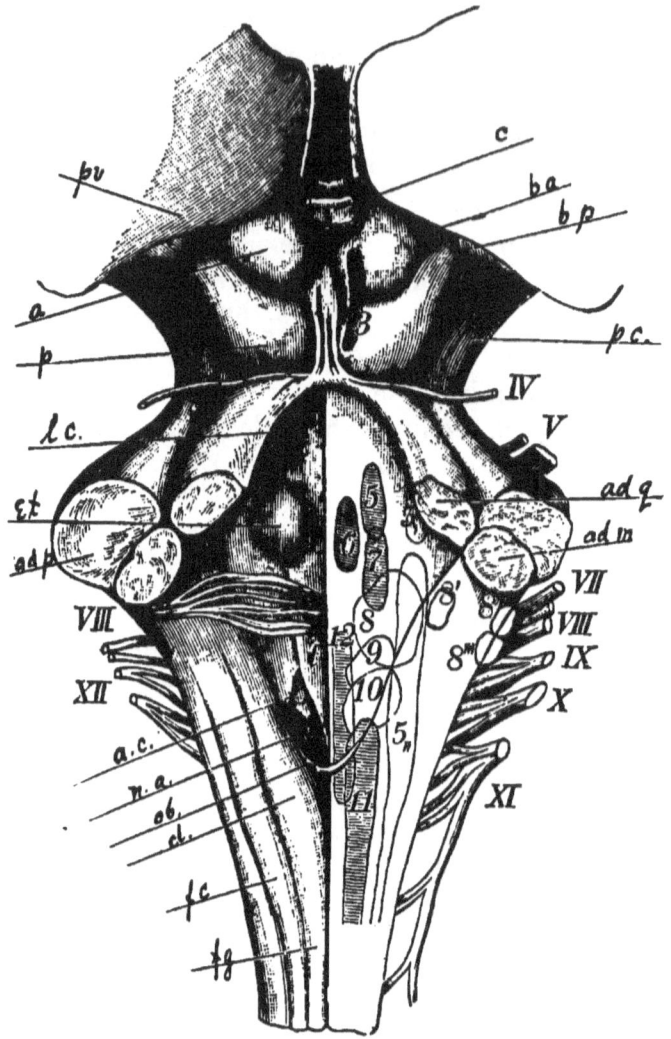

BULB OR MEDULLA OBLONGATA. (Reproduced from Landois).

c. Conarium or pineal gland.

pv. Pulvinar or cushion, i. e., lower part of thalamus opticus.

a and *p*. Four hills (Corpora Quadrigemina). *a*. Anterior hill. *p*. Posterior hill.

b a. Brachium conjunctivum anticum, i. e., tracts of nerve-fibres leading to the anterior hill.

b p. Brachium conjunctivum posticum, i. e., tracts of nerve-fibres lead-ing to the posterior hill.

pc. Pedunculus Cerebri, nerve-tracts to the hemispheres.

There are three pairs of Peduncles on which the small brain hangs:

ad p. Ad pontem. Connection with the bridge.

ad m. Ad medullam oblongatam. Connection with the Medulla oblongata, and further down with the spinal cord.

ad q. Ad corpora quadrigemina. Connection with the posterior hill.

l c. Locus cœruleus, bluish spot.

cl. Clava, a club-shaped bundle.

f. c. Funiculus cuneiformis, being a part of a nerve-bundle called "the Rope" or *corpus restiforme.*

f. g. Funiculus gracilis, the continuation of the clava.

e t. Eminentia teres. A tubercle covering the nuclei 5, 6, 7.

t. Funiculus teres.

n a. Nucleus accessorius.

o b. Obex. The bolt, crescent-shaped oblique fibres.

a c. Ala cinerea, a layer of gray substance of triangular shape. This portion of the fourth ventricle is called *calamus scriptorius* from its fancied resemblance to a pen.

The Roman numbers represent the nerves and the Arabian numbers their respective nuclei in the deeper layers of the medulla, where the nerves originate.

The first nerve is the olfactory. It enters the hemispheric part of the brain through several roots.

The second nerve is the Optic nerve which stands in connection with the thalamus opticus and the Four hills.

These two nerves do not appear in the adjoined figure.

3. Nucleus of the oculo-motor or third nerve is the main source of motor innervation in the most important muscles of the eye. The nerve passes to the front between the two crura; accordingly the nerve (*III*) is not visible in the adjoined cut. Other ocular nerves are the fourth and the sixth.

4. *IV.* Trochlear nucleus and nerve. A motory nerve going to the trochlea, the hollow of the eye innervating the muscle which makes the eye roll.

5. *V.* Trigeminus nuclei and nerve. A nerve rising from two nuclei and dividing into three branches, going to the face. It serves motory impulses as well as for the reception of sensory impressions.

6. Abducens nucleus. The nerve, because passing out in front, like the third nerve, is not visible in the cut. It is a motory nerve and innervates the muscle that moves the eye toward the side.

7. *VII.* Facial nerve. A motor nerve for the muscles of the face.

8. *VIII.* Acusticus nucleus and nerve, the sensory nerve of hearing.

9. *IX.* Glossopharyngeal nucleus and nerve, a sensory nerve, receiving mainly the impressions of taste.

10. *X.* Vagus nucleus and nerve, a mixed nerve of motor and sensory fibres innervating the heart and the lungs.

11. *XI.* Accessory nucleus and nerve. A nerve, communicating with other nerves, having mainly a motory character.

12. *XII.* Hypoglossus nucleus and nerve. The motor nerve for the tongue, being of special importance in man because it regulates the mechanism of speech.

most important centres will always cause instantaneous death.

The *medulla oblongata* possesses to some degree the faculty of adaptation to circumstances as has been proved by the famous frog-experiment. A decapitated frog in which the spinal cord and *medulla oblongata* are preserved, all higher centres being severed, will scratch itself with its right leg, if irritated on the right side of its back. When the right leg is amputated, it will after a few vain attempts with the stump, try to remove the irritant by means of its left leg.

This experiment proves that the soul does not dwell in one part of the nervous system alone ; but that every part is endowed with soul-life. Every ganglion is a seat of soul-life. The activity of every reflex centre is no mere physiological phenomenon. The lowest reflex centres of irritable substance possess the power of adaptation to circumstances ; the *medulla oblongata* being a higher, a superordinated and more complex centre, possesses this in a greater degree than simple ganglions. Yet there is one further step needed for changing irritability into distinct and definite feeling. This is created through the possibility of comparing the present irritation with the memories of former irritations—not only of the same kind, but of all kinds. Such a possibility is established in the brain, which is the coördinative organ of soul-activity.

The brain is a storehouse of all kinds of memories. All irritations received in the peripheral sense-organs are, as it were (to use Meynert's expression) *projected* into the hemispheres. There they leave traces or vestiges : every different impression leaves a vestige of its own ; and these vestiges are living memories, pictures of impressions, i. e., structures of a special form produced through irritations of a special form. These memories are so to say deposited in the brain and represent the outside objects through contact with which they have been produced. Being representative of things or of natural phenomena they are symbols of the surrounding world and make cognition possible.

The mechanism of the brain is so arranged that all the different memories are properly interconnected thus making a comparison among them easily possible.

CEREBELLUM AND PONS.

THE Small Brain (or *Cerebellum*) together with the Bridge (*Pons Varolii*) encircles the medulla oblongata like a thick ring, being thickest at the posterior part. The Pons overarches, bridge-like (hence its name), the medulla in front. It receives in the nuclei of gray substance embedded in its fibres, many nerves from the pyramidal tracts and thus forms an intermediate station between the cerebrum and the lower motory mechanism.

Some of the nerves that originate here stand in relation to the Pons. Thus, the fifth nerve (*trigeminus*) breaks with its motory as well as sensory fibres through the Pons ; and a disease in either arch of the Pons always affects to a greater or less extent the sensibility and motility of the opposite part of the body.

Between the two lobes of the Cerebellum there is a narrow central portion which, because of its worm-like appearance, is called *vermis* or worm. The upper worm culminates in the *monticulus* (mountain), the lower worm in the *uvula* (or grape).

The names as well as structures of the different parts of the Small Brain and the relations of the Pons may be studied in the adjoined diagrams.

*   *   *

The functions of the different parts of the Cerebellum are little explored. We know however that irritations produce vertigo and rolling motions. Animals in which the Cerebellum is injured, show an uncertainty in their movements similar to that observable in a drunkard. The adjoined pictures (reproduced from the Encyclopedia Britannica) show two pigeons;

PIGEON WHOSE CEREBELLUM IS REMOVED.

PIGEON WHOSE HEMISPHERES ARE REMOVED.

from the one the Small Brain and from the other the Hemispheres have been removed. The former shows all signs of intelligence : its motor apparatus are in all their details uninjured ; yet the power of properly coordinating the various motions is entirely gone. Thus the pigeon lies helplessly sprawled on the ground. The other pigeon stands firmly on its feet ; it flies if thrown into the air ; it walks steadily if through some

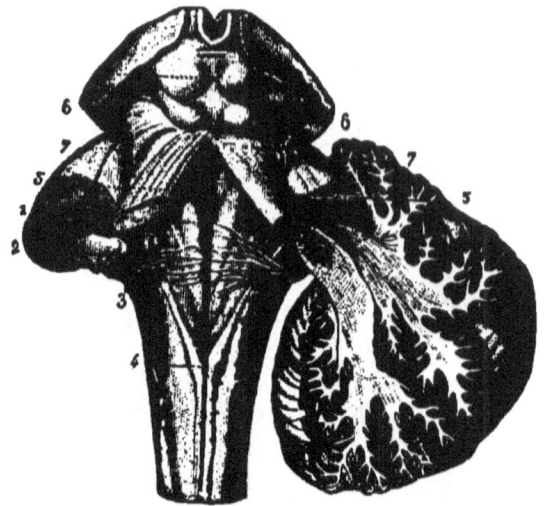

CEREBELLUM. DORSAL VIEW. (After Sappey.)

1. Bottom of Fourth Ventricle, the roof of which is formed by the cerebellum.

2. Striae acusticae, the roots of the auditory nerve.

3. Left lower Peduncle, rising from the medulla, and overlapping in its further progress the upper peduncle, as seen on the right side.

4. Clavae funiculi gracilis, the Clubs; the swellings of the clavae are caused through nuclei imbedded in their fibres.

5. Upper Peduncles, connecting the cerebellum through the red nucleus with the posterior hill, the thalamus, and most likely also with the hemispheres.

6. Laqueus or fillet, a tract of nervous fibres, originating on the dorsal side below the Four Hills. It passes slantingly to a lower part of the ventral side. The fillet consists of fibres from the auditory nerve, the trigeminus and the spinal cord, the latter part being motory. The others connect the activity of their respective nerves with the thalamic region.

7. Brachia ad pontem, the thickest among the three pairs of bands which pass into the cerebellum. It connects the Small Brain with the Bridge.

The dotted line at the top represents the corpora quadrigemina or Four Hills.

The left and middle part of the cerebellum is cut off. The gray and white substance in the interior of the cerebellum is so arranged as to produce the figure of a tree, called *arbor vitae*, the tree of life.

irritation it is made to move ; in a word the power of co-ordinating the most complex motions is preserved. Yet all movements are executed apparently without consciousness and without the faintest sign of intelligence.

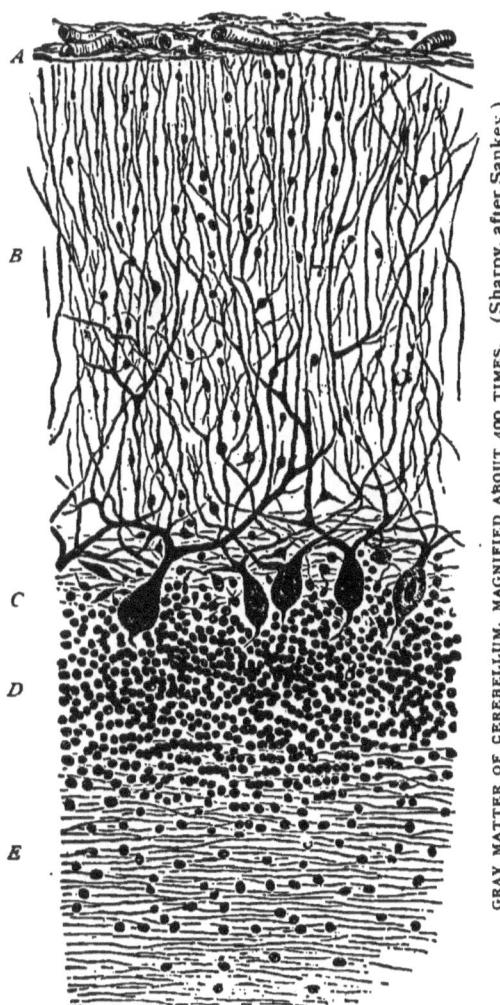

GRAY MATTER OF CEREBELLUM, MAGNIFIED ABOUT 400 TIMES. (Sharpy, after Sankey.)

A. Pia mater of cerebellum, the enveloping membrane. *B.* Outer gray layer. *C.* Great ganglionic cells *D.* Inner grayish-red, or so-called granule layer. *E.* White fibres.

The great ganglionic cells send out large branching processes into the outer gray layer, becoming finer the nearer they approach the surface. The ultimate ramifications together with a kind of connective tissue substance form a most delicate matrix of fibres, among which a number of small corpuscles are interspersed.

The connection of the ganglion-cells with the inner grayish red or granule layer consists of very fine fibres which are soon lost to view among the densely grouped granules.

A few scattered granules are found also in the white substance.

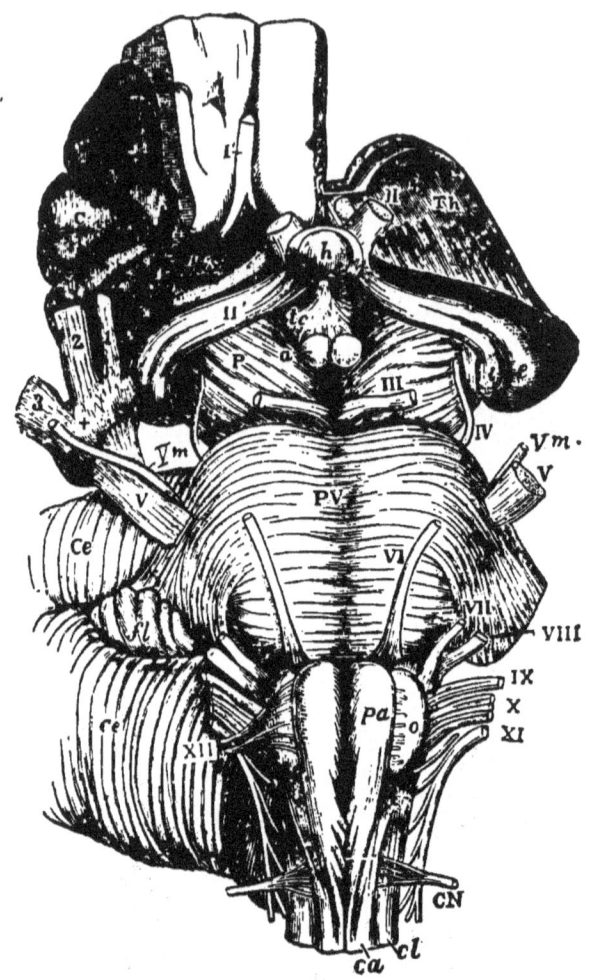

PONS AND ITS RELATIONS.

The Roman numbers indicate the nerves in their order.

The fifth nerve (*trigeminus*) divides in the Gasserian ganglion (marked x) into three sensory branches :

    1. The ophthalmic branch ;

    2. The supra-maxillary branch ;

    3. The infra-maxillary branch ;

V m. Motory branch of the fifth nerve.

C. Lobes of the cerebrum. Hemispheric region.

The gray layer between the roots into which the first (olfactory) nerve divides is called *substantia perforata* (marked x x).

Th Thalamus opticus.

h. Hypophysis. Here the optic nerve decussates. Its decussation is called chiasma, having the shape of a Greek Chi, χ.

a. Corpora candicantia or mammillaria.

i. Corpus geniculatum interius.

e. Corpus geniculatum exterius, being the ganglions of the second, or optic nerve. The optic nerve divides into two parts, the exterior stands in close connection through the corpus geniculatum exterius with the thalamus and passes into the anterior Hill of the corpora quadrigemina. The interior passes into the posterior Hill.

t c. Tuber cinereum.

P. Peduncles of the brain or crura cerebri.

P, V, Pons Varolii.

p a. Anterior pyramid of medulla. The decussation of the pyramidal tracts below the pyramids is plainly visible.

o. Olivary body.

C. N. First cervical nerve.

c. l. Lateral column of spinal cord.

c. a. Anterior column.

C. e. Lobus lunatus anterior of cerebellum.

C. e'. Digastric lobe of cerebellum.

fl. Flocculus or tuft, a small lobe of cerebellum.

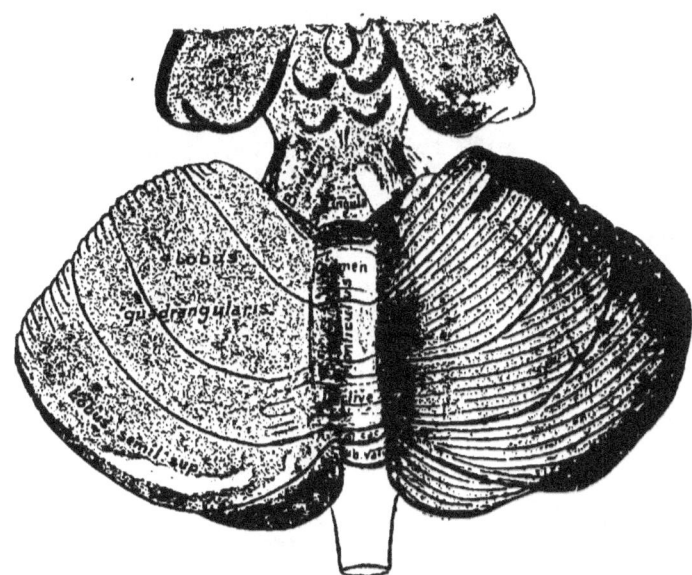

CEREBELLUM. Superficial view from the dorsal side. (Edinger.)

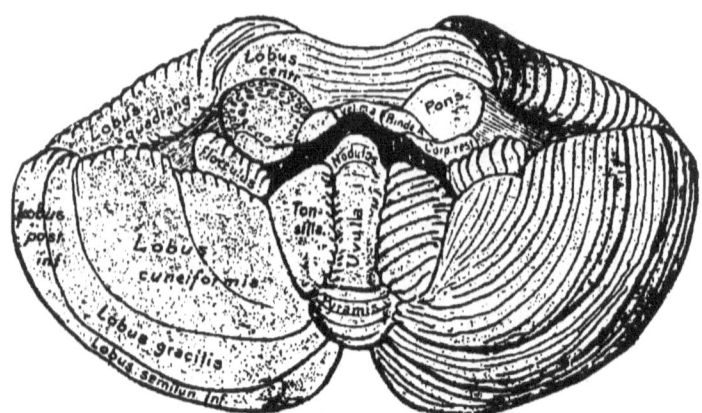

CEREBELLUM. Superficial view from the ventral side.   (Edinger.)

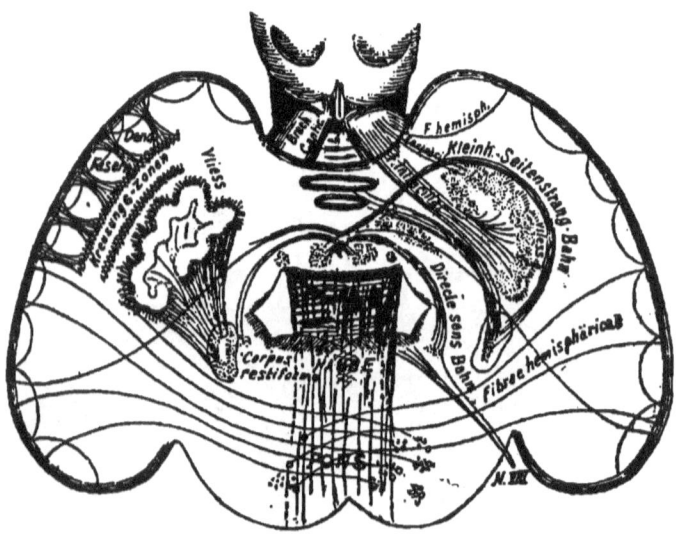

DIAGRAMMATIC SECTION THROUGH BRIDGE AND SMALL BRAIN.

(Reproduced from Edinger.)

It represents the most important results obtained by Benedict Stilling with regard to the paths of the various fibres in the cerebellum.   The medulla has been severed and pulled out of place in order to show the Bridge and Small Brain at once.   Thus the upper peduncles (*brachia cerebelli anteriora*) appear in the wrong place.   They must be conceived as belonging much lower. They enter the cerebellum at the hole in the middle.   (Compare for a correction of this displacement the other drawings of the cerebellum.)   Little additional knowledge upon this subject has been gained since Stilling.

THE THALAMIC REGION OF THE BRAIN.

THE upward continuations of the medulla are called the *Crura* (singular *crus*), the legs of the brain. They are the stems on which the Brain stands. These Crura consist on each side of two parts : the front part shows coarse longitudinal fibres emerging from the upper margin of the Bridge, called *crusta* (the crust) ; the hind part, covering the crusta, is called *tegmentum*, (German *Haube*, cover). Between both, on the upper surface of the crusta, where the tegmentum covers it, is seen a dark portion, called *locus niger* (the black spot).

The dorsal part of the tegmentum shows a narrow tunnel called *aquaductus Sylvii*, which connects the third and fourth ventricles. The upper roof of the aquaduct is overarched by the two fillets, which here decussate, and upon which the Four Hills rise.

Out of the tegmentum on each side a thick ganglion grows, called *thalamus opticus*, the lower part of which is the cushion or *pulvinar*. The Thalamus receives ascending fibres not only from the tegmentum but also from other sources. Through the external optic ganglion (*corpus geniculatum exterius*), it stands in connection with the optic nerve ; through the *taenia semicircularis* with the olfactory ; and through the fillet (*laqueus*), with the auditory nerve.

The anterior two of the Four Hills are in some way related with vision as a sensory process ; while the posterior hills exercise a decided influence upon the motory actions of the eyes.   Animals in whom all the parts down as far as the apparatus of the Four Hills have been removed, exhibit not only all the usual reflex motions against light (e. g., contraction of the iris), but are also able to regulate other motions by what they see.   When trying to escape they avoid ob-

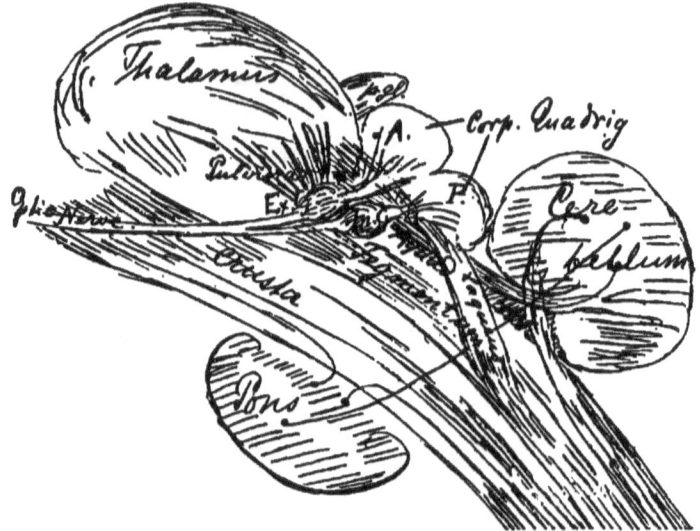

DIAGRAM SHOWING THE RELATIONS OF CEREBELLUM AND PONS TO THE
THALAMIC REGION.

The stem of the brain (or *crus cerebri*) consists of the crusta which lies in front, and the tegmentum which covers the crusta.

The optic nerve divides into two branches.   The superior branch passes into the *corpus geniculatum exterius* (the external optic ganglion) which stands in connection with the thalamus—this part of the thalamus is called *pulvinar* (cushion)—and passes into the Anterior Hill (*A*) of the corpora quadrigemina. The lower branch passes through the *corpus geniculatum interius* into the Posterior Hill (*P*).

The fillet (*laqueus*) consists of three nerve bundles that connect the Four Hills and perhaps also the thalamus with (1) motory fibres of the spinal cord, (2) the trigeminus, and (3) the auditory nuclei.   A decussation of the fibres of the fillet takes place under the Four Hills.

stacles placed in their way, they follow with their head the motions of a light, etc. Thus it appears that the Four Hills, independently of the higher brain-organs (especially the Striped Body and the Hemispheres), exercise some regulative influence upon ocular and other muscular motions.

According to Dr. Luys's hypothesis, the Thalamus ought to be considered as a condenser of sensory impressions, and the Striped Body (*corpus striatum*), a condenser of motory impulses. This, however, agrees neither with anatomical facts nor with pathological and experimental observations. It is irreconcilable with the results of Meynert's investigations. "Neither can," says Wundt, "the connection of all sensory tracts with the Thalamus be proved, nor, on the other hand, is its connection with motor tracts to be doubted." The fillet (*laqueus*, Germ. *Schleife*) consists of several tracts among which there are motor nerves entering in their peripheral course the spinal cord.

Prof. Schiff proved by experiment that if in an animal one Thalamus is cut through, a disturbance will be observed in the direction of the animal's walk and in the position of its legs. Instead of walking on in a straight line, it moves in a circle. If the section is made through the posterior third of the Thalamus, the animal will turn towards the side of the non-injured half of the brain ; if it be further in front, it will turn in the opposite direction. The French call these strange disturbances " *mouvements de manège,*" because they are like the epicyclical manœuvers of horses in circuses.

These motions are determined by an abnormal position of the body, as can be observed even when the animal is at rest. If the section is made through the hind part of one Thalamus, the animal turns its fore-feet round towards the side in which the injury has been made, while neck and vertebral column are turned in the opposite direction. "An animal" (says

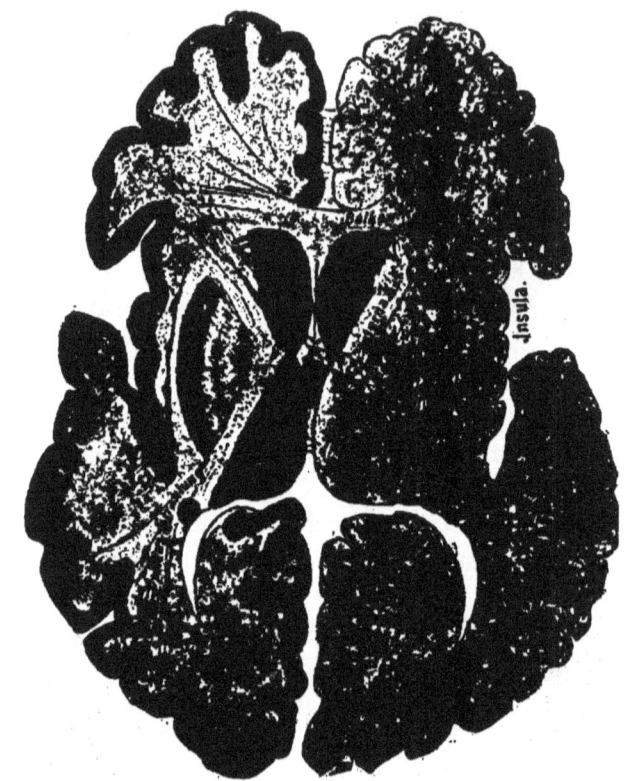

HORIZONTAL SECTION OF THE BRAIN, THROUGH THALAMUS AND CORPUS STRIATUM, SLANTING DOWN ON BOTH SIDES FROM THE MEDIAN LINE. (After Edinger.)

The nucleus caudatus is on both sides cut in two places. The thicker section, joining the two parts seen in the cut, is its head, the smaler its tail. The head borders in front on the descending part of the corpus callosum (*Balken*). Its tapering body stretches along the thalamus, so as to separate the concave surface of the thalamus from the corona radiata.

The lenticular body consists of three stripes, the outer one being the shell or putamen, the two inner ones the globus pallidus.

The lenticular body and nucleus caudatus constitute the Striped Body.

A bundle of radiating fibres, passing to the occipital lobe, are the paths of the optic centre. The claustrum or Wall is a gray layer of unknown functions situated underneath the insula.

Wundt, from whom this account is taken) "will naturally move in the indicated abnormal direction, if it gives the same quantity of innervation to the intended movements as before, in a similar way as a ship will be thrown out of a straight course by a turn of the rudder." If the anterior part of the Thalamus be injured, the neck and feet take a position just in the inverse direction ; hence the inverse movement.

The Thalamus, accordingly, is a reflex centre that controls or influences certain motor nerves ; and we consider it as the organ of co-ordination for the nervous tracts of the tegmentum. An animal whose Hemispheres and Striped Body are removed, is able to execute all motions however complex ; a fact which ought to be impossible according to Dr. Luys's theory.

Dr. Luys, it seems, was induced to propound this hypothesis because lesions of the Thalamus, although they cause disturbances, do not produce any paralysis. This, however, will find a sufficient explanation, if we consider that, in the extremely complex brain mechanism, there are other channels which will send sensory impressions to the hemispheres even if the co-ordinative centre of the tegmentum and other sensory nerves be excluded. An injury to the Thalamus may produce disturbances, as in the experiments above described. Yet these disturbances can and indeed they will be corrected after some time if but the other tracts that connect the hemispheres with the sensory organs remain uninjured ; and thus the symptoms will eventually disappear. The rotatory motions (*mouvements de manège*) will cease to be noticeable within six weeks, and this fact, it seems to me, corroborates our supposition that the Thalamus is an organ of co-ordination inserted between the tracts of the tegmentum and the optic nerve on the one side and the hemispheres on the other. Its function, however, can be performed by the Hemispheres as well—perhaps with a greater effort of conscious attention—and a patient, suffering from a lesion in the Thalamus may become accustomed to it.

This would explain why the pathological reports of post mortem examinations in which a degeneration of the Thalamus has been proved, throw little, if any, light, upon the subject.

For special students of physiology, the following passage, quoted from Dr. C. Wernicke (*Lehrbuch der Gehirnkrankheiten I*, p. 191), may be of interest :

" In the case of a girl of fourteen years, a tuberculous subject, Meynert observed a pathological condition of the head, spinal column, and upper extremities, lasting seven weeks, which he thought analogous to the condition produced by Schiff's section of the posterior part of the left thalamus in animals. His diagnosis was accordingly, degeneration of the left thalamus. The head and spinal column were turned to the right, the head having also a downward inclination, and there was a slight curvature of the spine pointing to the right side ; the right arm was flexed and the left kept extended. If by manipulation the opposite movement was executed, considerable resistance was experienced. Afterwards the left arm was also flexed but now offered little resistance to extension.

" The posture of this girl, whose mind was previously affected, seemed to rest on fixed ideas ; but it could be voluntarily given up, upon the occasion of rare exercises of will power to which she could be brought. Consequently there was no paralysis.

" The state of affairs experimentally produced by Schiff and which he has attributed to paralysis, Meynert did not conceive as such. For a rabbit prepared in this way was, as Schiff reports, still able to wipe mustard from its nose, with the paw supposed to be paralyzed. Moreover the same change of position took place in animals also, the hemispheres of which Schiff had previously removed. According to Schiff's own view such animals are not capable of voluntary motion but only of reflex motions. Under these circumstances, the paralysis of flexors or extensors could not possibly make the antagonistic groups predominant. Consequently some other explanation of this change of position was necessary, and Meynert finds it in the supposition of an interruption of certain paths of muscular sensation. That such paths must be contained in the thalamus, respectively in the Four Hills, is proved by the experiments of Goltz. Frogs whose hemispheres are removed, and in whom the mentioned ganglia are preserved show a wonderful adaptation for restoring the disturbed equipoise, if the place on which they sit is put out of its equilibrium. In frogs whose hemispheres are intact, the thalamus must accordingly be a centre of the muscular sensation in which this disturbance takes place.

"A lesion of the thalamus as produced in the experiments of Schiff, according to this conception, leads consciousness astray concerning the position of the body. This girl had no muscular sensation in certain muscular regions, and she tried to attain it, through forced contraction of these very same muscles, the flexors of the right, and the extensors of the left arm. In the left thalamus accordingly, the flexors must decussate, whilst the extensors do not. The former would correspond to the roots of the tegmentum, decussating in the thalamus through the posterior commissure, the latter to the *laminæ medullares*, which do not decussate. If the degeneration extends to the left side, the flexors of the left arm are attacked also ; in that case the muscular sensation of both extensors and flexors was missing. Hence the rigidity of the arm was changed during the progress of the disease to a loose condition of flexion easily overcome.

The Four Hills and the Thalami are the most important parts of the thalamic region, yet there are a few more structures which deserve at least a passing mention.

Between the Thalami and the Four Hills on the dorsal side appears a small body shaped like a pine-cone, which is called epiphysis or pineal (i. e. pine-cone-shaped) gland. This pineal gland (*conarium*, Germ. *Zirbel*) is interesting not only because, being the only part of the brain that appeared single, the philosopher Descartes considered it as the seat of the soul, but also because later researches have proved it to be a rudimentary eye.

The pineal gland is the larger, the lower an animal ranks in the scale of evolution ; it corresponds in certain amphibia to an aperture in the skull, and a kind of lizard has been discovered in which under the skin the rudimentary eye is still preserved.

This eye in the back part of the head must have been very useful when our ancestors still lived in the depths of the sea. Enemies who approached from behind could be discovered before it was too late. But when our ancestors changed their element and lived on the shore, they had to expose their third eye so much to the burning rays of the sun, that they kept it shut for ever. And it became gradually a rudimentary organ.

There is another body hanging on the ventral part of the brain, called hypophysis or pituitary body. It is a slimy mass of unknown functions. One thing about it is certain, namely, that it does not belong to the brain ; it does not consist of nervous substance. In some of the lower animals (viz., in the vertebrates that are not mammals) it lies much lower and stands in no connection with the brain whatever. According to the investigations lately made by Flesch and Dostojewsky, this body is similar in structure to some extremely active glands and thus it appears probable that it is not a rudimentary organ like the pineal gland, but still serves some physiological function.

The hollow space between the Thalami is called the third ventricle, the walls of which are formed by layers of gray substance. The ventricle at the bottom assumes the shape of a small funnel, called *infundi-*

bulum. The surrounding gray mass of the Infundibulum is called from its ash-gray color *tuber cinereum.*

The infundibulum, according to Gaskell, most likely
represents the primitive terminal mouth of the ar-
chaic intestinal tube. In mammals the hypophysis is
coalesced with the *tuber cinereum.*

Behind the hypophysis on the ventral side, at the
base of the brain, exactly where the Crura of the brain
pass upwards, we find two white little elevations, one
on each side, called *corpora candicantia,* the shining
bodies, or *corpora mammillaria,* the breast-like bodies.
These white little mountains are ganglionic masses
covered with white layers. They contain several
ganglionic centres, receiving nerve bundles from different directions. These bundles are:

1. The bundle of Vic d'Azyr, connecting the interior of the thalamus with the corpora candicantia.

2. The fibres of the tegmentum, coming from the
corpora quadrigemina and passing through the red
nucleus (*nucleus ruber*) in the subthalamic region.

3. Pedunculus corporis mammillaris, connecting
the medulla oblongata with the corpus mammillare.

The fibres of the *fornix* here rise upwards and
then turn backwards and extend behind the thalamus so as to form an overarching vault; they connect
the thalamus with the hippocampus, i. e., the marginal convolution of the hemispheres at the base of
the brain.

Another connection of the Thalamus with the subthalamic region is the *fasciculus retroflexus,* also called
Meynert's bundle, which connects a small ganglion,
the ganglion habenulae in the Thalamus with the *ganglion interpedunculare.* A decussation of this fascicle

takes place shortly above the ganglion interpedunculare.

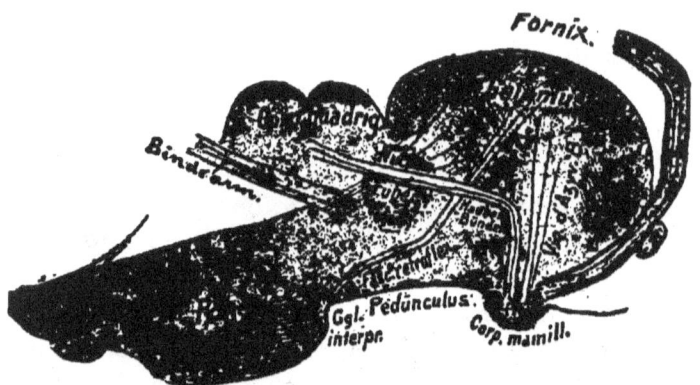

THE THALAMUS AND ITS RELATIONS. (After Edinger.)

The prefixed diagram explains the situation better than words. Formerly it was believed that the bundle of Vic d'Azyr was the beginning of the fornix descending from the thalamus and rising again into the corpus mammillare. Gudden's experiments have disproved this view and show that the bundle of Vic d'Azyr does not descend but rises into the thalamus.

The region around the red nucleus being situated underneath the thalamus is called the subthalamic region. It is a province of the brain, which being the meeting place of many intersecting tracts exhibits very complicated conditions. It is a labyrinth of interlacing fibres, some rising out of the nucleus restiformis, some out of the capsula interna, and some out of the thalamus. They here and there gather into small centres of gray substance, the import of which is but little known.

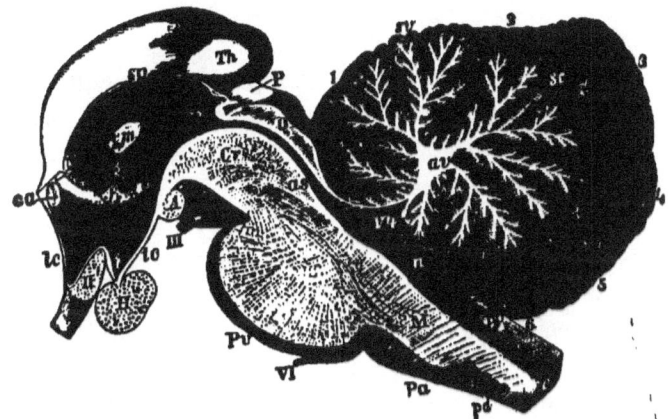

SAGITTAL SECTION OF THIRD AND FOURTH VENTRICLES. (After Reichert)

Th. Thalamus opticus.

P. Pineal gland (*conarium.*)

Q. Corpora quadrigemina, or Four Hills.

sp. Habenae conarii, the reins of the pineal gland. Thin nerve-fibres originating in the thalamus and entering the pineal gland.

cm. Commissura media ; the middle or gray commissure, being the place where the gray substance of the two thalami is connected.

c. a. Comissura anterior. The anterior commissure (seen here in a cross section) consists of white fibres. Its anterior part is formed by crossing fibres of the olfactory nerve. Its posterior part connects both temporal lobes of the hemispheres.

cp. Posterior commissure. Three distinct little bundles of white fibres, connecting both thalami.

l. c. Lamina cinerea, a band of grayish fibres.

II. Cross section of the optic nerve in the chiasma.

A. Corpus mammillare or corpus candicans. Its ganglionic nature is better seen in Edinger's diagram, "The Thalamus and its Relations." (*p. 146*)

a s. Aquaductus Sylvii, the tunnel between *V3* and *V4.*

n. Inferior medullary velum, covering the lower part of the Fourth Ventricle.

av. Arbor vitae, or the tree of life in the small brain.

sc. Folium cacuminis.

sv. Superior vermis; upper part of the worm.

1, 2, 3, 4, 5. 6. Lobes of cerebellum.

III. Third nerve.	*Pv.* Pons Varolii.
VI. Sixth nerve.	*Cr.* Crus cerebri.
f. Root of fornix.	*m.* Medulla oblongata.
H. Hypophysis or pituitary body.	*pp.* Clava.
t c. Tuber cinereum.	*e.* Medullary canal.
V3. Third ventricle.	*Pa.* Pyramid.
V4. Fourth Ventricle.	*p. d.* Pyramidal decussation.
i. Infundibulum.	

THE HEMISPHERIC REGION.

In ascending above the Thalamus we rise into the highest and most important province of the brain, into the hemispheric region, consisting of the cortex and the striped bodies or *corpora striata*.

If we pursue the course of the fibres of the crusta upwards, we notice that on each side they break through a thick oval body (the *corpus striatum*) and then, above the corpus striatum they radiate fanlike, and disperse in all directions. The narrow passage through the striped body, filled with these thick bundles of white fibres, is called the *Capsula interna*, and their fanlike dispersion above the striped body is called the *corona radiata* or crown. One smaller bundle of nerve fibres passes round the striped body to the frontal lobe of the brain, and this tract is called *capsula externa*.

The corpus striatum is thus divided by the *capsula interna* into two parts, which after their shape are called the lenticular and the tailed body—*nucleus lentiformis* and *nucleus caudatus*. The lenticular body appears in a lateral view, if looked at from the island of Reil, like a slightly oval lense. It is situated outside the internal capsule. The tailed body shaped like a big comma whose head lies in front and whose tapering tail stretches backward and downward, lies inside the internal capsule. The nucleus caudatus is in its thicker frontal part continuous with the gray matter of the hemispheres; it is also intimately connected with the shell (or putamen) of the lenticular

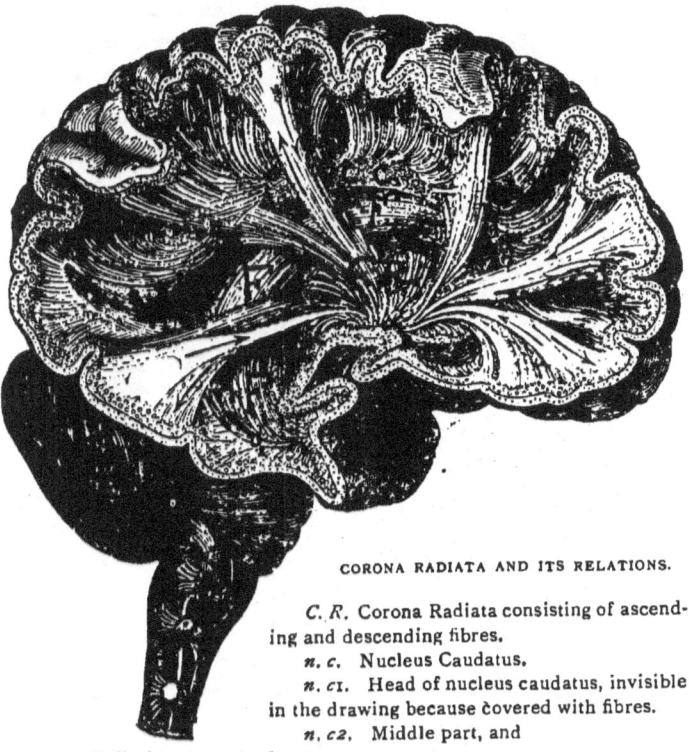

CORONA RADIATA AND ITS RELATIONS.

C. R. Corona Radiata consisting of ascending and descending fibres.

n. c. Nucleus Caudatus.

n. c1. Head of nucleus caudatus, invisible in the drawing because covered with fibres.

n. c2. Middle part, and

n. c3. Tail of nucleus caudatus.

x. Represents the place where the lentiform body lies buried underneath the protruding fibres.

C. C. Corpus Callosum, connecting the two hemispheres with each other.

F. F2, F3. Fornix, or the Vault; thick bundles of white fibres, rising in the marginal circumvolution of the temporal lobe (*gyrus hippocampi*), overarching the thalamus and descending to the corpora candicantia, underneath the front part of the thalamus.

The lateral ventricle lies between the fornix, the tailed body which forms its floor, and the corpus callosum which forms its roof. The right lateral ventricle is separated from the left through a double-walled membrane, called *septum lucidum.* Each lateral ventricle possesses three cavities which are called its anterior, lateral, and posterior horns.

V. Lateral ventricle, posterior horn.

v1. The anterior horn of the lateral ventricle, between the corpus callosum above and the front part of the fornix below.

v2. The lateral or middle horn of the lateral ventricle, its floor being the lower part of the fornix.

i. Insula Reil, being the deepest portion of the Fissure of Silvius.

•

body, and it engirds in its tail-like elongation the thalamus opticus from which it is distinctly separated by a sharp groove (*stria terminalis*) in which runs a small bundle of white fibres, *tenia semicircularis* which is the continuation of the olfactory nerve rising from

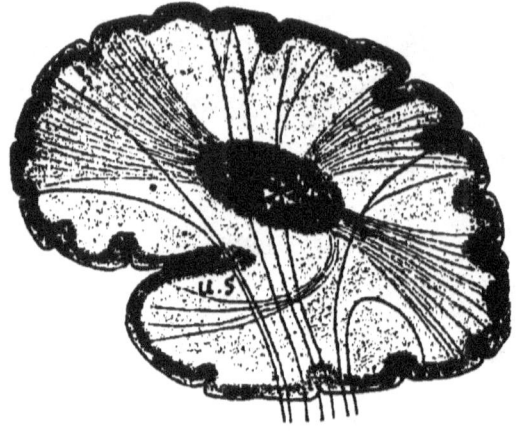

THE CORONAL CONNECTIONS OF THE THALAMUS WITH THE CORTEX.
(Diagrammatic. After Edinger.)

There are four groups of nerve-fibers: the anterior, posterior, superior, and inferior stems. The last one is marked *U. S.* All these bundles pass through the internal capsule.

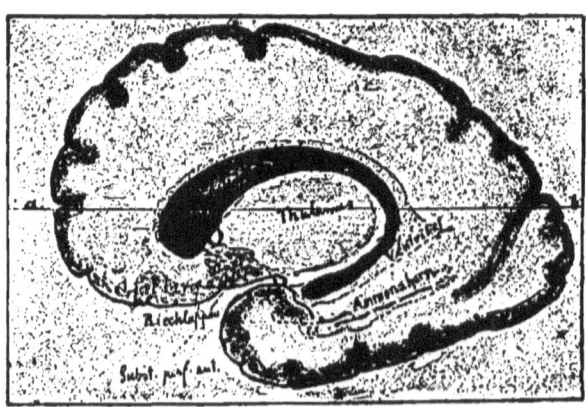

NUCLEUS CAUDATUS. (After Edinger.)

the olfactory ganglion. The nucleus caudatus forms the floor of the posterior horn of the lateral ventricle, and its tail ends in an eminence, called the amygdaloid tubercle.

A great part of the coronal nerve fibres rise from the thalamus. These nerves connect the thalamus with almost all regions of the hemispheres; near the thalamus they are gathered in bundles called the stems of the thalamus.

For further information we refer to the adjoined illustrations and diagrams, representing the brain, in coronal, sagital, and horizontal sections.

Coronal sections are such as run parallel to the

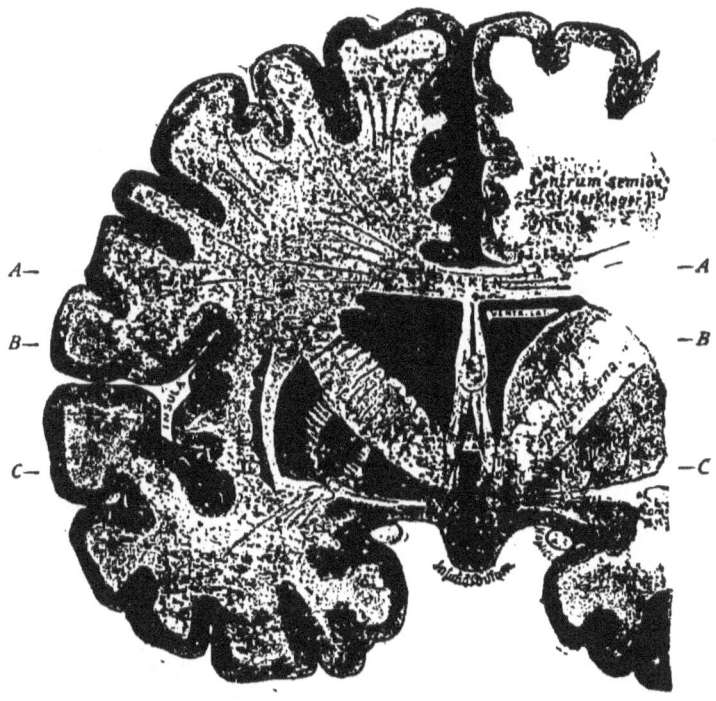

CORONAL SECTION OF BRAIN. (After Edinger.)

AA, BB, CC Indicate the three horizontal sections on pp. 153, 154, 155.

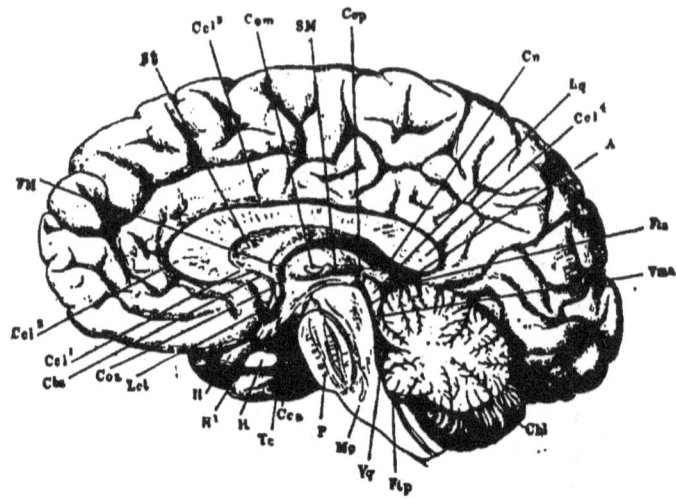

SAGITAL MEDIAN SECTION OF BRAIN.

F. M. Foramen Monro, the entrance from the third ventricle into the lateral ventricle.

S. M. Sulcus Monro, a groove of the third ventricle in the thalamus.

St. Septum pellucidum, a membrane forming the inner wall of the lateral ventricle. Each ventricle having its own septum pellucidum, there are two septa directly facing each other. The space between them is wrongly called the ventricle of the septum pellucidum. This space is, in fact, no ventricle, but must be conceived as the continuation of the fissure between both frontal lobes. The continuity of this fissure with the ventricle of the septum pellucidum has been interrupted by the growth of the corpus callosum. The corpus callosum (the commissural fibres joining both hemispheres) is little developed in lower mammals, it is strongly developed in the monkey and is still more prominent in man.

Ccl. 1. Rostrum or Beak, lowest part of the corpus callosum.

Ccl. 2. Genu or Knee of corpus callosum.

Ccl. 3. Upper surface of corpus callosum.

Ccl. 4. Splenium or Wedge; posterior part of corpus callosum.

Cba. Peduncles of corpus callosum.

Com. Commissura Media, connecting the two thalami. (Gray substance).

Coa. Commissura anterior, inter-connecting the temporal lobes.

Cop. Commissura posterior ; white fibres connecting both thalami.

Lct. Lamina cinerea terminalis ; part of tuber cinereum, originally the top and terminus of the primitive brain (as explained in the development of the brain).

II. Optic nerve.
Hr. Chiasma of optic nerve.
H. Hypophysis or pituitary body.
Tc., Tuber cinereum.
Cca. Corpus candicans.
P. Pons.
Mo. Medulla oblongata.

Vq. Fourth ventricle.
A. Aquaductus Sylvii.
Fta. Incisura pallii, sup. vale.
Ftp. Vallecula, posterior vale.
Lq. Four Hills.
Cn. Conarium or pineal gland.
Cbl. Cerebellum.

coronal suture of the cranium. For instance a vertical section through both ears is a coronal section.
Sagital sections are such as run parallel to the sagital
suture of the cranium. The sagital suture stands like
an arrow on the string of a bow at right angles upon
the coronal suture.

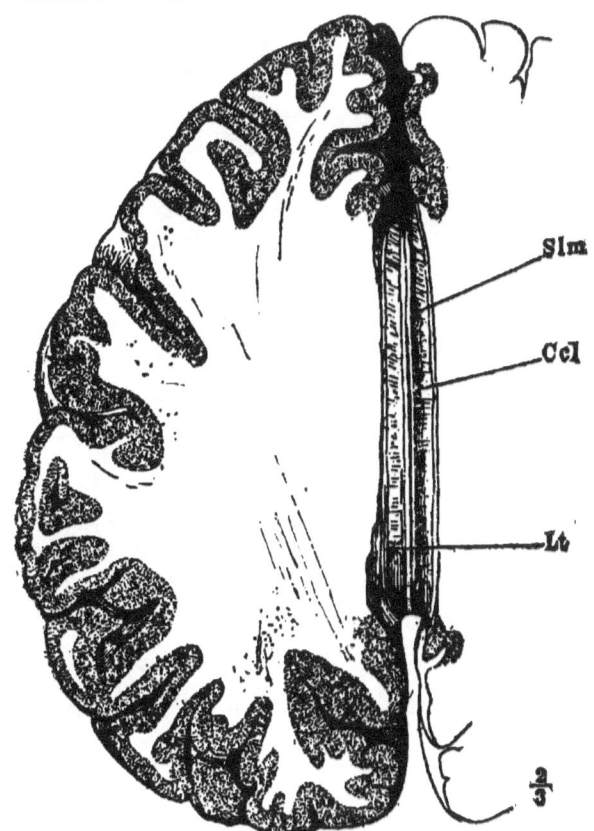

FIRST HORIZONTAL SECTION OF BRAIN. (After Henly.)
Indicated in the coronal section by an imaginary line to be drawn through
AA, and laying bare the corpus callosum (Germ. *Balken*).

Lt. Ligamentum tectum, Striae longitudinalis Lancisi.

Slm. Striae longitudinalis mediales; white longitudinal fibres, interlacing
in several places, running along in the middle of the corpus callosum. The
mass of white substance between the cortex and corpus callosum is called
Centrum Semiovale.—Ccl. Corpus callosum.

Cerebellum.

SECOND HORIZONTAL SECTION OF BRAIN. (After Edinger.)

Indicated in the coronal section by an imaginary line to be drawn through *BB*, laying bare the thalamus and nucleus caudatus.

The occipital lobes in reality appear as close together as the frontal lobes, so as to cover the cerebellum.

The Fornix rising in front from both thalami shows a cross-section in *F.II*. The fornix overarches the thalamus and descends to the marginal convolution on the base of the brain, which is visible in *F.I* only. This convolution is called the Gyrus Hippocampi. The gyrus hippocampi passes from the occipital lobe into the front lower part of the temporal lobe, where it is called Gyrus Uncinatus or hooked circumvolution.

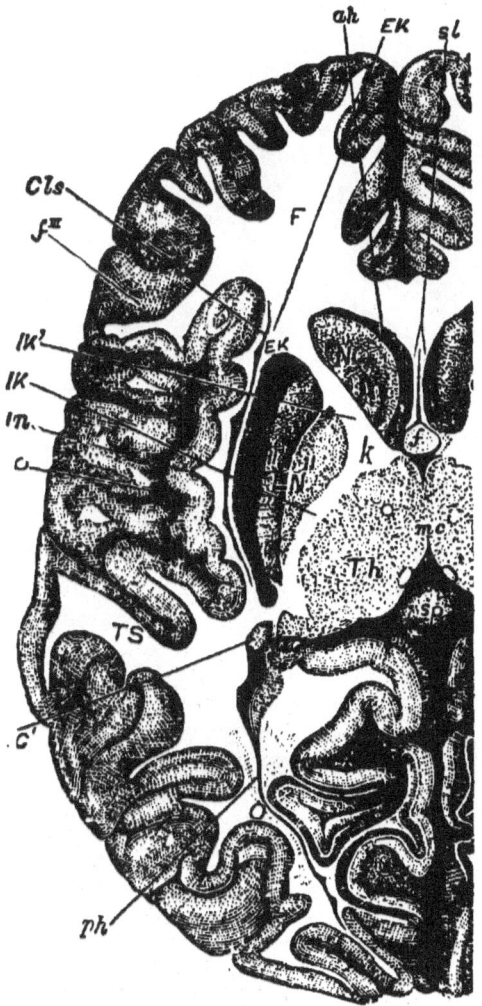

THIRD HORIZONTAL SECTION OF BRAIN. (After Flechsig.)

Indicated in the coronal section by an imaginary line to be drawn through CC.

Th. Thalamus.	*I. K.* Internal capsule posterior
Mc. Middle commissure.	limb.
f. Fornix.	*K.* Knee of internal capsule.
sl. Septum lucidum.	*E. K.* External capsule between
sp. Splenium.	lenticular body and claustrum.
N. C. Nucleus caudatus.	*Cls.* Claustrum.
ah, Anterior horn of lateral	*In,* Insula,
ventricle,	*o,* Operculum.

FOR CUT SEE PRECEDING PAGE.

ph. Posterior horn of lateral ventricle.
C'. Tail of nucleus caudatus.
L. N. Lenticular body.
I, K'. Internal capsule anterior limb.

F. Frontal lobe.
f III. Third frontal circumvolution.
O. Occipital lobe.
T. S. Temporo-sphenoidal lobe.

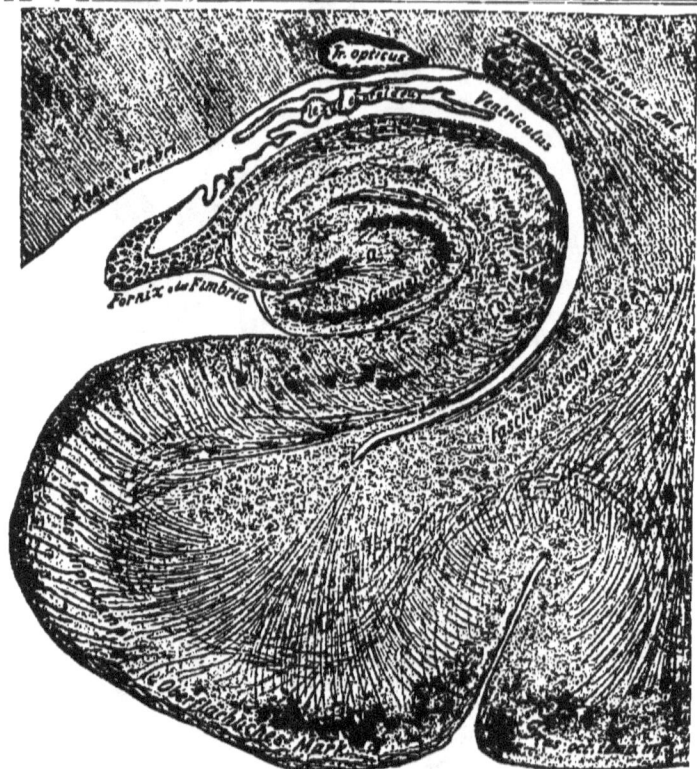

CROSS-SECTION THROUGH GYRUS HIPPOCAMPI. (After Edinger.)

The gyrus hippocampi is accompanied by a smaller circumvolution. the gyrus dentatus, (or fascia dentata) which is almost bare of all gray substance. It produces by protrusion inside a ridge in the lateral ventricle, called Horn of Ammon, or pes hippocampi major. The fornix rises from fibres originating in the gyrus dentatus, where it is called Fimbria.

All the marginal circumvolutions of the hemispheres; viz., the gyrus fornicatus, which surrounds the corpus callosum, its continuation, the gyrus hippocampi with the fascia dentata, and the cornu Ammonis, and also the nerve-fibres of the striæ Lancisi are strongly developed in animals in whom the function of smell is prominent. In the fœtal stage and in infants they are comparatively large; in the adult man they are almost atrophied. In the dolphin who has no olfactory bulb, they are found in a state of retrogression.

THE CORTEX AND ITS RELATIONS.

THE end-stations of the innumerable fibres of the corona radiata are the gray cells of the Cortex. These gray cells form the ganglionic element of the hemispheres. In the human brain they are associated among themselves by many systems of commissural fibres, which although extremely complex and numerous, are yet very economically arranged. Almost every province of the brain stands in direct relation with other provinces.

The white fibres of the brain accordingly consist first of ascending, and secondly of descending nerves, all of which are gathered together in the capsules. A dissection of these bundles would therefore destroy the connections of the Cortex with all the lower centres of the nervous system. Through these narrow passages all sensory impressions rise into, and all voluntary motor impulses descend from, the hemispheric region. But besides the ascending and descending fibres, there is a third class which we call commissural fibres, serving the purpose of inter-communication among the cortical cells, and establishing relations also between the cortex and the hemispheric ganglions (*nucleus caudatus* and *nucleus lentiformis*).

There are commissural fibres which interconnect the two hemispheres. The most important tract of these nerves forms a thick and broad body of a tough structure, called *corpus callosum* (German *Balken*). A

•

smaller tract of this kind is the anterior commissure.
Fibres of the anterior commissure inter-connect both
temporal lobes, while the corpus callosum appears to
bring all other parts of the one hemisphere into relation with the corresponding parts of the other.

The most important bundles that associate the different provinces of the same hemisphere are the *fasciculus arcuatus* (arching bundle), the *fasciculus uncinatus* (the hooked bundle), the *fasciculus longitudinalis inferior* (the lower longitudinal bundle) and the *cin-
gulum* or girdle.

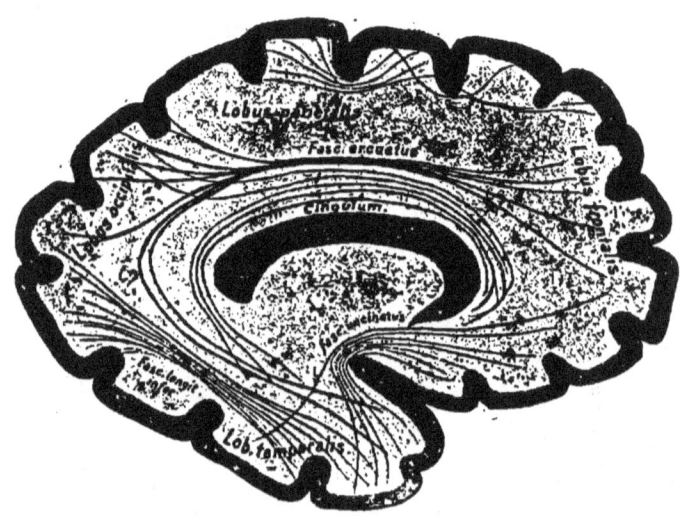

COMMISSURAL FIBRES OF THE HEMISPHERES. (After Edinger.)

According to experiments made by Charcot, a dissection of two-thirds of the front part of the internal
capsule produces paralysis, while a dissection of the
posterior limb, the third and hindmost part of the
capsula interna, is accompanied with anæsthesia.
This proves that the anterior fibres of the capsule are
mainly motor, and the posterior fibres sensory nerves.

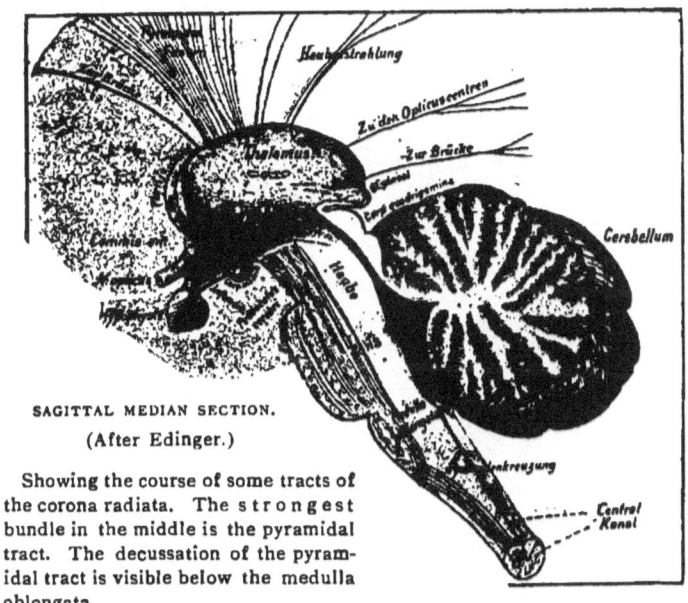

SAGITTAL MEDIAN SECTION.

(After Edinger.)

Showing the course of some tracts of the corona radiata. The s t r o n g e s t bundle in the middle is the pyramidal tract. The decussation of the pyramidal tract is visible below the medulla oblongata.

The rays of the tegmentum (*Haubenstrahlung*) rise from the tegmentum (*Haube*).

There are two connections with the Pons (*Brücke*).

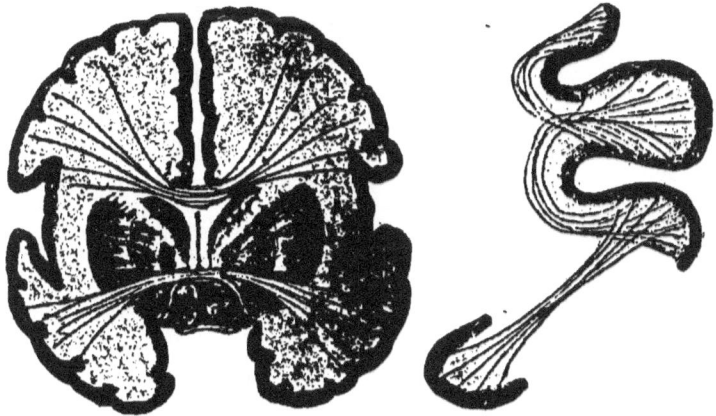

CORONAL SECTION THROUGH THE BRAIN,

Showing the connections between both Hemispheres by the corpus callosum and the commissura anterior. (After Edinger.)

FIBRÆ PROPRIÆ.

(After Edinger.)

Nerve fibres connecting adjacent circumvolutions.

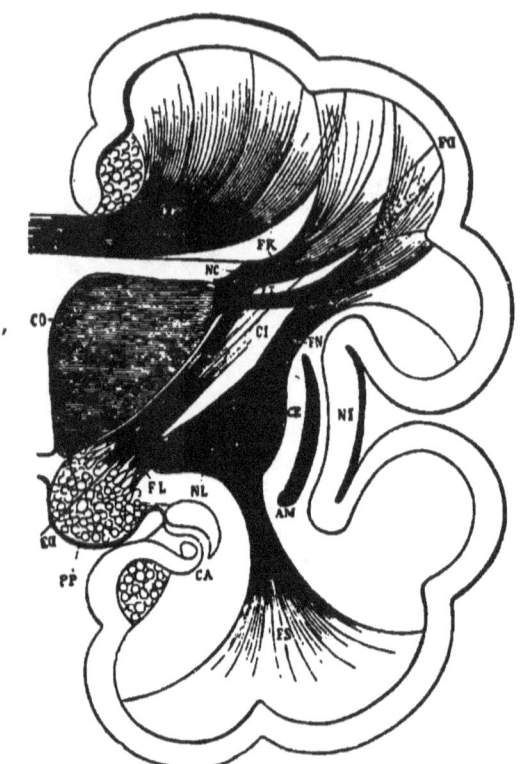

FIBRES OF THE HEMISPHERES.

Diagram of the connections between the Striped Body and the Cortex.

(After Huguenin, reproduced from Charcot.)

NC. Nucleus caudatus.

CO. Thalamus opticus (French, *couche optique*).

NL. Nucleus lentiformis, having three segments.

AM. Claustrum (French, *avant mur*).

CI. Capsula interna.

CE. Capsula externa.

PP. Crus cerebri

CA. Cornu Ammonis.

NI. Insula.

FL. Fibres of crus in connection with nucleus lentiformis.

FN. Fibres of nucleus lentiformis in connection with cortex.

FK. Fibres of nucleus caudatus in connection with cortex.

FD. Direct fibres, establishing a direct connection between cortex and crus.

CC. Corpus callosum.

STRONGLY MAGNIFIED SECTION
OF CORTICAL SUBSTANCE.
(After Edinger.)
(Taken from the frontal lobe
of a human brain.)
The most superficial layer
of gray cells (1) is covered
with a net-work of extremely
fine white fibres (tangential
fibres); the cells of the lower
strata are the larger, the
deeper they are situated.
The second layer passes gradually into the third, containing large pyramidal cells.
The fourth layer contains
smaller cells.

These four layers are inter-
sected by white fibres which,
enumerating them from be-
low, Edinger calls, a) radii
or medullar rays; b) inter-
radiary net-work; c) Grenna-
ry's layer (called after Gren-
nary who described these
fibres); d) superradiary net-
work; and e) tangential fibres.

The right part is prepared
with Weigert's Haemotoxy-
line, the left part with Gol-
gi's sublimate, showing on
the left side the fibres and on
the right side the gray cells
only. There are many more
gray cells than appear in the
diagram. Their number is
reduced in order to show
their relations more clearly.
The gray cells appear somewhat larger than they ought
to, because the sublimate
employed, according to Gol-
gi's method, not only colors
the gray substance, but fills
the hollow spaces round the
cells and their processes
also.

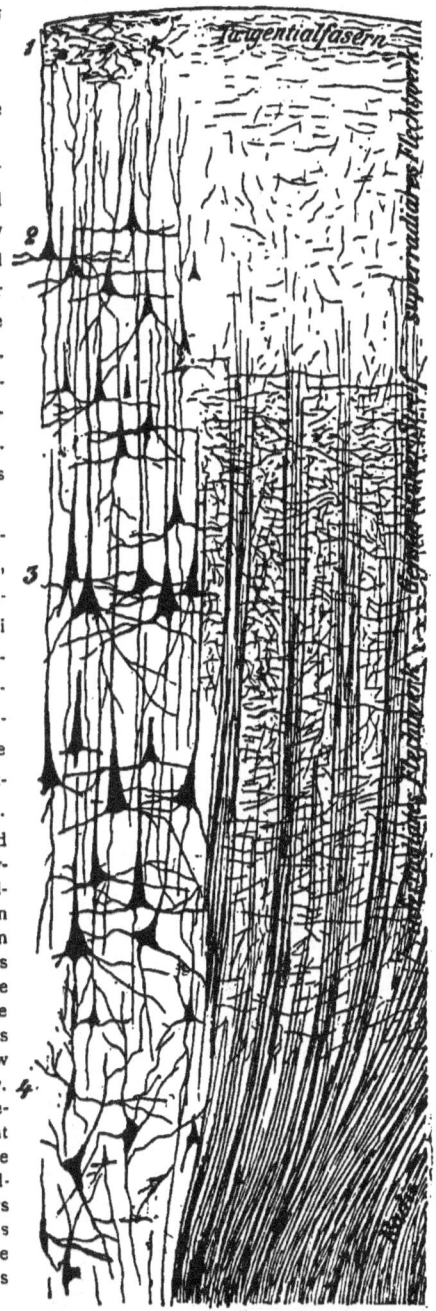

The Cortex, or gray substance of the hemispheres, is a very complex substance, which shows a great variety in the different parts of the brain. It consists of several layers of gray cells of different size embedded into white fibres. The adjoined diagram represents a strongly magnified section of the Cortex, taken from the frontal lobe, and prepared with two different chemicals. The left side makes the gray cells come out strongly, while the white fibres disappear. In the left side, on the contrary, the gray matter disappears, while the white fibres come out so as to be plainly visible.

•

LOCALIZATION OF BRAIN ACTIVITY.

I.

FISSURES AND CONVOLUTIONS.

It is commonly acknowledged that the hemispheres are the seat of all psychic activity. This, however, is true in a limited sense only. Properly speaking man does not think with his brain alone; he thinks with his entire body. Yet in the brain, especially in the hemispheres and the hemispheric ganglions (*nucleus caudatus* and *nucleus lentiformis*), his psychic activity is concentrated. The co-operation of every part of the organism is necessary to produce thought as the final result at the centre of the organism's activity.

Flourens proposed the theory, that the hemispheres performed their functions in a way such that the entire cortex is always engaged in any kind of mental work performed. If part of the cortical substance be lost, Flourens maintains that all the functions will be proportionately affected.

Goltz adopted Flourens's view to the extent of holding, that in case of a loss of cortical matter some homologous substance would perform the functions of the portion lost. The vicarious activity of brain-substance appears to be a well-established fact, although it does not take place to such an extent and in such a way as Flou-

●

rens supposed. "The different parts of the hemispheres are," as Prof. Hering says, "like a great toolbox with innumerable kinds of tools. Each single cerebral element is a particular tool. Consciousness may be likened to a workingman whose tools gradually become so numerous, so various, and so specialized that he has for every detail of his work a tool which is specially adapted to perform just this kind of work very easily and accurately. If he loses one of his tools, he still possesses a thousand other tools to do the same work although with more difficulty and loss of time. Should he lose these thousand also, he might retain hundreds, with which he can possibly do his work still, but the difficulty increases. He must have lost a very large number of his tools if certain actions become absolutely impossible."

*   *   *

Gall was the first to propound a localization of the different psychic functions. He started from the supposition that the skull being the case of the brain ought to show its formation, and he founded upon this supposition his phrenology. The skull shows indeed the formation of the brain, but it shows its outward shape only; and even that imperfectly, because different craniums vary very materially in thickness. Yet in judging about the formation of the brain, the internal structures are of much greater importance. Gall's phrenology, being in fact a kind of cranioscopy, is now entirely abandoned.

It is strange that most of the meritorious discoveries of this great scientist are little known outside of a narrow circle of specialists, while the error of his phrenology has become a favorite idea among half-scientific people and has made his name extremely popular.

Gall's idea of a localization of the different functions of the hemispheres has been revived in later years, yet upon another basis and in an entirely new shape. The modern conception of localized brain-functions is based upon experiments and affords at the same time a more precise and definite idea of the *modus operandi* of the brain.

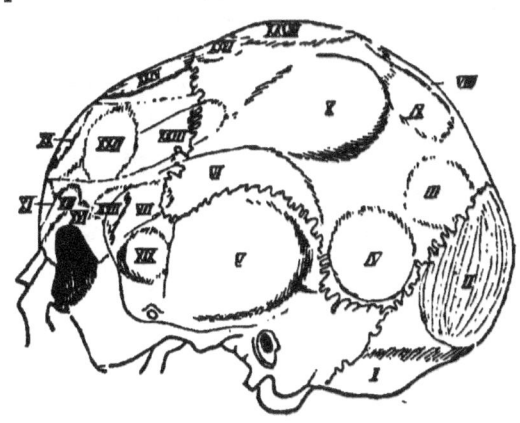

PHRENOLOGY. (After Gall.)

I.	Sexual instinct.	XV.	Language.*
II.	Love of children.	XVI.	Painting (sense of colors).
III.	Friendship.	XVII.	Music.
IV.	Self-preservation.	XVIII.	Numbers and arithmetic*
V.	Homicidal impulses.	XIX.	Mechanical abilities.
VI.	Smartness.	XX.	Comparison.
VII.	Acquisitiveness.	XXI.	Profoundness.
VIII.	Ambition.	XXII.	Wit.
IX.	Vanity.	XXIII.	Poetry.
X.	Circumspection.	XXIV.	Goodnaturedness.
XI.	Memory for objects.	XXV.	Imitation.*
XII.	Sense of locality.	XXVI.	Religion.
XIII.	Memory for persons.*	XXVII	Enthusiasm
XIV.	Memory for words.*		* Do not appear in the cut.

The outward surface of the cortex looks like a a tract of land in which many rivers and brooks have produced furrows. The furrows are called *sulci* or fissures, and the ridges between them are called convolutions. The fissures are produced to effect an economy óf space ; in so far as by their presence the area of cortical substance is greatly increased without any considerable increase of the size of the head ; and it has been observed that the higher the intelligence of an animal is, the richer is its brain in convolutions.

The immediate cause of the fissures are the arteries. The cortical substance is in greater need of arterial blood than any other part of the body. The more work an animal has to do with its brain, the more blood is needed in the cortex. Thus the arteries surrounding the superficial structures of the hemispheres become stronger and sink deeper, and the fissures are produced as if to form a natural system of irrigations. The fissures are, as Seitz calls them, nutrimentral channels,* *Nährschlitze.*

The names of the different parts of the hemispheres, their lobes, convolutions, and fissures may be studied in the adjoined diagrams. The most important fissures are the fissure of Rolando or *sulcus centralis,* which is the province of the motor centres, and the fissure of Sylvius, which, together with the adjoining part of the third frontal convolution in the left hemisphere, is the centre of speech.

The attempts at localizing the different functions of the cortex have been but partly successful. The most prominent workers in this line of investigation are Fritsch and Hitzig, Ferrier, Exner, Goltz, Munck, and others. The results are shown in the diagrams of the following chapter on pp. 170 and 171.

---

* Johannes Seitz : *Ueber die Bedeutung der Hirnfurchung.* Leipzig and Wien, 1887.

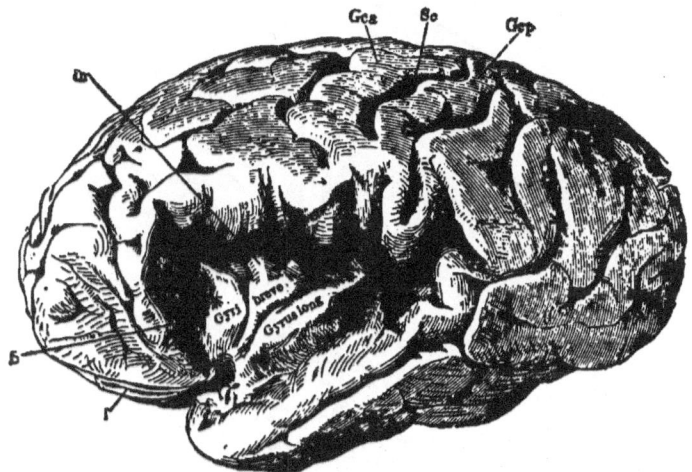

THE LEFT HEMISPHERE. (After Henle.)

The fissure of Silvius is drawn aside so as to show the extent of the Insula. The insula contains one long and two short convolutions, called *gyrus longus* and *gyri breves.* The cortical substance which covers the insula in *a* is called *operculum.*

In. Insula.
Sc. Sulcus centralis, or fissure of Rolando.
Gca. Gyrus centralis anterior.
Gcp. Gyrus centralis posterior.

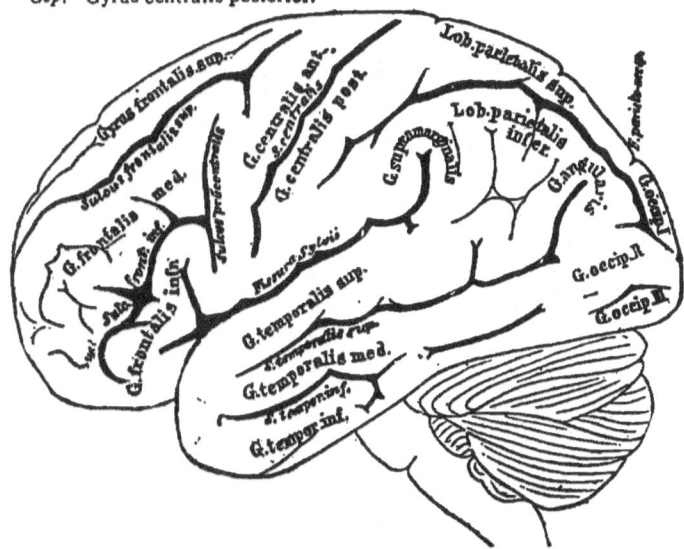

SIDE VIEW OF THE BRAIN. (After Ecker.)

The convolutions and lobes are in Roman letters, the fissures in Italics.

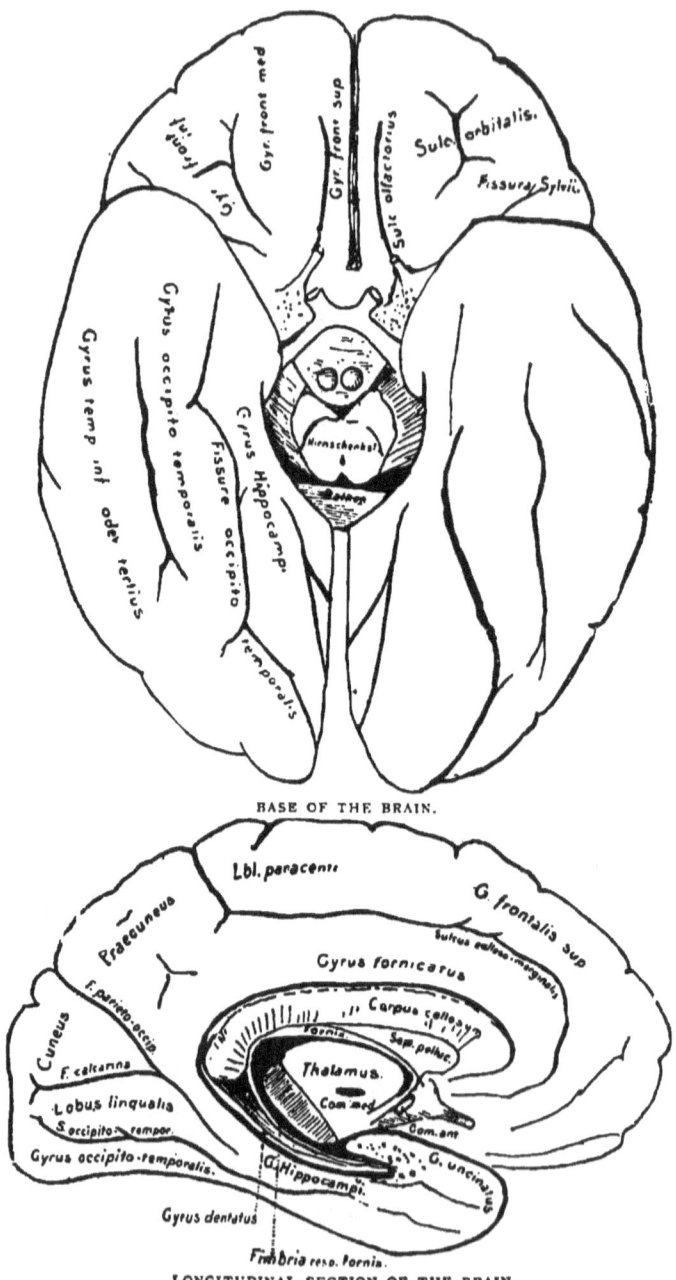

BASE OF THE BRAIN.

LONGITUDINAL SECTION OF THE BRAIN.

II.

MOTORY AND SENSORY CENTRES.

THE most important motory regions of the human brain are, according to all authorities on the subject, situated around the fissure of Rolando. There is less agreement concerning the sensory centres. The optic centre is situated, according to Meynert, Munk, and Huguenin, in the first, second, and third occipital lobes ; according to Exner, in the first and second only, and in the upper part of the cuneus.

The acoustic centre lies in the temporal lobes. Irritations of these centres cause hallucinations of hearing. In post mortem examinations Huguenin found the temporal lobes of deaf patients in an atrophied condition.

The centres of taste and smell are, according to Ferrier, supposed to be situated in the *uncus gyri fornicati.*

The tactile centres, according to Trippier, Exner, Petrina and others, must be sought for in the regions of their respective motory centres.

The frontal lobe does not contain either motory or sensory centres. It seems to be in the service of more abstract kinds of mental activity, and is most likely also the seat of affectionate and emotional centres. Defects of this part, be they acquired or inherited, are as a rule accompanied with idiocy or lack of intelligence. Monkeys in whom the frontal lobes were removed, showed no irregularities in the exercise of their motory and sensory functions ; yet they appeared more whimsical and less affectionate than before.

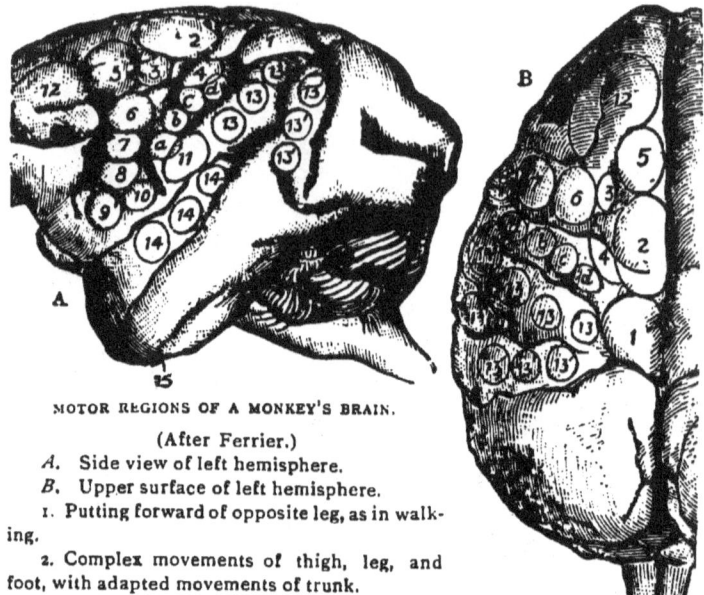

MOTOR REGIONS OF A MONKEY'S BRAIN.

(After Ferrier.)

A. Side view of left hemisphere.

B. Upper surface of left hemisphere.

1. Putting forward of opposite leg, as in walking.

2. Complex movements of thigh, leg, and foot, with adapted movements of trunk.

3. Movements of tail.

4. Retraction and adduction of opposite fore-limb.

5. Extension forward of opposite arm and hand, as if to reach or touch something in front.

a, b, c, d. Successive complex movements of fingers and wrist, ending in clinching of fist.

6. Supination and flexion of forearm, by which the hand is raised toward the mouth.

7. Action of the zygomatic muscle by which the angle of the mouth is retracted and elevated.

8. Elevation of the ala of nose and the upper lip, with depression of lower lip so as to expose the canine teeth on the opposite side.

9. Opening of mouth with protrusion of tongue.

10. Opening of mouth with retraction of tongue.

11. Retraction of angle of mouth.

12. Eyes opening widely, pupils dilating, head and eyes turning toward opposite side.

13, 13′. Eyeballs moving to opposite side, pupils generally contracting.

14. Sudden retraction of opposite ear.

15. Torsion of lip and nostril on the same side. This place is situated in the subiculum of Cornu Ammonis.

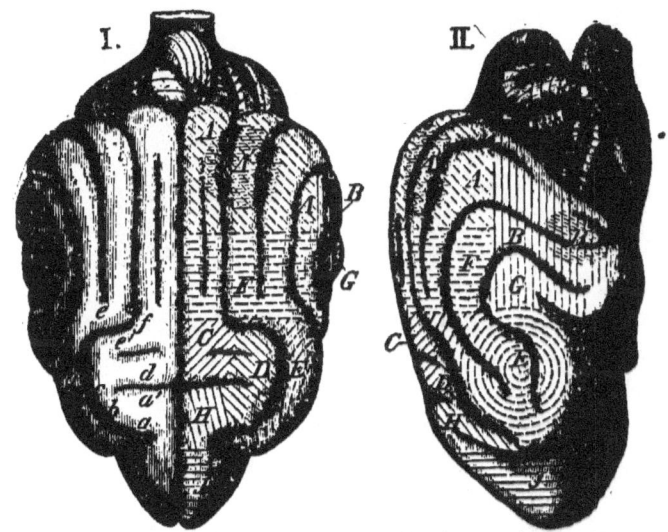

DOG'S BRAIN. (After Munk.)

A-J. Indicates Sensory Centres.
A. Vision.
B. Hearing.
C-J. Touch of.

C. Hindlegs.
D. Forelegs.
E. Head.
F. Eyes.

G. Ears.
H. Neck.
J. Trunk.

a-f. Indicate motory centres.
a. Neck.
a'. Back.   [Foreleg.
b. Extensors and Adductors of
c. Flexors and Bronators of Foreleg.

d. Muscles of Hindleg.
e. Focialis.
e'. Upper region of Facialis.
f. Muscles of the eye.
g. Muscles of chewing.

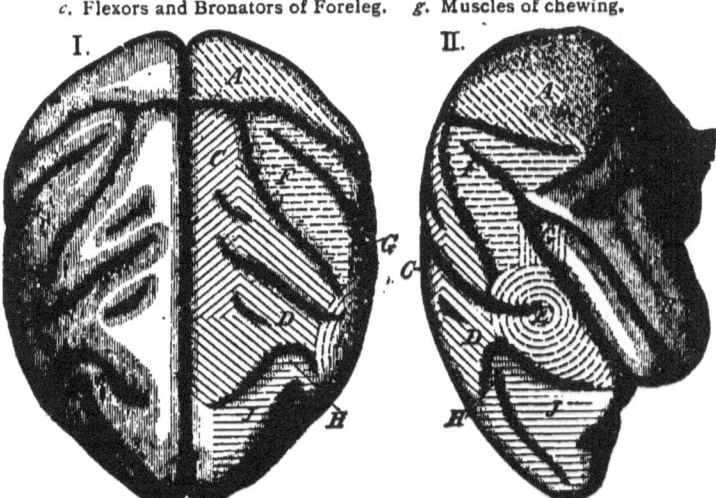

MONKEY'S BRAIN. (After Munk.)
Explanation the same as in the preceding cut

III.

LOSS OF BRAIN SUBSTANCE.

IT is strange that a man may lose large portions of the cortical substance of his brain, without showing any apparent loss of faculty.   If the motor centres are injured, the effect will always be an impairment of the voluntary motions of the opposite side ; yet the loss of sensory or other centres in one hemisphere will not be noticeable so long as the other hemisphere remains sound—except that such half brained persons will tire more quickly than normal people.   We may explain this strange fact by comparing it to the condition of a man who has lost one eye.   If the loss of the eye were not noticeable (perhaps because the man wears an excellently imitated artificial eye), it would by our ordinary methods of observation be very difficult to detect the loss.

The following facts from which this rule is deduced, are collected in Hermann's " Physiologie," Vol II, 2. p. 333 :

" Berenger de Carpi tells of a young man into whose brain a body four finger-breadths in width and as many in length had been driven so deep that it lay concealed by the matter of the brain.   When it was removed a certain amount of cerebral substance was lost, and thirteen days afterwards a second discharge occurred spontaneously.   The man recovered, showed no diseased symptoms, lived for a long time afterwards, and attained high distinction in the Church.

" Longet knew a general who through a wound in the skull near the crown of the head had suffered a considerable loss of brain-substance.   This defect permanently manifested itself by a depression in the part of the skull affected. The general preserved his activity of mind ; his correct judgment in professional matters exhibited no traces of disease ; only he was wont to tire quickly when engaged in intellectual work.

"Quesnay tells of an old servant whose right parietal bone was crushed. Every day cerebral matter oozed from the wound, and was removed. On the eighteenth day the patient fell out of bed, which resulted in further considerable losses of brain-substance. On the thirty-fifth day he got drunk ; a fresh emission of cerebral matter occurred, which was caused by the patient's tearing away in his intoxication the bandage about the wound. On the day following it could be seen that the defect reached almost to the *corpus callosum.* The patient got well ; his psychical functions were restored to their complete activity ; but he remained paralyzed on his left side.

"During the blasting of a rock, a crow-bar three feet and seven inches long and one and a quarter inches thick struck a young man, and penetrating the head in the neighborhood of the joint of the left jaw, passed through the skull and came out on the same side in the region of the forehead, having thus run through the hemisphere of the brain. The man got well, lived twelve and a half years afterwards, and apart from the blindness caused by the injury to the eye he showed no indications of abnormality, except certain fits of peevishness, caprice, and obstinacy.

" A whole hemisphere may be removed, without injury to the psychical functions. But in that case disturbances of the motory functions on the opposite side appear regularly to set in.

" A psychically normal individual that—as it happened—was paralyzed since his birth on the right side, died of phthisis. Upon dissection the place of the right hemisphere was found to be filled with some kind of serous fluid."

IV.

THE CENTRE OF LANGUAGE.

There is a region in the cortex, a lesion of which produces almost without any exception disturbances and even loss of speech. It is accordingly called the

•

Centre of Language.   This region is situated in the
island of Reil at the bottom of the fissure of Sylvius
and extends over the parts adjacent to the island, especially the third frontal convolution.

The centre of language is unilateral and must be
sought as a rule in the left hemisphere.   However
there are some exceptions. We have reason to believe
that left-handed people are right-brained speakers.
Left-handed people who had lost the power of speech
were found to have suffered injuries in the right hemisphere, but whenever their left hemisphere happened to be affected they had not lost the power of
speech.

Loss of language, or aphasia, may have various
causes, and will accordingly present different symptoms.
It need not at all be due to a derangement of mental
powers but may be a loss merely of the motor capacity
of speech.   In that case it is more properly called
paralysis of speech.   The patient may still be able to
write what he means.   Yet the ability to write may
be lost also; this disease is called agraphia. Agraphia
is not a paralysis of the hand ; it is a paralysis of the
memories of penmanship.   The hand may be able
to perform all the single motions necessary for
writing, but the patient has lost the power of co-
ordinating these movements so as to write words;
he is like an uneducated man who has not learned
how to write.   In that case the patient may be able
to communicate through gestures or pantomime.
Should the power of making gestures be lost also, the
patient may nevertheless know everything he wants
and may possess full clearness of his mind ; he may
think of the words even which he intends to use (as
we know from patients who have recovered from such

diseases), yet he is not able to communicate his thoughts.

Quite different from these forms of a paralysis of speech is the amnestic aphasia which is caused by an obliteration of the word-memories themselves. In that case, the patient can perhaps read and repeat, he can pronounce every word correctly, he can also write from dictation. The different motor centres are unimpaired, yet the words, or certain categories, are no longer at the patient's disposal. They are as if forgotten, blotted out of his memory, and wrapped in oblivion. Amnestic aphasia usually shows in post mortem examinations a destruction of the first frontal convolution on the left side where it is in relation with the island of Reil.

As a special form of amnestic aphasia we may consider the state in which ideas are not associated with their words. The ideas as well as the words are still extant, yet their connection is destroyed, the fibres of association are interrupted.

We quote from Hermann's " Physiologie " Professor Exner's report of the present state of investigation concerning the cortical centre of speech. Professor Exner says :

"If a man gives an appropriate answer to a question, the following things must, it is evident, take place within him :

(1) He must hear the words spoken ;

(2) These words must awaken in him the ideas that belong to them ;

(3) From the mental operation conducted with the help of these ideas, a resultant product must issue ;

(4) This product must be clothed in words ;

(5) The central innervations necessary to the utterance of these words must be brought about ; and finally

(6) These innervations must arrive at the proper muscles in their proper order and intensity.

" If the first requisite is not fulfilled, we are dealing with a deaf person ; if the last is not fulfilled, most probably with a patient suffering from some affection in the *crus ;* if the mental operation mentioned under (3) is not accomplished, it is a case of dementia ; all other interruptions or disturbances of the above-mentioned processes, viz. (2), (4), and (5), lead to aphasia.

"Cases of diseases occur that are only to be interpreted upon the supposition that the power of comprehension of words mentioned under (2) has been lost. We have here to do with patients that are very well able to speak words but do not understand them, though their hearing be good. An example will illustrate this : *

" 'A woman 25 years of age, ten days after parturition, while violently straining to relieve her bowels, suddenly became unconscious. When consciousness returned she exhibited no symptoms of paralysis, but was suffering from aphasia and paraphasia.†

" 'It was with difficulty, or not at all, that she found words to speak with ; she confounded or mutilated them, said " Butter "instead of "Doctor," omitted words and syllables, supplied others, used the infinitive for the determinate moods, and conjugated irregular verbs regularly. Not understanding a single word at first, she was taken to be deaf. It soon turned out however that she heard a knock at the door and even the ticking of a watch as distinctly as ever before ; she distinguished the bells of two different apartments of the house by their sound, etc., etc.'

*This case is from Schmidt (Allgemeine Zeitschrift für Psychiatrie, XXVII, p. 304, 1871); cited from Kussmaul's *Störungen der Sprache*, p. 176, Leipzig, 1877—a work to be recommended to all who are interested in the present state of knowledge upon this subject.

† This word denotes a disturbance of speech in which, instead of the words that fit the sense, other, improper words, or wholly meaningless combinations of words, are employed.

" In cases of aphasia like this, the patient stands in a relation somewhat like that in which we would conceive an intelligent animal to stand that hears well enough the language of the people about him, but does not understand it. The patient cannot properly be compared to a well person that hears a foreign language, since the latter when the name of an object is told him retains the same ; but not so a person suffering from aphasia. As Kussmaul pointed out, these forms of aphasia prove that the locality of the brain with which the sensation of the sounds of single vowels and consonants is connected, is a different one from that in which an acoustical word-image is apprehended as the symbol of a concept."

" No case has come to my knowledge," Professor Exner continues, "in which this 'word-deafness' has not also been combined with 'word-blindness'; that is to say, if a patient has lost the power to associate the words he has heard with their proper ideas, he is also unable to do this with written words, although he may be able to see as well as a person in the normal condition.* In this, and in many another connection, the case of Lordat has acquired much interest and celebrity. Lordat, who was himself professor of medicine, suffered several months from aphasia, and afterwards explained in detail the condition in which he found himself during this period of illness.

" In the same way that the understanding for spoken and written words can be lost, so can the power of comprehension of figures. An accountant was able

---

* Yet cases are known, as mentioned above, in which a paralysis of speech is not connected with a paralysis of writing or making oneself understood by signs. For an instance of aphasia not accompanied by agraphia see infra the case of the young clerk. (p. 179).

to read the number 766 figure for figure, but did not
know what it meant that the figure 7 stood before the ·
two 6's. So the understanding of written musical
notes can be lost, although the patient be still able to
play well by ear.

* * *

"In a second form of aphasia it is impossible for
the patient to clothe the results of his thoughts in words
[mentioned above under (4)], whether it be to utter
the same or to put them in writing. In most cases
of this kind the word is simply forgotten. If it
be told the patient, he can repeat it and even write it,
but immediately forgets it again. By reason of the
last circumstance this form of aphasia is easily distinguishable from that first mentioned.

· "It is striking that at times only single words or only
nouns, very frequently names, disappear from the
memory and are not again to be acquired. It also
comes to pass that only parts of words are forgotten.

" Thus, Graves tells of a case, where a man, six-
ty-five years of age, after an apoplectic fit forgot all the
proper names and substantives he knew but still recollected their initial letters. He accordingly compiled
an alphabetically arranged dictionary of the substantives necessary for purposes of ordinary intercourse,
and whenever in conversation an object occurred to
him that he wanted to speak about he looked it up in his
dictionary. If he wanted to say Cow for instance, he
looked up his word under C. So long as he saw the
printed name with his eye he could speak it, a moment
afterwards he would be unable to do so.

" The extent to which the impairment may be modified and limited in the field of language, appears from
a case of Lasègue, who came across a musician who was

totally aphasic and agraphic, but could take down in notes a tune that he had heard.

"A third form of aphasia is characterized by the circumstance that the patient is able to clothe his thoughts in words but is not able to bring about the central innervations necessary to the utterance of the same [referred to above as process (5)]. That the patients execute mental operations and also clothe the results of the same in words, appears with certainty from the fact that they are able to write them down. On the other hand they are also unable to repeat words spoken to them, and in their efforts to do this they show that the different parts of the mouth are able to execute voluntary movements—they distort their mouth and twist the tongue about, but produce only inarticulate sounds.

"'A vigorous young clerk in an attack of unconsciousness had lost completely the power of speech ; no other pathological symptoms appearing. He executed with facility all movements of tongue and lips. As his duties were such that they could be attended to with the pen, he kept his position. He gave his physician a carefully prepared account of his affliction.'

"With these patients it is not a question of inability to find the innervations for certain letters as such, but the difficulty is with the *words*, which they are powerless to form. That this is true will appear from the fact that many patients with whom a remnant of speech has still remained (and who, therefore, are still able to utter single words, or it may be mutilated words), although they have the power to speak a word yet cannot speak that word when a syllable has been left out or the order of the syllables changed, nor enunciate a syllable when the order of the letters has been changed ; for instance, if a patient can pronounce only the syllable *tan*, he is in that case unable to say *nat.* Secondly, this will appear from the fact, that a patient who has command of a few words will be able to pronounce a certain letter in one word and not in another.

" The following case of a patient Le Long—taken from Broca—will serve as an illustration of the condition last described as well as of cases of incomplete aphasia. ' Le Long had command of only five words, which he would add by way of supplement to the expressive gestures he usually employed ; they were *oui, non, tois* (for *trois*), *toujours*, and *Le Lo* (for Le Long) —three complete words, accordingly, and two mutilated ones. With his *oui* he expressed affirmation, with *non* negation ; with *tois* he expressed numerical concepts of all degrees, being able to indicate by a dexterous employment of his fingers the number he had in mind ; with *Le Lo* he denoted himself ; *toujours* he used when he was unable to express his thoughts by the aid of the other words he commanded. Le Long pronounced the *r* in *toujours* correctly, but omitted it in *trois*, as children do that have not yet overcome the difficulty of uniting the *r* with the preceding *t* ; he had lost beyond recall this knack of articulation. The nasal sound that he articulated in *non* he could not give to the last letters of his own name.'

" It is also a remarkable phenomenon, that patients who ordinarily have command of only a few words, in moments of excitement bring out and perfectly articulate more, and sometimes even ejaculate a very long oath. Jackson reports, that aphasic patients who are unable to answer ' No ' to ordinary questions, suddenly find the power of utterance of this negation when aroused to it by ridiculous questions—as 'if they are a hundred years old.'

*   *   *

"The processes that we have spoken of up to this point, the disturbances of which lead to aphasia proper, take place in the cortex. If the conduction towards the muscles of the innervations properly induced in the cortex is impaired, the power of speech is also naturally affected ; the language of the patient becomes forced, letters are omitted, the patient stutters, lisps, and at last becomes completely unintelligible ; yet this is not a case of aphasia. [This is paralysis of speech.] These disturbances of the paths of conduction may be effected in the medullary matter of the cerebral hemispheres ; most frequently, however, they must be sought in the nerve-nuclei of the medulla oblongata, especially in the nucleus of the hypoglossus as well as in that of the facialis accessorius and of the vago-accessorius.

"As regards now the localization. of the functions of speech in the cortex, this is a question that has been so frequently discussed during the past few decades, that it is impossible in this place to give a complete presentation of the views and arguments that have been held and propounded for and against the same. We must confine ourselves to a review of the results that may be derived with certainty from the experiments of pathologists.

"The view at present held with regard to the position and extent of the cortical province of speech, is based upon innumerable data derived from dissections of the brains of aphasic patients. It has gradually arisen through the comparison and co-operative completion of the experiments of various investigators.

" The first after Gall to assign to language a province in the brain was Bouillaud, whose theories were based upon observations and the data of dissection : Bouillaud fixed the seat of articulation of words in the frontal lobes. He did not succeed however, despite a struggle continued through many years, in establishing this idea, manifestly in consequence of the miscredit that it awakened by reason of its similarity to Gall's views. This was also the fortune of M. Dax and of his son G. Dax, who endeavored to prove by the help of a rich collection of pathological cases, that disturbances of speech regularly occur upon lesions of the left hemisphere but not upon lesions of the right. A reversion of the general opinion set in when, in the year 1861, Broca, originally an opponent of Bouillaud, adopted the doctrines of the latter in all their principal points, and more accurately fixed them by affirming that it was the gyrus frontalis inferior sinister which must remain unimpaired if the power of speech is to be retained. The circumstance that it is the left hemisphere in whose province the special function of language belongs, he later brought into connection with the fact, that people as a rule employ this hemisphere more,as well for mechanical operations as in writing, all of which is done by preference with the right hand.

" From that time on, the doctrine of the localization of the function of speech became almost generally accepted, and the only question then before scientists was, to determine with greater precision, by means of new and thoroughly examined cases, the territorial limits of this function, its individual deviations, and the conditions of preference of the left hemisphere.

" The posterior part of the gyrus frontalis inferior sinister and the island of Reil of the left side, must be regarded as the actual cortical province of speech : it is exceptional that lesions of these parts do not produce disturbances of speech. On the other hand, disturbances of speech sometimes occur even when the lesion does not affect either of these two cortical regions. But in these cases the lesions are almost always in the adjacent portions of the cortex. It is manifest that, in such exceptional cases, we have to do with important individual deviations, and that the cortical province, as it must be inferred for other reasons, is not the same in all persons.

"There is a very great number of cases which sufficiently demonstrate the part played by the left inferior convolution ; I shall cite here but a very striking one, reported by Simon. By a fall from a horse, as was found out from a section afterwards made, a man had driven a splinter of bone from the roof of the skull into the convolution in question. No other injury to the skull was discoverable. The man had arisen immediately after his fall, and was about to mount his horse again, when a physician who accompanied him asked that he submit to an examination. No symptoms of disease whatsoever, except speechlessness, were noticeable. He was able to communicate, however, by signs. He died later in consequence of inflammatory affections which followed the injury to the brain.

"According to statistics compiled by Lohmeyer, in every fifty-three cases of aphasia there are about thirty-four in which the left inferior frontal convolution is either alone the actual seat of disease or somehow stands in connection with it.

* * *

"The remarkable fact that in the production of speech the left hemisphere is so much more directly engaged than the right, is firmly established : Séguin calculated, from a collection of two hundred and sixty reports of cases of this type, that the number of instances in which aphasia arises from lesion on the left side, stands in proportion to the number of those in which impairments occur on the right side, as 14·3 :1 ; with reference to which it must be remarked that—as has been shown by other calculations—no deception is here caused by the possible circumstance that in general more injuries occur on the left side than on the right.

"This fact, which does not wholly agree with the ideas that we are accustomed to entertain of the cortical functions in general, we must accept as such, and seek only an incomplete analogy in the circumstance referred to by Broca, that our left hemisphere must be more skillful and more practiced in the execution of mechanical operations than the right. An incomplete analogy, we say, by reason of the fact that the direct innervations of the right hand are effected unilaterally by the left hemisphere, the innervations of the muscles of speech, on the other hand, take place bilaterally.

"But to a certain extent the analogy holds. If as the result of early lesions, or from birth, the motory cortical province of the right arm is lacking, the individuals thus affected train the left arm—that is the right hemisphere—to perform mechanical tasks. Cases to this effect have been reported by Moneau, Kussmaul, and others. The same, we must presume, holds good of language. Also in two cases on record, the disturbance of the cortical province of speech dated from childhood; and the fact that notwithstanding this these people could speak well, is undoubtedly only to be interpreted in the following way, that the island, the lowest frontal convolution, etc. of the *right* hemisphere had taken charge of the functions of language.

"In this connection a case reported by Schwarz is of interest. In a well-developed three-year old girl, during convalescence from measles, speechlessness with partial paralysis of the right arm suddenly set in. The lesion accordingly lay in the left hemisphere. The condition of the patient improved, yet the girl had to learn to talk again from the very beginning,. and in so doing acted like the normal child that is learning to speak.

"The left side, accordingly, does not exercise the exclusive prerogative of the superintendence of speech.

"The analogy is still further applicable. It appears that so-called left-handed individuals, who as contrasted with the majority of men have trained their right and not their left hemisphere to perform mechanical work, also employ their right hemisphere in speech. Pye Smith, Jackson, and John Ogle, Mongié, Russel, and Wm. Ogle have observed cases that appear to substantiate this. Left-handed people, namely, had become aphasic through lesions on the right side of the brain, and—a fact which proves more—where in a collection which Wm. Ogle made of one hundred cases of aphasia there were three left-handed men, in the case of each the lesion affected the right hemisphere."

v.

EXPERIMENTS UPON ANIMALS.

It is a strange fact that the hemispheres as well as the corpus striatum exhibit no sensitiveness to pain whatever. They can be cut, irritated, or maltreated in any way without causing direct suffering.

Experiments have been made to deprive animals (mostly pigeons, hens, and frogs, but also dogs) of their entire hemispheres. A pigeon without its hemispheres stands firmly on its feet if only the cerebellum remains unimpaired, but has lost all signs of intelligence. It behaves as if it were asleep. It will stand quietly in one place for hours and hours.

A brainless pigeon is without clear consciousness because it has lost all the memories to which sensory irritations may be referred. Yet it is not entirely void of feeling. The sensory and motory nerves perform their functions as usual, and with perfect harmony. The pigeon "quivers if a pistol is shot off near by ; its eye winks at the approach of a flame, and the pupils contract. It turns away from ammonia vapor" (Landois). Its consciousness however, if consciousness it can be called, is limited to the moment and to that one sense-impression which takes place at the moment. This sense-impression remains isolated, it cannot be compared with former memories. Thus it remains ununderstood, and is quickly forgotten.

Hens endure the operation better than other birds. For a few hours, they lie exhausted ; then they rise and remain in a sitting posture. Again, after hours, they walk about, scratch the floor of the room, and after a few days they begin pecking for food, although there may be nothing on the ground. Some hens learn again to eat and drink, if water and food is put into their bills, and thus can be kept alive as living automatons for several months. (See Exner in Hermann's "Physiologie," Vol. II, Part II, p. 199.)

Frogs preserve perfectly their equilibrium after removal of their hemispheres. If turned on their back, they will rise to their feet. If irritated, they will make two or three jumps, with a view to escaping. If thrown into water, they will swim until they touch the wall of the basin ; then they will creep up on the edge, where they remain. In all motions producible as direct reflexes upon their proper irritations, they show a perfect mastery of their limbs and harmony of movement. Yet without irritation there is no motion; there is no spontaneous voluntary action whatever. A brainless frog, if left to itself, will remain quietly on the spot where it has been placed, as if asleep ; it will take no food, betrays no consciousness of hunger or thirst, shows no sign of fear, and unless artificially fed, will in time dry up like a mummy.

That which in animals and in man appears to us as spontaneous and voluntary motion, is the result of cerebration among the memory-pictures of the cortex, acting, as we suppose, in co-operation with the corpora striata. When the memory-pictures have been removed, an animal is unable to act except in response to sensory impressions, that is by direct reflex-motions.

* * *

Goltz invented a new method to remove the hemispheres of animals, which has the advantage of causing less irritation than the scraping them out with a knife or a sharpened spoon. He injected through small apertures in the skull a jet of cold water, and thus succeeded in washing out the cortex without injuring other parts. Goltz distinguishes two kinds of effects : those which after some time pass away and those which remain for good. The former are mere temporary disturbances, while the latter alone can be considered as a loss of functions which have their seat in the removed parts.

A dog that has been deprived of the greatest part of his cortex is, as Goltz expresses it, an extremely complex reflex-mechanism that eats (*fressende Reflexmaschine*). He behaves like a perfect idiot, walks slowly and awkwardly, with the head downwards. His sense of touch all over the skin is obtuse. He shows a lack of information concerning the surrounding world and his own body which is mainly noticeable when he is fed. He sees, but like a sleep-walker who avoids obstacles without being aware of what they are. He hears, for he can be roused from his sleep by loud calls, but he hears like a man who is but half-awakened from a profound sleep and has not as yet recovered his full consciousness. The disturbances of all the other senses are analogous. He howls when hungry, but does not search for food. If fed, he eats until his stomach is full. He shows no indications of sexual instinct, and is generally without any interest or sympathy.

VI.

MEYNERT'S THREE SYSTEMS OF PROJECTION AND PSYCHICAL ACTIVITY.

THE motory as well as sensory centres of the hemispheres must be considered as psychical regions; that

is, they are the places in which the action of the nervous mechanism may be and often is accompanied with
consciousness. This is corroborated by the fact that
an irritation of these regions does not produce the
usual result in new-born animals ; their psychic activity
is not as yet developed and a few fibres only are differentiated in the white nerve-substance of their hemispheric region. In further support of this the circumstance can be adduced (according to Schiff), that these
cortical centres cease to work if the animal manipu-
lated upon is kept under the influence of chloroform
or other narcotics.

Consciousness is the most complex and concentrated form of feeling. Feelings, we can fairly assume,
may take place in all the innumerable cells of our body
so long as they are alive. But these feelings are extremely weak and by far the greater part remains isolated. Feelings, we assume, depend upon a special
form of activity in animal substance. The sensory
fibres of the nervous system are a mechanism constructed to co-ordinate and concentrate the various
feelings ; while the motor fibres co-ordinate the reflex-
activity in such a way that it may be subservient to,
that is, it may act upon irritations received from certain co-ordinated centres of feeling. The final concentration of both activities, sensory as well as motory,
takes place in the hemispheric region and it is in this
final concentration that consciousness is produced.

Meynert considers the whole nervous mechanism of
man as "three superordinated systems of projection."
The first or highest system of projection is the corona
radiata, comprising all those tracts which connect
the hemispheric ganglions, the thalamus, and the Four
Hills. As the second system of projection Meynert

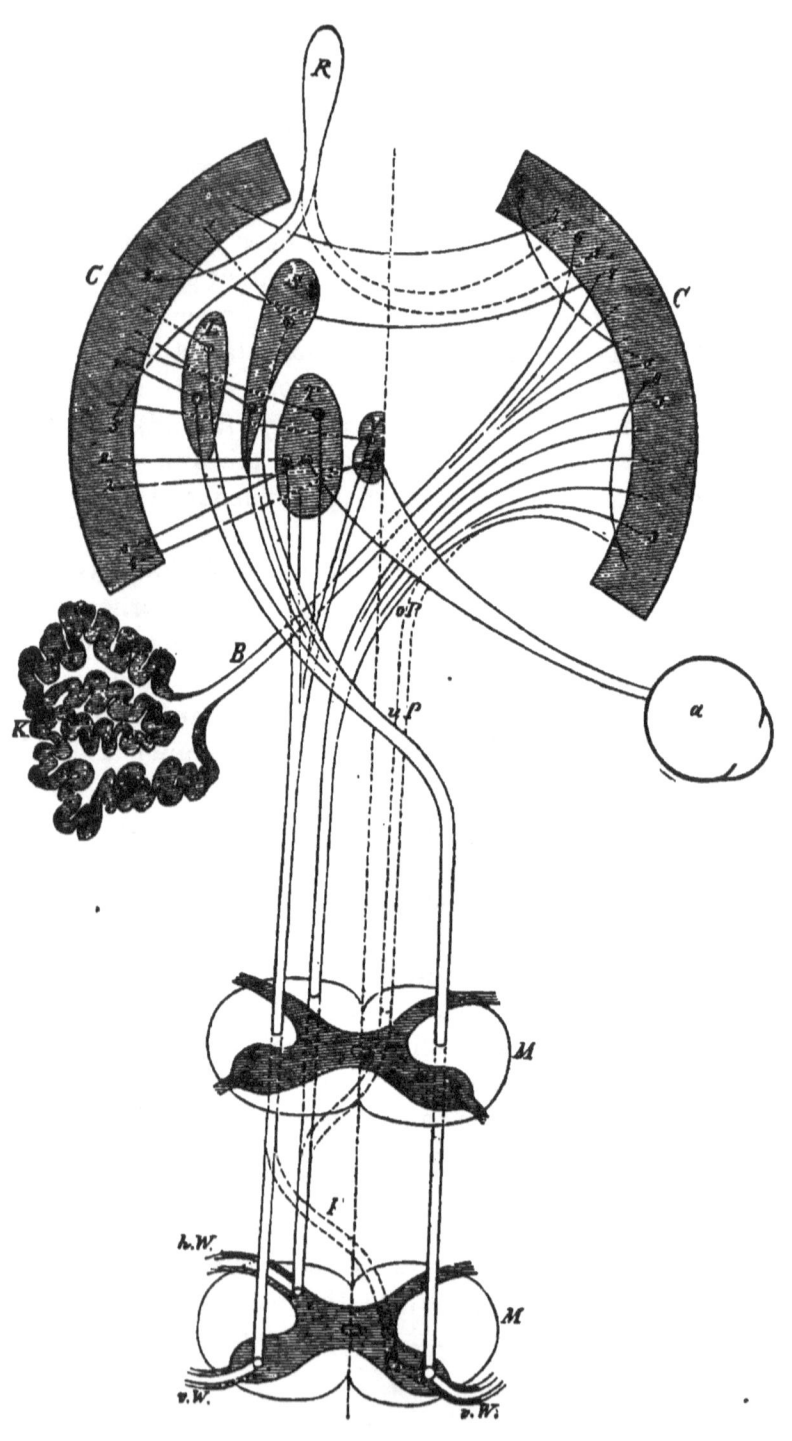

MEYNERT'S REPRESENTATION OF THE NERVOUS SYSTEM.

(After Meynert's investigations; reproduced from Hermann's Physiology, Vol. II, part II, p. 303,)

C. Cortex of hemispheres.

L. Lenticular body.

S. Tailed body (nucleus caudatus).

L. and *S* are the hemispheric ganglions, called Striped Body.

T. Thalamus.

V. Four Hills.

R. Olfactory nerve (*Riech-Kolben*).

A. Eye.

K. Small Brain or Cerebellum.

B. Brachium ad Cerebellum. (*Bindearm.*) Tracts connecting the Small Brain with the hemispheres.

hW. Posterior (sensory) roots of spinal cord,

vW. Anterior (motory) roots of spinal cord.

MM. Two sections of the Medulla in the spinal cord.

1. 1. Voluntary motor tracts, passing into the lenticular *L* and tailed bodies *S*, whence they issue downwards. They form part of the crus cerebri crossing over to the other side in the inferior pyramidal decussation (*u. P.*), and descend to their respective anterior roots in the spinal cord.

2. 2. Involuntary motor tracts. They pass from the cortex into the Thalamus *T* and the Four Hills *V*, whence they issue downward to their anterior roots forming part of the tegmentum. If there is any decussation in these involuntary tracts, it can take place in the spinal cord only as indicated in the dotted lines near *I*.

3. 3. Sensory tracts, crossing to the other side and forming the superior pyramidal decussation, in *oP*.

4. 4. Optic tracts.

5. 5. Olfactory tracts.

6. 6. Cerebellar tracts of *B*.

7. 7. Commissural fibres, connecting both hemispheres.

8. 8. Commissural fibres interconnecting the different provinces of one hemisphere.

describes the course of fibres from the great ganglions (viz., thalamus, Four Hills, and corpus striatum) to the central gray substance which forms the walls of the aquaductus Sylvii and the bottom of the fourth ventricle.

In the accompanying diagram representing Meynert's view of the nervous system, the lines connecting T (thalamus) with vW (anterior root of spinal cord) are paths of reflex motions descending from the thalamus. Their presence is proved by the fact that after the destruction of the voluntary motor tracts an involuntary mobility is preserved which can be produced through simple reflex-action so long as the thalamus remains unimpaired.

The third system of projection are the fibres below the central gray substance, namely the motor and sensory nerves which connect this part of the nervous system with the periphery.

The cerebellum forms a central organ of its own, being in connection with the hemispheres, the pons, and the medulla.

Every system of projection from the most peripheral to the most central, from the third to the first, is a further concentration of feelings and of their corresponding motor reflexes. The first system, which is the highest and most centralized, is alone the seat of consciousness. Accordingly no feeling, no sensation, nor any motion, can become conscious unless it be projected into the hemispheric region. All sensory irritations which do not rise into, and all motory reflexes which do not originate from this highest region—remain unconscious.

We say that no nerve-activity except that which is projected into, or takes place in, the hemispheres can become conscious; but we do not say that all the nervous activity of the hemispheres does become conscious. Many most complex actions, motions as well as sensations, and even long chains of logical reasoning, which can have their seat in the cortical substance only, are performed unconsciously. Accordingly, it is but a small part of the cerebral activity that enters into consciousness. Only the mountain peaks of cerebral nerve-activity, if they rise through a process of further co-ordination above the great mass of subconscious states, are illumined by a glow of concentrated feeling or consciousness.

Meynert's investigations have been modified of late by Wernicke,* in so far as Wernicke demonstrates that the Shell (putamen) of the lenticular body and the nucleus caudatus do not receive fibres from the corona radiata. They form no intermediate stations between the hemispheres and the periphery. This function has to be limited to the inner stripes of the nucleus lentiformis (which are called the globus pallidus). The Shell forms a terminus of its own quite analogous to the cortical region.

We have some reasons to believe that the Striped Body, in its terminal structures in the Shell and Caudate Body, performs a special and most important function of cerebral activity. This, it appears, can only be the function of consciousness. Whether our hypothesis is justified or not, we must leave to those who are competent to judge. We shall in the following chapter explain the reasons that have suggested the proposition of our theory, and shall be glad if specialists will take the matter in hand and give their opinion as to its tenability.

* Wernicke. *Lehrbuch der Gehirnkrankheiten*, Cassel, 1881.

WHEN unable to go to sleep, we try to force ourselves to do so by inhibiting all thoughts; we attempt, as
it were, to empty consciousness of all its contents. Yet
this is very difficult, for as soon as one thought has been
suppressed, another makes its appearance ; and if this
second thought is refused admittance a third one
succeeds in forcing its entrance. A constant battle
has to be waged to keep down all mental activity.
Thoughts, pictures or abstract concepts, and memories of all kinds rise again and again. We can never
attain a state of pure consciousness which is void of all
contents. When we succeed in suppressing all mental
activity, we fall asleep. Every attempt to think of
nothing, no less than every attempt to confine thought
for any length of time strictly to one monotonous image or idea, is a kind of self-hypnotization.

When we walk along on a road which exhibits no
noteworthy variety to the traveler, we may proceed
without observing anything. We walk almost unconscious of our movement. Yet, if the road divides before
us, doubt arises in our mind as to which way we shall
take. Doubt is a problem that requires settlement, and
if it is not settled it causes, so long as the doubt lasts, a
state of tension which makes us conscious of the situation. Consciousness is an intensified state of feeling
caused through tension. It lies between a want and
its satisfaction. Satisfaction not being immediately
attainable, feelings are no longer in a state of equilibrium, and it is this tension which concentrates and in-
tensifies feeling into consciousness.

It appears that consciousness never arises without a certain tension. Days spent in an idyllic life flow away almost unconsciously; there is little friction, there are no problems to be solved ; there are no unsatisfied wants, or if there are any, they are quickly and easily attended to. There is no need of consciousness, there is not much tension to call it into play, so life passes dreamlike as a tale that is told. The more life is burdened with problems that demand a man's full care and deliberation, and the stronger are his attempts to solve the problems of his situation, the more intense will his consciousness be.

It appears to me very doubtful whether conscious beings could exist in a world—if such a world were possible at all—where the struggle for existence was unknown ; for it is the struggle for existence that presents the first and most imperative problems to living and feeling beings.

Man is a creature full of needs, and while attending to these needs he has developed and constantly does develop a not inconsiderable amount of consciousness. If he had no needs he might degenerate into a half-vegetative state of existence like that into which certain parasitic infusoria have fallen, which, their sole wants being fulfilled, cease to exhibit even the most general symptoms of animal life, i. e., free motion.*

We may compare the tension of consciousness

---

* " There is, for instance, the female of the bark louse (Coccus) which, when fully developed appears as an entirely immovable body, not unlike a shield, as though it were an excrescence on the leaves of the plants upon which it sits. Its feet are degenerated. The proboscis of this creature is imbedded into the tissues of the leaf, the sap of which it sucks. The whole psychical activity of this parasite consists in the pleasure of sucking the sap and in coition with the males, who move about. The same is true of the grublike females of *Strepsiptera*, who, without wings and feet, pass their parasitic lives immovable in the bodies of wasps." Translated from *Hæckel*, " Anthropogenie," p. 702.

originating from an unsatisfied want, to a vacuum.
The vacuum of such a want in man's mind causes
memories and combinations of memories, old and new
ideas, to rush in in order to fill the vacuum. The more
difficult the satisfaction of a want is, the more consciousness and intelligence must be developed. For
long chains of representative feelings, observations of
present facts, the revival of memories and new combinations of memories require much attention. Every
thought which has been attended to loses its interest,
and the mental equilibrium is restored, unless (as
happens usually) the settlement of one problem gives
rise to another, thus producing a new tension. If the
vacuum were once definitely filled, the tension would
cease to draw new thoughts into its sphere. All change
would be stopped and a state of unconsciousness super-
vene.

Consciousness and intelligence work together under
normal conditions, but both are quite distinct functions. Consciousness is a concentrated or intensified
feeling which often, but not always, accompanies certain motions, sense-impressions, and also intellectual
work. We have no states of consciousness that are
without any contents. There are, however, sense-impressions, motions, and intellectual functions, which
are not accompanied with consciousness. Consciousness, accordingly, is an additional element that sometimes is and sometimes is not attached to certain mental
operations.

Considering anatomical, physiological, and psychological facts, it appears as the easiest explanation
to regard the Striped Body as the organ in which the
additional element of consciousness is produced.

The experiments of physiological psychology by

Wundt, Münsterberg,* and others, prove that the paths of unconscious cerebration are shorter than those of conscious cerebration. Mental activity, if its action, like a simple reflex motion, takes place automatically, passes down through certain nerve-fibres, which in their passage through the internal capsule do not enter into the Striped Body.† It is certain that some of these fibres enter the Thalamus, whence they descend to the anterior roots of the Medulla oblongata. Mental activity, however, which is accompanied with consciousness, must take a roundabout way. It needs more time, and we can fairly conclude that the mechanism of its action is more complicated. The question thus offers itself, whether there is a special organ, the function of which produces consciousness, and, if we have to look for an organ of consciousness, where must it be located?

We believe that in the Striped Body, (mainly those parts that exhibit an analogous structure to the cortical substance,) is to be found that place which in situation and anatomical conditions answers best to all the requirements that can be made in regard to an organ of consciousness. We suppose that a motor centre in the brain, if irritated, all conditions being normal, will produce motions (as has been experimentally proved); but there are two possibilities offered : 1) the reflex action can descend directly through the internal capsule without becoming conscious, (the path designated in Meynert's diagram as 2. 2.); or, 2) it may first enter into the Striped Body, where the additional element of consciousness is acquired. The different states

---

* See Münsterberg. *Beiträge zur Experimentellen Psychologie*, Freiburg Mohr.

† See Meynert's Diagram, 2, 2, in the preceding chapter.

of consciousness will, in that case, originate in the Striped Body. Yet their nature will depend upon the various nerve-structures from which the irritation of the Striped Body proceeds.

For a consideration of the merits of this hypothe-sis we adduce the latest investigations of Wernicke, a specialist in brain diseases. He says in his *Lehrbuch der Gehirn-Krankheiten:*

" The caudate body and the third stripe of the lenticular body consist mainly of the same finely granulated glia substance as the cortex. As in the cortex, so here between the ganglionic cells are found large masses of pure gray substance. The fibres rising therefrom are, although medullary, of extremely fine tissue. It is for this reason that the fibres of the caudate body in their passage through the white substance of the internal capsule are marked as reddish tracts, a circumstance that makes it easy to discover their course.

"The interior stripes of the lenticular body possess only slight, if any, trace of these tissues. They consist, as Meynert noticed, almost entirely of purely nervous elements, (l. c., p. 41).

" We must distinguish rigorously between the third stripe con-taining the main mass and the other two interior stripes. The latter alone can be considered, as Meynert suggests, as an intermediate station. The third stripe and also the caudate body are in no direct relation with the corona radiata. . . . . Some fibres of the second stripe can be traced into the corona radiata, but there are com-paratively few. By far the greater part of the two interior stripes has no relation to the corona, but remains an internodium of the fibres descending from the third stripe and the caudate body. These two ganglions are the main sources of the radiary fibres in the lenticular body. . . . . Thus they form a terminus (*Ursprungsge-biet*) of their own, analogous to the cortex for descending coronal fibres ; and these coronal fibres rising in the caudate body and [in the putamen of] the lenticular body find an intermediate station in the two internal stripes of the lenticular body," (l. c., p. 40).

The Striped Body is, as Wernicke shows, in no direct connection with the corona radiata. Yet the corona radiata is not the sole path of communication possible between the Striped Body and the cortex. There are other and more direct connections of a more intimate nature than can be afforded by a system of descending fibres. The Striped Body ontogenetically considered is continuous with the gray matter of the hemispheres and the connections established in this way are preserved also in the stages of a further differentiation.

A clear conception of the Striped Body and its relations to the corona radiata as well as the cortex, can be more easily obtained by a study of the adjoined diagrams.

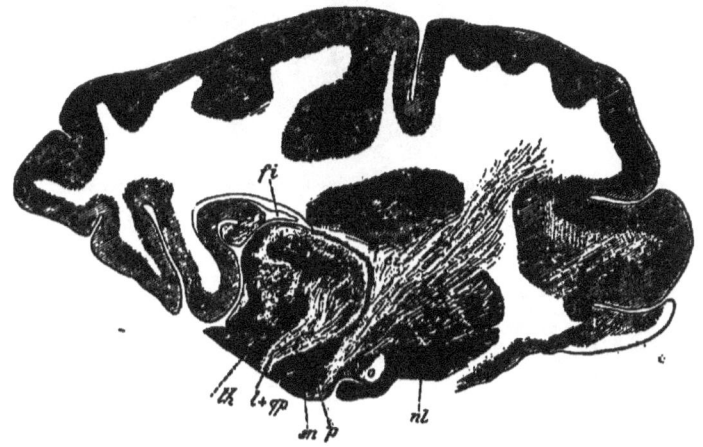

SAGITTAL SECTION THROUGH THE BRAIN OF A DOG. (After Wernicke.)

The corona radiata descending into the internal capsule (*ci.*), sends no fibres into the third stripe. Some fibres appear to enter the third stripe; but they do not. Yet there are fibres that enter the first and especially the second stripe.

aR. Outer olfactory convolution.

fi. Fornix, identical with Fimbria, to the edge of the hooked convolution.

nl. Lenticular body with three stripes. *I. II. III.*

nc. Caudate body.—*th.* Thalamus.—*ci.* Internal capsule.—*f.* Foot of the corona radiata.—*p.* Pes cerebri.—*o.* Optic nerve.—*sn.* Substantia nigra.— *l+qp.* Upper fillet connecting the thalamus with Posterior Four Hills.—*cgc.* Corpus geniculatum, exterior external ganglion of the optic nerve.

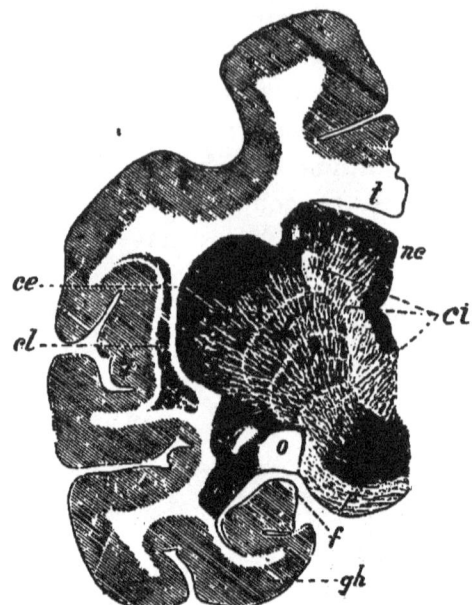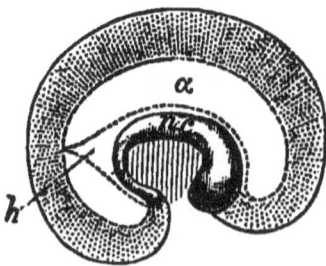# THE SOUL OF MAN.

200

FRONTAL SECTION OF THE BRAIN OF A MONKEY. (After Wernicke.)

Showing the connection between the nucleus caudatus and the second stripe of nucleus lentiformis.

i. Insula.
cl. Claustrum.
ce. External capsule.
t. Corpus callosum.
nc. Head of caudate body.
ncī. Tail of caudate body, continuous with the temporal process of the lenticular body.
I, II, III. The three stripes of lenticular body.
o. Optic nerve.
ci. Internal capsule.
p. Pes cerebri.
sn. Substantia nigra.

INTERIOR OF THE HEMISPHERE-VENTRICLE.

(After Wernicke.)

Showing the close connection of the Striped Body with the Hemispheres. The head and the tail of the Striped body appear as continuations of the cortex.

a. The primitive ventricle.
h. The definitive ventricle.
nc. Caudate body.

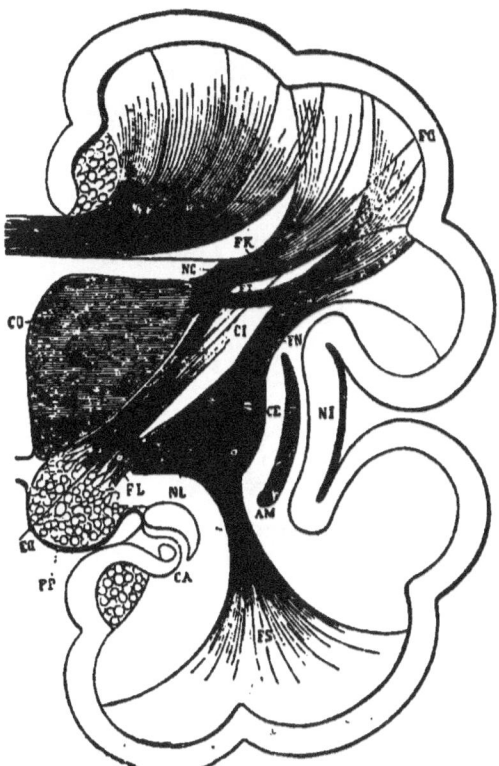

Showing the connections of the cortex with the Striped Body.

FS. FN. Connections with third stripe of lenticular body.

FK. Connection with caudate body.

(For further explanations of this cut see the chapter "The cortex and its Relations.")

The connections between the Striped Body (especially the third stripe) and Hemispheres seem to bear the character of commissural associations. It is not a connection through coronal fibres, which would denote that the Striped Body is to be considered as a mere internodium, an intermediate station between the highest system of projection and lower stages. It is rather an independent mechanism attached to the field of cerebral activity. Not only the anatomical structure of certain parts of the Striped Body is similar to cortical regions, but also its connections bear the character of the connections between one cortical region and other cortical regions.

The Striped Body must be the organ of some brain activity that in its kind forms the highest terminus in a hierarchical system ; judging from its size and structure the Striped Body must perform an important work of a very specialised kind.

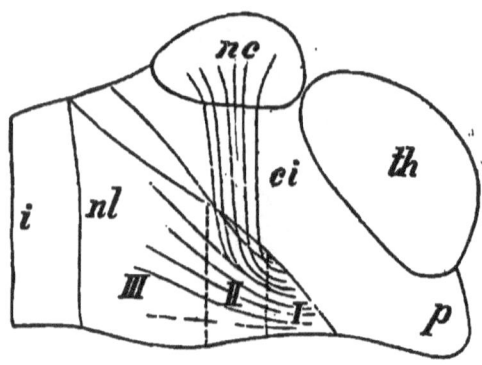

DIAGRAMMATIC REPRESENTATION OF THE FIBRES IN THE CAUDATE AND THE LENTICULAR BODIES. (After Wernicke.)

I, II, III. The three stripes of the lenticular body — *nc.* Caudate body. —*ci.* Internal capsule.—*p.* Pes cerebri.—*th.* Thalamus.—*i.* Island.

The connections between the Striped Body and the Hemispheres, it seems, bear more the character of commissural associations, which interconnect the different provinces of the cortex. They are quite distinct from the coronal fibres. If the nature of these connections were similar to those established by the corona, it would indicate that the Striped Body had to be considered as a mere internodium or intermediate station. Wernicke's investigations indicate that its office must be higher ; they must rather be of a co-operative than a subordinate nature.

Since certain tracts of voluntary motions originate in the Striped Body (see Meynert's Diagram in the

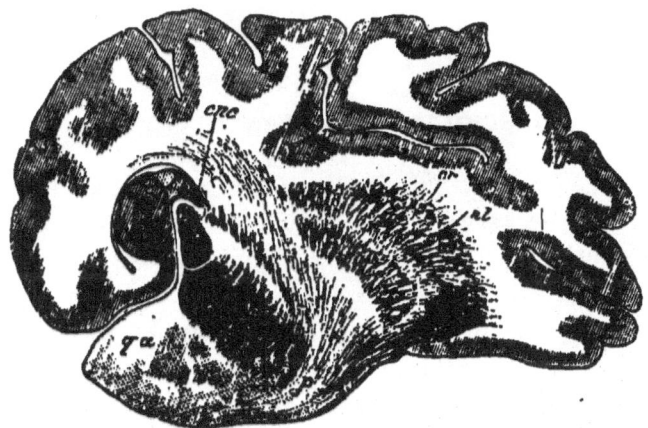

SAGITTAL SECTION THROUGH THE BRAIN OF A PIG. (After Wernicke.)
(Natural Size.)

Showing the course of fibres in the internal capsule. The greatest mass is a continuation of the corona radiata, originating in the cortex. Part of these fibres enter the Thalamus, while the rest pass directly down into the pes cerebri (*p*). A great number of fibres are plainly seen to originate in the Striped Body.

nl. Nucleus lentiformis—Lenticular body.

II, III. Two stripes of lenticular body. The first stripe does not plainly appear.

p. Pes cerebri.

cr. Corona radiata.

cnc. Cauda nuclei caudati, tail of caudate body.

f. Fornix.

th. Thalamus.

qa. Anterior of the four hills.

cge. Corpus geniculatum, exterior external ganglion of optic nerve.

preceding chapter), while the memories of these motions must have their seats in the motor region round the fissure Rolandi, (see Ferrier's Diagram in the chapter "Motory and Sensory Centres") we assume that the additional element which changes unconscious motions into voluntary acts of conscious motions, is a function taking place in the Striped Body.

•

VIII.

CONSCIOUSNESS AND INTELLIGENCE.

The cortical activity is generally supposed to represent the terminus of Meynert's three systems of projection ; and it is at the same time said to be the place in which the activity of soul-life becomes conscious. Yet this great and wide area of gray matter cannot properly constitute the central seat or organ of consciousness; it represents rather the store-house of old experiences ; it is the seat of intelligence.

Intelligence, physiologically expressed, is a great wealth of well-associated, i. e. well-interconnected and systematized, memory-structures. Consciousness and intelligence are not identical. We know for certain that intelligence and consciousness are radically different. Long chains of logical reasoning may take place without any consciousness. We may also, and often we do, unconsciously execute most complex movements that are expressive of intelligence in so far as they adapt themselves to special circumstances. In jumping, if we have any practice, we measure with our eyes correctly any given distance, and the motions of our limbs will be exactly adapted to the occasion ; and yet does this process of judgment only in rare cases enter into consciousness. Word-memories have unquestionably their seat in the cortex, and yet there are many instances where fervid oratory flows from the lips of a speaker with unconscious ease. Similar acts of unconscious mental activity are performed in all kinds of gymnastic exercises, by piano players, and in innumerable other ways. While writ-

ing an author spells correctly without being in the
least aware of it ; and indeed all conscious thought is
everywhere permeated by, interlaced with, and, as it
were, carried on the pinions of, the activity of unconscious intelligence.

The function of consciousness consists in a certain
strong stimulation of the different ideas registered in the
hemispheres. The nervous battery which discharges
these irritations, causing thereby now in this now in
that part of the cortex an increase of blood circulation,
we have called the seat of consciousness. Accordingly
consciousness, physiologically considered, would be the
effect of this nervous battery upon those nervous
structures with which at the time it stands in connection.

The seat of consciousness must be situated in some
ganglionic organ of co-ordination. And we believe
this organ can be sought for only in the Striped Body,
perhaps in the shell of the nucleus lentiformis. The
Striped Body being a part of the hemispheric region
must, for ontogenetic and other reasons, stand in some
such relation to the hemispheres. The corpus striatum develops in the same ratio as the hemispheres,
and if it is irritated by an electric current the result
appears to be the same as when the motor centres of
the cortex are all excited at once (Landois). Destruction causes hemiplegia (paralysis on the opposite
half of the body), which often is accompanied with
hemianæsthesia. Further verification of this hypothesis, that the organ of consciousness is to be sought
for in some part of the Striped Body, must be expected from pathological and experimental observations.

Consciousness, if extraordinarily intense and con-

centrated, is called attention. Attention is nothing
but a concentration of feeling in order to prepare for
and execute an act of motion. Attention is not motion. It
is rather a temporary suppression of motion, but its
final end and purpose is always the execution of some
motion or a series of motions adapted to given conditions.*   Reading, studying, observing in order to understand something, are as much motions upon which
conscious mind-activity can be concentrated, as is the
catching of prey by animals.   In a state of attention
all feeling is focused upon one aim, in order to prepare in an act of deliberation a specially adapted motion.   After due preparation this state of mind serves
as an irritant for the execution of the intended motion.

The unity of consciousness, accordingly, must be
conceived as the product of concentration.   Many
feelings converge upon one point, aimed at by the irritant for action.   The effect of their co-operation is an
attitude of which concentrated action or desire for
action directed upon one common aim is the characteristic feature.   Consciousness, therefore, is neither
a material nor mental essence, but it is a special
state of mind.   The unity of consciousness is not
an original and innate quality which makes attention possible ; its unity is a unification.   The unity of
consciousness is no intrinsic quality of mind ; it is imposed upon the mind by the object of attention, which
like a magnet attracts all its tendencies to motion, and
thus produces in them and among them a systematic
arrangement so that they all are subservient to one
plan of action.

The physiological mechanism of consciousness is

---

* See Th. Ribot's " Psychology of Attention." English translation published by The Open Court Publishing Company.   1890.

an unsolved problem still. If our hypothesis, that the Striped Bodies must be considered as the organ of consciousness, should be confirmed and proved, the question might be raised, Why can we not concentrate our attention upon two different objects at the same time? Why cannot one corpus striatum concentrate the consciousness of one hemisphere upon one kind of work, while the other concentrates that of the other hemisphere upon some other subject?

A satisfactory answer to this question cannot be given until we know more of the construction and mechanical action of the brain and especially of the cortical ganglions. Until then we must be satisfied with a preliminary answer. If consciousness is the common direction of mind-activity, its unity need not be constituted by, or rest upon, one unique organ. Thus a carriage may be drawn by two horses, hitched side by side and directed towards one common goal. If consciousness or attention (i. e., the concentration of consciousness) is not a unity but a unification, we need not search for one single and unique organ of consciousness, as did Descartes, who for this reason assumed the seat of the soul to be the pineal gland. Being simply a state of mind produced through a certain attitude of concentration, consciousness may have its seat in two or even in several organs. It will obtain so long as a common direction governs the single parts of an organism; and it need not depend upon the uniqueness of its organs.

We can illustrate the state of attention by the phenomenon of vision. If our attention is concentrated upon one object which we see before us, we need not, like the marksman, shut one eye; but we may let the axes of both eyes so converge that the object of our at-

•

tention is placed at the centre of vision of both eyes.
The unity of vision and also of consciousness consists
in this convergence ; and although there are two pictures, one on each retina, and two cortical images, one
in each hemisphere, the object is nevertheless perceived as one only. . The concentration of mental activity may take place in both Striped Bodies at the
same time. So long as it converges upon one object, so long as it is concentrated upon one and the
same idea, it will be felt as a unitary state of consciousness.

It is more than probable that the mechanism which
produces this mental convergence of consciousness
works as automatically in normal brains, as does the
co-operative adjustment of the motions of our eyes.
And in spite of the wonderful result produced, it may
be, and I am firmly convinced that it is, not much
more complicated than the unification in the activity
of our two organs of vision.

COMPARATIVE PHYSIOLOGY OF THE BRAIN.

THE question has often been discussed which part of the brain contains the physiological conditions which distinguish man from his lower fellow-beings. The idea that these conditions reside in the forehead is a most popular belief; yet the great physiologist Meynert concludes, that, all abstract reasoning being impossible without language, the reasoning capacities of man must have their central seat in the region of speech which is situated round the *fossa Sylvii*, consisting mainly of the insula, the operculum, and the first frontal convolution.

The frontal lobe, accordingly, contains some functions which are not at all the exclusive prerogative of man. It is true that the human head alone is distinguished by a strongly marked frontal development. Yet there are several reasons which make man's forehead rise so proudly. Among them the development of the frontal convolutions is one, but by no means the most prominent reason. The frontal lobe of man is 42, of a monkey 35, of a bear 30, of a dog 32 per cent. of the whole brain. The rise of the human forehead is chiefly conditioned by the strong development of the insula and the whole region around the fissure of Sylvius as well as of the lenticular body, upon which the insula rests. The growth of these parts raises the cortex which covers them and thus

makes the forehead rise. In addition to these facts
we notice that the temporal lobe, like a thick wedge,
is pushed forward so as to lift the whole brain still
higher.

The region of the fissure of Sylvius appears very
low in a sheep, and the temporal lobe (In the diagram
of a sheep's brain *S par.*) lies behind it in a longitudinal direction. Let us imagine that we could turn
the hindpart of the *Sulcus parallelis* in the brain of a
sheep downward and forward so as to approach the
olfactory bulb. By this process we should change the
brain of a sheep so as to resemble the brain of a dog
or a fox. In the brain of a monkey the end of the
temporal lobe (*Tm*) is turned forward, so as to be
directly behind the fissure of Sylvius. In man it protrudes so much that it lies below and a little in front
of the fissure of Sylvius.

The brains of carnivorous mammals, (for instance,
the brain of a fox,) show a very regular arrangement.
The fissure of Sylvius (*R p*) is surrounded by four
horseshoe-shaped convolutions. In man their arrangement is much modified but still traceable. The
first horseshoe alone is fully preserved in its lower,
temporal course, (*Sl'*); it still reaches (in arc I)
round the fissure of Sylvius, but the greatest part of
its upper or parietal portion has disappeared. The
second arch (arc II) corresponds to the *Sulcus interparietalis* (*Sip*) and *Sulcus occipitalis exterior* (*S. occ. e*).
Its horseshoe form is still well preserved in the monkey's brain, while it is scarcely recognizable in man.
The frontal part of the next arch, situated between
the second and fourth horseshoe-shaped furrow, corresponds to the posterior central convolution in the
monkey and in man, (limited in front by the Central

Fissure *C.*). Man possesses here another well discernible central convolution (called the anterior central convolution *C. a*).

There is scarcely any frontal lobe in the fox's brain, except the convolution which surrounds the anterior branch of the fissure of Sylvius (*Ra*). It is crossed in its upper part by a horizontal fissure (*cm*). These changes in the arrangement alter the

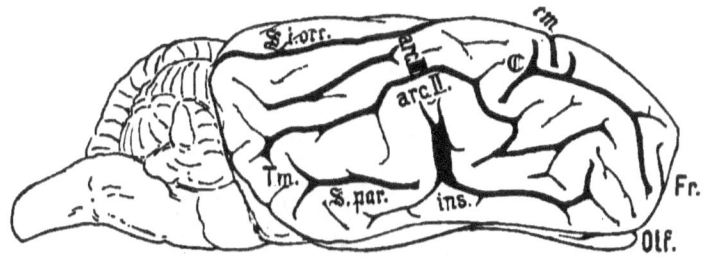

BRAIN OF A SHEEP.

ins. Insula. Above the insula is found the posterior branch of the fissure of Sylvius.

S. i. occ. Sulcus interoccipitalis.

S. par. Sulcus Parallelis.

Fr. Forehead. *Tm.* Temporal lobe.

O.f.; *arc II, arc III*; *C*; *cm·* have the same signification as the following diagram, "Brain of a Fox."

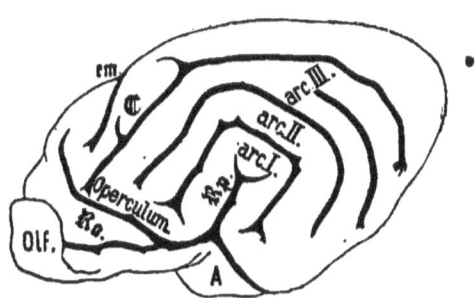

BRAIN OF A FOX.

Olf. Olfactory bulb.—*arc.I.* Arcus parietalis primus.—*arc.II.* Arcus parietalis secundus.—*arc.III.* Arcus occipitalis.—*C.* Sulcus Rolando.—*cm.* Sulcus Calloso-marginalis.—*A.* Gyrus uncinatus (hooked convolution).—*Rp.* Ramus posterior fissuræ Sylvii.

direction of the fissure of Sylvius, which is almost vertical in the sheep. In carnivorous mammals and in the monkey it forms with the base of the brain an angle of about 45 degrees while in man it is almost parallel to the base of the brain.

This comparison shows that man's brain is distinguished by a special development of the frontal; the monkey's brain by a special development of the oc-

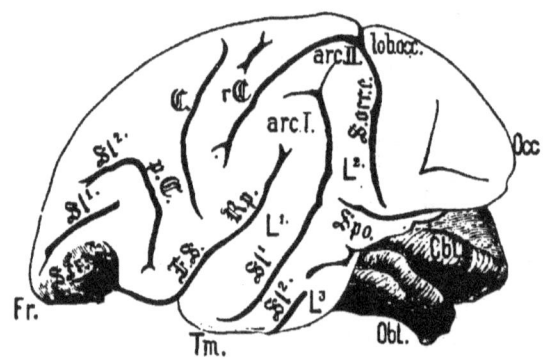

BRAIN OF MONKEY. (*Cercocebus griseoviridis.*)

Fr. Forehead.
Occ. Occiput.
Tm. Temporal lobe.
S. cr. Sulcus cruciatus.
Sl1. (In the frontal lobe) first frontal fissure.
Sl2. Incipient second frontal fissure.
The same letters are used in the temporal lobe for the first and second temporal fissure.
p.C. Sulcus præcentralis, appearing in connection with the incipient second *sulcus frontalis.*
C. Sulcus centralis.
F. S. Fissura Sylvii.
Rp. Ramus ascendens of Fissura Sylvii.
arc. I. Anterior parietal arc.
arc. II. Posterior parietal arc.
lob. occ. Lobus occipitalis.
rC. Sulcus interparietalis.
S. occ. e. Sulcus occipitalis exterior.
S. po. Sulcus præoccipitalis.
L1, L2, L3. First, second, and third temporal convolutions.
Cbl. Cerebellum.
Obl. Medulla oblòngata.

cipital ; and the fox's by a development of the parietal lobes.

"Had these proportions no meaning," says Meynert, "comparative anatomy would be a loss of time and serious men should leave it alone."

One of the most important modifications in the arrangement of the different parts remains still to be noted. This is the change from the horizontal arrangement where (as in the sheep) the cerebellum and

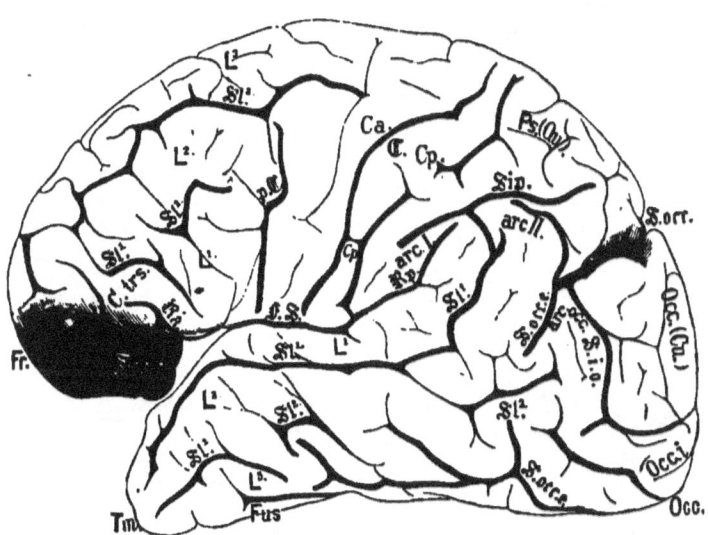

BRAIN OF MAN.

Fr. Tm. Occ.—Scr. Sulc., F.S., Rp.,—Sl1, Sl2; in frontal lobe and *Sl1, Sl2*, in parietal lobe ;—*L1, L2, L3*, in parietal lobe—*pC; C; arc. I, arc. II : S. occ. e*; the same as in the preceding diagram, "Brain of Monkey."

C. trs. Gyrus transitorius. Transitory convolution surrounding *R.a* Ramus anterior, the anterior branch of Fissura Sylvii.

Ca. Cp. Anterior and posterior Central convolution, separated by *C.*

Sip. (In the preceding diagram *rC.*) Sulcus interparietalis.

Ps. (Qu.) Lobus parietalis superior, commonly called Quadratus.

S. occ. Sulcus occipitalis interior.

Occ. (Cu.) Gyrus occipitalis superior, commonly called Cuneus.

Occ. i. Gyrus occipitalis interior.

S. i. o. Sulcus interoccipitalis.

arc. oc. Arcus occipitalis.

•

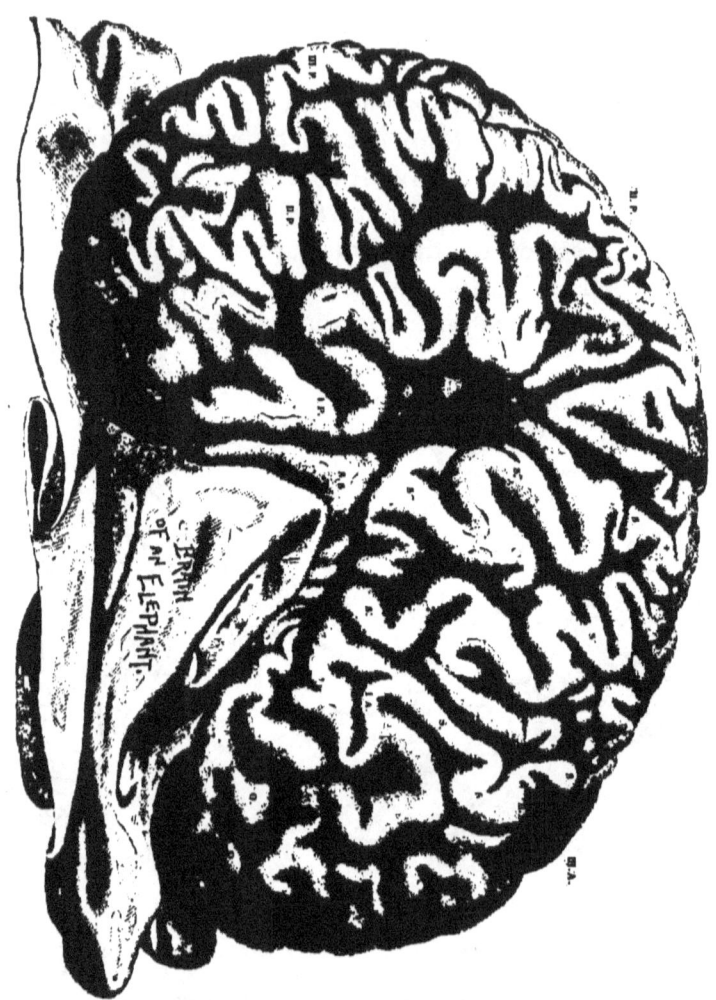

BRAIN OF AN ELEPHANT.   (After Leuret and Gratiolet.)

S.S. Fissure of Sylvius.—*S.S. S'S'. S''S''.* First, second, and third superior convolutions.—*I A, II A, III A.* First, second, and third anterior convolutions. —*I P, II P, III P.* First, second, and third posterior convolutions.—*O. O.* Sub-orbital convolutions.—The first superior convolution (*S.S.*) corresponds to the Fissure of Rolando in the brain of man and monkey.—The second and 'third superior convolutions interrupt the continuity between the corresponding anterior and posterior convolutions.—M. Leuret says on the subject : "If we suppress in our mind the superior convolutions up to the place where the cross appears in the diagram, and if we imagine that the anterior convolutions are continuous with the posterior convolutions, we have an arrangement as it appears in the ruminants and solipeds."—The same author says : " No animal, not even the whale has a brain so large as the elephant. Even man himself is inferior to this animal, not only with regard to the whole volume of brain, but also with regard to the number, extent, and undulations of the cerebral convolutions."

Medulla Oblongata lie in one line with the elongated brain, to the erect position which brings the medulla directly underneath the hemispheres and places the cerebellum below the occipital lobe. This mechanical change of so momentous consequences, must evolutionally have begun long before it could have been acquired by exercise, since the incurvation of the pons in the human embryo which thrusts both pons and cerebellum forward, thus producing the conditions that determine the further development of the brain in a supra- and not in a juxta-position, takes place at a very early period.

The importance of this change will be appreciated when we consider that the rise of the head causes a creature to rely more on its eyes and less on its nose. The animal of scent becomes an animal of vision, ultimately liberating its anterior extremities for work. The jaws recede and the different parts of the brain are piled upon one another so as to shape the hemispheres into a dome-like cupola. The senses also cease to be arranged one behind the other. Eye, ear, and nose form a triangle, the eye being situated at the top.

The nose being removed from the ground naturally turns downward toward the earth which for the animal of scent has been the main source of information ; for there is nothing to be scented in the air.

The conclusion of Meynert, whose authority we have closely followed in this article, is that the human organisation can be explained neither through exercise of functions alone nor through natural selection, but, according to Weismann's theory, through the development of special virtual faculties of the germ.

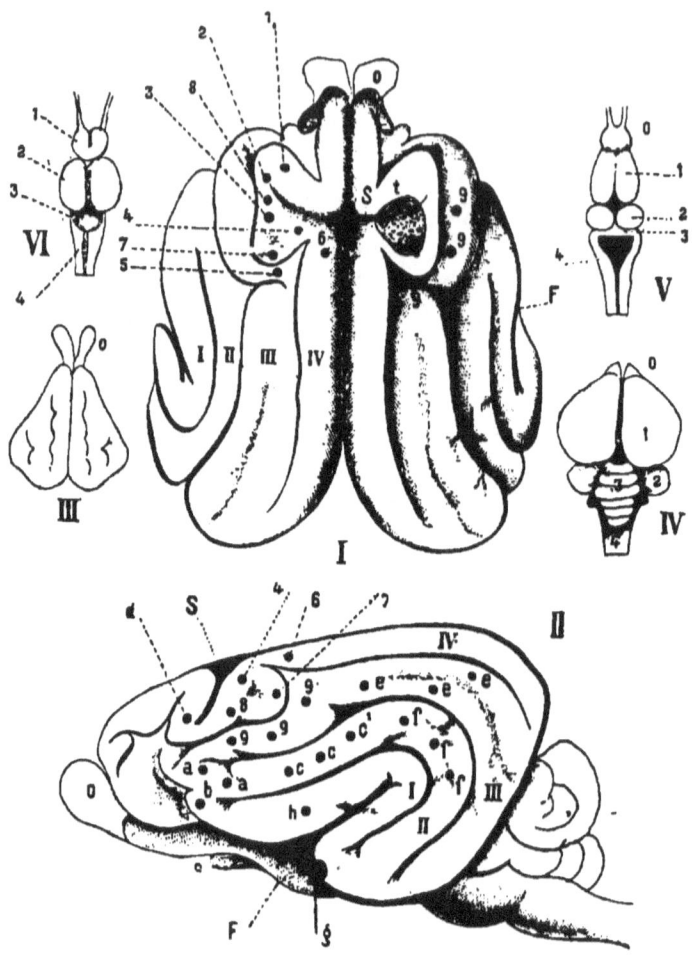

DIAGRAMS SHOWING THE GROWTH OF THE HEMISPHERIC REGION IN PROPORTION
TO AN INCREASE OF INTELLIGENCE.   (Reproduced from Landois.)

I. Brain of a dog dorsal view.
. II. The.same lateral view.
III. Brain of a rabbit.
IV. Brain of a pigeon.
V. Brain of a frog.
VI. Brain of a carp.

Iń III-VI.
o. Bulbus olfactorius.
1. Cerebrum.
2. Lobus Opticus.
3. Cerebellum.
4. Medulla Oblongata.

The diagrams I and II show the motor centres of the dog's brain.
I, II, III, IV, are the four horseshoe-convolutions.
S. Sulcus cruciatus.
F. Fossa Sylvii.
p. Optic nerve.

MOTORY CENTRES. (After Fritsch and Hitzig.)

1. Muscles of the neck.
2. Extensors and flexors of forepaw.
3. Flexors and rotators of forepaw.
4. Muscles of hind leg. (Luciani and Tamburini.)
5. Facial nerve.
6. Wagging the tail side ways.
7. Retraction and abduction of foreleg. (Ferrier.)
8. Lifting of the shoulder and extension of foreleg. (The motion of walking.) (Ferrier.)
9.9. Orbicular muscle of the eyebrows. (Ferrier.)

ZYGOMATICUS AND CLOSING THE LIDS.

a. Retraction and elevation of the corners of the mouth.
b. Centre for the mouth and tongue. It opens and closes the mouth, extending at the same time the tongue.
cc. Retraction of the corners of the mouth.
c'. Lifting of the corners of the mouth.
d. Opening of the eye.
e. Opening of the eye and turning the head aside.
f. Centres of hearing.* (Ferrier.)
g. Centres of smell.* (Ferrier.)
t. Thermal Centre (in 1 after Landois and Eulenburg) shows increase of temperature.

Landois says : "The degree of intelligence in the animal kingdom is according to the size of the hemispheres of the Cerebrum in proportion to the mass of the other parts of the central nervous system. If we take only into consideration the brain, it shows that those animals possess the higher degree of intelligence, in which the hemispheres of the cerebrum have the greater preponderance over the mid-brain. The latter represents with the lower vertebrata the optic lobes, with the higher the four hills. (Joh. Müller).

"In the above diagram, figure VI represents the brain of the carp, figure V that of the frog, and figure IV that of the pigeon. In all these figures the hemispheres are numbered 1, the optic lobes 2, the cerebellum 3, and the medulla oblongata 4.

"In the carp the cerebral hemispheres are smaller than the thalami, with the frog the latter are superior in size. With the pigeon the cerebrum extends behind as far as the cerebellum.—Analogous to these proportions is the degree of intelligence of the above named animals. In the brain of the dog (fig II) the hemispheres cover the four hills, but the cerebellum lies behind

---

* The centre for smell and hearing are situated in other regions according to Munk.

the cerebrum.   In man the occipital lobe of the cerebrum overlaps the cerebellum.

"Meynert happily represented these proportions in another manner. From
the cerebral hemispheres fibres, as is known, pass downwards through the
Pedunculus cerebri, namely through the ventral part of the Pedunculus,
called the Pes. This is separated by the Substantia nigra from the dorsal
part of the same, called tegmentum, which stands in connection with the four
hills and the thalami. The greater the cerebral hemispheres, the more
numerous are the fibres running through the pes."

The tegmentum in the guinea pig is about ten times larger than the pes,
that of the dog and the monkey, five or six times. In man the pes is about
the same size as the tegmentum, which proves that the reflexes coming down
from the cerebrum are that much more numerous.

"Finally the degree of intelligence depends on the number of convolutions
in the hemispheres. While with the lower animals, as the fish, the frog, the
bird, the convolutions are wanting (Fig. IV, V, VI), we see in the rabbit two
shallow convolutions in each hemisphere (Fig. III.) The dog shows a richly
marked cerebrum. Remarkable is the wealth of convolution in the elephant,
the cleverest and noblest of animals. Even in the invertebrata, as in some insects with high instincts, convolusions have been observed in the cerebrum.
Yet it must not be forgotten that even many stupid animals, as cattle, possess
richly convoluted hemispheres." (Cattle in the wild state, we may add, were
most likely in possession of a higher intelligence. This perhaps accounts
for their having inherited their convolutions.)

"This observation concerning convolutions holds good also of men of
high intelligence, but brains rich in convolutions are also found in stupid
persons.

"The absolute weight of the brain cannot be used for the estimation of the
degree of intelligence. The elephant has the *absolutely* heaviest, man has the
relatively heaviest brain."

There is a startling agreement between Professor
Weismann's biological views and Ludwig Noiré's
theory concerning the origin of reason.   Noiré says
that language, i. e., the mechanism of thought has
produced reason ; man thinks because he speaks. And
according to Weismann's theory, Meynert says that
man became a sight-animal because the mechanism
of his brain arrangement forced him into an erect walk,
thus developing the higher senses of his organization.

FECUNDATION AND THE PROBLEM OF SEX-FORMATION.

HUMAN soul-life may be compared to an ellipse. It is determined and regulated from two centres ; the one of which is consciousness, the other the sexual instinct. The sun of man's individual existence stands in the former, the physical immortality of the race is to be found in the latter, and it would be difficult to decide which of the two is of greater importance.

It does not lie within the plan of this book to enter into the difficult field of sexual problems, which owing to the subconscious character of its phenomena, is in most of its phases still a *terra incognita.* Yet we do not intend to leave this great field entirely out of sight, and shall in the following pages briefly indicate the dominant physiological facts in the domain of propagation.

Every organism has developed from a single primitive cell. This primitive cell is called the ovum, or egg. There are some organisms that consist so to speak of an ovum only; and these unicellular beings are, according to Weismann, endowed with potential immortality. When in the course of a further evolution organisms grow more complicated, a division of labor takes place, and we must distinguish in that case between those cells that serve the function of reproduction, or

•

the sexual cells, and those that build up the body of
the individual, or the somatic cells. The potential immortality with which life in its lowest phases is endowed, continues in the sexual cells, and Naegeli has
therefore compared humanity to a creeping plant,
which at given intervals sends out buds and shoots.
The creeping plant is represented in the sexual cells ;
the shoots that grow therefrom are the individuals.
The shoots die off, but the creeping plant continues
to exist and to send out new shoots thus preserving
the life of the race.

The formation of new cells in plants has been
carefully studied by botanists, and is in its main
features well known. New cells may develop by a
simple division of the mother cell, or by a complex
division after a conjugation of two cells. The former
is agamic reproduction ; the latter, sexual reproduction. But whether the division of a cell does or does
not take place after sexual conjugation, the mother
cell must have previously gone through a process
which J. Sachs calls "cellular rejuvenescence." A
certain portion of the watery elements (cell-sap) is
expelled, and if the cell contains a nucleus, this nucleus is dissolved in the protoplasm ; and thus the cell
returns into a youthful state, where its elements can
be recombined into new formations. Examples of this
process will be found in the development of the spores
of many kinds of Algæ and in similar plants of the
lowest orders. The adjoined diagram represents *Stigeoclonium insigne* (*A*), containing in its cylindrical cells
green colored protoplasm, which is called chlorophyll. The chlorophyll is arranged in stripes of
very definite outlines (*A cl*). The rejuvenescence
begins (in *B*) with a contraction of the cells. The

protoplasm loses its definite form and gathers into a
solid ball from which the cell-sap is pressed out. (*B*,
a and *a'*.) The protoplasm is then rearranged and
the new formation protrudes through an aperture in

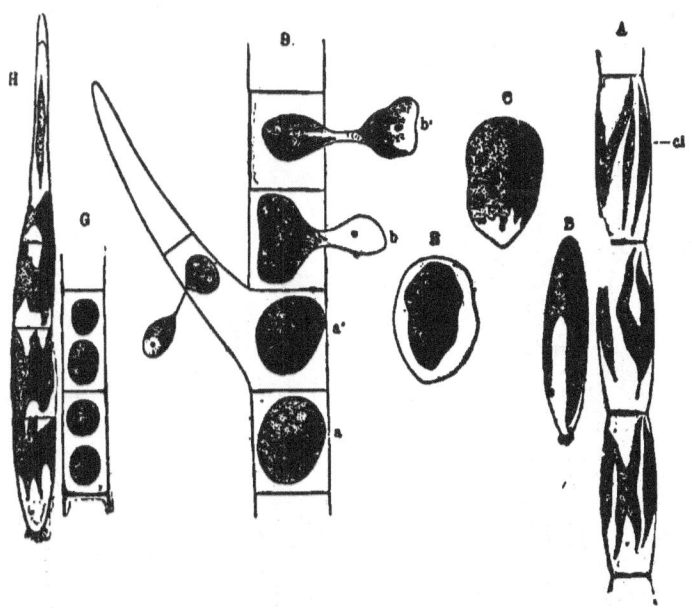

FORMATION OF CELLS IN STIGEOCLONIUM INSIGNE.

A. Several cells of the Alga. *cl*. green protoplasm (*chlorophyll*) embedded
in colorless protoplasm.

B. Showing the contraction of the protoplasm (*a* and *a'*). Some protoplasm protrudes through the cell wall (*b* and *b'*).

C. Free spores without the membrane.

D. Full-grown spore.

E. Encysted spore.

G. Two cells of a filament ready for segmentation.

H. Young Alga.

the cell (*B*, *b* and *b'*.) Thus far this new formation
remains passive, its form is determined by outward
conditions. But as soon as it is released from its
mother cell, (as seen in *C*,) it roams about ; its motions in this case being caused by inner conditions.

The young spore soon becomes encompassed in a
membrane (*E*) and for a few hours keeps growing, its
growth being mainly in length (*D*). Then it settles
into a condition of rest. Its further growth by a division of cells is represented in *H.*

The simplest process of conjugation is found in
another alga, *Spirogyra longata,* which is very common
in stagnant water. Its filaments consist of rows of

I.   II.

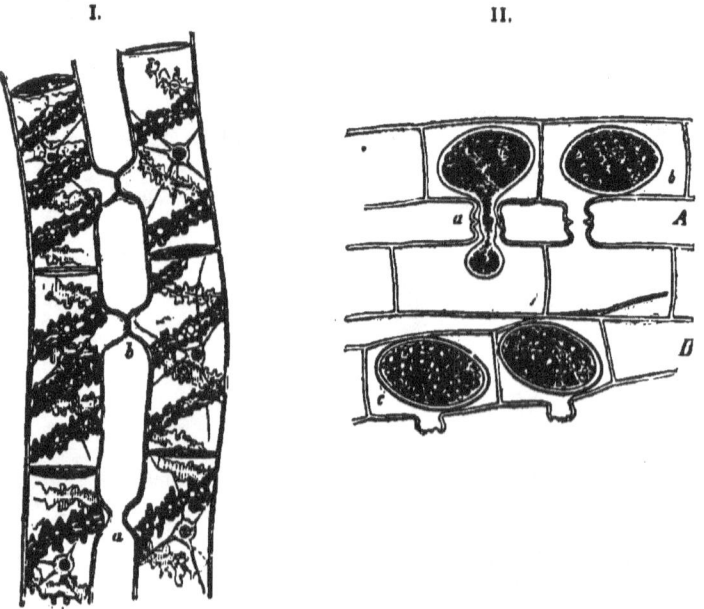

SPIROGYRA LONGATA.

I. Cells of two filaments in an early stage of conjugation, showing the spirally coiled chlorophyll-bands, in the chlorophyll-granules of which lie rings of
starch-grains; they contain also small drops of oil. This is the condition of
the chlorophyll after the action of strong sunlight; the nuclei are also to be
seen in the cells, each surrounded by protoplasm, threads of which reach the
cell-wall in different places;.*a* and *b* are the protuberances in the different
stages.

II. *A.* Cells in the act of conjugation; at *a* the protoplasm of one cell is
passing over in the other; at *b* this has already taken place.

B. The young zygospores surrounded by a cell-wall; the protoplasm
contains numerous drops of oil.

cylindrical cells, each of which contains a protoplasm-sac. This sac encloses a relatively large quantity of cell-sap, in the midst of which is suspended a nucleus enveloped in a small mass of protoplasm and attached to the sac by threads of the same substance. In the sac lies a spirally coiled chlorophyll-band at intervals showing, thicker portions (chlorophyll-granules) which contain starch-grains. The conjugation always takes place between opposite cells of two more or less parallel filaments. The first stage is the formation of lateral protuberances (*I*, *a*), which continue to grow until they meet (*I*, *b*). The protoplasm of each of the two cells in contact then contracts. The protoplasm of the one which contracts first will as a rule pass over into the other.* The protoplasm of the two cells thus being combined, rounds itself into an ellipsoidal form, and contracts still more by expelling the water of the cell-sap. This may occur simultaneously in the two conjugating cells. Next, the cell-wall opens between the two protuberances, and one of the two ellipsoidal protoplasm-masses forces itself into the connecting channel thus formed, gliding slowly through it into the other cell-cavity. As soon as it touches the protoplasm-mass of the other cell, they coalesce. (*A a*). After a complete union the united body is again ellipsoidal and scarcely larger than either protoplasm-ball from the union of which it was formed. During the union a further contraction has evidently taken place with a renewed expulsion of water. The coalescence gives the impression of a union of two drops of water, although the protoplasm is never fluid in the physical sense of the word. The conjugated protoplasm-mass covers itself with a cell-

* Strassburger. Ueber Befruchtung und Zelltheilung, 1878,

wall and forms a zygospore, which germinates after a repose of several months and then develops a new filament of cells.*

Sometimes it happens that several cells combine. Conjugations of three or more cells have been observed in Myxomycetes and some Fungi. In the case of *Spirogyra longata* both combining elements are apparently equal. The higher we rise in the development of plant life, the more unequal the two elements become, and the more apparent is the distinction between a male and a female germ—the antherozoid and the

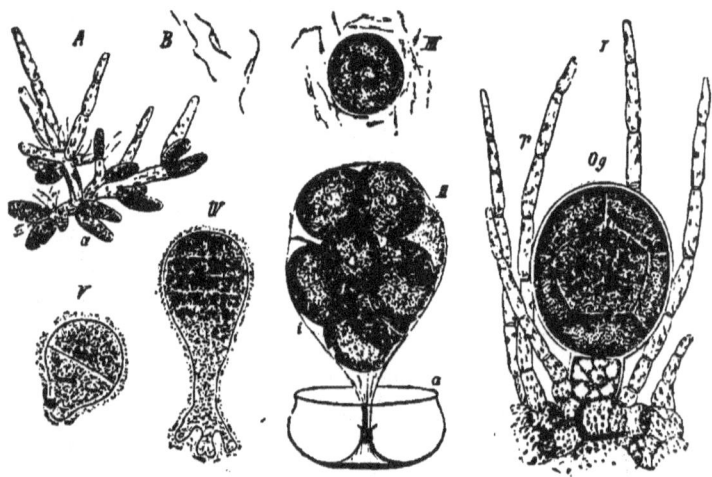

SEXUAL REPRODUCTION OF FUCUS VESICULOSUS.

A. Branched hair-bearing antheridia.

B. Antherozoids.

I. An oögonium *Og* with paraphyses *p*.

II. The exterior membrane *a* of the oögonium is split, the inner membrane *i* protrudes containing the oöspheres.

III. An oösphere escaped, with antherozoids swarming round it.

V. First division of the oöspore or fertilised oösphere.

IV. A young plant resulting from the growth of the oöspore (after Thuret, *Ann. des Sci. Nat.* 1854, Vol. ii).

* Compare Julius Sachs's, Textbook of Botany, English translation, pp. 9 and 10.

oösphere. The former is also called a spermatozoön, the latter an ovum ; terms which are applied in the same sense to the animal world.

The lowest animal organisms, such as the amœba, propagate by division ; but here also an antecedent rejuvenescence of the protoplasm has been observed. The process of sexual propagation is here very similar to that in higher plants, as exhibited in the diagram of *Fucus vesiculosus (III)*.

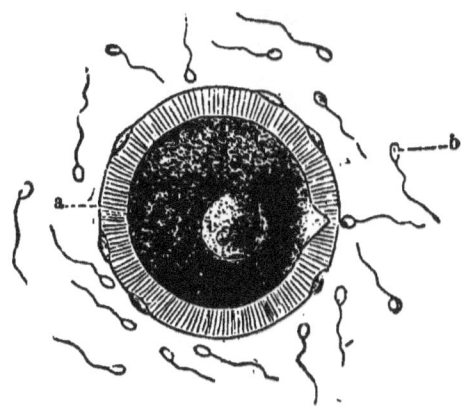

FECUNDATION OF EGG OF HOLOTHURIUM,

a. The egg.—*b*. Spermatozoa.

In the internal generative organs of higher animals one among the many cells of a Graafian follicle develops into a female germinal cell, called the germinal vesicle. The germinal vesicle can easily be distinguished among the other cells by its unusual size. It is surrounded by a greater number of cells which form an elevation called the cell-hill.

The eggs of vertebrates (of fishes, reptiles, amphibia, and birds), which develop outside of the mother organism, are wrapped in different kinds of envelopes which afford a protection to them during the first stages of their growth. The germinative cell alone is the ovum, or egg-cell proper. The mature egg of birds consists of a yellow mass, called the yolk, which is enveloped in the yolk-membrane and surrounded by a whitish mass, called the white of the egg. Both have a mere nutritive value. In one spot the white

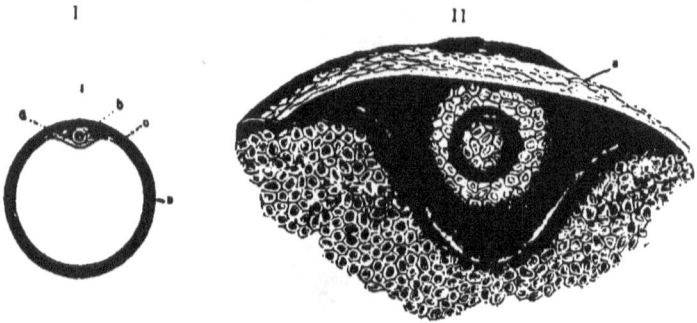

I. GRAAFIAN FOLLICLE.

a. blastoderm (membrane of the follicle).—*b.* Ovum (egg-cell).—*c.* Segmentation-cavity.—d. Cell-hill.

II. CELL-HILL. (Strongly magnified.)

The ovum (*a*) is embedded in transparent cells.

substance appears to sink deep down into the yellow yolk. This part is popularly called treadle, because it was formerly believed to be produced by the tread of the cock. It contains the germinative disc, having the shape of a lense or flattened globe, and this disc is the egg-cell proper, having a yolk of its own, a germinal vesicle and germinal spot.

Before impregnation can take place, the ovum must be prepared for it by a process of rejuvenescence. In some animals (especially in certain insects, but not in higher mammals) parthenogenesis takes place ; that is, the ovum develops a new individual without the assistance of the male sperma. The preparation for impregnation has been best observed in the ova of sea-urchins and star-fishes. The rejuvenescence sets in without the interference of the male element. The process, as described by Selenka, begins with lively motions in the yolk of the ovum ; processes protrude from the outer transparent layer of the yolk into the gelatinous zone, forming very delicate rays. After

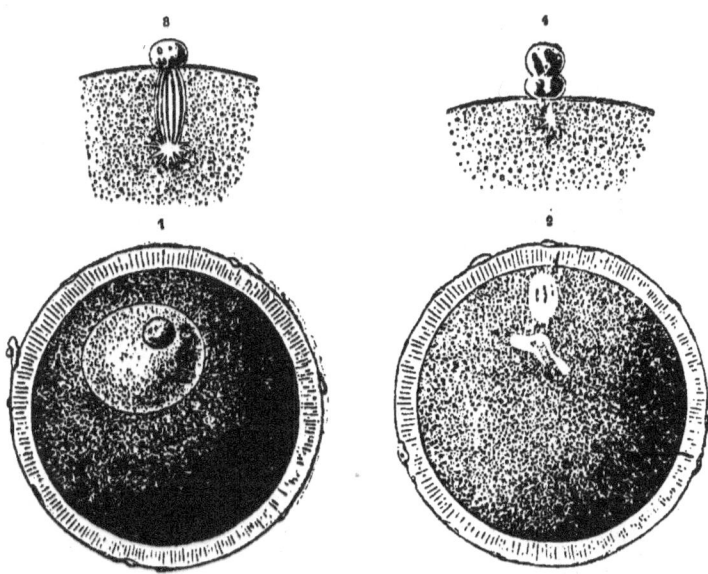

EGG OF A STAR-FISH. (*Asterias glacialis.*)

1. Full grown egg.

2. The same. The nucleus in a state of dissolution and about to form the polar spindle.

3. Segment of the egg, showing the polar spindle after having thrown out the polar body.

4. The same, after having thrown out the second polar body.

some time the rays recede and leave minute pores which may serve partly to effect increased respiration, partly to facilitate the entrance of the spermatozoa.

The state of maturity being attained, most important changes are observed in the germinal vesicle. The germinal vesicle of a mature egg exhibits all the essential qualities of a nucleus. (See the diagram of the egg of the star-fish, *Asterias glacialis*, 1.) The protoplasm of this nucleus, which is wrapped in a mem- ˙ brane, develops a system of cavities in the shape of meshes, called vacuoles. The germinal spot rests in the middle of this net-work, attached to the membrane by many delicately intertwined threads ; and thus the nucleolar plasma is reduced to a state much resembling that of vegetable cells.

According to the observations of Fol and others, the nucleolar membrane soon wrinkles, most likely in consequence of some such process of contraction and expulsion of watery elements out of the vacuoles as has been distinctly observed in plant-cells. The contours of the germinal vesicle grow paler and more irregular ; soon the vesicle disappears and most of its elements—those of the germinal spot not excluded— are intermingled with the surrounding yolk. The place at which the germinal vesicle has been dissolved, however, remains visible as a transparent spot composed of a finely granulated diaphanous substance, irregular in shape and without definite delimitation. This transparent spot forms the centre of a process which eventually ends in the reconstruction of a new nucleus. The process begins with a movement of this transparent spot towards the surface of the egg, forming a spindle-shaped figure, the polar spindle (*Richtungsspindel*) and excreting two little bodies called the polar bodies (*Richtungskörper*).

The two poles of the spindle-shaped figure produce a differentiation of the protoplasm ; they attract small transparent masses, so that, for some time, the appearance of dumb-bells is presented. The two knobs soon assume the shape of suns connected with the long fibres of the spindle.

Auerbach, the first observer of this phenomenon, called it the "caryolytic figure"; Fol calls it "the double star," or "amphiaster." In these double stars the polar bodies are formed. When the double star approaches the surface of the yolk, its membrane protrudes forming a small elevation. And now out of that pole of the spindle which is in contact with the surface, one polar body is excreted under vigorous contractions of the outer layers of the yolk. A second polar body is formed at the same pole where the star has disappeared and is expelled in the same way, leaving one star only in the ovum at the other end of the spindle.

The two most important views as to the meaning of the polar cells are those (1) of Balfour and Van Beneden, and (2) of Weismann. The first-named authors suppose that the egg, being a product of both sexes, is primitively hermaphrodite. By the extrusion of the polar bodies, the male portion of the egg is thrown out, and the remainder thus becomes unisexual (female), and ready for the entrance of the spermatozoön. This process would thus be a contrivance for the prevention of parthenogenesis.

Weismann distinguishes in every animal body two kinds of cells, *somatic* and *generative (or sexual) cells*. As all the cells arise as products of the segmentation of the ovum, they are originally quite similar morphologically, and each would thus consist of a "somatic" and of a "generative" portion. In order that certain of them should give rise to definite generative cells, it is necessary that the formative element, which would give rise to the somatic portion, should be got

•

rid of, and this is effected by the extrusion of the polar bodies.

The first hypothesis presupposes that in partheno-genesis no polar bodies are formed. Weismann has lately, however, proved their existence in the partheno-genetic summer eggs of Daphnidæ, and this view is consequently rendered improbable. In the develop-ment of the male generative cells, a certain portion of each primitive seminal cell also remains passive, not giving rise to spermatozoa.

The significance of the polar bodies is apparent from the rôle which the remaining part of the polar spindle has to play. It is no indifferent material that has been thrown out, but elements of the greatest formative faculty; for the remaining star constitutes that part around which the new nucleus is to be formed. The substance of the star gathers into two light grains, around which other similar grains are formed. They coalesce and thus form the new nu-cleus of the ovum. The new nucleus slowly recedes from the periphery toward the centre or near the centre of the ovum, and when it settles into a state of rest the ovum is ready for impregnation.

The process of rejuvenescence is in itself sufficient to produce segmentation, and in many of the lower animals parthenogenesis takes place. Parthenogene-sis, however, is confined to the invertebrates. In all the vertebrates, an admixture of the generative pro-ducts of the male is an indispensable condition to the development of the ovum.

As an example of the process of conjugation we select Selenka's observation of the impregnation of the egg of a sea-urchin (*Taxopneustes variegatus*), which he removed fresh from the mother organism and

placed in water, so that male germs could approach it.
A spermatozoön succeeds in forcing its entrance, as
a rule, at the very same place of the elevation which
originated through the expulsion _of the polar bodies.
The tail of the spermatozoön remains outside. A star
is formed by the transparent mass of the protoplasm

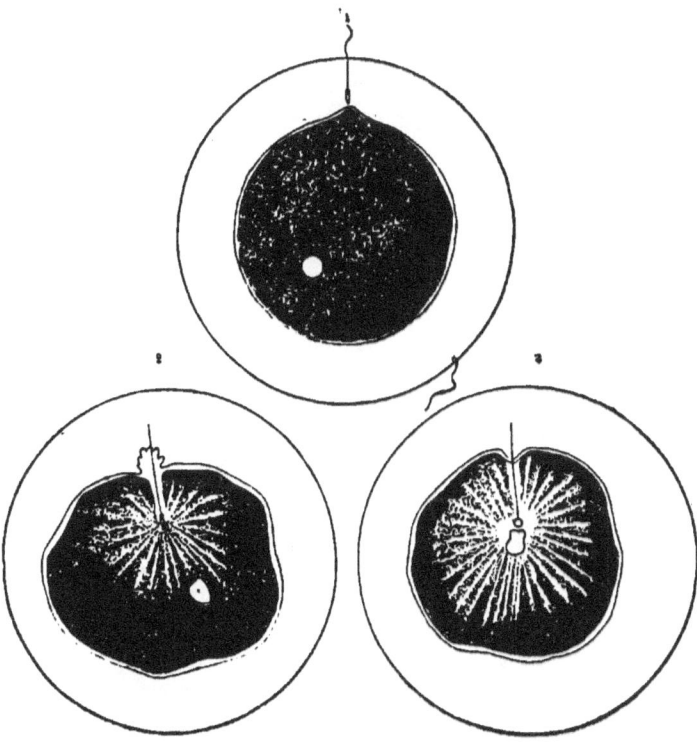

FECUNDATION OF THE EGG OF A SEA-URCHIN. (*Toxopneustes variegatus.*)
(Strongly magnified.)

1. Full grown egg after the removal of the polar bodies; a spermatozoön
is approaching the protrusion formed by the expulsion of the polar bodies.

2. The spermatozoön penetrates into the interior; a sun of transparent
protoplasm gathers around its head; the whole cell is in a state of violent
perturbation.

3. The spermatozoön's head is dissolved into the substance of the cell;
the neck is enlarged forming the sperma nucleus. The sperma nucleus and
the nucleus of the ovum approach each other and will soon be united into
one.

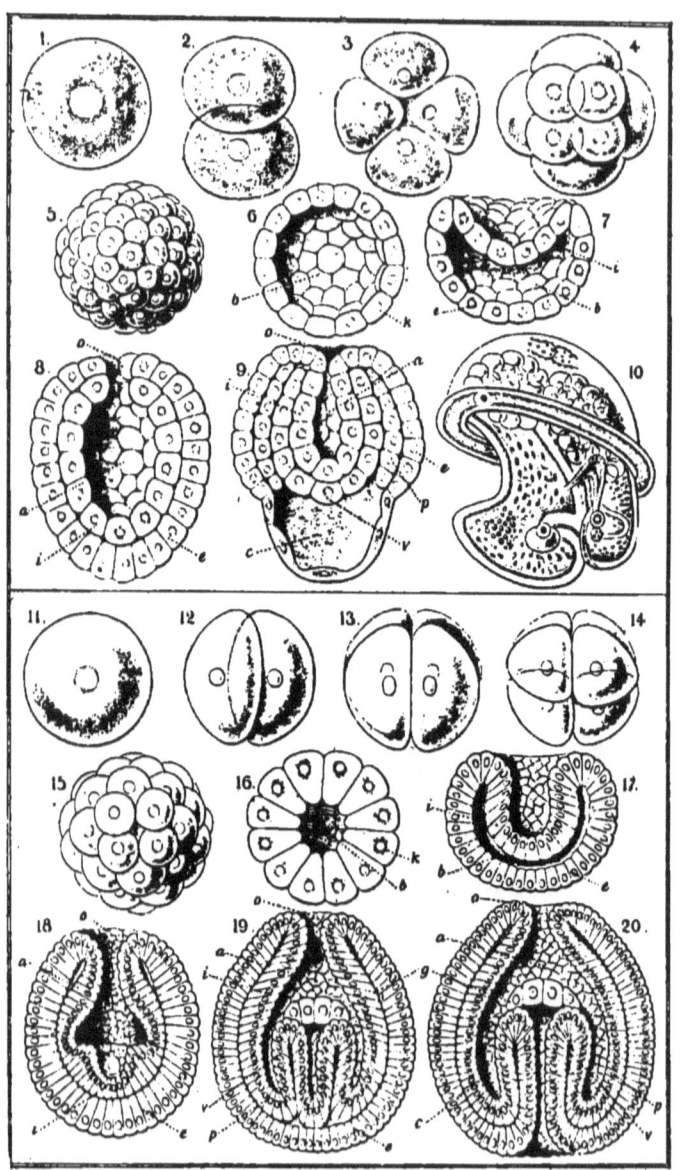

which gathers round the head of the spermatozoön, and at the same time a contraction of the yolk sets in. The head of the spermatozoön and the nucleus are attracted to each other. The pointed top of the spermatozoön is dissolved and absorbed by the yolk. The round neck increases in size and forms a second nucleus, called sperma-nucleus in distinction from the nucleus of the ovum. The nucleus of the ovum forms a hollow cavity, shaped like a diminutive crater which receives the sperma-nucleus. The sperma-nucleus sends out several finger-shaped processes toward the nucleus of the ovum, and amid a constant change of form coalesces with it into one nucleus, called the segmentation-nucleus. The first segmentation-nucleus divides into two equal parts, each of which forms a new centre for the division of the ovum into two halves. The process of segmentation continues until the morula stage is reached, whereupon the gastrula is

---

GASTRULA-FORMATION OF THE POND SNAIL (*Lymnaeus*) AND THE ARROW WORM (*Sagitta*).

Gastrulation, which comprises the first five stages of germination of the Metazoa, is represented in this plate in its simplest and most primitive form, as the development of the archigastrula (Fig. *8* and *18*); all the remaining stages of germination are to be regarded as secondary modifications of this primary form. Figures *1-10* show the gastrula-formation of a mollusk, the common pond snail (*Lymnaeus*), after the researches of Carl Rabl; Fig. *11-20* of a worm, the arrow worm (*Sagitta*), after the observations of Gegenbauer and Hertwig. The letters have the same signification in all the figures.

a. Progaster.   *i*. Entoderm.   *c*. Coeloma.
o. Prostoma.   *g*. Gonocyta.   *p*. Parietal membrane.
e. Ectoderm.   *k*. Blastoderm.   *v*. Visceral membrane.
b. Blastocoeloma.

Fig. *1* and *11*, primitive cell (*Cytula*) or "fecundated egg-cell," (also called "first stage of segmentation").—Fig. *2* and *12*, bipartition of the Cytula.—Fig. *3* and *13*, quadripartition of the same.—Fig. *4* and *14*, division of the same into eight segmentations or blastomeres.—Fig. *5* and *15*, mulberry-germ (*Morula*).—Fig. *6* and *16*, bladder-germ (*Blastula*) hollow ball in section.—Fig. 7 and *17*, hooded-germ (*Depula*), invagination of the blastula.—Fig. *8* and 18, cup-germ (*Gastrula*) in section.—Fig. *9* and *19*, Coelom-larva (*Coelomula*) in section.—Fig. *10* and *20*, Larva with aperture and hindpart.

formed which in its further development, will soon exhibit the rough outlines of the animal that is to grow
from it.

*   *   *

With regard to the formation of sex by the two
elements of fecundation it would seem as if the female
egg tended to produce male, and the male spermatozoön to produce female individuals. According to this
hypothesis a predominating influence on the part of
the egg would produce male offspring, and a predominating influence on the part of the spermatozoön
would produce female offspring. A man in that case
is not exclusively a male individual, he is potentially
a woman ; and, *vice versa*, a woman is potentially a
man. If a man could have children without the co-
operation of woman, they would be female, and if a
woman could have children without any intercourse
with man, they would be males. A boy in that case
would be more the son of his mother than of his father,
and a girl more the daughter of her father than of her
mother.

The fact which 'most obviously suggested this
theory of a reciprocal production of the sexes is the
strange phenomenon that the queen-bee of a hive lays
eggs without impregnation. All these eggs develop
into drones. The queen lays eggs that produce female bees,—queens or workers,—only after fecundation. Thus it is apparent, at least in the sexual life
of the bee, that the male element alone can serve for
the reproduction of the female, while the female (even
without any male intercourse) contains all the conditions to reproduce the male.

The embryo appears in the first stages of its development as neutral ; it possesses a kind of sexual

indifference, so that it appears impossible to foretell its eventual character. Yet this is no evidence that later circumstances during pregnancy are alone decisive. It may be that later circumstances will favor the male or the female, (as is actually the case with certain plants,) so as to effect the formation of sex indirectly in the one or the other way.

Experiments have been made by Knight * with melons and cucumbers ; and he produced male blossoms through warmth, light, and drought, and female blossoms by means of shade, humidity, and manure. Mauz succeeded by the same means in changing the sex in diœcious specimens.

Ploss has proposed the theory that as a rule by poor nutrition more boys are produced, and by opulent food more girls. It is not impossible and almost probable that hunger or at least a scarcity of food exercises a stimulating influence upon the sexual life, and increases the vigor of the reproductive functions, so that the female mother will bring forth male offspring.

Thury maintains, that the egg if fecundated at an early period of its existence will produce females, and if fecundated at a later period, it will produce males. He proved his view by having cows fecundated in the first days of rut. They gave birth only to cows, while those fecundated in the latter days of their rut gave birth to bulls.

Baust, in perfect agreement with Thury's theory, states on the basis of private observations, which are naturally very limited, that the conceptions effected during the first three days after the menses produce

---

* This observation and the facts following are reported in the *Naturwissenschaftliche Wochenschrift*, III, 133.

only girls, those effected after the eighth day only boys, while those between vary.

It is not impossible that the young egg is comparatively weak and plastic, that it constantly keeps gaining in strength, or rather in stability, so that there is a chance for the spermatozoön to supplant more of its elements in the beginning than later on.

. Hofacker has called attention to the relative ages of the parents. The more a father is advanced in years in comparison with the mother, the more the number of boys predominates. If a father is younger than the mother, the girls are more numerous.

Sadler has proved that this rule holds good upon the average for the English peerage, and Kisch has come to a similar conclusion on the basis of statistics attainable in calenders and reports of royal and aristocratic families.

Kisch's statement is summed up as follows: "If the man is at least ten years older than the woman, the latter being at the height of her reproductive vigor (viz., at an age of 20-25 years) there are more boys than girls. This proportion remains although not quite so pronounced if the woman is older than twenty-six years. However there are more girls than boys even if the man is older, if he has not yet reached the height of his reproductive vigor. The excess of girls is most decided if the man and the woman are of the same age. If the woman is older, there is a small excess of boys."

Kisch's rule may hold good upon the average. Nevertheless there are flagrant exceptions. The present German Emperor, for instance, although equal in years to the Empress, has five boys and no girls.

These facts again seem to prove that upon the

whole the greater strength of the female element favors the production of male children, and *vice versa.*

In spite of all the fluctuations that take place in the relative numbers of the sexes in limited circles, the average numbers in whole societies remain about equal. This fact induced Düsing to seek the origin of the sex in the relations of the single individuals to the whole community. He maintained that if male individuals predominate, female births will exceed male births and vice versa.

Düsing founded his theory upon the observations of Mr. Fiquet, a Texas breeder at Houston. Fiquet says: "It is a common occurrence that happens daily in the numerous herds which live in our American prairies that a strongly used bull will produce steer calves, while in the herds where many bulls are kept cowcalves predominate." In thirty cases, on ground of this observation, Fiquet has succeeded in producing a certain sex without fail.

The theory of Fiquet and Düsing does not explain the origin of sex, it sums up certain observations. But if the theory is correct it finds its best explanation in the hypothesis that the stronger of the two elements in fecundation always reproduces, not its own, but the other sex.

THE NATURE OF SOUL-LIFE.

INTO psychological discussions, of late, have been introduced the terms 'double personality,' 'double soul,' and 'double ego.' They serve for explanations of certain problems, but give rise, in their turn, to other problems; and to many minds the difficulties seem rather increased than diminished by the introduction of these strange combinations of words that tend rather to mystify than to clear our ideas. Indeed, authors are not lacking who deal with psychological topics as if there were a psychic fluid floating about us, or as if beside the conscious, subconscious, and unconscious activity of the soul, there existed a super-conscious sphere of psychical manifestation. On the basis of these hypotheses of course everything becomes possible, and the human body may easily be considered as the haunting-place of two or several ghosts.

We shall abstain here from controversial discussions and limit our explanation to a statement of the most important facts of soul-life.

In a certain sense each one of us—every higher organized creature—possesses a double soul. Organization produces a union of many organs, the interaction of which constitutes the unity of the organism. But the parts that constitute the organism are not at all annihilated by their coalition. Every single cell

continues to exist as an individual in itself. All together form a community and the work of every cell
is divided between caring for its own growth and
health, and contributing to the common weal of the
whole organism. In return for its work, it is bene-
fited by advantages that it would not possess if it
lived a solitary life.

Thus in every organism there exist two spheres of
soul-life. The one consists of the activity of the constituent parts; the other is that produced by their co-
operation. We call the former the sphere of the peripheral, the latter that of the central soul-life; and in this
sense adopt the term 'double soul.'

The peripheral soul is the separate psychical activities of the constituents of an organism; the central
soul is the product of their common activity. The
peripheral soul is the foundation upon which the central soul stands, or rather it is the ground from which
it grows. The central soul did not come from fairy-
land, a stranger, to inhabit for a time the human body
in company with the peripheral soul. The central
soul was born in its present abode; the body in which
it lives is its home, and the duality of soul-life, thus,
is not that of a composition, but that of a disintegra-
tion. It does not designate a descent of some unknown
power that comes from above; it is the rising of aspirations that are lifted from below to higher spheres.

Some time before the terms double ego and double
soul were employed by modern psychologists, Professor Hæckel had spoken of the double soul of the
Siphonophore, a Medusa of the Mediterranean sea.
The Siphonophore, consisting of many single individuals and yet exhibiting unitary perception and will,
is popularly called a colonial sea-nettle.

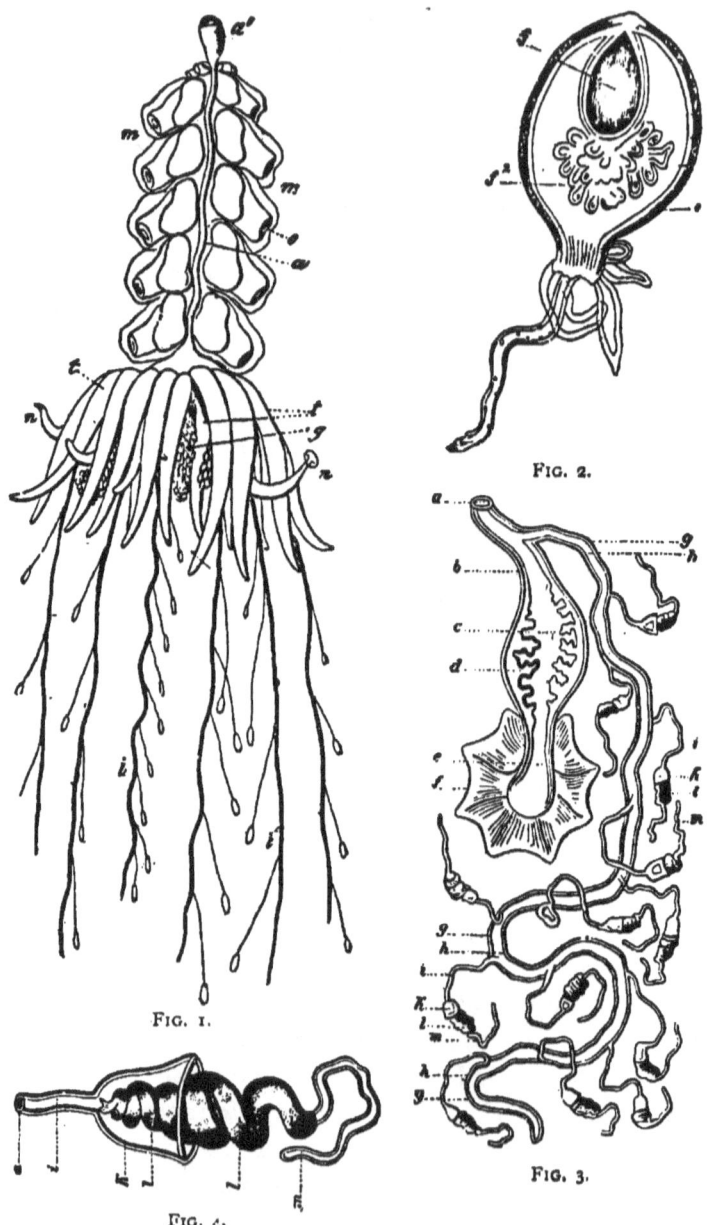

FIG. 1.

FIG. 2.

FIG. 3.

FIG. 4.

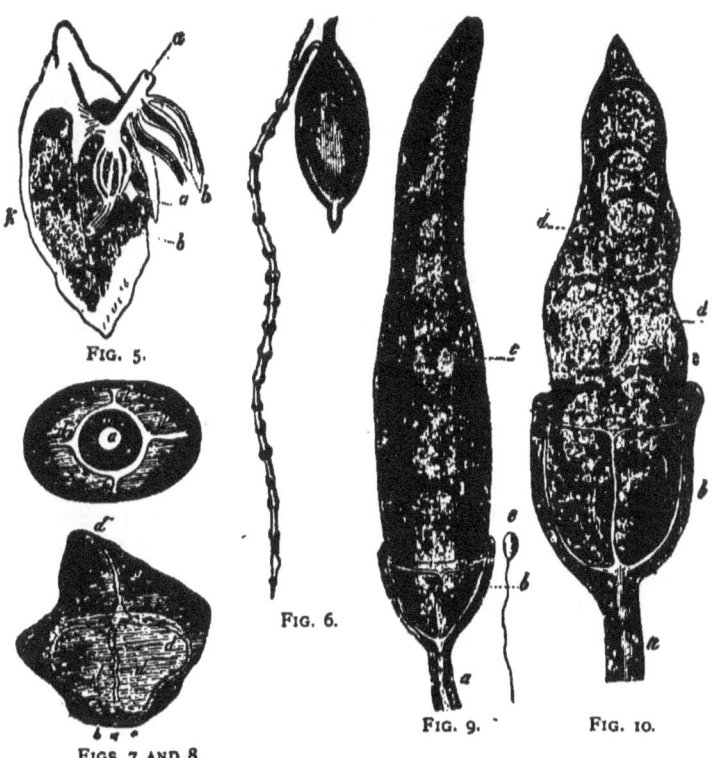

FIG. 5.

FIG. 6.

FIGS. 7 AND 8.

FIG. 9.   FIG. 10.

A COLONIAL SEA-NETTLE OR SIPHONOPHORE CONSISTS OF:

A STEM (fig. 1 *a*). It is an elongated hollow polyp, closed at the lower end and having an air-bladder (fig. 1 *a'* and fig. 2) at its upper end.

THE AIR-BLADDER (fig. 2) consists of an outer skin *c*, and an air-bag *f*, with a villous appendix (*f* 2).

LOCOMOTORS OR PROPELLORS. Fig. 1 *m*, (fig. 7 seen from below, fig. 8 from the side.) Motion is caused when from the orifice (fig. 7 *a*) the water is expelled, fig. 7 and fig. 8 *b* the web, *c* and *d* contracting fibres.

FEEDERS OR NUTRITIVE POLYPS (fig. 1 *n*, fig. 3 *a* to *f*). Connection with the stem *a*; skin of the feeder *b*; intestines *c*; liver glands *d*; throat *e*; mouth *f*. The assimilated food flows through *a* into the cavity of the stem, whence it is distributed through the different orifices (fig. 2 *a*, 3 *a*, 4 *a*, 5 *a*, 9 *a*, 10 *a*) to the other polyps.

PREHENSILE FILAMENTS (fig. 1 *i*, fig. 3 *g* to *m*, and fig. 4). Skin *g*; hollow interior *h*; arms *i*; bell-shaped envelope of the arm *k*; nettle-battery *l*; nettle-filament *m*.

SHIELD, OR PROTECTING POLYP (fig. 1 *o*, fig. 5 *k*). It covers the feeders *b*, and the feelers *h*.

FEELERS OR SENTIENT POLYPS (fig. 1 *t*, and fig. 6).

MALE AND FEMALE POLYPS (fi. 1 *g*, fig. 9 and fig. 10). Their bells *b*, their stomach *d*, sperma *c* is formed in the walls of the polyp The stomach of the female is filled with eggs.

Professor Hæckel says :

"The Siphonophores or colonial sea-nettles are found floating on the smooth surface of the tropical seas, yet only at certain seasons and not in great numbers. They belong to the most gorgeous formations of nature's inexhaustible wealth, and whoever has been fortunate enough to witness the sight of living siphonophores, will never forget the glorious spectacle of their wonderful forms and motions. These siphonophores are best compared to a floating flower-bush, the leaves, blossoms, and fruits of which look like polished crystal-glass of the most graceful forms and delicate colors.

"Each single appendage of the floating bush is a separate Medusa, an individual in itself. But all the different Medusæ of the community through division of labor have assumed different specialized forms. One part of the Medusa-community controls simply the natatory function (m), another the reception of food and digestion (n), a third sense-perception (t), a fourth defense and aggression, a fifth the production of eggs, etc. All the different functions which a single Medusa performs, are in the present case thus distributed among the different citizens of the sea-nettle colony ; and all the individuals have transformed their bodies to accord with their respective duties.

"As in a community of ants, so in the Siphonophore-republic, a number of differently formed animals have combined into a kind of higher social organization. But, while in the republic of ants, which is of a much higher order, the ideal bond of social interests and that of a political sense of duty unites all the individuals as free and independent citizens, in the Siphonophore-republic the members of the community are by bodily connection riveted like slaves directly to the yoke of their communal unity. Still, even in this close coherence each person is endowed with an individual soul of its own. If severed from the common stem, it can move about and live and have an independent being. The entire sea-nettle, as a whole, also possesses a will of its own—a central will, on which the single individual depends. It possesses a common sensation which at once communicates the perceptions of the single individuals to all the others. Thus, each of the Medusa-citizens might well exclaim with Faust :

'Two souls, alas ! do dwell within my breast.'

"The egoistic soul of the individual lives in compromise with the social soul of the community.

'' Woe to any Medusa, that in the infatuation of egotism would break away from the communal stock in order to lead an independent life ! Unable to perform all the particular functions that are indispensable to its self-preservation, most of which were performed by its several fellow-citizens, it needs must soon perish, if it be detached from its old companions. For one Medusa of the Siphonophore can only float, another only feel, a third only feed, a fourth only catch prey and repel enemies, etc. Only the harmonious coöperation and the reciprocal support of all its members, only the communal consciousness, only the *central soul*, linking all together in bonds of faithful love, can impart a lasting stability to the existence of both the individuals and their totality. In the same manner also in human affairs, only the faithful fulfillment of political and social duties by the citizens of a country ensures the permanent existence of civilized states."

Man no less than the colonial sea-nettle possesses a double soul. The peripheral soul of man consists of the many different activities of such cells as do not stand in a direct relation to the central soul-life of his organism. And by central soul we understand that part of our mind, which makes up the sphere of consciousness.

The spheres of the peripheral and the central soul are not distinctly separated by a definite boundary. The transition from the one to the other is almost imperceptible, and although there is an enormous amount of peripheral soul-activity that is never illuminated by, and apparently can never be accompanied with, consciousness (let me only mention the nervous activity of all the details of digestion, the work done by the kidneys, the liver, etc.,), there is also a vast neutral territory which is now conscious, now unconscious. The main tracts of this neutral territory, which, according to our wants, may not be or may be connected with consciousness, might fairly be included in the term central soul.

There are innumerable nerve-ganglions in our body, whose work is steadily performed without our being conscious of it. Indeed, it is the smallest part of the psychical processes going on within us, of which we become conscious. This fact by no means proves that unconscious activity proceeds without any feeling. It proves only that the feeling of these peripheral ganglions stands in no direct connection with the conscious life of our central soul. The feeling of peripheral ganglions must be of a lower kind, it is extremely vague and dim in comparison with that of central soul-life, where, by a specialization, it has become extraordinarily strong. Sometimes, however, in abnormal conditions of things, caused by disease, the feeling of the peripheral ganglions may be so intensified that we do become conscious of it in the form of pains and the various kinds of aches.

The peripheral and central soul-life continually intertwine. The labors of conscious activity that may have been performed with the intensest attention, will sink down into the night of unconsciousness, and *vice versa*, unconscious memories of the past, that seem irredeemably lost to our recollection, continue to live ; they sometimes combine with other, kindred or antagonistic, ideas, and then their logical results only, the product of their combination, unexpectedly and suddenly flash up on the surface of our conscious being. And we—*i. e.*, in this case, our central soul—do not know whence they come. They haunt us like voices of spirits from a distant beyond.

Our conscious ego covers a very narrow space. Only one or two and certainly no more than a few ideas can at one and the same time be accompanied with consciousness. How poor would we be, if our mental existence were limited to that. Happily, we can constantly derive new vigor and recreation from the spheres of our unconscious soul-life.

Could we look into the interior of a human brain, and did we understand all the many vibrations and motions of the nerve-substance, we would undoubtedly be struck with the quantity of unconscious work that is being carried on there all the time. We should observe how many millions of memories (every one of them having a special structure of its own) are constantly nourished by the oxygen-freighted corpuscles of the blood which surround them in the delicate capillaries.

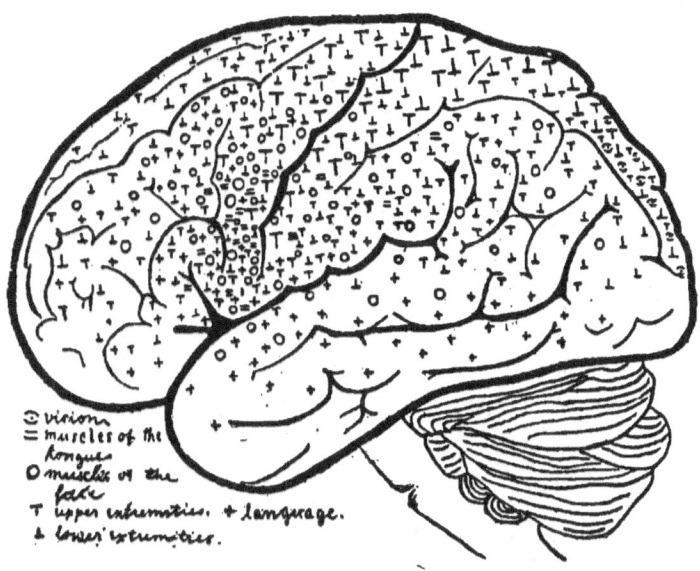

LOCALIZATION OF CERTAIN FUNCTIONS ACCORDING TO EXNER,
IN ORDER TO SHOW THEIR DISTRIBUTION.

The places where the different kinds of memories are located do not form, as has been supposed, distinct provinces separated by definite boundaries.

They are promiscuously distributed, yet there are corners where memories of the same kind are thickly crowded. In the parietal circumvolutions of the cortex, round about the fissure Rolando,* we see the movements of our limbs in their most complicated combinations. Below the fissure of Silvius are images of sound. There are all the old nursery rhymes, college songs, sonatas, and operas, that have delighted us. Near by are the words of our mother tongue. They live deep in the folds of the fissure Silvius, in the third frontal circumvolution and are largely dispersed over the sphenoidal lobe. All the verses of our childhood, of which we have not thought for years and years, are there still preserved. The front corner of the sphenoidal lobe is the seat of smell,† perfumes, and odors—disagreeable and pleasant. The hind part of the cortex in the occipital lobe‡ is full of images, it glows with colored pictures of all kinds. There are the dear old faces of our friends, there are landscapes and all manner of instantaneous photographs of former sights and experiences. In the three frontal circumvolutions those.thoughts are throbbing that are of a more abstract order. There are philosophical reflections and mathematical problems. Now and then one or the other idea looms out like a memorial of a national victory more powerfully than the rest. They are the memories of successful thoughts, of happy solutions of difficult problems. What an astounding throng of different structures, and all alive and consisting of feeling nerve-substance !

---

* *Gyrus centralis, lobulus præcentralis,* and the regions about the *præcuneus,* according to Fritsch-Hitzig and Ferrier.

† *Gyrus hypocampi,* according to Munk ; *gyrus uncinatus,* according to Ferrier.

‡ According to Munk and Ferrier.

This is the physiological aspect of the brain. Psychologically considered our mind is an immense empire of innumerable spirits that here live together in the narrow space of about a quarter of a cubic foot. Spirits they are, because they are psychical existences, they are framed by the memories of organized substance. Yet at the same time they are material realities; they are living forms of bodily presence, sustained by the nourishing currents of the blood.

This vast spiritual empire in the human brain is excellently provided for with highways and by-ways for intercommunication. The communications are called by physiologists commissural fibers, by psychologists associations. If it so happens that in the state of unconscious activity a certain number of ideas associate, and then if they have formed a new unity (the solution of a problem, a discovery, an invention or a poem), their life becomes more excited so that they make themselves felt. They are ushered into our consciousness like an inspiration from heaven. Is it to be wondered at that the poet, the artist, the prophet are under the impression that they are instruments merely in the hands of a Greater One than themselves? They feel influenced by a foreign and a supernatural power, over which they have no control. And this is true in a certain sense. As the limbs and the whole body of a child grow without the assistance of his consciousness, or as plants germinate and blow and bring seed, so the thoughts of a man in the shape of delicate brain-structures which are the organs of his feeling and thinking, grow and develop even in spite of him, even if he should attempt to oppose their development. It is not *we* who make our thoughts think, but our thoughts are thinking, and their thinking is sometimes accom-

panied˙ with consciousness. Therefore, we should say,
as Lichtenberg proposes, "it thinks," just as we say :
"it lightens," or "it rains."

Experimental psychology has furnished us with .
many new data of abnormal soul-life through pathological observations and hypnotic experiments. How
odd and incredible, indeed, at first sight, almost impossible, do these recent acquisitions of psychological
research appear. And yet they find their parallels in
well known and common facts of mental activity—in
facts that every one can verify by his own experience.
If the facts are but clearly stated in their parallelism,
what a flood of light do they shed upon all the problems of abnormal soul-life !

CENTRAL AND PERIPHERAL SOUL-LIFE.

THE experiments of M. Alfred Binet* prove that in the limbs and sense-organs of hysterical persons we can provoke various complex movements of adaptation which are performed without consciousness. There are certain details of vision that escape consciousness, yet are perceived by the eye. Similarly the anæsthetic hand, a hand that from a nervous disease is deprived of sensibility, jots down in automatic writing impressions which it receives. The hand is called anæsthetic because the patient knows nothing about it ; it is not in connection with his consciousness. M. Binet proves that feeling is not extinct in it ; for it has a feeling of its own and its psychic acts show a certain intelligence or adaptability.

The experiments of M. Binet are instances of peripheral nerve-activity not entering into the sphere of central soul-life.

Experiments of a similar kind were made by the late Mr. Gurney, one of the founders of the Society for Psychical Research of London. From an account† of his experiments on "Intelligent Automatism," reported, in the main, in Mr. Gurney's own words, we quote the following :

* Published in THE OPEN COURT : No. 100, "Proof of Double Consciousness in Hysterical Individuals " ; No. 101, "The Relations Between the Two Consciousnesses of Hysterical Individuals " ; No. 102, " The Hysterical Eye "; and No. 112, "Mechanism or Subconsciousness ? "

† *Spectator*, June 30, 1888.

"Mr. G. A. Smith, the 'hypnotiser,' sent off one of the patients into a mesmeric sleep, and in this sleep the patient was told that he was to write some particular word, or to count the number of *e*'s in a particular verse, or to do a particular multiplication sum when he awoke. . . . . Then he was wakened and at once engaged in reading aloud, or counting backwards, or doing something that engrossed his full attention ; but his right hand was placed on the planchette (an instrument on wheels containing a pencil), the paper and planchette being always concealed from the subject's eyes, so that he could not know, unless he were able to guess from the blind movements of the instrument under his hand (which guessing was made very difficult by the occupation found for him), what letters or figures (if any) the instrument was tracing. ' As a rule, he was always offered a sovereign to say what the writing was, but the reward was never gained.' On being sent back into the mesmeric sleep, he recalled the whole process, though in the waking state he could never tell what the movements of the planchette under his hand were engaged in producing. Here is Mr. Gurney's account of the results as regards the arithmetical sums worked by what he calls the 'secondary intelligence ' :—

"The sums given were simple, as most of the 'subjects' were inexpert at mental arithmetic. There were 131 sums in which three figures had to be multiplied by a single one ; of these 52 were quite right, 28 had three figures in the answer right, 18 had two figures right, and 14 had one figure right only, whilst 12 were quite wrong, and 7 were either so illegible and muddled as to be undecipherable, or only a small stroke or curve was made at all. . . . . In some cases the sum itself was correctly written, but no attempt was made to put the answer. . . . . A few sums of other kinds were also given : of 14 simple additions (of about the following difficulty : $4 + 7 + 9 + 11 + 13$), six were done correctly, two were quite wrong, and the remaining six were either not done at all, or the answers were illegible scribbles. . . . . Another case illustrates the very distinct memory, on re-hypnotisation, of what had been written. Wells was told to work out the sum, ' 13 loaves at 5d. each,' and instantly woke as usual. He wrote, ' 13 loaf at 5d. is 5s. 5d.' When hypnotized again, and asked to say what he had written, he replied, ' 13 loaf—oh, I've put *loaf* instead of *loaves*— at 5d. is 5s. 5d. I've written the 13 twice—see—but I crossed it out.' He then proceeded, by a long roundabout process, to work the problem out, arriving at the correct answer again.

" Another form of experiment was to tell the 'subject' to count the number of times a certain letter occurred in a given verse. Thus, Wells was told to write down the number of times the letter *e* occurred in the verse—" Mary had a little lamb, etc.," and then, after saying-the verse once quickly through to show that he knew it, he was instantly awakened and given *Tit-Bits* to read. Whilst thus engaged he wrote, *The letter E comes 11 times*—which is right. The same experiment was tried with Parsons, who also was kept occupied by being set to read immediately upon waking; but he was not so accurate, and wrote down '12.' He was completely successful, however, when told to write the number of *e*'s in

> ' God save our gracious Queen,
> Long live our noble Queen,
> God save the Queen,'

and wrote 11, having read excellently the whole time."

Concerning Mr. Gurney's explanation of these facts, the same account adds:

" His inference is that these trances induced by mesmerism, or whatever we like to call the peculiar influence which special persons seem to possess of rendering others unconscious,—separates the mind of the patient into two separate planes of consciousness, each of which is capable of accomplishing such simple intellectual tasks as the subject's education has fitted him to perform, but nevertheless without the privity of the other, so that the man is apparently subdivided into two men, one of whom is reading aloud, and the other working a sum or counting the number of *e*'s in a stanza, though the man who is doing the sum has little or no knowledge of what his *alter ego* is reading aloud ; while the man who is reading aloud has no knowledge at all of the operations of the *alter ego* who is doing the sum."

According to our view these two souls are not two different beings, but they are psychic activities performed in two different spheres—the spheres of central and peripheral soul-life. If the activity of peripheral soul-life is not connected with that of the central soul-life, the central soul can know nothing about the processes that take place in the peripheral regions of our mind. Accordingly we call them *unconscious*. If the peripheral nerve-activity is indirectly, yet not too distantly, connected with the central soul, we may have a dim idea of its proceedings. Thus, we do not know whether the nerves of our intestines are now secreting particles of fat or albuminoids or any other substance, yet we can know upon the whole whether or not they are in a state of health. Such conditions we call *subconscious.*

The experiments of Mr. Gurney as well as those of M. Binet corroborate the fact that every nervous ganglion is a brain in miniature, as *vice versa* the whole brain is but a centralization of many ganglions. All nervous substance exhibits, in the performance of the psychic functions of irritation and reflex motion throughout, a marvelous adaptability to circumstances. Thus, the decapitated frog, when his back is irritated on the right side by a feather saturated in a solution of hydrochloric acid, scratches the spot and removes the irritant.

This might be called a simple reflex motion and can perhaps be explained as purely mechanical. Formerly it was believed to take place without any consciousness. But now it is known, that if the frog's right leg be amputated and his back be again irritated, after several unsuccessful trials to remove the irritant by his right leg, he will use his left leg.

This is plainly a process of adaptation to circumstances. The central soul of the decapitated frog, as can be proven by other experiments, has been removed ; but parts of the peripheral soul still continue their activity in the spinal cord so long as the nervous substance remains in a condition of comparative health. And the activity of the peripheral nerve-substance cannot be merely mechanical as are the movements of a machine; judging from the experiment of the frog, they must be psychical at the same time. The mechanism of nervous reflex-motions lives and feels. Even the peripheral ganglions possess a kind of consciousness of their own, dim though it may be.

There is no difference of kind between the peripheral and central soul, there is a difference of degree only. And the difference that obtains is undoubtedly produced by a division of labor. This will at the same time explain the fact that the lower a nervous system is, the more independent are its peripheral ganglia. The central soul-life is less differentiated in a frog than in man, and still less in a colonial sea-nettle.

The decapitated-frog experiment is in so far to the same purpose as Mr. Gurney's and M. Binet's experiments, for it proves the independent action of peripheral soul-life without any interference of, or connection with, central soul-life.

The phenomena of peripheral and central soul-life are not a coördinated duality; they form a hierarchical, *i. e.*, a super-ordinated system. The central soul rises from the peripheral soul. The former being taken away, the latter may continue to exist; but we see no possibility for the central soul to exist, if its foundation, the peripheral soul, is withdrawn. We can remove the spire of a church-steeple, and let the base stand, but we can not remove the base and have the spire remain in its place. Thus the central soul of consciousness, being the combined product of a certain part of the activity of the peripheral soul, can not lead an absolute life of abstract existence. It subsists and can subsist only upon condition of the peripheral activity of the nervous system.

How closely the central and the peripheral activities

are interwoven, can be learned from the facts of post-hypnotic suggestions. Mr. Gurney's experiments were purposely so arranged as to make the execution of a post-hypnotic suggestion an act of automatic and unconscious intelligence. This, however, is a special case only and indeed an exception.

Post-hypnotic suggestions, as a rule, rise from the peripheral sphere of unconscious life into the region of consciousness. There they appear as if created out of nothing in no other manner than inspirations may come to a poet. The central soul is in possession of certain data ; but it can, out of itself merely, give no account of their origin. A number of conscious ideas are a living presence in the mind, and that is all that from consciousness alone can be learned. Their factors may be, and usually are, hidden in the depth of unconsciousness. The result only of nervous activity becomes conscious, but not the details of its conditions. Consciousness knows least of all about the nervous fibers, the brain-cells, and their distribution.

The subjects who have received post-hypnotic suggestions deal with them very differently. They either execute them withcut heeding what they do, almost unconsciously ; or, especially if the suggestions are absurd, they try to suppress them. Some succeed in doing so, some yield to their impulse after a vain struggle. Some execute them, and if asked why they act thus, they either invent a plausible motive or answer that the idea just struck them to do it.

We quote an example from Forel's latest publication on Hypnotism :

"I said to a hypnotized patient : ' After awaking the idea will occur to you to place a chair upon the table, and then to tap me on the left shoulder with your right hand.' I then ordered him to do several other things, adding : 'Count as far as six, and awake. The patient counted and when he reached six, opened his eyes drowsily, saw a chair and stared at it.—Often there arises a conflict between reason and the powerful impulse of suggestion. Either the former or the latter will gain the upper hand according as the suggestion is natural or unnatural and as the hynotized subject is suggestible. Our hypnotized subject after having stared at the chair for awhile, suddenly rose, took the chair and placed it on the table. I said : ' Why do you do this ? ' The reply always varies according to the culture, temperament, and quality of the hypnotized subject and of the hypnosis. One will say : 'I followed my impulse.' Another : ' The idea occurred to me.' A third alleges an a posteriori motive saying, the chair had been in his way, it had bothered him. A fourth after the performance of the action, loses every recollection and appears to awaken at that very moment. Particularly in the last instance the subject has the staring glance of a somnambulist , it is more or less rigid, his movements are automatic, and do not cease to be so until after the performance of the act.''

Another curious instance mentioned by Dr. Forel is the following :

''To a hypnotized woman I said on a Monday : ' Next Sunday morning precisely at quarter past seven you will call on me. You will see me in a sky-blue coat, with two long horns on my head, and you will then ask me, when I was born.' Next Sunday I was sitting in my study, and had forgotten the whole affair. My patient at thirty-five minutes past seven knocked at my door, entered, and burst into laughter. I at once recollected my suggestion, which now was actually realized, exactly in the manner it was given.''

In the waking state the central soul plays a dominant part. This is accomplished positively as well as negatively ; positively by concentration and negatively by inhibition. The consciousness of the central soul can be and usually is concentrated upon one object, *viz.*, the object of attention. But all the many sensory impressions that are received in all quarters of the periphery would greatly detract from the clearness of attention, if they were constantly permitted to enter the sphere of the central soul and to interfere with its activity. The central soul, if concentrated upon a subject of interest, sees fit not to heed other things, it suppresses their observation.

For instance, I am writing now and do not notice certain noises about me. I look up from my paper to collect my thoughts, but I do not observe the scenes outside of the window upon which I look. They are indifferent to me, and if afterwards asked what I had heard or what I had seen, most likely I should not be able to tell. I heard the noises—the word "I" here signifies my ears; I heard certain words but I did not listen—the word "I" here signifies my consciousness. I saw certain things, but I did not look; so I cannot tell what I heard or what I saw. My consciousness on the one hand, and my eyes or ears on the other, are two different things.

It may happen, however, that the sound of a word that I did not heed lingers in my memory still. I recall the sound, and now I perceive its meaning too. A certain scene that I glanced at in an absent-minded state, may have impressed itself strongly enough as afterwards to come up in my recollection. Some persons passed by; my eye had seen them, but I had taken no notice of them. Being asked whether a certain acquaintance of mine had been among them, I might then positively know that he was.

If we could ask the eye, it would certainly always be able to tell what it had seen. If we could look into the memories registered in some of the sensory ganglions, we could know what scenes were photographed by the eye; for every scene upon which the eye looked is registered in nerve-substance. We can, however, not expect to recollect a sensation that was prohibited to enter, and thus never entered, our consciousness. The following account from Max Dessoir,*is of special interest.

" Several friends were at my house, and one of them, Mr. W——, sat apart reading, while we others were talking together. Suddenly the conversation turned upon a name X——, which particularly interested Mr. W——. He abruptly turned round, and asked what had happened to Mr. X—— He declared, that he knew nothing of our previous conversation ; and that he only had heard the name mentioned. Then, with his consent, I hypnotized him, and in the state of deep hypnosis I asked him again, and to our great astonishment he coherently related the whole trend of the conversation that had taken place while he was reading."

In another passage Dessoir says :

" The idea of the husband when his wife scolded him for having mislaid the house-key at the inn, was after all not bad. " Wait—said he—until I get drunk again, and I shall certainly find out where I left it."

It is noteworthy, that in dreams as well as in states of intoxication, certain people seem upon the whole to reveal always a similar character which, however, may greatly differ from their normal condition. The conscious life of the central soul being extinguished, and the inhibition that in the waking state is constantly exercised being abolished, the peripheral soul-life oozes out in its originality, and however it may differ from the waking state it shows again and again, under similar circumstances, naturally similar traits of character. There is accordingly a truth in the Latin proverb :" *In vino veritas.*"

The same may be said about dreams. Dreams reveal to us characteristic features of our peripheral soul-life.

* *Das Doppel-ich*, p. 19.

DOUBLE PERSONALITY.

CONSCIOUSNESS, or the centralized and intensified feeling of the central soul, does not remain equally the same throughout our life. It is sometimes more, sometimes less, intense. Its highest state of concentration, when it is most intense, we call attention, and a mental condition in which concentration is lacking, we call a distracted or absent-minded state. The Germans in this sense speak of a person as being "dispersed," *zerstreut*, when his attention is not focused upon one central idea, but is dimly distributed over a larger field.

The object of attention is that idea in which and to which at a given moment our entire psychical activity converges. It may be called the centre of the central soul. It is that part of our soul which, being the content of the present state of consciousness, represents at the time our ego.

The object of attention can and usually does change rapidly. Indeed a certain power of self-control is necessary to fix attention upon one object for any length of time. The importance of the power of attention can scarcely be overrated, and M. Ribot quotes with approval Helvetius, who says: "All intellectual differences between one man and another spring only from attention."

The *central* soul, the ego proper of man, his conscious personality, is not limited to the present state of consciousness. It possesses the peculiar quality, that the present state of consciousness is connected with the most important memories of former states of consciousness. In other words, central soul-life is a continuous process, and its continuity is felt, it is conscious. The continuity of the central-soul is its history in shape of living memories, that stand in connection with its present.

The facts of our life are thus represented in our mind in the shape of a series of memories, and it is this series of memories that constitutes our personality.

It is but natural that under normal conditions every man should have a personality of his own. A man's personality is the history of his life and the sum total of his experiences. The memories of former experiences influence our actions even now. They guide us in our decisions and are constituent parts of our present state of consciousness.

If a certain sensory impression is perceived,—for instance we read a certain sentence in a book,—the impression is recognized as something we had heard or seen before. Most likely every word is familiar to us, the combination of words in this sentence alone is new. All the memories of these words are awakened, not only the memories of the letters, the written words, but also of the sounds ; then the memories of the conceptions are revived, the thought-images of which these words are symbols, and with them all those mental activities that are therewith associated. Thus the state of our present consciousness is in a constant contact with the past, it grows upon and it adds to it.

The memories of old experiences and the reactions upon certain conditions in former situations are the foundation from which our wishes and desires, our hopes and longings, rise ;—they are the elements of that which as one whole is called character—in a word they constitute our conscious personality.

* * *

Consciousness does not act continually. The activity of the central soul sinks at regular intervals below the level of consciousness. It goes to sleep every night, and the existence of the central soul, it thus appears, is for a short time periodically wiped out.

We know that sleep is by no means a state of inactivity ; but while in a waking state the life of the central soul is predominant, in sleep the peripheral soul develops an unusual activity. It performs the work of restoration. The peripheral organs clean the brain of its waste materials and restore the loss of its consumption, by building up those living nerve-structures that contain the energy which during the waking state is drawn upon.

In the deepest sleep all consciousness disappears, but in lighter slumbers part of the borderland between peripheral and central soul-life remains active, and then forms in the subumbra of dreams a new centre of its own, which may be called the dream-ego. The dream-ego need not be, and, indeed, as a rule, it is not connected with the normal ego of the waking state, so that usually we have a vague recollection only that during sleep we were dreaming of something but cannot tell what it was.

The ego of the dream possesses a chain of memories of its own, which perhaps has never been connected with the memory-chain of the conscious ego in the waking state. In that case, if we do not know of what we dreamed, we cannot properly speak of our having forgotten the dream. We never knew it, for it was never in connection with our consciousness. Yet should we, on the day after the dream, happen to see one of the objects that appeared in the visions of our slumber, we might be enabled by this observation to recollect the whole dream.

We can easily understand this fact, for the sight of the object that we dreamed of brings the waking consciousness into contact at one point with the memory chain of the dream-ego. Thus an association is produced between both, and the whole chain of the dream-memories or a great part of them can be hauled up, as it were, to the surface of conscious recollection.

* * *

There exist certain cerebral diseases, in which, the continuity of the present state with past memories is interrupted through an impairment of the brain. In such cases a new chain of memories is usually formed, and the unconnected states of consciousness combine among themselves into a new ego, which (not unlike the dream-ego) on its own part is not connected with the original, normal ego. Certain important memories that constitute the normal personality being wiped away, the new ego may in all its main characteristics be vastly different from the normal ego. When the normal ego reappears, it knows nothing of the second ego. It will continue its existence from the moment it had ceased, and takes as little notice of the other ego as a man in the waking state bothers about the dreams of the previous night, of which he knows nothing. Both states, the normal and the abnormal ego, may alternately appear, just as the waking-ego and the dream-ego may come and go. It is as if a dream-ego of a sleep-walker had acquired a continuity of its own. In such a case besides the normal personality another personality is formed in one and the same body.

Certain activities and habits,—namely, those that are usually performed unconsciously,—remain common to the normal and abnormal personality, but the two egos constitute separate spheres. Physicians who have observed and described such states, most forcibly and correctly designate this phenomenon as cases of "double personality," and we explain them as a doubling of "the central soul within one common peripheral soul."

Ribot quotes the following remarkable instance * of a young American woman from the "Philosophy of Sleep," by Macnish :

" Her memory was capacious and well stored with a copious stock of ideas. Unexpectedly and without any forewarning, she fell into a profound sleep, which continued several hours beyond the ordinary term. On waking she was discovered to have lost every trace of acquired knowledge. Her memory was *tabula rasa;* all vestiges, both of words and things, were obliterated and gone. It was found necessary for her to learn everything again. She even acquired, by new efforts, the art of spelling, reading, writing and calculating, and gradually became acquainted with the persons and objects around, like a being for the first time brought into the world. In these exercises she evinced considerable proficiency.

---

* We do not cite here the famous case of Dr. Azam's Felida X——. The statement of the case does not appear well defined and seems to be self-contradictory in important points. It seems strange that, according to the account, the patient's memory in the abnormal condition covered also that of the normal, while the reverse did not take place. And yet Dr. Azam states that a radical change of character took place; while the patient appeared modest and decent in the one, she was coquettish and frivolous in the other. Such a change is not possible without the obliteration or at least impairment of cortical brain structures—which after all are memories, if not of actual experience yet of instruction and education.

" After a few months another fit of somnolency came upon her. On rousing from it, she found herself restored to the state she was in before the first paroxysm ; but was wholly ignorant of every event and occurrence that had befallen her afterward. She is as unconscious of her double character as two distinct persons of their respective natures. For example, in her old state she possesses all the original knowledge, in her new state only what she acquired since. . . . . In the old state she possesses fine powers of penmanship, while in the new she writes a poor, awkward hand, having had neither time nor means to become an expert."

In this manner there are formed two entirely different and independent chains of recollections. When the one appears, the other disappears. This duplication can be due only to a temporary interruption of consciousness with its chain of memories, thus causing the obliteration of the conscious personality. Peripheral soul-life continüing its activity, forms a new concentration and produces another central soul which in the course of its development has to create its own material. The patient thus appears to lead a double life, by possessing two central souls, which are encompassed by one and the same peripheral soul.

How much the cases of double personality, rising from the obliteration of normal personality, are similar to the formation of a dream-ego, may be learned from an instance quoted by M. Ribot in his " Diseases of Personality," where a constant change of personality is effected. He says :

" An insane woman of Charenton, possessing very remarkable power and originality of mind, from day to day would change in personality, in condition, in life, and even in sex. Now she would be a young lady of blood royal, betrothed to an emperor ; anon a plebeian woman and a democrat : to-day a wife and in the family-way ; to-morrow still a maid. It would happen also that she would think herself a man, and one day she imagined herself to be a political prisoner of importance, and composed verses upon the subject."

•

The cases of double personality are similar to the cases of a double soul, in so far as both show two or more distinct consciousnesses.   Yet, while the case of a double soul may exhibit the normal symptoms of the peripheral and the central activities of the soul in their isolation, a case of double personality shows an unusual and a continuous rise of a second central soul with a new and distinct chain of memories rising from the subconscious spheres of peripheral activity. This being possible only if the normal central soul is temporarily extinct, its appearance must be considered as the symptom of a severe and most probably fatal disease of the brain.

The phenomenon of double personality is a special and an abnormal case of double soul-life, it is a case in which by the weakness of central soul-life part of the peripheral activities usurp the centre for a certain period.   It is like a change of party in the government of the mind ; other elements representing new ideas and principles with traditions of their own, assume the executive power.   The symptoms of independent peripheral activities are like the individual exertions of private citizens.   A duplication of personality accordingly can be effected only by ousting the original personality that is in possession of the central executive powers in our body, represented in the motor regions of the hemispheres and controling the muscles of our limbs, especially the organ of speech.

The inference that can be drawn from the fact of double personality seems to be, that the peripheral soul-life of an organism has the intrinsic tendency to build a central soul out of its own materials.   Could we amputate the central soul of a man, *i. e.*, his conscious personality, the subconscious and unconscious activities of his nerves would again grow together or at least show the tendency to grow together and become focused in a new centre. Similarly a tree, the top of which is cut down, will send forth new branches to replace the loss.

* * *

The result of our investigations confirms the proposition that all nervous activity is in a certain way psychical. Even its so-called unconscious functions are processes accompanied with a kind of feeling. Accordingly, they are (considered by themselves) to a certain extent conscious. They can not properly be called conscious, because by "conscious" we mean the strongest and most concentrated kind of feeling, and not mere irritability. Yet the irritability of organized substance is the germ from which consciousness is developed.

If the work performed by the many different minor ganglions of the peripheral parts is called unconscious, this should only mean that the feeling remains isolated in the peripheral sphere, and that it is not known to, *i. e.*, it stands in no connection with, the larger central ganglions. The activity of the central ganglions and the activity of such parts as are at the time in connection with them, are the constituent elements of our consciousness.

The central consciousness being stronger than the rest eclipses all the others. So the stars disappear before the rays of the sun, although they continue to remain in their places. If we speak of our ego, or of our personality, we think first and almost exclusively of that part of our mind which we have defined as our central soul.

There is no doubt that the different parts of living

substance have by division of labor lost certain properties to such an extent that they scarcely retain the
rudimentary features thereof. Feeling is one feature
only of organized life. While the dim feeling of irritability has been concentrated in a central consciousness; it is more than probable that in certain and perhaps in most parts of the peripheral activity of the soul
it has simultaneously been reduced to a minimum.

In our great cities we have often occasion to observe in the evenings pictures of magic lanterns used
as advertisements in the streets or on public squares.
We may often be puzzled whence the picture comes;
whether the lantern stands in front in a hidden place
on the opposite side of the street, or whether it stands
behind the picture. The effect only appears and all
the many rays of light which are intercepted by the
white screen, are imperceptible. No wonder that the
lantern in former centuries was considered as a magic
instrument.

The Psyche with its glowing, its brilliant, and ever
changing life similarly appears as a wonder that cannot be accounted for. Not knowing whence it came,
we are almost driven to the conclusion, that here is
the inscrutable interference of an extra-natural power.
Nevertheless, patient inquiry will after all convince us,
that there is no exception to, no annihilation of, natural
law. The same natural powers are at work in our
soul as in the surrounding universe.

Our central soul appears to us like the white Alpine
summit when seen from afar. It can scarcely be distinguished from a roseate cirrus-cloud that hovers free
in the air. Nevertheless, the Alpine summit rests on
solid rock and stands firmly upon the ground from
which it has risen. We see only the snow-covered top

and are not aware of its granite base. Yet the base is there, and though it appears dark to us, it consists, in the main, of the same material as its top in its majestic grandeur.

Certainly, nature manifests herself in our soul in a peculiar and extraordinary way. Nature seems to be concentrated here in all her glory and, if anywhere, here she demonstrates that she is no chaotic agglomeration of dead matter, but a living power, everywhere conforming to law.

Law is not imposed upon nature, but is immanent in nature. It is, fundamentally, nothing but the fact that nature is consistent; nature remains faithful to herself. Thus being a law unto herself and being a living power, she naturally makes life grow according to law *i. e.*, she organizes in living organisms. Living organisms therefore can truly be said to be created in the image of the living cosmos. They are microcosms and can be looked upon as revelations of the macrocosm, of the immeasurable All.

This is the more true, the higher an organism is, and most of all it is true of man. We cannot doubt that there is a scientific truth in the words of Moses, when he says : " So God created man in His own image, in the image of God created He him."

WHAT IS HYPNOTISM?

IN recent times a number of quite unexpected disclosures have been brought to light by the aid of hypnotism. The wonderful reports about hypnotic experiments at first seemed so highly incredible, that, perhaps justly, they were received with distrust. They seemed to merit general disbelief. But, the experiments were repeated and again and again proved successful. At the present time we have at our disposal an abundance of well-accredited facts. England, Germany, Switzerland, Italy, and particularly France, have been the theatre of eager researches. Nor has America remained altogether unconcerned in the matter. In recent years the literature relating to this subject has reached fabulous proportions.

The more conversant we have become with hypnotic phenomena, which at first appeared quite abnormal, the more occasion have we had to convince ourselves that, after all, they are not more wonderful than other phenomena of life. The phenomena, at all events, which after strict, critical investigation and experimental treatment have been confirmed and retained as facts, are easily arranged under the head of biological and psychical laws, with which we are familiar in our daily experience.

At the very threshold of the new science we are embarrassed by the different answers which are given to the question, "What is hypnotism?" I have sought in vain after a simple and precise definition among the most prominent authors of the department. The psychologists of France and Switzerland are divided into two hostile camps, from both of which the ingenious founder of scientific hypnotism, M. Charcot, seems to keep equally aloof.

M. Charcot considers the hypnotic state as a *psychosis, i. e.*, a diseased state of the soul, and has become more and more convinced (according to accounts that have appeared in French and German journals) that the therapeutic employment of hypnotism leads to injurious results, or, to say the least, its efficacy is very doubtful.

The two hostile schools, one at Nancy, the other at Paris, unite in their opposition to Charcot's view, that the hypnotic state is a psychosis. The Nancy school is headed by Prof. Bernheim, the Parisian by Dr. Luys. Prof. Bernheim looks upon hypnotism as throughout psychical; he resolves all its facts into products of suggestion; while Dr. Luys believes to have produced physiological and even extra-physiological changes in his hypnotic subjects. Both schools devote their entire powers to establish hypnotism as a panacea for innumerable ailments that visit humanity. Hence their opposition to Charcot.

The question, "What is Hypnotism?" is answered by Bernheim as follows:

"The hypnotic state is a peculiar, psychical condition, which can be provoked artificially, and which to a varying degree *augments suggestibility ;* i. e., it has the power of influencing any single idea received by the brain in such a manner that under all circumstances the subject strives to realize the same." *

* We quote this definition from a report of the Psychological Congress of Paris in the "*Internationale Klinische Rundschau,*" Vienna, August 25, 1889;

He adds :

" All the different processes can be reduced to one ; *viz.*, suggestion. . . . . There are hypnoses without sleep."

Dr. Forel is a follower of the school of Nancy. He also declares that :

"The vague conception of hypnotism must ultimately be recognized as the idea of *suggestion.*"

But suggestibility can also be observed in persons that are not hypnotic. Have the masses in France been hypnotized perhaps by Boulanger, because by augmenting their suggestibility, he has prompted them to all kinds of whimsicalities? Surely not. Suggestibility is a general phenomenon of soul-life, which can be observed everywhere, but which appears in a special, and indeed in a morbid, condition in the hypnotic state.

The idea of suggestion, it seems to me, is much vaguer than that of hypnotism. If suggestion were the core of hypnotism, if it were its characteristic feature, every teacher who imparts knowledge, and plants ideas in the minds of children, would be a hypnotizer.

Dr. Luys embraces in his definition all the details, that he actually has, or believes he has, observed in the hypnotic subject. Hence his definition is overloaded, and that which is essential is not carefully distinguished from that which is unessential. That which is perfectly accredited is introduced together with observations of doubtful character. Dr. Luys says :

" Hypnotism is an experimental extra-physiological state of the nervous system. It is an artificial neurosis which is developed in a predisposed subject, a pseudo-sleep which is imposed, and dur-

Dr. Bernheim's book on suggestions not containing a proper definition— although he maintains repeatedly that "hypnosis must be reduced to its real foundation, which is suggestion."

ing which the subject that is experimented upon, loses the notion of his own existence and the external world."

The last part of the definition applies to sleep no less than to hypnotism; and in the first part the expression "extra-physiological state of the nervous system" appears to have the greatest weight.

This is not the place for subjecting the expression "extra-physiological" to analysis and criticism. We cannot adopt an expression that is of a negative kind. Instead of elucidating·it perplexes, and, in addition, we cannot admit experiments exhibiting extra-physiological states to that class of facts which have been and can be verified by repetition.

Here is the difference between the Nancy school and the Paris school. The Paris school maintains that the phenomena of hypnotism depend upon physiological changes; they represent extra-physiological states: effects are produced such as anæsthesia, hyperæsthesia, contractures, hemilateral or bilateral transfers, rigidity by the use of magnets, or by the touch of medicines contained in glass tubes. The Nancy school denies all these propositions, and Dr. Bernheim declares, that "all the pretended physical phenomena of hypnosis are of a psychical nature. Catalepsy, transfers, contractures are effects of suggestion only."

The simplest definition, which at the same time completely covers the matter at issue, is the following:

Hypnosis is sleep produced at will from artificial fatigue.' And hypnotism is the scientific treatment and investigation of hypnotic states.

* * *

In many respects we agree with both the Nancy and the Paris school; even where it seems that they are irreconcilable. There are, no doubt, physiological changes taking place in the nervous system in natural sleep as well as in artificial sleep; but at the same time we recognize that all nervous activity is psychical, although it may not be in connection with the central soul of consciousness. Yet the term "suggestion," in one respect too wide, is in other respects too narrow, too special. It does not cover the characteristic features of soul-life in the state of dreams and of sleep. Dr. Bernheim overlooks this difference. In the preface to the second edition, he goes so far as to identify sleep and suggestion. He says: "Sleep itself [meaning thereby natural sleep] is only the effect of suggestion."

This is a palpable error.

* * *

What then is sleep?

Sleep is a reduction or total obliteration of consciousness. Natural sleep regularly follows in normal conditions upon fatigue. A person becomes tired after having exhausted a certain part of the potential energy stored up in his body, and especially his brain. Sleep, accordingly, is the state of restoration of lost energy during an apparent inactivity of our mind, accompanied with the more or less marked disappearance of consciousness.

We can artificially produce sleep by alcoholic drinks or by different kinds of drugs, such as morphine and opium. This is called *narcosis*. The narcotic state, especially if produced through alcoholic blood poisoning, seems to be the result of a fatigue, produced through an abnormal combustion that takes place in the brain after the introduction of such materials as possess a strong affinity for oxygen.

The extinction of consciousness can also be accomplished through a disturbance of the conditions of nervous activity. A deprivation of oxygen, or an inhibition of the blood circulation at once renders persons unconscious.

Hypnosis is distinguished from normal sleep by being provoked artificially and at the discretion of the hypnotizer. Further it differs from narcosis so far as the means employed are not of a material but of a psychic nature. Thus, terror can hypnotize. As experience teaches, men and animals can be rendered motionless through fright. Monotony likewise lulls asleep those who allow themselves to be swayed by its impression ; gentle swinging or rocking, the aspect of uniform views, prairies, deserts, large corn-fields, and continuous sounds, as the ceaseless murmuring of waves, cause sleep in persons who yield to their monotony. In the same manner unexpected, exceptionally violent emotions (sudden, startling sounds, glaring, dazzling light), or intense concentration upon a single idea may also cause unconsciousness.

When one all-absorbing idea that happens to be of a religious nature engrosses consciousness, the state of mind is, by ascetics and penitents, called ecstasy.

The concentration of ecstasy upon a single idea is akin to and yet, as a rule, vastly different from the concentration of attention: as can be observed for instance in a close student. The former is monotony or uniformity in general, the latter "monotely,"* or uniformity of aim. The former is an enforced inactivity, the latter an exceedingly strained activity. The worker in a state of attention considers systematically one and the same object in all its different relations, and does not tire in his absorption in the matter at

---

* From τέλος, end, purpose, aim.

hand; the ecstatic penitent absolutely drops all relations and distinctions, he loses himself in a passive
contemplation or intuition enforcing through monotony absolute cessation of all activity, be it in thought
or in deed.   But the consequence of both is in several
points similar.   Both are forgetful of all other things
and both will in time succumb to fatigue.

Besides these means of producing sleep, the Nancy
school added that of suggestion.   People are made to
believe that they will fall asleep, and lo! they actually
do fall asleep.

There is much truth in Prof. Bernheim's theory of
suggestion, but we must beware of its one-sidedness.
The suggestion of sleep will undoubtedly often make
people sleep if it produces the feeling of fatigue.   Without producing real fatigue, the effect of suggestion appears to me very doubtful.

The animal and the human soul are hierarchical
organizations of living substance.   Innumerable organisms, performing physiological and psychical functions, are coördinated and super-ordinated, so as to
form one system that finds its centralization in the
summit of the hierarchy which we call the central soul.

Living substance is, as we know, extremely unstable and the function of life consists of two processes
which are closely interwoven; the one is building up
structures containing potential energy, the other breaks
them down and spends their energy.   The former is
the alimentary or trophic, the latter the vital, or the
active, process of organized life.   Fatigue is expenditure of energy, involving a want of rest for restoration.

Sleep is the break-down of the top of our soul-or-
ganism; it is a temporary abolition of the central soul.
The hypnotizer causes this break-down, either by the

shock of sudden fatigue, applied to the very centre of consciousness or by leveling the central soul by cutting away the summit of the psychic hierarchy through monotony. He fills it with an idea or sensation so vast, so vague, so broad, that there is no mark of distinction for a centre, there is no occasion for a rise of the soul's activity in one spot. The hierarchy is destroyed at its top, the central soul disappears and all psychic life is dissolved in peripheral activities.

*   *   *

Hypnosis, that is, sleep induced through psychic agencies, betrays symptoms similar to those of natural sleep and of narcosis.

Charcot distinguishes three phases of hypnosis :

1. Somnambulism ;
2. Catalepsy ; and
3. Lethargy.

All three phases of hypnotism display striking resemblances to corresponding states of sleep. Lethargy corresponds to the deep, dreamless sleep, while somnambulism represents the light slumber of the dream, in which the normal consciousness is obliterated and makes room for the rise of a dream-consciousness. Between both states catalepsy represents an intermediate condition.

In the cataleptic state consciousness has become extinct as in lethargy, but certain functions of the nerves remain active. The limbs are pliant and plastic like wax ; they easily assume any position and persist in any motion imparted to them.

The acts of falling asleep and of awaking take place in a regular succession of a series of transitional states, which sometimes may be passed through swiftly, al-

NORMAL	ABNORMAL
Attention	Ecstasy
CONCENTRATION	OF MIND
Docility	Suggestibility
THE HEIGHT OF	SELF-CONSCIOUS-NESS
Wake-Dream-ing Visions	Hallucinations
MINIMUM OF	WAKING CON-SCIOUSNESS
Dreams Sleep-walking	Somnambulic State.
MINIMUM OF	PSYCHIC ACTIVITY *
Dreamless Sleep	Cataleptic State
MINIMUM OF	NERVOUS RE-ACTIONS †
Profound Sleep	Lethargic State
MINIMUM OF	NERVOUS ACTIVITY‡
Trance	Hypolethargic State
Danger	of Death

* Here insensibility overcomes the subject. "Psychic" is used in its usual and narrower sense. Psychic denotes that which is feeling. The highest kind of psychic activity is consciousness and self-consciousness; the lowest kind of feeling that we can reproduce in our recollection is the dim shadow of a dream. Any feeling that we suppose to exist below this point can be called "psychic" only if the word is used in its broader and original meaning of "pertaining to the activity of the soul." The feelings manifested beneath this point, are better called irritability of organized substance.

† Here torpor sets in; the greatest number of reflex motions cease to respond to their proper stimuli; only such as breathing and the beating of the heart continue.

‡ Here not only the beating of the heart and breath become low, but the trophic activity of the nerves appears arrested. Hence danger of death.

most suddenly indeed, but which cannot be skipped by leaps.

The state of consciousness is like the surface of the quicksilver column in a barometer or thermometer. May it ever so suddenly fall or rise, it has to pass through all the intermediate degrees.

Fatigue causes the diminution of our power of concentration. We no longer prohibit the rise of ideas that distract our mind and so we commence to dream awake. Our muscles cease to obey and our head sinks down, we commence napping. Light slumber with dreams yields to deep and ever deeper sleep until all consciousness vanishes. Our central soul has apparently disappeared. But the nervous activity of the peripheral spheres has not yet ceased entirely. Its psychical manifestations become lower ; but the more pronounced the sleeper's inactivity appears, the stronger seems to grow the trophic or nutritive faculty in sleep. There is no expenditure of energy and the time of rest is employed in building up the broken-down nerve structures, and in restoring the energy that was spent during the state of activity.

Thus the natural result of sleep is the gradual disappearance of fatigue. The more the loss of expended energy is restored, the readier will a sleeper be to awake. By and by some of his memories will be revived ; he will dream again, and at last, when the greatest part or all of the broken-down nerve-substance is rebuilt, the faintest noise or a weak ray of light will be liable to resuscitate him from his sleep into full consciousness.

The activity of the soul having remained for a certain time below the zero of consciousness seems to be pressed upward again through the restoration of its vitality from the basic periphery to the higher summit of central soul-life. This applies to normal sleep as well as to the hypnotic and even to narcotic states.

The parallelism between hypnotic and natural states can be explained most easily and quickly by the annexed diagram which is symbolically arranged as a psychometer—an indicator of the stages of soul-life. The scale shows the order of the phases of psychical activity as they rise from and above one another.

LETHARGY, CATALEPSY, SOMNAMBULISM.

The LETHARGIC and cataleptic states are of less interest in a psychological treatise than somnambulism. We shall only mention, that in lethargy, along with the disappearance of sensibility, there can be produced a peculiar muscular rigidity. The skin can be compressed into a fold, and perforated by a pin, without causing pain, and the subject may become stiff as a board. The cataleptic state is characterized by a plasticity combined with a certain rigidity. The subject is like a painter's manikin. He remains even in the most awkward positions in which he is placed, and continues mechanically to perform motions imparted to his limbs.

The difference between the cataleptic and the lethargic state is one of degree, not of kind.

The rigidity of the limbs seems to increase with the loss of sensibility. In the lethargic state the muscular contracture is more than double* that of the normal state. Dr. Luys designates this as a transformation of nerve-forces†, as if the nerve-energy, which is

---

* Dr. Luys says: "In a series of experiments practiced upon this subject (Esther), I found that one can produce a deflexion of the bent forearm in the normal state with a weight of 10 to 12 Kilogrammes. In the state of lethargic contracture, 20 to 25 Kilogrammes are necessary, and on this point the muscle is not deflected, but the whole body is bent."

† "On est amené à constater qu'il y a là véritablement un phénomène de transformation des forces nerveuses qui se manifeste dans des états nouveaux."

distributed according to the economy of the organism, as a rule, in an equal manner, were exclusively utilized to contract the muscles. The explanation of Luys becomes probable, in consideration of the fact, witnessed by other experimenters also, that, the deeper the sleep the more nerve-force will be at disposal. Thus sensibility may increase also. For instance, in the optic nerves, anæsthesia or insensibility can in lethargy be replaced by hyper-æsthesia, *i. e.*, an unusual and extraordinary sensibility. Dr. Luys calls it *une sorte de hyperesthésie compensatrice.*

Persons, who are left to themselves in a lethargic state, seem to awaken spontaneously, and complain of an intense sensation of cold. Some subjects have slept longer than twenty-four hours, and it may be assumed that there is danger in the experiment.

The state of ultra-lethargy shows symptoms of the most ominous kind. A total exhaustion prevails, respiration ceases, and the pulse becomes extremely low. All nervous activity, even the nutritive functions of regeneration, are more and more suspended.

The somnambulic state is by far the most interesting, because it displays psychical peculiarities that afford abundant parallels, not only to normal dreams and sleep-walking, but also to the narcosis of intoxication, and to insanity. Accordingly, the theoretical psychologist, not less than the practical philosopher, the moralist, the educator and the physician of the insane, will here find the clue to many obscure problems of soul-life, and at the same time valuable hints that can be turned to use in their professions.

THE REALITY OF DREAMS.

WE constantly observe the fact, that in dreams we see, hear, smell, taste, and feel as if we had to deal with substantial objects. Our visions are as real to us in a dream as the things we perceive in the waking state.

How does this happen?

Physiology teaches, that a sensory impression upon the skin irritates the nerve. Let us suppose, that a few rays of light have fallen through the cornea upon the retina. The irritation is thence transferred to a ganglion, and from the ganglion into the central ganglions of visual irritations, *viz.*, the anterior lobes of the Four Hills, or corpora quadragemina (*C. Q.*), and in the optic thalamus (*th*). Here, we suppose, is the place where the irritation is felt as a visual image; we now call it a *sensation*.

Accordingly a sensation is the sensed effect of some phenomenon upon a sentient being; it is an image, a sound, a touch, a smell, or a taste that has become conscious. If a visual sensation is called an image, we must bear in mind that it is not a passive or inactive imprint, but it is the sum of all the movements and of their memorial residua, made by the organ of sight in order to map out the outline, the form, and other qualities of an object.

It would be incorrect to say that the elements of a sensation are motions of the sensory nerves, for besides the motions there is another element in sensation which we call feeling. We call the whole process sensation and by feeling we understand that passive element which accompanies sensory movement, and which is known by experience to every sentient creature.

EXPLANATION OF THE DIAGRAM.

Visual impressions received on the retina travel along the optic nerves through a ganglion to the thalamus (*th*) as well as to the anterior lobes of the Four Hills (the *corpora quadragemina*) (*C. Q.*). The intermediate ganglion is called "the external *corpus geniculatum.*" (It appears in the adjoined diagram as the internal. In reality the external optic ganglions (*corpora geniculata exteriora*) lie outside of and almost directly above the internal. If they had been thus represented, the diagram could not with any distinctness show the connections of the nerves.) In the anterior lobes of the Four Hills or in the thalamus, perhaps in both, sensations of sight must be supposed to take place. Details as to the latter point are not yet known.

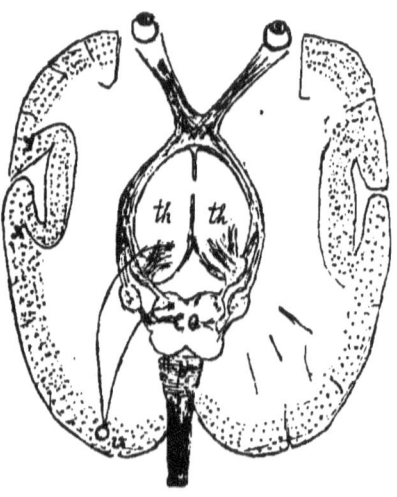

DIAGRAM SHOWING THE MECHANISM OF VISION.

That part of the thalamus, in which the fibres from the external optic ganglion immerge, is called "pulvinar."

The posterior lobes and the internal optic ganglions, which are connected with them, act, according to Wundt, as motory agents of the organ of sight. Gudden has pointed out that they have no connection with sensory functions.

According to Wernicke (*Lehrbuch der Gehirn-Krankheiten* I, p. 70, et seqq.), the band of white fibres which connects the Four Hills as well as the pulvinar of the thalamus with the cortical centre of vision must be considered as a continuation of the optic nerves. It is the path for the transmission of visual sensations to the cortical centre of vision. *v.*

x indicates the sensory, and *y* the motory centre of speech.

Although a sensation may be fully accompanied with consciousness, it is without value to us so long as it remains an isolated sensation. We do not know and cannot know what it means. It is without significance. In order to give significance to a sensation, it must become a perception.

Sensations are dispatched from the central ganglions to special localities of the brain. The visual sensation goes to the centre of vision in the cortex (v). Here exist a multitude of old visual memories, that have been registered there. The sensation that just arrived travels on the path of least resistance to the place where the cerebral cells through similar impressions are predisposed to receive it. The new sensation stimulates the old memories of a similar kind. Its form fits into the forms of certain old memories and thus it revives them, it excites them into new life. When the sensation has been received among the memories of former sensations, and when it is felt to be the same as a special kind of these former sensations, we call it a *perception*.

The distinction which we make between sensation and perception will be elucidated by an experiment made by Prof. Munk. A dog whose centre of vision was extirpated had lost all visual memories of the past. He had not, however, lost the power of sight ; his visual sensations were apparently uninjured, but they are new to him as though all his former experiences, gained through sight, had been wiped out.

Prof. Munk says :

. . . . '' After extirpating the cerebral cortex of a dog on both sides at the place A ' (Fig. p. 285) and when, on the third or fifth day after the lesion, the inflammatory reaction is past, the hearing, smell, taste, motion, sensation, etc., of the animal do not present any abnormity whatever ; only in the domain of the visual sense are we struck by a peculiar kind of perturbation. The dog will move about freely and easily whether in the house or in the garden, without ever running against an object, and if we heap up obstacles in his path, he will regularly avoid them, or if they cannot be avoided, he skillfully overcomes them, by creeping through, for example, beneath a foot-stool, by carefully leaping across the foot of his master, or over the body of any animal obstructing his way. But the sight of human beings, which formerly he used to greet with joy, now leaves him indifferent, and likewise indifferent the sight of the dogs with whom he was wont to play. The restless and rapid movements he executes, are prompted by hunger and thirst, and yet howsoever keenly the latter are felt, he no longer as of old hunts about the corners of the room, where he used to find his food, and if we place a plate of food and a dish of water in the middle of his path, he again and again turns away and takes no notice of them. Food, when held up before his eyes, leaves him unmoved, so long he does not smell it. A finger or lighted match, when brought near to his eyes, no longer causes him to blink. The sight of the whip, which formerly would regularly send him into a corner, does not frighten him in the least. He had been trained to give his paw, whenever a hand was moved past one of his eyes ; but now one may move one's hand in whatever way one will, but the paw does not stir until we call aloud "Paw!" And there are many more observations of the same kind.

There can be no doubt as regards their meaning. By the extirpation of a part of the brain, the dog has become "soul-blind," *seelenblind;* that is, he has lost the old visual representations he possessed,—the memory-images of his former visual perceptions, so that he no longer knows or recognizes what he sees. Yet the dog sees, the visual perceptions reach his consciousness, attain the state of sensation, and cause the rise of representations concerning the existence, form, and position of external objects, so that there are acquired anew other visual representations and still other memory-images of the visual perceptions.

One might maintain, that, as regards his visual sense, our act of intrusion has transported the dog back to the condition of earliest youth, to the condition of a puppy, whose eyes have just been opened. As the puppy must learn to see, that is learn to know what he sees, so also our dog again must *learn* to see, except that its ripe capacity of motion, the advanced development of the other senses, etc., may shorten the time of his apprenticeship. And an apprentice he appears in fact. Our restless, goggle-eyed dog, with neck stretched forward, and moving incessantly to and fro, when the fever is past, will stare at every object around him cautiously testing and prying into every nook ; and thus he acts both in lying

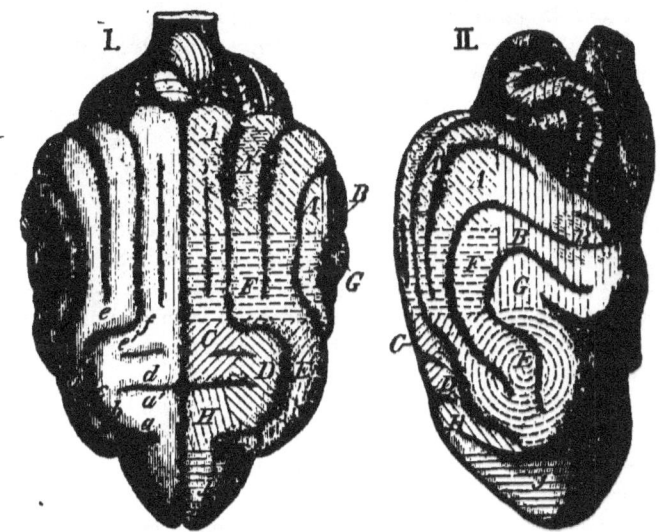

BRAIN OF A DOG, ACCORDING TO MUNK.

A, Centre of vision.
B, Centre of hearing.
C–I, Sensory Regions.
C, Hind legs.
D, Fore legs.

E, Head.
G, Ears.
F, Eye.
H, Neck.
I, Trunk.

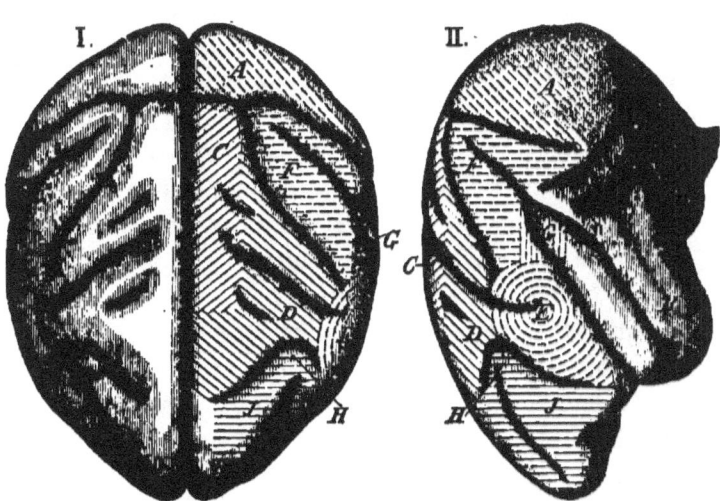

BRAIN OF A MONKEY, ACCORDING TO MUNK.
Description as in the preceding cut.

down and in moving, the latter of which he seems to prefer. And first of all he will have set himself right concerning the things that are most important to his existence. We need to duck his head only once or twice into the pail till his nose touches the water, and thereafter, when thirsty, he will always find the pail of his own accord. The same is true of the plate from which he feeds. And thereafter by slow degrees he learns to know human beings and surrounding objects,—first large, later smaller objects. The more he has learned anew to see, the less his unrest becomes, and the more moderate his curiosity. Things, concerning which he does not anew gather fresh experiences, remain unknown to him : He remains startled by the sight of a staircase when he is confronted for the first time by such an object, after the lapse of weeks just as after the lapse of a few days. He will shun the whip after a few days' acquaintance, or only after weeks, all according as sooner or later he has felt its effects upon his back. If nothing that is subject to experimental test has been withheld from his knowledge, our dog in some three or five weeks after the operation mentioned will have been restored in the region of the visual senses, and can no longer be distinguished from other healthy animals of his species."

The registration of many perceptions of the same or a similar kind cannot be better explained than by a comparison to composite photographs, although the simile must not be regarded as a sameness. One memory is laid upon the other as one photograph covers the other, on one and the same sensitive plate. The common features in all pictures appear stronger, while the particular and individual traits either disappear from weakness, or being contradictory to one another become blurred and are lost sight of.

This is the origin of generalizations that takes place in animal brains. All perceptions grow together into one general idea and if we speak not of a single, but of a whole, class of perceptions of the same kind, we call it a *conception.*

Conceptions attain their compactness and unity by

being named. The whole group of many perceptions is united into one idea by being comprehended under a common word symbol. Thus language becomes the mechanism of abstract thought and the speaking animal will be a rational being.

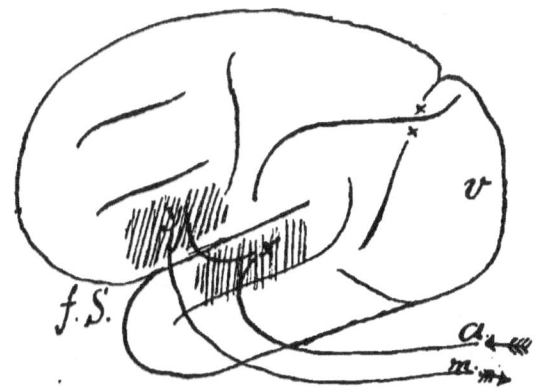

DIAGRAM SHOWING THE CORTICAL MECHANISM OF SPEECH ACCORDING TO WERNICKE.

x, Sensory centre of speech ; $a\,x$, Line of acoustic transmissions ;
y, Motory centre of speech ; $y\,m$, Line of motor impulses to the
$f\,s$, Fissure of Sylvius ;   muscles of speech.

We add that x is associated with other centres-of the cortex, for instance with v, the centre of vision. With the sound of the word dog, all the visual memories of dogs which we have seen are awakened.

Physiology has taught us that our perceptions do not take place in our sense-organs but in the hemispheres of the cortex ; they are the combined result of the present state of conscious sensations and of old memories with which they can be associated. This explains easily why hallucinations and dreams must naturally appear no less real than the sensations in the normal state of waking consciousness.

It is but in agreement with all the other facts of nervous activity that, if a sensory fibre is irritated in sleep (be it by an internal or an external cause), and if the irritation is transmitted to its cortical centre, it will produce there a re-awakening of former memories in the same way as a sensation does. This re-awakening is perceived as a present sensation, and not being contradicted by the testimony of any of the senses, it appears as real. Indeed it is (considered as a percept) as real as a sensed perception can be. It is produced by the same organs in the very same place.

We have been taught by experience to find the corresponding objects of our sense-percepts outside of ourselves. Thus they are projected to the place of their supposed origin. Is it not quite as natural that dream-visions should be treated in the same manner ? They are projected to a place where their origin under normal circumstances must be supposed to be.

An irritation at any place along the whole line of a sensory nerve-fibre produces a sensation which is imagined to take place at the origin of the nerve. To that point the irritation is always projected—even if that part of the nerve no longer exists. If a special nerve in the stump of a limb or along the line of the nerve up to its cortical centre is hurt, the pain appears as real and at the same time is as distinctly specified or localized in the missing limb as if the latter still existed. An irritation in the nerve of the big toe is felt in the big toe even after the amputation of the whole leg, as if foot and toe were still in connection with the body. In fact, the pain *is* real and so is the vision of a dream. But the cause of the pain is wrongly interpreted, and so is the cause of a vision.

Let us suppose, that the enemy of a certain country had been able to bribe the telegraph-operators, and the latter had sent to the capital a spurious dispatch about some great victory. Would not in this case the report of the victory, the joyous celebration and measures taken in consequence thereof, be just as real and positive, as if the victory were true? When the sensory organs in their totality or in part remain inactive, and the central organs are set into motion through internal incitements, the result will be precisely the same as if the incitement had come from the sense-organs.

Every recollection that a man has, is an image of former sensory impressions. Certainly, it is weak in comparison with the present sensation, it is faded and dim. Nevertheless it is a real image. And when the image of a memory is revived not by mere association through commissural fibres, but through the same sensory fibres, which in the waking state transmit sensations, it is but natural that the image will appear as vivid and as present as a real object.

Maury has sought by experiment to produce dreams of a certain kind.* He begged a friend to remain beside him in the evening, and as soon as he fell asleep to excite certain sensations in him, without telling what they were to be, and to wake him after giving him time to dream. On one occasion eau-de-cologne was given to him to smell; he dreamed that he was in a perfumer's shop, then the idea of the perfume aroused that of the East, and he dreamed that he was in Jean Farina's shop at Cairo. The nape of his neck was gently pinched, and he dreamed that a blister was applied to it, which recalled to mind the physician who had attended him in childhood. When a hot iron was brought near his face he dreamed of stokers. When he was asleep on another occasion, a person present ordered him in a loud voice to take a match, and he dreamed that of his own accord he went to find one.

* Maury, Sommeil et Rêves, p. 127.

It appears as a natural consequence of this view that we can dream such things only as we have experienced. Our dreams are confined to the materials stored up in our memory ; yet this material can be so rearranged, it can so appear in new combinations, that we may sometimes be astonished at the originality of our dreams.

The wealth of intellectual life also depends upon the store of memories hoarded up in the hemispheres. The sensations which we receive at present and which become conscious in our mind, derive all their significance from their associations with former sensations. When we see an old friend of ours and hear his words, it is not the present sensation alone that excites us. His appearance and the timbre of his voice are recognized as identical with old memories, and may thus arouse a storm of awakening recollections in all the corners of our brain. How many memories of olden times have been, as it were, asleep in our mind, but in a moment, when by some association they are connected with the present state of consciousness, they rise like spirits from the depths of unconscious existence,—like spirits and yet in such a vivid manner that the past seems to become present and the imaginary appears as real.

Gœthe describes the awakening of old memories most beautifully in his dedication of Faust. In his old age thinking of the beloved ones of his youth, Gœthe says :

> Again ye come, ye hovering Forms ! I find ye
> As early to my clouded sight ye shone !
> Shall I attempt this once to seize and bind ye ?
> Still o'er my heart is that illusion thrown ?
> Ye crowd more near ! Then be the reign assigned ye,
> And sway me from your misty shadowy zone !
> My bosom thrills, with youthful passion shaken,
> From magic airs that round your march awaken.

Of joyous days ye bring the blissful vision ;
  The dear, familiar phantoms rise again,
And, like an old and half-extinct tradition,
  First Love returns, with Friendship in his train.
Renewed is Pain : With mournful repetition
  Life tracks his devious labyrinthine chain,
And names the Good whose cheating fortune tore them
From happy hours, and left me to deplore them.

The present surroundings of the poet disappear, while the memories of the past rise in his mind and become reality again. Gœthe concludes the poem with these lines :

What I possess I see far distant lying,
And what I lost, grows real and undying.

These stanzas are not mere figures of speech. They depict the awakening of old memories as they rise in the mind of the poet gradually filling the actual present with their reality.

DREAMS AND HALLUCINATIONS.

In the artificial sleep of hypnosis the dream-images are as perfectly real as in natural sleep, and in post-hypnotic suggestions the images likewise appear equally real, to such a degree, that a subject is very seldom able to distinguish them from reality. It seems as if even a fever-patient could more easily discern between truth and delirium than the hypnotic subject.

Concerning the reality of suggested hallucinations Professor Forel says:

I have frequently made the following experiment. During the hypnosis I told Miss L., that on awaking she would find two violets in her lap, both of them natural and beautiful, and that she would give me the prettier flower; but I laid a real violet on her lap. On awaking she beheld two violets; one was brighter, more beautiful, she said, and therewith she gave me the corner of her white pocket-handkerchief, but kept for herself the real violet. I now asked, whether she believed that both violets were real or, whether one of my supposed presents, known to her from previous experience, were among them. She said, that the brighter violet was not real, because on the pocket-handkerchief it looked so flattened.

In this case the subject could distinguish to some extent the hallucination from reality. Forel continues:

I repeated the experiment with the suggestion of three real, equally dark violets, not at all flattened, but fragrant, with stem and palpable leaves; but I only gave her one genuine violet. This time Miss L—— was completely deceived, and was utterly unable to tell me, whether one of the violets or two, or indeed all three, were real or suggested ; all three, as she thought, were this time genuine ; at the same time she grasped with one hand the air, and held the genuine violet in the other.

Hence we learn, that when we suggest sensations for all the senses, the illusion is complete.

For example, I hand to another hypnotized lady a real knife, and tell her, that there are three. Though fully awake she is absolutely unable to distinguish the supposed three knives one from another, not even if she employs them for cutting, if she touches them, or drums on the window-pane. When other persons later derided her on the score of her illusion, she grew angry, and firmly maintained, that there had been three knives, that I only later had hidden two of them ; she had seen all three knives, felt, heard them, and would not yield on this point."

Bernheim once gave to a patient of his hospital in an hypnotic state the following suggestion :

" In six days, during the night between Thursday and Friday, you will see the nurse come to your bed and pour cold water over your feet." On the following Friday, she loudly complained that the nurse had poured cold water on her feet during the night. The nurse was called, but naturally denied it. He then said to the patient :—" It was a dream, for you know how I can make you dream ; the nurse has done nothing."—She emphatically declared, that it was no dream ; for she had clearly seen it, felt the water, and become wet."

Beaunis relates the following suggestion, which may at the same time serve as a natural explanation of second sight :

" On the afternoon of the 14th of July, 1884, I hypnotized Miss E., and gave her the following suggestion : " On the first of January, 1885, at 10 A. M., you will see me ; I shall come to wish you a Happy New Year; after that is done I shall immediately disappear."—I did not mention this suggestion to anybody. Miss E. lives in Nancy. I was myself in Paris on the first of January, 1885. That day, Miss E. told a friend, a physician and several other persons, that on the same day, at 10 A. M., when she was in her room, she heard somebody knocking at the door. She said : ' Come in !' and to her astonishment saw me enter, and heard me with a cheerful voice wish her a Happy New Year. I immediately went out ; she at once hastened to the window to see me leave the house, but did not see any further trace of me. To her surprise, she also noticed that I, at that season, had come to her in a summer dress. (The same clothes that I wore at the time of the suggestion.) Her attention was in vain called to the fact that I was in Paris on the first of January, and could not have come to her on that day. Nevertheless she maintained that she had seen and heard me, and she is still convinced of that, in spite of my declarations that it was impossible."

One of the strangest facts as to the reality of hallucinations is the observation of Messrs. Féré and Binet, that the laws of optics hold good for suggested images as well as for real ones. Thus they suggested to a hypnotized subject that she would see a portrait on a table. The subject when awakened saw the portrait, and when Dr. Féré placed a prism before her eye, she was greatly astonished to see the portrait double. Dr. Féré informs us that the subject had no education and could not possibly have any idea of the qualities of a prism. Other instruments had in the same way their natural effect. The mirror reflected the suggested image, while an opera glass brought it nearer, and if inverted, projected it to a greater distance. Yet upon close examination, it was found that the magnified picture only showed larger proportions, but revealed no finer details than could be seen with the naked eye.

There is, accordingly, a difference between dreams and hallucinations. Dreams are, as a rule, products of inward incitements solely. Suggestions, however, are associated with certain external sensations. If the suggestion is given that a subject will see a bird on her hand, she will see, before a mirror, the reflection of her hand and with the hand also the bird reflected. Whatever change the object suffers with which the suggestion is associated, the same will be observed in the suggestion.

There is a story about a man who when going to bed put slippers on his feet and armed his eyes with spectacles, because he used to dream that he stepped into glass-splinters which caused him much pain. He did not notice the glass in his dreams, because of his shortsightedness.

We are not informed of the success attending his remedy, but if the frequent occurrence of the odd dreams had to be attributed to an itching in his soles, if, as we suppose it did, the pain existed first and the dream consisted in an interpretation of the pain, the ingenuous method of protecting his feet with slippers, it is most probable, was of no avail.

It would be different if a hypnotic subject had been told that the surface of the lawn was strewn with glass. In that case he would feel innumerable wounds in his feet, if he walked over the lawn bare-footed, but he would be protected against the pain if he saw that a thick leather sole remained between himself and the grass.

The reality of dreams, which subjectively considered cannot be distinguished from the reality of sensations, is the source of many errors in philosophy, as well as religion. Schopenhauer * derives from this fact his idealism. The subjectivity of the world, (*i. e.*, the world in so far as it is my conception, the world as it appears to me) is mere appearance (*Erscheinung*) ; it "is in this respect akin to dream"; Schopenhauer says, "it belongs to the same class. The same cerebral function which in sleep produces an objective, vis-

* *Welt als Wille und Vorstellung*, Vol. II, p. 4.

ible, and palpable world must be no less active in the production of the objective world in the waking state."

Schopenhauer claims, and undoubtedly he is right, that there is a remarkable difference between dreams and the play of our imagination. Yet it is a difference of degree not of kind. The imagination of the savage is real and objective like the images of dreams, while the imagination of the philosopher and the inventor is more abstract. The poet—at least the modern poet —may often stand between both. Even such a man as Goethe, critical though his mind was, could not entirely free himself from visions. Yet we must remember that the account of his vision is reported in a book which he entitled *Wahrheit und—'Dichtung.'* It seems probable that memory-pictures appear real only when innervated by the nerve-fibres that rise from the central ganglions of the brain. These nerve-fibres being the usual channels for the transmission of sensory impressions, it seems natural that the effect of their innervation is the same whatever the cause of their irritation may be. The commissural fibres, however, that serve the purpose of association, cannot have a stronger effect in dream than in the waking state. The innervation by commissural fibres awakens conceptions and images only in such a way as they appear in our imagination.

The savage who is almost incapable of abstract thought, will naturally be limited to an imagination of palpable visions, while the thinker or the inventor, whose brain is filled with commissural fibres, can better dispense with the dreams of the waking consciousness and exercises his imagination chiefly in abstract thought.

The life-like corporeality of dreams appears natural

when we consider the physiology of sensations and the kinship that obtains between sensations and dreams. There is no evidence, as Schopenhauer imagines, for our possessing a special organ of dream which he supposes to have its seat in the great sympathetic plexus ; and still less can it prove that the soul is endowed with the power of producing an extended world out of itself. Schopenhauer says, " As the stomach and the bowels change everything which they digest into chyle, thus the brain reacts upon all irritations by producing tridimensional images, subject to the law of causality." We see no possibility that a being whose sensations were always tridimensional, should have four-dimensional visions in his dreams.

The different nerves, it is true, possess special energies, which make them react always in the same way as sensations of light in the optic nerve, or as sensations of sound in the auditory. Yet this special energy is not purely subjective; it is the inherited product of objective impression upon the subject. It is an acquisition of the experiences of former generations. The objective reality of sound waves cannot be doubted merely because the subjective sensation of sound is an inherited "special energy" of the nerve apparatus of hearing. If it were indeed merely subjective, we would be obliged to accept the consequences of the extremest Idealism, that the whole world is a dream and that there is no difference between dream and reality.

From our standpoint dreams find their natural explanation; and the arguments brought forth by Idealism fall to the ground.

In concluding this chapter we call attention to the fact that the life-like reality of dreams must be consid-

ered as the origin of man's belief in ghosts. In Homer
we find the following passage :

> " Hush'd by the murmurs of the rolling deep,
> Achilles sinks in the soft arms of sleep.
> When lo ! the shade, before his closing eyes,
> Of sad Patroclus rose. He saw him rise
> In the same robe he living wore. He came
> In stature, voice, and pleasing look the same.
> The form familiar hover'd o'er his head,
> " And sleeps Achilles (thus the phantom said:)
> Sleeps my Achilles, his Patroclus dead ?
> Living, I seem'd his dearest, tenderest care,
> But now forgot, I wander in the air,
> Let my pale corse the rites of burial know,
> And give me entrance in the realms below."
>   " And is it thou? (he answers) To my sight
> Once more return'st thou from the realms of night?
> O more than brother ! Think each office paid,
> Whate'er can rest a discontented shade ;
> But grant one last embrace, unhappy boy !
> Afford at least that melancholy joy."
>   He said, and with his longing arms essay'd
> In vain to grasp the visionary shade !
> Like a thin smoke he sees the spirit fly,
> And hears a feeble, lamentable cry.
> Confused he wakes ; amazement breaks the bands
> Of golden sleep, and starting from the sands,
> Pensive he muses with uplifted hands :
>   "'Tis true, 'tis certain ; man, though dead, retains
> Part of himself ; the immortal mind remains ;
> The form subsists without the body's aid,
> Aërial semblance, and an empty shade !
> This night my friend, so late in battle lost,
> Stood at my side, a pensive, plaintive ghost :
> Even now familiar, as in life, he came ;
> Alas ! how different ! yet how like the same ! "

Dreams were considered as caused by the hovering
phantoms of the departed spirit. This we know is an
error. Yet let us not forget, that there is a truth even
in this superstition. The vision of our dream is a
reality, although there is no ghost standing at our
bedside. The images of the deceased continue to live
in our brains, they continue to influence our actions and
prove themselves in many cases most powerful pres-
ences. Shakespeare depicts in several of his dramas,

how real are the ghastly shadows of innocent victims in the imagination of the murderer. And how often is the memory of a mother a veritable blessing to her child, better and more valuable than the inheritance of wealth and worldly goods.

———

SUGGESTION· AND SUGGESTIBILITY.

Two means can be employed for provoking hallucinations in a hypnotized subject; *first*, the panto-
mimic attitude, and *second*, the verbal suggestion.
We can impart to the subject a certain position that is
closely associated with the memories of the state of
mind to be provoked : a clenched fist, for example, is
associated with the notion of anger. But it is much
more convenient to produce hallucinations through the
words that are connected with this or that mental
state. A verbal suggestion attacks at its very centre
the idea that is to be aroused. Thus the alarm of
"Fire" suddenly raised in a crowded theatre, will
create the wildest confusion, and the most dangerous
excitement. The unexpected but impressive and
natural shout "a mouse" will cause terror among a
company of ladies. Some will at once jump upon
chairs, before the truth or untruth of the terrible an-
nouncement can be ascertained ; and if, perchance, a
slight rustling in the paper basket is heard, witnesses
will probably come forward who have seen a mouse in
bodily form, and who in perfect good faith would
maintain upon oath the truth of their statement. Such
witnesses, it cannot be doubted, have seen a mouse,—
the real image of a mouse,—but it was only a hallucination.

The suggestion given to hypnotic subjects, works

in a manner that is not much different. It is the awakening into a vivid reality of certain images in their mind. The suggestion, therefore, is upon the whole limited to the material found in the brain of the subject, and consists mainly in combinations of extant ideas. It may, accordingly, be perfectly possible to suggest to an untutored individual the conceit, that he or she is a great mathematician; but, by virtue of this, the subject will by no means really become such. To make this possible, one should indispensably have to suggest to him all the single propositions and lessons that are laboriously learned at school. Suggestion can only occasionally add something entirely new and even then it is a mere trifle in comparison to the memory-material which it employs.

A most remarkable phenomenon is the post-hypnotic suggestion, which, like an alarm-clock, is set to take place at a definitely fixed point of time. The French call it *suggestion à échéance.* The suggested idea remains unconscious, and at the time determined spontaneously appears with astonishing accuracy.

Dr. Frederick Björnstrom relates the following episode of an experiment performed by Drs. Liègeois and Liébault:

Liègeois has succeeded with a suggestion of one year's duration. On October 12, 1885, he hypnotized in Nancy a young man, Paul M., already before subjected to hypnotic experiments. At 10.10 A. M., he told him during the hypnosis that the following would happen to him on the same day one year later. "You will go to Monsieur Liébault in the morning. You will say, that your eyes have been well for a whole year, and that for that you are indebted to him and to M. Liègeois. You will express your gratitude to both, and you will ask permission to embrace both of them, which they will gladly allow you to do. After that, you will see a dog and a trained monkey enter the doctor's room, one carrying the other. They will play various pranks and make grimaces, and it will greatly amuse you. Five minutes later, you will behold the trainer with a tame bear. This man will be rejoiced to find his dog and his monkey, which he thought he had lost ; in order to please the company, he will let his bear dance also—an American grizzly bear, of large frame but very gentle— and you will not be afraid of him. Just as the man is about to leave, you will ask M. Liègeois to let you have ten centimes to give to the dog, who will beg, and you will give them to him yourself."

Liègeois and Liébault, at whose clinic the experiment was made, naturally kept the suggestion a secret, so that the somnambulist might not get any knowledge of it.

One year later—on the twelfth of October, 1886—Liègeois was at Liébault's before 9 A. M. At 9.39, as nobody had arrived, the former considered the experiment a failure and returned to his rooms. But at ten minutes past ten, the youth, Paul, who had better remembered the hour, came to Liébault and thanked him, but also asked for Liègeois. The latter arrived immediately, called by a messenger. Paul arose, rushed to meet him, and thanked him also. In the presence of fifteen or twenty reliable witnesses, the hallucinations now clearly developed themselves in Paul as they had been predicted one year before. Paul saw a monkey and a dog enter ; he was amused by their antics and grimaces. Then he saw the dog approach him, holding a box in his mouth. Paul borrowed ten centimes from Liègeois and made a gesture as if to give them to the dog. Then the trainer came and took away the monkey and the dog. But no bear appeared. Nor did Paul think of embracing any one. With the exception of these two details, the suggestion had thus been fulfilled. The experiment was ended. Paul complained of slight nervous weakness. In order to restore him, L. hypnotized him ; but took the opportunity during the hypnosis, to ask for information about what had just happened.— "Why did you just now see that monkey and that dog ?"—"Because you gave me suggestion of it on the twelfth of October, 1885."—"Have you not mistaken the hour ? I thought I said at 9 A. M."—"No, it is you who remember wrong. You did not hypnotize me on the sofa I am now occupying, but on the one opposite. Then you let me follow you out into the garden, and asked me to return in one year ; just then it was ten minutes past ten, and it was at that hour that I returned."—"But why did you not see any bear, and why did you not embrace Liébault and me?"—"Because you told me that only once, whereas you repeated the rest twice."

All those present were struck with the precision of his answers, and Liègeois had to acknowledge that Paul's memory was better than his own. Awakened after ten or fifteen minutes, Paul was entirely calm and had no remembrance of what he had just said during the hypnosis, nor did he remember what happened before the hypnosis in consequence of the suggestion of October 12, 1885.

Post-hypnotic suggestions can be given not only so as to produce harmless hallucinations, but also to prompt the subject to the execution of crimes. In Dr. Charcot's clinic a patient was ordered to kill an assistant physician and a slip of cardboard was suggested to her as a dagger. The woman promptly obeyed the command and after the performance of the deed gave a fictitious reason for committing the crime, never doubting that she had acted on her own account.

* *
*

Suggestibility is an attitude which can be observed in normal soul-life, not only now and then, as an exception but as an everyday occurrence. It is man's disposition to receive and accept ideas. The best "drummer" for a business-house is he that most surreptitiously insinuates to his customers the belief that they stand in need of his goods. The best teacher is he, that, in the simplest manner possible, imparts to his pupils the knowledge which he possesses. The best preacher or orator is he who most strongly impresses his moral injunctions upon his hearers. In short, suggestion is met with wherever ideas are transplanted from brain to brain.

Suggestibility in its highest stage of normal soul-life is called docility. It constitutes the receptiveness of the soul, the faculty of receiving, assimilating, and appropriating ideas. When this receptivity is joined to clear consciousness, the new ideas will not be received simply, they will be compared with the old ones, and either arranged among them in proper order or rejected as conflicting ideas. In such case they are relegated to the lumber-room of the brain among those concepts which we class as absurdities and errors. But when, in sleep or in hypnosis, the activity of consciousness has been reduced, and when the memorial chain of past experiences has been broken, receptivity also is lowered to an indiscriminate and uncritical reception of anything that offers itself; thus we see, that both in the dreamer and in the hypnotized subject any absurdity may find ready entrance. All control, all critique is lost, when a comparison with old experiences has been rendered impossible.

The three phases of hypnotism, in their variety and with their numerous transitional states, can be characterized in the following manner:

The suppression of consciousness (*i. e.*, the consciousness of the central soul) is common to all three states. In the hypnotic state we encounter an automatic-mechanical working of intelligence. If we say to an hypnotized subject, "you have murdered a man; look, there is blood still clinging to your hand," he proves unable to coördinate this idea with other notions. Therefore he accepts it without criticism as a fact. He not only believes the suggestion, but he even acts accordingly. He washes his hands, and devises plans with logically correct arguments, often showing great intelligence in the effort to escape the consequences of his imaginary transgression. With individuals, in whom religious feelings and ideas are strongly developed, there is evinced a readiness to take upon themselves the consequences, and to expiate the deed by submission to punishment. But in every case the somnambulic process of reflection is effected with the same regularity and with the same intelligence as if the individual were in full possession of his consciousness. Nay, the process is accomplished more swiftly, because the inhibition which in various ways occurs through the presence of consciousness falls out entirely. The ideas that once have been stimulated, be it fear or hope, or conceptions liable to rouse fear or hope, will work with mechanical exactness, according to the dynamical power which the brain-structures that represent these ideas in the subject, possess.

The somnambulic state is a process of intelligent automatism; it is a phenomenon of mental deliberation with the exclusion of a centralized consciousness.

DIAGRAM SHOWING THE MECHANISM OF SOMNAMBULISM.

EXPLANATION.

Centralized consciousness, which manifests itself in conscious sensation as well as conscious will, is excluded. A suggestion is given by certain sensory impressions ($S I$) which produce an *I*rritation of their sensory ganglion, taking place in the ascending line, *i. e.*, the *S*ensory *N*erve, at $I S N$. It is thence transmitted to the memories of the hemispheres. There it takes effect as a suggestion. (*Sugg.*) Not being properly coördinated with other ideas, it is readily accepted without any critique. The wary guardian, consciousness, being asleep, there is no inhibition to check the progress of innervation. As in the case of sleep-walking, the ideas awakened innervate directly and unhesitatingly the motor ganglions (the *I*nnervation taking place in the descending line, representing the *M*otory *N*erve, at $I M N$), which at once produce muscular motion ($M M$).

EXPLANATION OF THE DIAGRAM.

NORMAL	ABNORMAL
Attention	Ecstasy
CONCENTRATION	OF MIND
Docility	Suggestibility
THE HEIGHT OF	SELF CONSCIOUS-NESS
Wake-Dream-ing	
Visions	Hallucinations
MINIMUM OF	WAKING CON-SCIOUSNESS
Dreams	
Sleep-walking	Somnambulic State
MINIMUM OF	PSYCHIC ACTIVITY
Dreamless Sleep	Cataleptic State
MINIMUM OF	NERVOUS RE-ACTIONS
Profound Sleep	Lethargic State
MINIMUM OF	NERVOUS ACTIVITY
Trance	Hypolethargic State
Danger	of Death

In the highest state of consciousness, attention is concentrated upon one object or idea; all thought that is not subservient to, or may interfere with this purpose, is checked. In the corresponding abnormal state this concentration is so absolute that it produces a kind of intellectual trance, called "ecstasy." Ecstasy is a fixedness or torpor of consciousness, which, as we learned in a former discussion on the subject, will lead to a real trance,—it will hypnotize.

A very high state of consciousness, which however need not be so high as that of attention, is the attitude of mind called "docility" in which sensations or ideas are perceived and correctly recognized. It is a state of receptivity. In the corresponding abnormal state, the ideas received are not compared with the memories of former experiences; they are accepted in good faith without discrimination.

The senses of a man in a state of fatigue become gradually dulled. They cease to perform their work with accuracy. At the same time thoughts become visionary; they turn up promiscuously, often without any logical connection, but following a very loose association which gives to their appearance the shape of fortuitous incidents. Single ideas or memory-images may still remain awake. They can under circumstances afterwards be remembered as dreams. In profound sleep all thoughts and dreams cease, while through the increase of the trophic [nutritive] functions in the nervous substance, the expenditure of energy is restored and a new rise of consciousness is prepared.

In the cataleptic state, besides consciousness, the activity of intelligent mentality is also suppressed. The nerve-process is, in this case, limited to simple reflex-motions. Man becomes a living muscular manikin,

which submits to being placed, at the hypnotizer's discretion, in any position.

In the lethargic state a great part of the mechanism
of the nervous reflex-motions is, in addition, rendered
inactive; the reflex centres of breathing, the beating of
the heart, and the trophic functions alone remain at
work. In a hypo-lethargic state even these last signs
of nervous vitality become low and the similarity of
the state to swoons and trances warns the experi-
menter of the danger to which the subject here is exposed—a danger which naturally forbids further experiments.

THE CO-ORDINATION OF MENTAL ACTIVITY.

WE may compare the hemispheres of the brain to a globe upon the walls of which all the many memories of former experiences are inscribed. There are images of concrete objects and symbols of abstract thoughts, but all of them are alive; and every one of them is directly or indirectly in a two-fold telegraphic connection with the outside world: every one of them receives and sends out dispatches; there are afferent and efferent nerve-fibers. The globe is irregularly illuminated, and often quite dark; for the living memories may perform their work unconsciously; every one of them is living and feeling; but the feeling remains comparatively low, so long as it is isolated. It is in such case not communicated to the central soul. In order to be conscious, it must be centralized, it must be connected with the organ of concentration which coordinates all ideas and thus locates the one that at the moment comes to the front.

A special idea (a sensation, or the memory of a sensation, or an abstract thought) being for a moment centralized among all the other ideas of a brain, attains a prominence and a strength in feeling which is called consciousness. Consciousness is nothing but exalted feeling; it is, so to say, condensed and centralized feeling. In its highest state which it attains through coördination we may call it self-consciousness.

The idea that at the time flashes up in consciousness may be compared to the centre of vision. The object which we look at is clear and distinct; yet it is not the only image present in the field of vision. The other objects grow more and more indistinct the farther they are from the centre and many things will remain unnoticed, although they are pictured upon the retina of the eye. Similarly the ideas in our mind that are grouped around the present centre of consciousness grow dimmer and dimmer and disappear at last in the gloomy twilight of unconscious vagueness. The intermediate states we call subconscious. Yet even those nervous structures which at the time are unconscious, must not be considered as utterly void of feeling. So long as they are alive they can in an instant be centralized, and thus come to the front in consciousness.

The mechanism of concentration, it seems, is located in a special organ. The operation of this mechanism may be compared to an electric battery which provides the interior of the globe with light.

Then the process of conscious thought would be like the illumination now of this and now of that spot in the structures of the hemispheres. That spot which at a given moment receives the full effect of the incandescence forms, as it were, a centre of brightness. But the vicinity about it also appears luminous, indeed the whole globe is, although dimly in its distant parts, lit from that one spot; and the subumbra increases with the distance from the centre. Yet it may be that here and there, where direct associations obtain, spots that are relatively brighter, will appear amid the dusk of the remoter regions. It is not always the same spot which forms the centre of brightness. The centre is changing and may rapidly change. As a rule it is all but impossible for it to remain the same for any length of time, because the energy of that one idea would soon be exhausted. Every concentration upon one idea is tiresome, and we know that concentration is one of the means employed by hypnotizers to produce artificially that state of sleep which is called hypnosis.

We have reason to believe that this function, which we have compared to the operation of an electric battery, is performed by a special organ of the brain. All the facts hitherto ascertained by observation and experiment seem to establish the theory that the large ganglions of the nervous system, the Cerebellum, the Thalamus, and Corpus Striatum, are, each in its way, organs of coördination. The Corpus Striatum we suppose to be the organ of coördination for the hemispheres. It is a ganglion, the structure of which is analogous to the structure of the hemispheres, not only in so far as it has grown out from the walls of the hemispheres but also because its gray substance (especially in the *putamen*) forms a terminus similar to the cerebral cells in the cortex, with which latter, furthermore, it is in various directions intimately connected.

Some psychologists suppose that in the somnambulic state the hemispheres are completely asleep. Yet this is apparently inconsistent with the theory that somnambulism is an intelligent automatism—unless we give up all our present notions about the operations of the hemispheres as the organ of intelligence. It is true that some physiologists consider the hemispheres as the seat of consciousness, and thus it seems that, if consciousness is asleep, the hemispheres should remain inactive. But the experiments of somnabulism, no less than other and kindred facts of unconscious

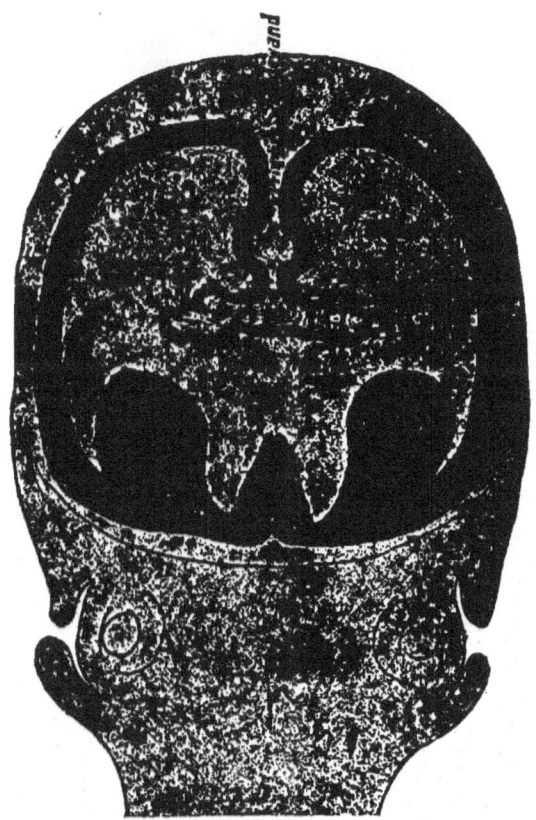

Diagram showing the growth of the Striped Body (*corpus striatum*) from the hemispheres. The drawing represents a human brain in a fœtus of two and a half months, according to Dr. Ludwig Edinger.*

soul-life, prove that acts of automatic intelligence are possible, and thus point to another solution. The piano virtuoso has the complex motions of his fingers not in his hand alone, but in his brain, in the storehouse of his memories. If he executes these movements unconsciously, the hemispheres of his brain do

---

* *Zwölf Vorlesungen über den Bau der nervösen Centralorgane.* By Dr. Ludwig Edinger. Leipzig: F. C. Vogel.

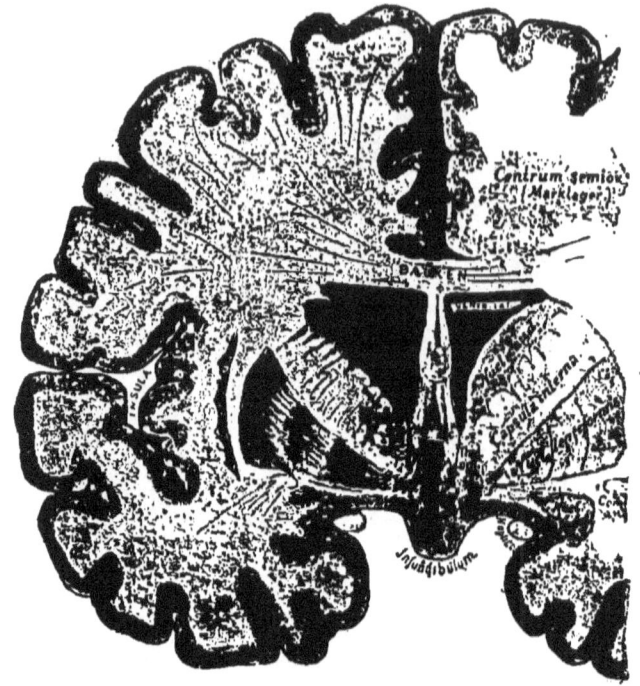

A VERTICAL SECTION OF THE HUMAN BRAIN :
Showing the situation and shape of the Striped Body in a full-
grown individual. It consists of two parts, the caudate body*
(*nucleus caudatus*) and the lentiform body (*nucleus lentiformis*),
divided by the internal capsule (*capsula interna*). The lentiform
body consists of three, sometimes of four, stripes, the outermost
one of which is called the shell (*putamen*).

not remain inactive. Yet the activity of the hemispheric structures is not always connected with the
consciousness of the central soul. After a longer process of conscious exercise, they have become sufficiently fixed as to work automatically. *Automatic*
means "self-moving," "self-acting," or "indepen-

*The caudate body has the appearance of a large comma, the biggest
part of which lies in front, with the tail turned backwards. The lentiform
body, in that part which lies opposite the claustrum appears as a lense.

MENTAL CO-ORDINATION.   313

dent." Acts of automatic intelligence are such as
are performed independently of the centralization of
consciousness.

Unconscious cerebration can no longer be considered as extraordinary. On the contrary, it is a distinctively normal feature of soul-life. All cerebration, it appears, remains unconscious, so long as it is not concentrated and properly coördinated, so long as it
remains unconnected with the centre of soul-life.

THE SUGGESTIBILITY OF CROWDS.

THE intelligence of an aggregate of people represents by no means the sum of their intellectual ability,
but only their average capacity; and if we could get
the exact measure of the understanding of crowds, we
would find that in most cases, it does not even reach
the average. One reason for this deficit in the intelligence of masses of people will be found in the fact
that nobody, if seriously taken to task, cares to identify
himself with the whole crowd. Thus many help to give
expression to an opinion for which they do not feel a
personal responsibility.

Great masses of people are for several reasons extremely suggestible. First, great masses are likely to
be composed of many men below the average of education, and people who are in possession of little knowledge are easily influenced by any opinion that is
offered with great self-assertion. A lack of knowledge
is always accompanied with a lack of critical power.
Thus, secondly, great masses are not likely to show
much opposition to new ideas, unless a new idea directly
and unequivocally threatens some one of their firmly
established prejudices. Thirdly, even where great
masses consist of learned men, of professors, doctors,
or other people who are generally accustomed to think
independently, it is not likely that the majority is thoroughly familiar with that line of thought in which the

speaker's argument moves. They may have been partly indifferent to the subject before he commences to speak ; or if they chanced to be interested in the subject, they had not as yet formed an opinion of their own. An opinion is now presented to them ready made, and the simplest thing in the world is to accept that opinion just as it is offered.

Schiller in one of his Xenions expresses a similar idea ; he says of some board of trustworthy men :

" Every one of them, singly considered, is sensible, doubtless,
But in a body they all act and behave like an ass."

Large bodies are always more likely to make mistakes than single individuals. Many cooks spoil the broth ; not only because there are too many opinions, but also because if they form one mass, all their knowledge together does not make up the sum but the mere average of their wisdom.

As a means of bringing the combined intelligence of a number of persons to bear on a special point, rules of discussion have been invented which make it possible for every opinion to be heard before the association as a whole decides upon the acceptance of a special idea or plan of action. And this is the only way any meeting can be conducted in which the critical power of the individual members is not to be suppressed, but the minds of all are allowed to co-operate.

There is a special art of suggesting ideas to large masses and we call it oratory. The art is very valuable ; and most valuable is it in a republic. It can be used for good and for evil purposes. An orator may suggest base ideas perhaps, with the same cleverness as noble aspirations.

We shall explain the different methods employed,

for two reasons: first, to shed light upon the art of
oratory as a method of suggestion for its practical use
in serving honest and legitimate purposes; and, secondly, to guard against the tricks of impostors, who
know how to gain the ears of an audience and lead
their hearers astray.

A suggester of ideas, i. e., an orator (be he teacher,
attorney at law, preacher, or drummer—the latter has
generally to be an orator to two ears only) must always
speak in the language of his audience; viz., his pupils,
his clients or the jury, his congregation, his customer.
He has—to use the expression of Experimental Psychology—to adapt himself to his "subject." It is
useless to talk Greek to an audience of farmers and it
would be absurd to speak in stilted phrases to a crowd
of sailors. The orator must place himself on the same
level with the intellect ot his subject; he must find a
common ground from which he may start; therefore it
is advisable to introduce first ideas that are familiar.
These first ideas being admitted as old friends, he can
gradually introduce others. Stump orators who flourish
and operate among the vulgar classes find it most convenient to gain entrance by flattery. An honest man
whose ideas will speak for themselves need not stoop
to such means. A drummer whose goods are worth-
less, commences to praise the taste of his subject and
adds that everybody of good taste gives the preference
to his merchandise. A wirepuller in a political cam-
paign extols the intelligence of the American nation
until everyone of his audience feels elated and proud
of being so intelligent. Then he ventures one step
further, declaring that no one but a fool can believe in
principles such as those of the other party.

The communication of ideas is an art. Yet the sub-

jects to whom ideas are communicated should understand the mechanical laws of that art. Knowledge is
a preservative, a protection against evil suggestions,
because it affords a means to discriminate between
good and evil.

An excellent example of the method how under most
difficult circumstances certain ideas can be suggested
to a mass of people that are not willing to accept them,
is the famous scene on the Roman forum in Shakespeare's *Julius Cæsar.* Brutus is demanded to give
an account of the murder of Cæsar, and he justifies
himself to the general satisfaction of his audience.
"Who is here so base," he asks, "that would be a
bondman?" Of course, every one wants to be a free
man, a Roman citizen. To the question "Why Brutus
rose against Cæsar?" he answers: "Not that I loved
Cæsar less, but that I loved Rome more. . . . As Cæsar
loved me, I weep for him; as he was fortunate, I re-
joice at it; as he was valiant, I honor him; but as he
was ambitious, I slew him."

Brutus's oratory is natural and it is grand in its
simplicity. Its fallacies are believed in by himself.
He committed a noble crime when he stabbed his
fatherly friend; and his speech is convincing because
it shows the nobility of his motive.

Mark Antony has a more difficult position; he is
looked upon as the defendant of an ambitious tyrant,
and it appears as specially objectionable to say anything derogatory of such honest men as Brutus, Cas-
sius, and the other conspirators. He therefore, declares it his intention only to perform the burial, which
none of the proud and free Roman citizens would deny
the meanest man in Italy. He praises the honesty of
Brutus and the conspirators, by whose kind permis-

sion he is allowed to speak. Here is the trick of his
oratory, and Mark Antony is fully conscious of it.
He does not start from a common ground ; but he
starts from an idea strongly supported by his hearers,
which is the very same idea that he is about to give
battle to, and to destroy. Mark Antony is open to the
charge of equivocation. He is not honest and square
like Brutus. He deliberately and cautiously instills
one drop of venom after another into the souls of
his "subjects" until they are full to the brim and cry
for vengeance on the murderers of Cæsar. It is true
he prosecutes criminals, and the criminals ought to be
punished. But his prosecution is not dictated by the
love of justice but by the desires of a robber to deprive his successful brother-robbers of their spoil.
After having stirred the free citizens, the proud Ro-
mans and masters of the world into a furious excitement, he says :

> " Now let it work. Mischief, thou art afoot,
> Take thou what course thou wilt.

This masterpiece of Shakespeare's dramatic genius
faithfully depicts the type of crowds. The conquerors
of the world had in Cæsar's time ceased to be free men,
they lacked the backbone of the contemporaries of
the Scipios, of a Cincinnatus, and of a Fabricius. They
allowed their sympathies and their votes to be turned
by any demagogue in whatever direction he pleased,
all the while imagining that they were free men, and
that they acted of their own accord. If the citizens
of a republic cease to be independent, if they are of a
suggestible nature, they are not worth their freedom,
and they will become the prey of unscrupulous wire-
pullers, or their government will soon cease to be a
republic.

There is a lesson for America! Our politicians even to-day use the basest flattery. They tell us that we are the greatest and most intelligent nation ; we are wise and independent. Having hypnotized their audience with such cheap and vile phrases, they instill their suggestions into the souls of the brave and the free with impunity.

Let every American citizen be wary. Whenever a stump-speaker begins to flatter, be on your guard, for it is almost certain that he is about to deceive you. Our people should do less shouting and more thinking in election campaigns, and every single individual who attends a meeting should feel himself responsible for the expressions of indignation or enthusiasm of the whole assembly.

A republic needs independent citizens, quick in comprehension, but slow in judgment, and tenacious in that which they have recognized as right. Every honest thinker must endeavor to counteract the suggestibility of the masses by the proper education of our people.

SENTIMENTAL ARGUMENTS.

One of the most effective methods of suggesting ideas, or plans, or propositions, is the employment of sentimental arguments. The results of a certain action is described, and the suggester (be he orator, or author, or politician, or demagogue, or preacher, or teacher, or a fantastic dreamer) dwells at length upon the details of his description, taking for granted that these must be the natural consequences of his scheme. He excites the sentiment, the sympathy, the hopes and fears of his " subject." And his subject whose critical powers are lulled asleep under the influence of some delightful dream, becomes an enthusiast for his scheme. Being anxious about the result, he forgets to examine whether the proposed scheme really leads to that result; and if he really makes an attempt to examine the validity and soundness of the plan, he has, in the meantime, become so infatuated and intoxicated with the beautiful vision depicted to him, that he has ceased to be impartial; he is no longer unbiased, and has become unable to examine the issue without a prejudice.

Sentimental arguments are dangerous, because they come to us like friends: they appear most innocent and harmless in sheep's clothes. The fleece of a sheep may hide a wolf or a real sheep, and which of the two would be the worse is sometimes difficult to tell. Ideas comparable to wolves make the man in whose brain they dwell, appear most dangerous, but those ideas that resemble the ovine species, I am inclined to regard as the greatest of all evils, for the heads in which they live and for society also.

A man whose opinion is founded upon sentimental arguments usually considers those fellow-mortals of his who are of a different opinion as rascals, for men who oppose this or that pet scheme must have, so it appears, a different sentiment. They seem to stand in opposition to the result of the scheme, and thus they must be, and are often declared to be, villainous rogues.

The fallacy of a sentimental logic is apparent to every clear-minded person, and we must accordingly be on our guard against it. Every man should make it a rule for his thinking, never to form an opinion on mere sentimental grounds.

The most insidious method of hypnotizers is what we may call "suggestion by insinuation." For instance : The hypnotizer introduces his ideas by hints rather than by a direct communication. He puts a question which implies the supposition of a certain fact. And the unwary 'subject,' while bothering about an answer, gets accustomed to the fictitious fact ; his imagination is set at work to depict certain details of the occurrence. Amid these details, worked out in his imagination, he forgets the main thing : namely, to investigate whether the fact is true itself. His account of the event is now based upon a fact. This fact is the memory of his imagination. The idea of such an event has become by insinuation a reality in his brain, he remembers it plainly, and being unable to discriminate between the memory of a real experience and a common report of an occurrence, he will, in best faith, take an oath upon the truth of his statement.

How dangerous suggestibility by insinuation is, our lawyers have ample opportunity to ascertain. From my own experience I know of a case where, in a trial for alleged murder, a Polish woman presented, upon the questions proposed, her evidence against the defendant in such a way that her whole testimony became a tangle of improbable and impossible statements. It was a dream, incidentally suggested in preliminary examinations by questions which intimated to her how it might have been. Her vivid imagination made her suppositions appear to her as real happenings, and in court she gave her evidence on oath.

There were questions like these.

"What time was it ? "

" It was half past four in the morning."

"Did you not yesterday say it was a quarter to seven?"

"No, I did not. I said it was exactly half past four."

In a preliminary examination she had said it was a quarter to seven, but in the meantime it had become manifest, that if it had been a quarter to seven all her testimony would be irrelevant.

"How do you know that it was exactly half past four?"

"When I saw this man, I looked at the clock to see what time it was, and the clock was exactly half past four."

It was not difficult to prove that from the window at which she was, it was impossible to see the spot where she fancied to have seen the man against whom she gave evidence. So it must have been a case of self-suggestion.

The worst insinuations are those devised from personal malice. Some villain, for instance, writes a letter to a man with the intention to throw suspicion upon his character. The tone of the letter is friendly; he writes with a pretense of kindness and frankness, yet among the sentences there are phrases like this : "You showed some anxiety about the matter and I am glad that I can be of service to you." Thus a statement is introduced together with an insinuation that the person addressed had some reason to be anxious about it. Whether this is true or not, the letter if read by others, or if perhaps later on presented in court, will throw suspicion upon the person addressed.

The method of insinuation is the more surreptitious, the more trivial the details are that are introduced in connection therewith. The details may be true, while the fact insinuated is perhaps absolutely false. If the truth of the details can be proved, the insinuation is most likely to find credit.

Villains who employ such means are liable to do great harm. There is one antidote only against the refined venom of such knaves, and that is independence of judgment. A man who is able to discriminate between true facts that are proved, and fictitious facts that are insinuated, will be able to see through the schemes of a trickster, and take his statements for exactly what they are—insinuations. They are not proved simply by being suggested, but require to be proved ; and if they can be proved to be false they are evidences of villany.

* * *

The lesson of this is that Psychology is a study too much neglected ; it is indispensable for every one who has to deal with people ; and who has not ? the physician, the clergyman, the employer of labor, the officer in the army, the professor, the merchant, the banker, almost every one has to deal with people, and, above all, the lawyer. Self-knowledge is not sufficient to make us free, it must be self-knowledge *and* the knowledge of other people ; it must be self-knowledge in the broadest sense, knowledge of the soul, of the motives that work upon, and can be employed to affect, man's sentiments. It is only knowledge that can make us free ; and knowledge will make us free. And because it makes us free, knowledge, and chiefly so psychological knowledge, is power.

THE SIGNIFICANCE OF HYPNOTISM.

THE entire mass of psychological data furnished by modern researches, and especially by hypnotic investigations, may be divided into three groups:

(1) The normal phenomena of soul-life, which can be observed in every-day life;

(2) Abnormal phenomena of soul-life, which can be reproduced under special conditions and thus admit of verification by experiment; and

(3) Abnormal phenomena of soul-life observed by certain individuals who are supposed, or claim, to be in possession of special gifts (such as second sight and telepathy).

The data of the first two classes alone can be considered as indubitable facts; those of the third class rest on a very weak authority, considering the innumerable illusions that can take place in individuals given to the belief in the miraculous.

The psychological data of indubitable character, i. e., the phenomena of every one's normal soul-life, and those experiments of psychic research which admit of verification by experiment, we have learned, exhibit a strong tendency to corroborate the monistic view of psychological phenomena. Dualism indeed is limited to the third class as a store-house for its weapons of attack, and psychologists of a dualistic bias have therefore taken pains to gather all attainable reports about telepathy and second sight as experienced by certain individuals of a specially spiritual nature. If dualists wish to convince the world of the truth of dualism, they must derive their proofs from the data of the two first classes, which are generally acknowledged as facts by science. These, however, seem to exclude a dualistic interpretation ; so strong is their evidence in favor of the inseparable unity of psychological and physiological phenomena !

Ideas are no disembodied ghosts created from supersensible or supernatural elements, they are real structures that live in our brain, possessed of a definite form and produced in the nervous substance through sensory impressions. In calling them ideas, we do not, however, as a rule refer to their physiological objectivity, which forms their bodily reality, but to their spiritual subjectivity : we refer to that indescribable phenomenon which every living being experiences when he feels and thinks. The whole empire of subjective experiences is called the *ideal*, while the processes of motion that take place in the world of objective existences, are called the *real.**

Dualism looks upon the real and the ideal as two distinct worlds which exist independently of each other. In the human body, it is conceded, they are united into a wonderful harmony. The ideal inhabits the real as a house ; the spirit animates the body for some time, but it may leave the body, as a prisoner leaves his prison, thenceforth to live as a pure spirit.

Monism looks upon the ideal and the real as two

---

* The word *real* may be used in a limited and in a more extended sense. In the former sense, when strictly confined to bodily objectivity, it excludes the ideal ; in the latter sense, when signifying all facts that can become objects of experience, it includes the ideal also. Thoughts and feelings are ideal ; and yet they are realities.

•

inseparable aspects of one and the same fact, they are two abstractions made for different purposes and abstracted from one and the same indivisible object. Monism considers the world as a living actuality, which naturally in an evolution from lower to higher forms evolves ever higher souls, thus raising the subjectivity of atomic life to the intellectuality of a human being.

When we speak of the ideal in man, (*ideal* is here used in the philosophical sense of the purely subjective,) we must bear in mind that the ideal and the real do not in actual life exclude one another. Feelings pure and simple without their proper physiological conditions do not exist ; thoughts without the thinking brain-structures in which they take place, are impossible. We might just as well speak of movement without a moving body. Therefore the ideal by itself, the thinking subject, abstract and absolute, is an absurdity. It does not exist. The thinking subject is always at the same time a bodily object of actual and material reality. Not only the thinking subject upon the whole, but every detail of the thinking subject's feelings, his sensations and thoughts,—every irritation felt, every idea thought,—every emotion taking place in the empire of the ideal, mean at the same time a special modification of nervous substance in the empire of the real. The parallelism between the real and the ideal is, so far as science has investigated, uncontradicted and perfect.

The ideal therefore is a special kind of reality ; and indeed it is the most important part, the most real and most actual element of reality. The ideal in its highest development, being the empire of feeling and thinking subjectivity, is the product of organized life. The non-organized elements can be said to contain the germs only, the mere potentiality to bring forth the empire of the ideal. In the sensations and thoughts of sentient creatures the different objects of reality are depicted ; they are mirrored therein as images, as ideas. The literal translation of the Greek word idea ($\varepsilon \tilde{\imath} \delta o \varsigma$) is image. The ideal is the realm of representations ; and the objects represented in the subjectivity of a sentient being, are the objective realities of its own body and of the things of the surrounding world.

The existence of the ideal gives meaning and purpose to the world of bodily realities. Sentient beings can make the objects around them subservient to their needs and comforts; and man, the first born son of nature, will have dominion over the earth in proportion as his ideas are correct images of things and of the relations among things.

The monistic view is thus corroborated through those results of psychology which can be considered as indubitable facts. An idea, being a bodily structure of nervous substance and being situated in the centre of the organism, viz., the brain, must be of paramount importance, even if we consider its activity as a mere physiological process. The brain is the capital of the body ; it is the seat of the government, whence orders are issued to, and obeyed in, all the various provinces of the different organs and limbs.

Facts being as they are, can we wonder that ideas of fear, of worry and anxiety produce pathological conditions in the body ?

It is well known that sudden or extraordinary terror may kill a person. Goethe describes in his *Erlking* how a child dies from fright in the arms of his father riding on horseback through a stormy

•

night. The boy imagines that the Erlking is attempting to snatch him away and thus he becomes a prey of the phantoms of his own imagination.

Similarly Gottfried Bürger describes the death of Leonore with masterly accuracy, as if he had studied in hospitals the deliriums of fever-patients. Leonore expects her betrothed home from the war, but she does not find him among those who return. In despair she beats her bosom and tears her hair, but in the hush of night she hears him knock at the door, she sees him enter, his horse is waiting and he takes her along over dale and hill, over rivers and mountains far away to be married—in the grave.

There is an old story about a court-fool (which may briefly be told without vouching for its truth). He was condemned to death by the sword. The duke, however, had pardoned him, but had given the order not to let him know. The fool's punishment should be, to go through all the terrors of execution. The executioner, then, should strike the blow not with a sword but with a sausage. When the fool, so the story goes, received the harmless stroke, he fell, dead, to the ground. He died from the fear of death.*

The physiological reality of ideas renders it necessary that the ideas of the central soul influence the unconscious activity of the peripheral soul. This is especially noticeable in certain functions, for instance in the movements of the digestive organs, which are not under the control of the will, yet are strongly and almost immediately influenced by certain states of mind in one or another way. Unusual wrath poisons the milk of a mother ; and great excitement so alters the

---

* The story is told in many different versions.

secretion of saliva that the bites of infuriated dogs or of other animals become extremely dangerous.

Almost all hypnotists report cases in which burns and blisters have been produced by means of suggestion. A certain part of the skin is touched with a harmless instrument or with the finger, and after a while an inflammation appears at the very same spot, reproducing the exact form of the contact. This proves that the trophic functions of the muscles and the skin, those functions that build the wasted tissues up again, and nourish them, stand in close connection with the nerves and depend upon their activity. We do not believe that the burn produced through suggestion is a real burn ; it is the perturbation of the trophic function of the nerves, caused through the idea that a reaction is necessary against an imaginary wound. Thereby redness is produced which has the appearance of inflammation.

The blood perspiration attributed to certain saints and the appearance of the holy stigmata on their bodies must likewise be explained as the results of suggestion : they are produced through the auto-suggestion of prayer and a strong concentration of the mind.

While terror, cares, and worry will have injurious effects, joyous and gay ideas may in the same way act as a medicine for good. The firm confidence of a patient in his physician, the strong hope of convalescence will under otherwise favorable conditions do a great deal in curing, and healing, and soothing. The mental disposition of a patient is of great and incalculable importance in the cure.

Man's imagination is no empty nothing ; nor is it a mere psychical and purely subjective illusion. Every single act of imagination is a real physiological process which can be made available to do a certain amount of work. There is some truth in the methods of faith-cure, yet we should be wary not to overrate the power of imagination. Ideas as physiological processes and in their physiological effects have a special and limited province; and we cannot expect that they should cure a cancer or set aright a broken leg.

Considering the great effects often produced under the spell of a properly directed imagination, several physicians in France, Switzerland, and in other coun-tries have proposed to use hypnotism and suggestion as curative methods for all kinds of diseases. They have been successful to some extent, although the ex-travagant hopes that hypnotism might be a panacea were by no means fulfilled. On the contrary, all the results hitherto obtained, it seems, are such as might also have been produced through the bringing on of natural sleep.

Extravagant reports about cures effected by such hypnotizers are not beyond the suspicion of self-de-lusion, and cannot be accepted without reserve. Most of our hypnotizers—among them even some of great name—suffer from the same disease as their patients; namely, from illusions. Many cures are effected on individuals who have an imaginary disease, which dis-appears under the influence of a counter-imagination. In such a case the disease as well as the cure is an hal-lucination of the patient in which his physician kindly shares.

There are other cases in which the patient suffers from a real disease, which seems to be overcome under the influence of hopeful and elevating hallucinations. The cure appears to be perfect for a time; yet there comes a relapse after a while against which no faith-cure or hypnotism will avail.

Natural sleep is undoubtedly one of the strongest and best curatives. Perhaps it is the very best medicine that can be employed. Hypnotism, it seems to me, should be resorted to by the physician only under such circumstances where natural sleep cannot be had.

The wonderful effects of natural sleep will find their explanation, if we bear in mind that in the state of rest together with the obliteration of consciousness the trophic functions of the nerves seem to increase in proportion as other activities cease. Sleep, therefore, is the state of re-generation, it is the restoration of the vitality expended during the period of activity. It is a process of hoarding up again in the tissues of the organism that potential energy which affords new life and fresh vigor to think and to act.

THE DANGERS OF HYPNOTISM.

In spite of the many astonishing results that have been obtained through hypnotic treatment, we nevertheless must beware of anticipating more than it really can be expected to achieve. It is perhaps natural that the idea of rest should act soothingly upon the nerves, but, still, we must not imagine that the illusion that we hear well will cure deafness, or the illusion that we possess excellent eyesight will remove the blindness of a cataract. A correct view of the nature of ideas will guard us from erroneous expectations of this kind, and physicians therefore will have to limit the application of psychical means (and especially of hypnotism and suggestion) to such physiological conditions that can directly or at least indirectly be reached and influenced by psychical methods. Psychical cures, accordingly, must be restricted in the main to nervous diseases.

We consider it as our duty on this occasion to caution against the abuse of hypnotism that is frequently practiced by half-scientific people and sometimes even by prominent physicians. Hypnotism, as a means of cure, should be employed as little as possible, and in such cases only where natural sleep cannot be produced ; and even then it must be employed with discretion.

Dr. Luys reports several cases in which patients hopelessly ill have been restored to health by the application of hypnotism. He speaks, for example, of a man who had been debilitated by insomnia. His digestion was impaired, his walk tottering, the nervous system prostrated, and his entire constitution was undermined. He had been given up by several physicians. Dr. Luys treated him several times in vain, but finally with success. The patient improved perceptibly, and soon was perfectly cured. To cure nervous diseases that are caused by insomnia, in fact, seems to me the main purpose to which hypnosis can profitably be applied.

There are also reported cases of inveterate vices and evil habits, (for instance dipsomania,) that are said to have been completely cured by means of hypnotic suggestion. And the applicability of hypnosis in certain desperate cases, when all other expedients have failed, may under exceptional conditions likewise be justified.

The rotating mirror invented by Dr. Luys seems to be the best and least injurious means of producing artificial sleep. It is an instrument with two wings not unlike the automatic fly-fan, only much smaller and studded with small glittering pieces of glass. The wings are fixed upon a pin, which when wound up sets them into a rapid revolving motion. The patient being comfortably seated in an arm-chair, is requested to stare at the mirror. The giddily rapid, monotonous rotation by and by tires the eyes and produces a feeling of fatigue, so that the patient is soon very likely to fall asleep.

It is more than doubtful whether the anæsthesia of the cataleptic condition should be employed in operations. Narcotics have hitherto proved by far more reliable and less injurious.

It does not seem advisable to employ the cataleptic state in cases of childbirth, as Dr. Luys and other French physicians have done. To be prepared for the occasion, it is necessary that many weeks previous to her confinement, the woman be hypnotized daily. If this were not done, the hypnosis would most likely not succeed at the critical moment. But this exemption from the throes of a few painful hours are bought at an exorbitant price! We have to consider that henceforth throughout the whole life the woman will remain predisposed to hypnotic states. And still worse : a fatal germ of the same predisposition is most probably implanted in the infant born.

A predisposition to hypnotism, at all events, must be regarded as one of the most dangerous kinds of disease. It is an extremely serious misfortune. A predisposition to hypnosis is a diseased, abnormal state of the nerves. Individuals who either by nature or through artificial methods possess a predisposition of this kind, are but to a limited degree their own masters. Not only the hypnotizer himself has an absolute control over them, but every stranger, by skillful manipulation, may influence their soul-life, and can render them serviceable to his private ends.

It is maintained by some hypnotizers that encroachments of this sort can be prevented, by imparting to the subject the suggestion, that he should not submit to be hypnotized by any one but his own hypnotizer or physician. But, as a matter of fact, every suggestion can be counteracted or modified by another suggestion. An impostor might easily introduce himself as the physician's deputy, and there are a hundred other means at his disposal. Once having been admitted into the confidence of the subject, he will quickly usurp the entire control over his or her soul.

We certainly should regard it as a national calamity if the majority of a people had acquired a predisposition to hypnotism. The independence of individuals would be destroyed, for that trait consists in the capacity to resist obnoxious suggestions. It is generally admitted by all psychologists that hypnotism affords an easy means for criminals safely to commit their crimes through unconscious middle-men as instruments of the deed. The danger of hypnotism is increased by the possibility of "timing" the execution of a post-hypnotic suggestion. Forel says upon the subject:

"The enormous importance of suggestion at appointed time or 'à échéance' is manifest. We are able for a definite period of time to predetermine the thoughts and resolutions of hypnotized subjects when the hypnotizer himself is no longer present; in addition one can give to the suggestion the appearance of a free decision of the will. One is further able to suggest to the hypnotized subject the belief that the impulse did not come from the hypnotizer. Nay, with highly suggestible people we are even able successfully to suggest the total amnesia of the hypnotization : 'You have never been hypnotized,' we may say ; 'if you are asked, swear before God, that in all your life you have never once been hypnotized ; I myself have never hypnotized you.'

"I am perfectly aware, that in this consists, perhaps, the most appalling danger of hypnotism in the administration of criminal justice."

The dangers to which hypnotic subjects are exposed in the respect that they may become instruments of crime in the hands of unscrupulous criminals, great though they may be, are trifles compared to the dangers rising from their own auto-suggestions. Hypnotic subjects cease to be able to control their own ideas. Hallucinations may come to them at any moment and lead them to crimes or to follies of all kinds.

Dr. Luys, who, if he is partial, is rather prejudiced in favor of hypnotism, says:

" Hypnotized subjects, by the very fact that they are under the influence of a quite special mental state, or even subjects that are neuropathic by nature, are apt to present this strange phenomenon, that through the automatic action of the cells of their brains they will produce truly autogenetic suggestions, just as insane persons are seen to create fixed and spontaneous ideas. At one time they will tell you, that they have met with some extraordinary experience, have received certain strange proposals, are acquainted with persons of high social standing ; or else, they will accuse some acquaintance of their circle of having spread abroad slander, of robbing, or of seeking to wrong them. Still, all these denunciations are made with a mien of absolute sincerity, and if one did not know such subjects from their peculiar psychological point of view, one might really be tempted to lend faith to their statements. It is precisely mental habits of this kind that frequently cause the society of hypnotic subjects to prove so irksome and well-nigh unendurable in the wards of public hospitals.

" This likewise constitutes a point of contact of hypnotism with insanity, because these cases of suggestions very frequently are produced either by sensorial illusions or by persistent hallucinations, and from this point of view hypnotic subjects present the exact state of mind of persons laboring under the hallucination of persecution."

The dangers arising from auto-suggestion and self-hypnotization are confirmed almost by every one who is familiar with the subject. Professor Lombroso,* of Turin, reports among many other instances the following case.

"An artillery officer, who was hypnotized at a public séance, afterwards became almost insane. From time to time he had attacks of spontaneous hypnotism at the sight of any shining object. He would follow a carriage lamp in the street, as though

---

* See Frederik Björnström, *Hypnotism*, Humboldt Library, No. 113, p. 123.

spell-bound. One evening, if his fellow-officer had not saved him, he would have been crushed to death by going directly towards an approaching carriage. A violent hysterical crisis followed this and the man had to take to his bed."

The whole purpose of a liberal education consists in the freedom, independence, and self-reliance of the individual. Accordingly, we can observe that in coun-tries where men and women are raised with a love of liberty and independence there are comparatively few symptoms of hypnotism. In countries in which children are brought up to become mere instruments in the hands of priests, the inclination to hypnosis is com-paratively strong. Let us not increase the natural tendency of weak characters to allow themselves to be guided blindly; and therefore let us be careful to avoid the dangers of hypnotism.

The growing generation should learn, neither to shut out new ideas nor indiscriminately to accept them, but to receive them with critique and to arrange them in proper order in the storehouse of general knowledge. This is necessary above all in a repub-lic in which every citizen is called upon to take part in the government of the state, in the election of the authorities, and in the framing of the laws.

PLEASURE AND PAIN.

KANT says somewhere, "Pleasure is the feeling of the furtherance, pain of the hinderance of life," and expresses in this sentence an opinion that has been in vogue among philosophers since time immemorial. But it is strange that neither Kant nor any other thinker has greatly troubled himself with a careful investigation of facts. The statement seemed so obvious, so direct and convincing, that it received almost universal admittance in philosophy; and was even employed as a corner-stone for ethics by Epicurus, Bentham, Spencer, Hœffding, and others.

Alexander Bain in his excellent work "Mind and Body," quotes Kant's definition and develops his own as follows (p. 59):

"States of Pleasure are connected with an increase, states of Pain with an abatement, of some or all of the vital functions."

Bain adds:

"There are, however, a few startling exceptions. For example:—Cold may be painful and yet wholesome, as in the cold bath, and under the keen bracing air. But this exception, on closer view, confirms the general rule, while rendering its application more definite. Cold undoubtedly depresses, for a time, one very sensitive organ, the skin, perhaps also the digestive organs; while, in moderate degree (that is, the degree constituting wholesomeness) it exalts, through the capillary circulation, the lungs, the heart, the muscles, and the nerves; and the contrast teaches us that as far as *immediate pleasure* is concerned, we lose more by depressing the functions of the skin and the stomach, than we gain by increasing the power of the heart, the lungs, the muscles, or even the nerves themselves.

" Another very remarkable exception is the painlessness of many diseases, together with the occasional absence of all pain, and even the presence of great comfort, in the sick bed and in the final decay of life. . . . .

" The connexion of pleasure with vitality, and of pain with feebleness or loss of function, does not apply to all organs alike ; some are comparatively insensitive, their degeneracy and decay seem unaccompanied with feeling ; while in others the smallest functional derangement is productive of pain. Muscular weakness does not give pain, unless we are compelled to efforts beyond our strength ; also the nervous system may be enfeebled as regards thinking power without producing discomfort, provided we are allowed perfect repose. . . . .

" Intellectual feebleness, decay of memory, and incapability of thought, are not painful in themselves. . . . .

" We often see patients in the last stage of consumption, still entertaining the most sanguine prospects of recovery ; a proof that, instead of being mentally depressed, they are in the opposite or joyous condition. . . . ."

There is no sufficient explanation for all these exceptions to Bain's law identifying pleasure with a growth and pain with a decay of the vital functions. Bain says that sometimes an acute smart will temporarily raise the energies ; it will have the effect of a stimulus. But this explains only a few instances, such as a cold bath or the influence. of keen, bracing air, and these instances may be used as examples to show that the cold bath in itself can by repeated indulgence and through its wholesome effects become a pleasure. First it becomes a want and then the satisfaction of this want itself, even without taking into consideration the wholesome after-effect, is felt as pleasurable. First it becomes a want and then the satisfaction of this want itself, even without taking into consideration the wholesome after-effect, is felt as pleasurable.

Mr. Bain does not, and I think he cannot, from his

standpoint, remove the innumerable difficulties arising from exceptions irreconcilable with his law.   The
degeneration of several functions, the decrease of muscular and nervous activity, and even the dissolution
by consumption are by no means always painful processes, and yet if anything they are decay, they are
abatement.   Certainly, the law is wrong, it is not derived from facts.   It is an a-priori statement to which
facts have to be fashioned in order to agree.

Pain is apparently due to a disturbance.   We have
for instance a hollow tooth ; the nerve is exposed and
the slightest irritation causes most violent pain.   There
is neither growth nor decay in the nerve, yet there is
suffering.   The decay of the osseous parts took place
without pain.   Now we go to the dentist and, supposing
that he is unable to save the nerve, he at once removes
all pain by the aid of a drop of cocaine, or carbolic
acid, or any other drug which causes the nerve to die.
Here is decay without pain.   When infants are teeth-
ing, there is growth combined with pain.   Whatever
the tooth may feel we do not know ; yet its growth
causes disturbances in the surrounding parts which
are perceived as pains.   It is a well-known fact that
in children growth is often accompanied with pain
which is felt in arms, legs, or other limbs.*

---

* Copulation, which is supposed to be a pleasure, is not growth, but a combination merely.   Modern researches by Weismann and others have shown
that it is a natural want rising from the insufficiency of an individual to propagate itself.   Its physiological condition seems to be the divided existence
of the reproductive germ, so that each sex posesses but one part.   The continuance and regeneration of life depend upon the activity of the germ. Thus
the restoration of the germ becomes a necessity and want of self-preservation.
The natural desire for fecundation (not the other sexual instincts, which
through heredity became strongly connected therewith) is an expression of
the yearning for immortal life.

If growth were a pleasure, then child-bearing in itself, apart from its
results should be the height of earthly enjoyment which perhaps should be

In a state of decay the vital functions are abating. The lower the vital functions become, the less pleasurable excitement, but at the same time the less pain will be possible. Decay far from being identical with pain is the annihilation of the possibility of pain.

Pain is caused through perturbation. The more violent perturbations are, the stronger the pain will be. There are wholesome and disastrous disturbances. Among the wholesome disturbances we count not only those which arise from growth, but also such as arouse our energies and indirectly promote our general welfare, disastrous are such as lead directly or indirectly to destruction.

Decay is often accompanied with great suffering, but the suffering is apparently not due to the decay itself, but to the struggle of the animal vitality in order to overcome the decay. The agonies of death are not caused by death but by life's resistance to death. The agony is stronger in youths exuberant with vigorous health, than in old men whose vitality is low.

Pleasure and pain are generally conceived like heat and cold,* as correlatives; and in some respects they are counterparts; they are the two extreme poles of our soul-life. But they are unlike heat and cold in so far as the one is not the same as the other differing only in degree.

Pleasure is wrongly considered as active, pain as passive. Prof. Bain attempts to show that pleasurable emotions display "the general erection of the body," while pain "leads to the relaxation of all the extensor

eclipsed by birth only—birth being growth beyond the limits of an individual. Child-bearing in itself, the growth of a new being, is neither pleasurable nor painful. It often becomes painful by the many disturbances which it is but too liable to cause.

* Bain says: Yet pleasure and pain are as opposite as heat and cold.

muscles" which, he says, are by far the largest. Yet, the flexors of the hand which contract in a fit of anguish, so as to ball the fist, are much stronger muscles than the extensors, and even if that were not the case, Prof. Bain must and does concede, that there is "still an active prompting under pain." He cannot, as he suggests, confine this active prompting to a relaxation of the flexor-muscles alone, for the cry of intense pain is to a great extent executed by the same muscles as the shouts of gay hilarity. Pain as well as pleasure are states of consciousness that accompany the reactions of the nervous system to certain irritations. Pain, it appears, is always caused through a disturbance, (whether this disturbance is good or bad is here a secondary consideration,) while pleasure is the gratification of a want.

There is much confusion shown concerning the nature of pleasure and pain, if the one is called an "accession of vital force," the other "a loss or deprivation of energy."* The different pleasures may be classed partly as the accessions, partly as a spending of vital force. Digestion is an accession, bodily exertion a deprivation of energy. Both are classed together as the most common pleasures of life. They are pleasures in so far as both are satisfactions of wants. A youth, who is glowing with vitality, has a natural want of bodily exertion, and a hungry stomach has a want of food. Take away the want and all that can be called pleasure in the acts disappears. It ceases to be a gratification.

It is generally acknowledged that there are pains which are wholesome, and pleasures which are disastrous. This does not prove that decay may sometimes

* Sir Charles Bell uses these expressions.

be wholesome and growth fatal; yet it proves that some disturbances are good and conductive to our prosperity, while, on the other hand, some gratifications of certain wants will be found to be injurious.

The gratification of natural wants cannot, upon the whole, be considered as injurious; although an occasional lack of their gratification will often under favorable circumstances lead to progress. Wants that are not at all or insufficiently satisfied, prompt the inventor to invent, and the courageous to discover new paths that will in the end make possible their gratification. In the evolution of mankind and in the history of civilization this factor, perhaps, has been too little recognized. Ungratified wants are always disturbances in human life, and the more natural a want is, the more disagreeably will the disturbance make itself felt. Every living being has the natural tendency to gratify its wants, and pleasure may be defined as the feeling that naturally accompanies the gratification of wants.

Now we must bear in mind that among the many wants of living beings there are not only lower and higher kinds of natural, but also unnatural, wants. The intensity of a pleasure does not depend upon its being of a higher or lower kind, but exclusively upon the intensity of the want.

The lower natural wants are called necessities of life, and it is noticeable that they cease to be intense pleasures, the more their satisfaction becomes ensured. The energy necessary for their gratification can thus be employed for the higher emotional and intellectual wants. Unnatural wants are the result of unnatural habits, but we can observe that their gratification is just in the same measure as in other cases pleasurable to the degree of intensity of the want.

It would be impossible to draw an exact line between natural and unnatural wants, although there are some about which there can be no doubt where to classify them. The truth is that there is a large group of indifferent habits which are not injurious. They may be considered by one who is accustomed to them, as natural, by another, who has never practiced them, as ridiculously unnatural. Thus the smoking of a cigar, the drinking of a glass of wine, may be to one an intense pleasure, while to the other it appears as an abomination. The performance of certain actions may be an enjoyment for one and a veritable torture to another. There are men who love their trades or their professions, others who abhor them. There are women who delight in attending to their household-affairs, while others loathe the work.

Pleasure and pain are unavoidable so long as life means growth. Every progress causes disturbances which must be readjusted. A state of perfect adaptation, of which Mr. Spencer speaks, is a dream which is not realizable, unless we dam life's great stream in order to convert it into a stagnant lake. But if we succeeded in that, we would be sure to produce worse evils and more disagreeable pains than all the happiness would be worth, which could possibly result from such a state of perfect adaptation.

Professor Bain says: "Inasmuch as we follow pleasure and avoid pain, if pleasure were injurious and pain wholesome, we should soon incur entire shipwreck of our vitality," but he finds it necessary to add, "as we often partially do, through certain tendencies that are exceptional to the general law." Do not, indeed, *most* shipwrecks in life occur because people indeliberately follow pleasure and avoid pain? And is it not for that reason that we have to preach morals? Some ethical philosophers attempt to base their morals upon the pursuit of pleasure and the avoidance of pain; but they start from the wrong supposition that pleasure is a furtherance, and pain an abatement of life. If pleasure and pain cannot be considered as a furtherance and an abatement of life, they can still less be identified with morality and immorality. It is true that the performance of moral acts should become a want of our nature, and in that case they would naturally become pleasures to us. But, so long as they are not yet natural wants, we must, nevertheless, follow the commands of right conduct. We certainly shall have a very questionable guide, should we follow our feeling of pleasure and pain in determining what is right conduct. Yet we should unhesitatingly obey the behests of our conscience,* without regard to pleasure and pain.

* I here hesitated whether to use the word "conscience" or "reason." I preferred the more popular expression "conscience," although it is so often employed by modern theologians in a mystical sense. The Apostle Paul certainly uses the word in the sense of "a reasoning upon right or wrong conduct." Speaking of the conscience of the heathen he characterises it as "their thoughts, λογισμοί, accusing and excusing one another."

THE THREE PHASES OF REFLEX-MOTIONS.

THE entire field of the activity of psychic life, which under normal circumstances can be connected with, or, as it were, illuminated by, consciousness, shows three different phases or stages, which like the steps of a ladder rise one above the other.

The first and lowest stage is that of simple reflex-motions, which are executed without necessarily entering into consciousness. Such reflex-motions are many kinds of muscular movements, the unconscious facial expression of emotions, winking, sneezing, coughing, sucking, chewing, swallowing, and vomiting. These reflex-motions may, or may not, be accompanied with consciousness. If we do not direct our attention to them, they, or at least some of them, may take place unconsciously upon the occurrence of the irritation by which they are provoked, and against which they must be considered as reactions. Most of these reflex-motions, also, we can bring about at will. In that case the mere thought of them may serve as an irritation to provoke the reflex-motion. The mere idea of the act becomes, as it were, an inner irritant that produces the reflex-motion.

The simple reflex-motions constitute what we commonly call 'reflex-motions in the strictest sense of the word.' Agreeably to their nature, they stand, as a rule, below the threshold of consciousness. Without

thinking of it, without being constantly aware or conscious of it, our heart beats, we breathe and wink, and
execute most complicated movements. In the adjoined
diagram we represent a simple reflex-motion, thus :

DIAGRAM OF SIMPLE REFLEX-MOTION.

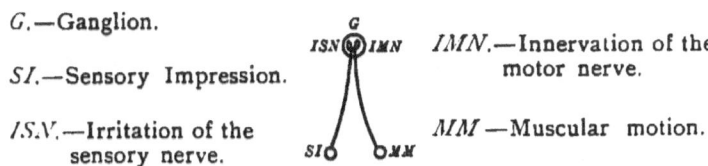

G.—Ganglion.

SI.—Sensory Impression.

ISN.—Irritation of the
    sensory nerve.

IMN.—Innervation of the
    motor nerve.

MM—Muscular motion.

The centres of the simple reflex-motions, physiology teaches, are situated in the bulb (*medulla oblongata*).

We shall now speak of the second phase.

Everybody, perhaps, is from his own experience
acquainted with some phenomenon in human soul-life
that might be designated as 'a direct and simple
reflex-motion of conscious will.' This occurs in those
unusual or extraordinary situations in which prompt
action is demanded, no time being left for deliberation;
for example, in the emergency of a sudden danger.
We assume, for instance, a father comes home from
work and finds the tenement-house in which he lives,
on fire. From a window he hears his child crying for
help. Without stopping to think whether he can, or
whether he cannot, save the life of his boy, whether
the staircase might be wrapped in flames, or whether
he can reach the place whence the cry proceeds, he
rushes into the house at the risk of his own life.

This is a reflex-action that passes through consciousness, but the impulse to action is so overwhelm-
ingly strong that it gives no time or opportunity for
any deliberation.

Irritations coming from sensory impressions, if connected with consciousness, in so far as they give information through some of the senses, are called *sensations*. An innervation of motory nerves or the initiative process of motions by muscular contraction, if connected with consciousness, is called *will*. That which causes a motor innervation accompanied with consciousness (an act of will), is called *motive*. A motive may be a sensation, it may be also the memory of, or a thought abstracted from, former sensations. The word "motive" conveys the proper idea of being that which sets in motion. The process of reflex-motion, if connected with consciousness, is called reflex-action, or simply *action*.

An act that is a simple reflex-motion of conscious will may be a direct action without deliberation, because of the strength and urgency of the motive which allows no time for reflection ; such is the case above described. But it may arise from a lack of intelligence also. Observers of animals know many instances where even higher-organized beings, such as apes and dogs, can speedily be provoked to actions, if only the proper motives are applied.

Æsop tells in one of his fables of a monkey-show in which a spectator spoiled the performance by throwing nuts among the actors. The sight of the nuts so strongly engaged the monkeys' attention as to exclude for the moment all other motives; they forgot their training and even their master's whip, and fell into a scramble over the nuts. Similarly Reynard the Fox, in the animal fable, entices Bruin the Bear with a prospect of honey, and Puss the Cat with the suggestion of mousing, to inconsiderate actions.

DIAGRAM OF SIMPLE REFLEX ACTION, BEING A REFLEX-MOTION,
CONNECTED WITH CONSCIOUSNESS.

SI.—Sensory impression.

ISN.—Irritation of the sensory nerve.

S.—Sensation.

W.—Will.

IMN.—Innervation of the motor nerve.

MM.—Muscular motion.

In the life of human society simple reflex-actions
are rare, though they may frequently be observed
among children, savages, idiots, and the so-called
quick-tempered people. In the mind of an educated
man every psychical irritation that acts as a motive
upon the will, before passing into act, has to run
through a shorter or longer process of deliberation.

DIAGRAM SHOWING AN ACT OF DELIBERATION.

SI.—Sensory impression.

ISN.—Irritation of sensory nerve.

S.—Sensation.

P.—Perception starting a chain of deliberation by
passing through the memories M^1, M^2,
M^3, and ending in

PE.—The plan of execution.

W.—Will.

IMN.—Innervation of the motor nerve.

MM.—Muscular motion.

The memories of former sensations are, as it were,
stored up in the mind ; they make up the stock of that
which goes by the name of *experience.* In so far as
they are arranged in a systematic order, they are called
intelligence. The richer the storehouse of memories
is, and the better they are arranged, or associated,

the quicker will the old experiences be at hand to interfere with, and perhaps to modify, reflex-actions.
The higher the intelligence of a creature is, the less
prone will it be to simple reflex-actions, and the
stronger will be the power of inhibition, so as to make
a process of deliberation possible, before the motive
passes into act. A reflex-action of this kind may be
called an "act of deliberation."

These three phases of reflex-motions represent three
stages of a more and more complicated activity of the
soul. The first considered by itself has its place below
the threshold of consciousness, although it may be
brought within its sphere : it may become conscious.
The second reaches to and stands upon the threshold
of consciousness; the third fills out the whole sphere
of consciousness and appears in orderly connection
with all the memories of experience.

*   *   *

Nature in all things proceeds with great economy.
This is particularly manifest in the function of consciousness.

We may compare consciousness to a light, which
illuminates certain activities of the human soul, but
leaves others to be performed in the gloom of unconsciousness. Consciousness itself has not the power to
accomplish a single one of all the activities which it
illuminates. It only accompanies them and sheds
light upon them, bearing now upon the one and now
upon the other object of attention, as they severally
appear at the focal point of our central soul-life. If
but the innervation of the respective fibres be accomplished, the motions of our bodies and even the
thoughts of our brains will take place just as well
without consciousness as with consciousness; not

otherwise than a machine, that is set a-going, will work in darkness as well as in light.

If all the activities that are performed within our body, or at least all those that take place in the highest and most unstable living substance—the nerves and the brain—were without exception connected with consciousness, what a prodigious chaos would our soul in that case exhibit! In the general turmoil we should not find a moment for deliberation. In the midst of so much excitement and work, no leisure would be afforded for the selection of that which at the time is most important and most needed. The new and extraordinary could not be discriminated from the mass of ordinary events that follow the settled course of routine. The restriction of consciousness to a narrow field is, therefore, a most excellent arrangement. And this arrangement has not the slightest disadvantage, because the limitation is not at all stable ; on the contrary, consciousness can be quickly shifted about, it can at a moment's notice be attached to any kind of psychic activity, as occasion may demand.

When a child is learning to play on the piano, how laboriously must he learn to distinguish every note and every key, and to associate the notes with the keys that belong to them ! His consciousness must again and again be concentrated upon the task with the most intense attention, and in spite of all his attention, how awkwardly do his hands blunder over the key-board ! Compare his play to that of an accomplished player. How swiftly and with what unconscious ease the virtuoso's fingers glide across the piano ! The same difference of conscious awkwardness and unconscious adroitness is noticeable in all arts and in all sciences. What enormous exertions of conscious thought the schoolboy makes in his calculations, while the mathematician operates with his formulas with unconscious certainty, like a machinist whose hand even in the dark is able to find and to use every screw and every lever of his engine.

When the mental activity of our present consciousness sinks down into unconsciousness, all the attention of the mind that is available can be directed upon new difficulties, and thus our thoughts gain sufficient freedom for better and higher, or more needed, work. When mental processes in the sphere of intelligence have become automatic, we call them acts of unconscious intelligence.

Unconscious intelligence works more rapidly than conscious intelligence, because its mechanism is simpler than where the same mental acts are accompanied with consciousness. And unconscious intelligence often works with more exactness than conscious intelligence, because, machine-like, it works with mechanical accuracy. In former times, so long as thinking was identified with consciousness, unconscious thought was the greatest stumbling-block of psychology. Since psychologists have learned to distinguish between the activity of intelligence and that of consciousness, they find no difficulty in the fact that unconscious thought is possible.

Lest the ideas ' unconscious thought ' and ' unconscious ' feeling be misunderstood, a few words may be added on the meaning of the word "consciousness." Consciousness is that intensified and concentrated feeling which constitutes the character of the central soul. Its condition is a coördination of all the feelings into a system grouping them, as it were, all together within the circumference of a circle, in the centre of which is located the present object of attention. There are many feelings that are too far from the centre to be singly discriminated; they form one indistinct mass of feeling concerning the general state of the whole organism. The German physiologists most appropriately call this indistinct mass of innumerable feelings " *Gemein-gefühl*"; the English language, wanting a good Saxon expression, had to resort to the Greek word *cœnœsthesis.* We shall as an equivalent term introduce the expression "general feeling" which appears to be more congenial to the spirit of the English language and less heavy than the foreign-sounding " *cœnœsthesis.*" *

Unconscious thought and unconscious feeling are by no means altogether bare of feeling; yet they are called unconscious, because, and in so far as these thoughts and feelings are not discriminated in their individuality, they disappear among the whole mass of the general feeling and cannot therefore be remembered in their individuality. The concentrated feeling of the central soul naturally can recall only those thoughts and feelings in their clearness and distinctness which appeared with clearness and distinctness, or in other words those which appeared in the centre of its system of coördination.

---

* The proper English translation for "cœnæsthesis," (κοινός, common, and αἰσθησις, feeling,) the German "Gemein-gefühl," would perhaps have been "common sense," or common feeling. The word "common," however, has acquired a specified meaning through the Scotch school of so-called "common-sense philosophers."

THE NATURE OF THOUGHT.

By thought is generally understood mind-activity;
it comprehends all kinds of operations that take place
among representative feelings. The prime condition
of thought, accordingly, is a certain stock of representative feelings. In the adult man these representative feelings are either concrete sense-images or abstract symbols, ideas, and generalizations.*

Philologists usually confine the term thought to
operations with abstract symbols exclusively; and they
are (or at least may be) fully justified in so doing
with reference to their special object of investigation.
The most important symbols of abstract representations are word-symbols or names. Thus it is obvious
that the evolution of thought in the narrower sense of
the term is inseparable from the development of language. Thought in the narrow sense of the word is
identical with abstract thought; as such it is the exclusive property of man. Thought as we understand
the term here, is not limited to the reasoning of
speaking beings. It is the common property of all
feeling beings, whose feelings have acquired representative value. Accordingly, thought is not possible
without feeling. We think in that we are aware of
certain states of ourselves, in short because we feel.

* Compare the second chapter of this work, in which "The Origin of
Mind" is discussed.

The interaction among feelings, the comparisons, combinations, separations, anticipations, and the calling into play of representative feelings, the function of exciting them into activity from a state of rest, constitute the nature of thought.

Thought is not feeling, and feeling is not thought. But there is no thought without feeling. Any sense-impression can stimulate thought into action; and the action that takes place among feelings is that which we understand by thought. For instance, I hear an indistinct ring of the bell, and at once a series of thoughts is evoked. The sensation just received is compared with the memories of other rings; an awakened memory is a feeling also. The sound is plainly distinguished from the ring of the dinner bell; it is recognized as that of the door bell, and at once other representative memories are called forth. With the ring of the door bell is closely associated the idea that somebody must be at the door; and this idea elicits several long strings of anticipations : It may be the postman with letters; from whom? How many possibilities crowd in! It may be a welcome friend or it may be an agent who will intrusively offer his goods.

All these operations are called thinking.* It is a matter of course that man's thought is to a great extent an operation with names; but it need not be, and indeed it is not always. Very often it is a pro-

---

* The limitation of the term thought to abstract thought, was made by Ludwig Noiré, with the avowed purpose of elucidating the origin of reason—viz: the ability of man to form concepts. The animal brain is in possession of images only, and man forms concepts (this was Noiré's answer) solely with the help of language. Human reason, he said, is language. Without language man would have no reason. Reason and language are inseparable, like the soul of an organism and the organized body of a soul. Having another purpose in view, we do not use the term thought in the limited sense, but understand by it all mind-operation.

cess that calls into play sense-images only. Yet it is characteristic of man that he can put his thought into language, and not until he has done so can he be said to have attained to a full clearness of his thoughts.

The ultimate purpose of thought is a proper reaction upon irritations, and this is attained, 1) by rendering distinct all the sense-materials offered, and 2) by calling to assistance all the memories pertinent to the present situation. Thus thought is a process of clarifying or articulating dim feelings in order to adjust reflex motions to special circumstances, in other words in order to change subsequently reflex motions into actions.

The process of thought as an interaction among feelings takes place in the very lowest animals. Unicellular micro-organisms which hunt for food·have certain dim feelings that represent, be it ever so vaguely, the means of satisfying their hunger. Repeated experience makes these feelings more distinct and changes them in a further evolution, first into clear sensations, and then, in man, into abstract concepts, generalizations, and other abstractions.*

Under the term feeling we comprehend all states of awareness, not only sensations, but also abstract ideas. Sensations are one kind and abstract ideas another kind of feeling.

Sensation is the product of two factors : the feeling subject and the sensed object. Thus every sensation of a feeling being has a foreign element in it. Abstract ideas seem to be free of this foreign element, and abstract thought appears as a purely internal act. Yet

---

* Generalizations are, as a rule, not distinguished from other abstractions. Yet there are very important abstractions which are by no means generalizations. There are abstract conceptions which are quite special and concrete ; for instance, the path of a comet represents an individual case. It is an abstract idea, but not a generalization.

it only *seems* to be free from this foreign element, for in truth, it is not free. It is free in so far only as the foreign element has in the meantime become our own. Abstract ideas have been derived from the memories of sensations, and these memories are part of ourselves. Yet they were imported into the thinking subject by former sensations. That internal kind of feeling which we call abstract ideas, would be impossible without former sensations and their memories.

Sensation possesses a distinctness that is lacking in dim feelings and still more so in mere sense-impressions which have not as yet acquired meaning. The distinctness of sensations is due to their being a repetition of a feeling perceived before. The oftener a feeling of the same kind is repeated, the greater will be its distinctness. Its form will appear more and more regular. Thus distinctness is the recognition of regularity, i. e., of conformity to law. Similarly the articulation of speech and song are due to the regularity, and the recognition of regularity in the production of sound-waves. We may, accordingly, consider sensation as the articulated feeling of specific sense-impressions.

* * *

Those physiological acts which are perceived subjectively as states of consciousness, or feelings (viz., sensations and abstract thoughts), we shall now consider in their mechanical connection with other physiological processes, especially their irritations and the reflex-motions that ensue. We shall in this connection when treating of feelings, i. e., of sensations and ideas, leave out of sight the subjective state of awareness, and consider them as objective processes, that take place while a feeling is perceived or an idea is thought.

THE MECHANISM OF THOUGHT.

Concerning the process of feeling in general and of articulate feeling in particular, we may state the following facts:

1. *Feeling* (i. e., that physiological process which subjectively is perceived as feeling), *is caused by irritation.*

2. *Feeling tends to motion.*

Feeling is a process that takes place between irritation and its reaction. Irritations may be either internal or external. External irritations are impressions produced by contact with the surrounding world; by the rays of light upon the eye, by waves of sound upon the ear, etc. Internal irritations are such as hunger and thirst.

Living substance, being irritable and endowed with memory, adapts itself to such conditions of contact with surrounding objects as are often repeated, and thus a regularity is produced, which by and by leads to distinctness. Living matter in its lowest forms is irritable throughout. Very soon, however, irritability is specialized as feeling in the sensory nerve-cells and eventually mounts to a clearness which is called consciousness. The highest form of feeling is attained when it appears in distinctly articulated speech. The operations of these articulated feelings are rational or human thought.

What is stated for feeling in general holds good for thought also:

1. *The process of thinking is directly or indirectly caused by irritations;* and

2. *It ultimately results in motion.*

The tendency of thought to pass into motion is called

will. Will, as all tendency to motion, must have a direction or an aim. The aim of will is called *purpose.* The motion produced by will is called *action.*

Thought need not directly originate from irritations, it may proceed from the memories of former irritations. Irritations certainly remain its ultimate foundation, and the substance of all thought throughout exists only because irritations have been previously received. The most abstract thought, our conception of form, and with it all purely formal sciences, even erroneous thought, the shadowy chimeras of the mind, have all ultimately originated from feeling of some kind. We arrived there through some process of abstraction. In this respect the old dictum of the schoolmen remains true forever : *Nihil est in intellectu quod non antea fuerit in sensu.* Nothing is in our mind which has not been before in our senses.

Certain feelings correspond to certain contacts. They thus become representatives first of the contacts, then of the objects themselves which cause the contact. Thus living creatures acquire a possibility of depicting their surroundings in their own substance. They can in their feelings map out the world in which they live. The different feelings become so many images of the objects to which they correspond. Not only the things of the outside world, in their effects upon ourselves, but also the movements of our members in their actions upon things external are portrayed in the feeling nerve-substance. Both together furnish all the data for our knowledge of the world.

Cognition, accordingly, may be characterized as a process of orientation in the world. The macrocosm outside is depicted in the microcosm within, and the more correctly the latter represents the former, the nearer it is to truth.

Our next statement derived from these considerations we formulate as follows : Feeling, and more so

3. *Thinking is a representative process.*

The process of orientation is of greatest importance to living beings, because it facilitates adaptation to their surroundings. They can pre-arrange certain adaptations in their thoughts ; they can make plans of their movements before the execution of the movements takes place.

4. *The mechanism of thinking consists in combining, in separating, and re-combining the representative images or symbols.*

Thinking is an inner experimentation with images and symbols of things, to the end of deciding, how an intended action (the reaction against the irritation) shall take place. Thus it becomes a great saving in the economy of animal activity. Instead of trying all possibilities in reality, until one is found that is best suited to the occasion, the images of things, obtained through the feelings of previous experiences, are associated and disassociated within the brain, until there results the desired combination, which thereupon is executed. Then the purpose of thinking is attained ; it ends in a reflex action against irritations.

Students, as a rule, are confined to their study. They represent the brain of a community and may be considered as the specialized organ of thought in mankind. It is natural, perhaps, that students and thinkers should often imagine that thinking exists for its own sake. Their opinion is repeated by those who may be called the dilettanti in the art of thought, and thus it happens to be a fashionable dogma of the time. Nevertheless it is an error.

5. *The purpose of thinking is adaptation to surrounding conditions.*

Thought, you may object, sometimes does not end in action, but in the suppression of action. Inhibition, however, is an action also. Thought should always end in the regulation or adjustment of our behavior toward our surroundings. If it does not, it is not the right kind of thought. Thought for its own sake is a disease. If muscles contract neither for a special purpose nor for the general purpose of exercise, we call the contraction a cramp. Thought for its own sake is a spasm of the brain.

Abstract thought is a still greater economy than thinking in concrete images, because it introduces the principle of economy into thought itself.* Images of single objects are substituted by more comprehensive symbols which find their best expressions in words, and one word-symbol represents many images. In this manner the representative process is enhanced. Words become representations of representations, and each further advance of human intelligence, as Ernst Mach has pointed out, will be characterized in some way as an "Economy of Thought."

Higher thinking, (thinking, $\varkappa\alpha\tau'$ $\dot{\epsilon}\xi o\chi\eta\nu$,) as we find it in the human brain, is called abstract thought, because it is conditioned by abstraction. Particular qualities that are common to several things, are mentally severed from the images of these things, and then combined into a new unity by a special symbol. The most natural symbols being words (in so far as they

---

* Economy of thought does not mean that we should think less but that thought should become more effective. By economy we are enabled with the same amount of thought to accomplish more work.

are most easily communicated), language is the means by which abstract thought becomes possible. Noiré said : "Man thinks because he speaks," *i. e.*, man thinks "in abstracts," because within his mind notions of abstract qualities by means of word-symbols have been combined into unities.

Still, in a different sense the inverse is also true : "Man speaks because he thinks." In this case thinking is employed in its broader sense. Man has learned to speak because his mind was filled with images, of which a great many similar ones naturally tended to combine. In the broader sense of the word all animals may be said to think ; in the strict sense of the term, man alone thinks.

THE RISE OF CONSCIOUSNESS.

WE CALL consciousness intensified feeling. Consciousness can only have arisen from feeling through an inhibition of reflex motion. It is, undoubtedly, the failure of the purpose of reflex motion to which living substance owes its higher development. If all reflex motions that react against irritations, had always answered their purpose, there never would have been a need of consciousness and the animal world would lead an unconscious, purely instinctive life not very much different from that of plants. Animal life would only consist in the performance of simple reflex motions.

Let us suppose that the reflex motion of coughing in a patient were attended with pain, by which the irritation in the throat would rather be aggravated than relieved, would not, as a rule, the patient seek to restrain the cough, and would he not, by and by, attain a point where the reflex-ganglion would resist the irritation and suppress the reflex-motion even in sleep?

Dr. Mœbius,* professor of zoölogy at the university of Kiel, relates an interesting experiment performed by Mr. Amtsberg, of Stralsund.

"A pike, who swallowed all small fishes which were put into his aquarium, was separated from them by a pane of glass, so that, whenever he tried to pounce on them, he struck his gills against

* *Schriften des Naturwissenshaftlichen Vereins von Schleswig-Holstein ;* quoted from Prof. Max Müller: "The Science of Thought," Vol. I, p. 10.

•

the glass, and sometimes so violently that he remained lying on his back, like dead. He recovered, however, and repeated his on-slaughts, till they became rarer and rarer, and at last, after three months, ceased altogether. After having been in solitary con-finement for six months, the pane of glass was removed from the aquarium, so that the pike could again roam about freely among the other fishes. He at once swam towards them, but he never touched any one of them, but always halted at a respectful dis-tance of about an inch, and was satisfied to share with the rest the meat that was thrown into the aquarium. He had therefore been trained so as not to attack the other fishes which he knew as in-habitants of the same tank. As soon, however, as a strange fish was thrown into the aquarium, the pike in nowise respected him, but swallowed him at once. After he had done this forty times, all the time respecting the old companions of his imprisonment, he had to be removed from the aquarium on account of his large size.

" The training of this pike was not, therefore, based on judg-ment ; it consisted only in the establishment of a certain direction of will, in consequence of uniformly recurrent sensuous impres-sions. The merciful treatment of the fishes which were familiar to him, or, as some would say, which he knew, shows only that the pike acted without reflection. Their view provoked in him, no doubt, the natural desire to swallow them, but it evoked at the same time the recollection of the pain he had suffered on their ac-count, and the sad impression that it was impossible to reach the prey which he so much desired. These impressions acquired a greater power than his voracious instinct, and repressed it, at least for a time. The same sensuous impression, proceeding from the same fishes, was always in his soul the beginning of the same series of psychic acts. He could not help repeating this series, like a machine, but like a machine with a soul, which has this ad-vantage over mechanical machines, that it can adapt its work to unforeseen circumstances, while a mechanical machine cannot. The pane of glass was to the organism of the pike one of these un-foreseen circumstances."

Deliberation before action and with it all higher kind of thought becomes possible only through an inhibition of reflex action. The tendency to act still continues, even if action itself is inhibited. The desire

to do a certain thing and the memory of pain or disappointment that inhibits it, come into conflict and a
struggle between them results, that will either lead to
the entire suppression of the intended act or it will
bring about an adaptation to circumstances. If the
latter takes place, the tendency to act has gained the
upper hand over inhibition, nevertheless the resultant
is different from what it would have been as a simple
reflex motion without having passed through the process of deliberation. It is modified and most likely
better suited to the circumstances.

One of the most important tasks of education is that
of accustoming youth to self-discipline. The will need
not and must not be suppressed or even weakened,
but there must be developed a still stronger power of
control which, if it be necessary, will inhibit impulses
of the will or, at least, prevent them from passing into
action before they have been submitted to a thorough
critical examination. This scrutiny consists in comparing all the resultant consequences of the intended
act with the memories of similar cases, be they of one's
own experience or implanted in the mind through information from other sources.

Men, in whom this process takes place, are not so
easily decoyed into actions, which later on they must
repent. Such a self-control makes it possible, that not
only the desire which at the time excites us will be
decisive, but all the other ideas, the memories and images that live in our mind, will also have an influence
upon the final decision. If impulses are thus controlled,
we behold, as it were, an orderly meeting, called to
order by a presiding officer, who by turns grants the
word to each and all present, who might have anything
to say concerning the matter under discussion. The

meeting consists of our own ideas, our hopes, our wishes, our longings, and aspirations, while the presiding officer is represented by our power of self-control. The mind of a man who is exclusively swayed by the influence of the moment, who easily yields to the present impulse, resembles the gathering of a mob where the most impetuous talker is always the leader. The sudden impulses of the will are then executed before the other side of the question can be heard. Such a man is limited to the situation of the moment; he becomes a sport of circumstances and a slave to his own passions. Moral freedom, that higher condition in which all ideas of our mind enjoy equal rights and perfect liberty, is possible only by an inhibition of action through self-control.*

The inhibition of a reflex motion does not annihilate the suppressed irritation; it makes it even more intense. A suppressed sneeze thus can provoke a very disagreeable sensation. In certain circles, where etiquette banishes sneezing as a breach of manners, people have discovered a means of suppressing the irritation by the aid of a counter-irritation. They press the bridge of the nose between the eyes, and by this simple method they free themselves from the tickling irritation that causes sneezing.

This will do for the suppression of a sneeze, but it is a different matter when the irritation appears in the form of hunger, which, if not satisfied, will keep increasing. It will again and again start a process of deliberation and consider every circumstance that may be turned to advantage. Hence the proverb says, that hunger sharpens the wit.

---

* For the treatment of the problem of Free will, see "Fundamental Problems," p. 191, et seqq. and pp. 389-397 of this book.

If the necessities of life cannot directly be satisfied, they must be indirectly. If their end is not immediately attainable, means must be invented, which on a longer, yet on a better and safer, way will after all accomplish the end. And the means that had to be inserted between a will and its end or purpose, made thinking necessary. Deliberation was wanted in order to introduce the means to the end, and thus it is want that produced in living creatures the development and further perfectionment of thought.

The strong impulse of self-preservation, and the impossibility of directly satisfying this craving, compel organized substance to rise from the lower state of a dim feeling to that of clear consciousness. Want is an inner irritation that can produce the most terrible pain and bring man to the verge of despair. Like the Sphinx of Œdippus, it cruelly sacrifices innumerable beings and thus sternly demands the solution of problems that will and must be solved under penalty of painful perdition. Thus guides the fear of death to a higher stage of life. But it guides only the courageous thinker, the Œdippus who by the power of thought is the victor in the struggle for existence. The faculty of thinking, and with it the clearness of conscious thought, has been forced upon us.

We learn from these facts that the philosophy of Deism which prevailed among liberals of the eighteenth century and is still in vogue to-day is an erroneous notion of God. The divinity that shapes our ends, the all-life that manifests itself in nature, is of a different kind than the deists imagined. The deists regarded God as an all-loving, benevolent father, whose purpose was the happiness of his creatures; God's good intentions, however, were too often frustrated through the malevolence and ignorance of men. In contrast to this view, it must be admitted, that the old orthodox conception of God is far more correct. The God of the Bible is free from the philanthropic sentimentality of the eighteenth century, and agrees better with positive facts. The God of the Old Testament is a stern master, who through servitude guides to freedom, and after visitations dispenses his blessings.

It must strongly be doubted, whether men amidst mere enjoyments, living in a state of constant happiness, would ever advance. Man received into his household certain animals, as sheep and oxen, and took good care of them. Their lot must now appear as more desirable than that of their previous state of freedom ; they are unacquainted with the hard struggle for existence, and upon their verdant pastures they have no evil foreboding of their imminent death. And even death itself, if they are destined for meat, is inflicted in the least painful manner.

If anywhere among living creatures there has been realized the ideal picture of undisturbed happiness, and of a pure enjoyment of life, it certainly is to be found among the herds on our cattle-farms. Yet, at what a price ! While the wild sheep and the wild bull are eminently distinguished from other animals by their intelligence, domestic sheep and oxen under the care of man have to such an extent become obtuse, that their very names have strikingly become the symbols of irredeemable stupidity.

The real God, who rules supreme in the evolution of cosmic life, is free from all sentimentality. He may certainly appear cruel in comparison with the ideal of a fatherly and philanthropic grandsire. He rather resembles a stern father, who does not, in a weak good-naturedness spoil his children, but educates them now with severity, now with kindness, in order to develop their powers. The history of evolution proves that he does not intend to bring up faint-hearted, sentimental children of happiness; he wants his sons to be intellectually and physically self-reliant, reared in the bracing atmosphere of freedom.

THE LIMITATIONS OF THE SENSES.

ONE of the strongest arguments in favor of agnosticism is based upon the same principle as that upon which positivism stands. We recognize that the ultimate data of experience and the basis of all knowledge are sensations. Sensations naturally depend upon the character of the senses; and the senses of man—indeed those of every possible living being—are adapted according to circumstances to special sensations only. "Now it is evident," the agnostic declares, "that our knowledge is limited to those natural processes which can affect our senses; yet it is precluded from all the rest. That which cannot affect our senses will forever remain unknown to us. It is unknowable."

The fallacy of this syllogism is apparent and can be pointed out by the mere statement of innumerable discoveries concerning such natural processes as do not affect our senses. The truth is that man's knowledge is not at all limited to his own direct sensations. By the power of his mind through reflection he can, and he constantly does, transcend that narrow sphere, and he gathers new material for his experience through indirect observations.

The senses are affected indirectly, if a thing is perceived by its effects upon other things. We lack for instance an organ to perceive the chemical rays of light. They have no perceptible effect upon our eye. Nevertheless we can indirectly be affected by them when we observe their effects upon the photographer's sensitive plate. Thus we bring a process that does not affect our senses within their range through indirect observation.

There are innumerable examples of a similar kind, and the assertion that a certain thing, this or that natural phenomenon, is unknowable has by the progress of science again and again been refuted.

Let me cite one instance only from the later history of science. Auguste Comte who, under the inappropriate name of positivism, some time before the invention of the word agnosticism, propounded and defended the agnostic idea of the Unknowable, declared that certain things must necessarily remain forever hidden from the knowledge of man, and he selected as an illustration that we could never know the chemical composition of the stars. Comte's assertion appeared very plausible ; the limitation of our knowledge in that line seemed to be beyond the shadow of a doubt. For there is no possibility of a chemist's ever getting a piece of, or taking a trip to, Sirius or to any other one of the stars. And yet such is the interconnection of all processes in the universe, that means were discovered to state most positively of what materials the stars consist. It was a strange irony of fate that while Comte was publishing his assertion of the agnostic view, two German scholars were analyzing the rays of the sun and the stars by a new method called spectrum analysis, which in exactitude rather surpasses the cruder method of an analysis in the crucible. It is true that our chemists cannot journey to the stars, but the light of the stars

travels to us and gives us information concerning the
substances of which they consist.

There is nothing in the world which does not produce some effect upon something. Imagine that a
certain something existed that did not in any way
whatever make its existence manifest—could it be
said to exist? I think not. The existence of a thing
and its manifestations are identical. The existence of
a thing, be it ever so insignificant, is real only by
manifesting its existence through certain effects. The
quality of producing effects is its reality.

We may fairly suppose that there are many things
in the world which have never as yet either directly
or indirectly affected us in a manner to make their
reality known to us. Yet all things in the world being interconnected, there is always the possibility that
their effects can somehow be brought to bear upon
our faculty of observation. Whatever exists is in so
far as it is real, knowable. There are certain things
which from a certain standpoint are unknowable, as
objects may from a certain point of view become invisible. A tree behind a house may be invisible to
to me but it is not invisible in itself. The Copernican
conception of the solar system may be incomprehensible to a savage, yet it is not incomprehensible *per se.*
Incomprehensibility is not a quality of things, not a
peculiar feature of all or of certain natural processes,
it does not attach to, it is not a quality of, the reality
of objects.

If things or natural processes appear to us as incomprehensible, the fault is not theirs but ours. If
the whole world is incomprehensible to us, it is no
proof that the world possesses the quality of being unknowable, but because we lack the quality of compre-

hending it; we ourselves in that case, are wanting in strength to formulate a unitary conception of all the natural phenomena which come within the reach of our observation.

Sensations are the effects of surrounding objects upon a sentient being. Sensations are the ultimate basis of all knowledge; they are the data of experience.

The duty of the scientist is to describe the facts of natural processes in such a way as to show their regularity; and the duty of the philosopher is to arrange all knowledge into one harmonious system which shall be a unitary conception of the world. Man must have a conception of the world not only because it behooves him as a thinking being to have such a conception, and because the demands of his mind have to be satisfied, but also because he is in want of a foundation for his conduct in life. Brutes follow their impulses, but man is—or ought to be—a moral being; he can regulate his actions according to certain maxims; and the maxims of individuals as well as of nations depend upon, they are derived from, their respective conceptions of the world. The various philosophies of all times and peoples find a practical expression in their ethics.

THE BASIS OF A POSITIVE PHILOSOPHY.

THE main error of metaphysicism is the vicious habit of metaphysical philosophers to start with postulates. They take a very broad abstract idea, such as the "Absolute," or "Being," or "Deity," or "God," or "the Infinite," and consider it an actual reality. Upon this abstract idea they build with more or less ability and boldness a complete system of other abstract ideas, and when it is finished they call it a philosophy. As a matter of course every philosopher builds a philosophy of his own. Why should he not? The building-material of castles-of-air is inexpensive— extremely inexpensive!

Many sensible people have turned their backs upon philosophy because they have discovered the hollowness of purely abstract reasoning, which is to no practical purpose in real life. Yet there is another view of philosophy, which in contradistinction to metaphysicism we call positivism.

Positive philosophy* rejects all kinds of postulates and starts from the positive data of experience. The data of experience are the several states of our consciousness. The elements of our states of consciousness are sensory impressions. A sensory impression fully realized in consciousness is a sensation. Sensations become percepts; many percepts of the same

---

* For the difference between Comte's positivism and that here proposed see the author's "Fundamental Problems," p. 173 and p. 75, note.

kind become concepts. Thus all the objects of our surroundings are mirrored in their relation toward us, and among themselves in the living substance of our brain. From the concepts of things abstractions are made; and by the help of our abstract thoughts we can recognize the finer relations that interconnect the phenomena of nature; we can trace the laws that govern the changes of their forms.

Abstract thought is the instrument of science which opens our eye to a deeper comprehension of the facts of nature. The relations that interconnect the phenomena of nature, and the laws that govern the changes of their forms, are not material things; they are not concrete objects like tables and chairs, yet they are nevertheless realities, they are facts and as such they are of great moment. The form of a thing is the most important part of it. The form of a watch is that which makes it a watch. The metal of which it is wrought is another and, truly, an indispensable, part, yet the metal is only the material of which the watch consists. * Similarly justice is an abstract idea. It designates certain relations among men that are of highest importance. Thus justice is a reality in life, and if there were no justice in our law courts, it would still be a most powerful reality, though it existed merely as an ideal in our hearts. And so the relations among things, as well as persons, as in the instance given of justice, are realities, although we know that they are not materialities.

* There is no mystery in the changes and in the new creations of form. We may say that the watch existed potentially even before it was invented; thus the organized life of organisms existed potentially in the non-organized substances before their combination. Yet there is no necessity, as Mr. Wake suggests in the essay, "God in Evolution," (Open Court p. 1997) for resorting to the supposition of a divine personality who created and preconceived the origin of organized life upon earth.

The meaning of positive philosophy is, that it requires every idea, every concept, every abstract thought to be legitimatized. If ideas have not originated from the data of experience, if there is no reality corresponding to them, they have no right to exist; and we are consequently entitled to treat them as mere illusions.

One great advantage of the positive method is that we can never forget, while adhering to it, the origin of abstract ideas. Existence, Cosmical Being, the Infinitude, Gravitation, Natural Laws, Virtue, God, etc., are abstracts; they are symbols for certain generalizations and qualities of, or relations among, concrete things. Considered as abstracts, they are invaluable possessions of our mind; considered as concrete things, they lead to self-contradictions.

Metaphysical philosophers are often awe-stricken at their inability to explain their possession of abstract ideas, and think they have come by them through divine inspiration. There are not a few who expect to find in reality some concrete thing that is infinite*; they enquire for the gravitating force behind the falling stone; and when, in their search, they get beyond their depth, the problem is declared insolvable. Facts may be as clear as a mountain-brook; they step into the brook, make its waters muddy, and then declare that it can never be clarified. It is painful to read, for instance, Mr. Spencer's expositions on motion, time, and space. He confounds the issues of his disquisition, and when he arrives at the conclusion "all is unknowable," "all is inscrutable," he seems not to be aware of the fact, that this result is the reflection of his own confusion.

---

* The Problem of Infinitude is discussed in "Fundamental Problems," p. 169, et seqq.

We can not consider as data of experience every assertion made by a visionary dreamer. We must suspect all assertions of so-called facts that stand in contradiction to other facts. The data of experience are such facts only that under the same conditions can be ascertained by every one, and can be re-ascertained and verified by experiment.

Positive philosophy seems to start with a poor capital; yet its foundation is solid, and in former publications* the author of this book has endeavored to develop some of the spiritual treasures which it yields. We found that neither religion, nor art, nor science, lost aught of their dignity by being deprived of their metaphysical tinsel crowns, which were wrongly deemed their most valuable ornaments.

It is commonly supposed that from the positive view all ideals disappear, that all higher and spiritual life vanishes. This is not so, and it has been our earnest endeavor to show that such concepts as God and Soul, Morality, Freedom, Responsibility, and Immortality, are deepened in their meaning. In so far as they are recognized as realities, they grow immensely in importance. In positive philosophy ethics finds for the first time a scientific basis.

Positivism is that view which is to supersede the idealism as well as the materialism of former ages; for it contains that which is true in both, avoiding their common errors. Positivism is the boldest and most radical philosophy that has ever been propounded, yet at the same time it is the only practical philosophy. From the cloud-land of metaphysics it turns our minds

* " Fundamental Problems, the Method of Philosophy as a Systematic Arrangement of Knowledge." Chicago, 1889. The Open Court Pub. Co.
" The Idea of God." (A Pamphlet.) Second Edition. Chicago, 1889. The Open Court Pub. Co.

toward the duties of real life. It is based on facts ; and it is a systematic arrangement of facts. The purpose of philosophy will be found in its being a guide for man's conduct in life ; it becomes the basis of ethics and is thus again applied to facts.

Positive philosophy recognizes no revelation, no intuition, no mysticism, no agnosticism ; it deals with facts and with facts only. On facts it builds its ideals ; and its religion rests upon a scientific basis.

Metaphysicism is a disease of philosophy, and it is indeed a fatal disease, for it leads straightway into the realm of the mystic Unknowable where all philosophy is at an end.

When a metaphysical philosopher descends from the cloud-land of metaphysics toward earth in order to apply his postulates to the realities of life, he becomes entangled into innumerable contradictions wherever he appears with his metaphysical principles. But a metaphysical philosopher is never dismayed. As soon as the public gets accustomed to the strange names of his metaphysical principles, he calls them philosophical truths and declares them to be absolute. From their disagreement with the facts of reality he concludes that they are unknowable. They are like God whom no one can see and live. People then bow down in silent reverence and our philosopher returns to the aërial heights, where he disappears glorified in the celestial fog of mysticism.

Metaphysicism is often decked out with many facts of the natural sciences. We must, however, be severe in drawing the color-line sharply. The various metaphysical systems may be different in style and grandeur, they may be different in name, and the borrowed plumage of natural science may be more or less brilliant, but in their principle one is exactly like the other ; they are built upon the foundation of mere abstractions to which no reality corresponds and they end as a natural consequence in contradictions which are not so much concealed as masked under the pretense of profundity. The credulous multitude is told that they have got into problems so deep, that they are insolvable. The contradictions of such systems, then, are openly paraded as the Unknowable, the Incomprehensible, the Inscrutable, the Inexplicable, or even the Mysterious and the Occult.

It is the rock of positive facts on which the proud galleys of metaphysicism strike before they sink into the realm of the Unfathomable. The ship that there founders, is irredeemably wrecked.

THE REACTION AGAINST MATERIALISM.

How does it happen that in our days, among large classes, not only in America but all over the world, there has set in a tendency to Spiritualism which manifests itself in many ways? A crude belief in spirits and spiritual manifestations exists ; mediums infest the country,·who communicate with the departed and impose upon the credulous in many ways. New creeds are preached, such as Christian Science and so-called Metaphysics. Faith-cure is practiced, and among the societies for psychical research scattered throughout the world there are some that vie with each other in the publication of incredible statements about telepathy and wonderful tales of second sight.

This movement may be called a reaction against materialism. Mankind, it seems, is growing tired of the crude materialistic philosophy that came to them in the name of science, and a reaction is taking place which, according to the education of the different people concerned, assumes the shape of a more or less crude superstition. It is noticeable that the reaction is strongest among the unchurched, among liberals and so-called freethinkers ; it is less marked among the adherents of the old creeds, the members of churches and religious congregations.

Science is *not*, as is so often claimed, materialistic ; yet to the unscientific, to the laymen, who are not thoroughly versed in its elementary truths, science naturally enough appears materialistic. The science that is transplanted from the laboratory or the study into the streets, rapidly ceases to be science. There are very few savants who take the trouble to be popular. Most of them confine their publications to men of their own class, and it is an exception that now and then a scientist addresses the whole of civilized mankind, and speaks or writes in a style that can be understood by business people and workingmen. The duty of popularizing, to a great extent, thus devolves upon men who have not grasped the whole truth of scientific discoveries, and who look at them from the outside only. They inform themselves about the rigid formulas, the exact statements of laws by which we can predict the slightest details of the movements of molecules and atoms. Perhaps they are also able to explain these formulas, and point out the mechanisms of action discovered through scientific investigation. Yet the spirit of science escapes them, they overlook the spiritual that pervades the mechanism. This it is that evoked the just sarcasm of Goethe, who says in Faust:

> " He who would study organic existence
> First drives out the soul with rigid persistence,
> Then the parts in his hands he may hold and class,
> But the spiritual link is lost, alas !
> *Encheiresin naturæ* this chemistry names,
> Nor knows how herself she banters and blames."

By materialism I understand that view of the world which explains everything from matter, and takes for granted that material existence is the only reality. Materialism overlooks the importance of the spiritual and does not consider it as a reality worth while troubling about. Spirit is, so materialists claim, an occasional function of matter only, the origin of which is not yet explained, yet it is certain that its existence is very fleeting.

Après nous le déluge! was the motto of the French materialists of the eighteenth century. "We need not trouble," they thought, "about our fate after death, for death is a finality; death ends all. Therefore, let us enjoy the present, let us eat and drink, for to-morrow we shall be no more. And if a deluge is to sweep over our graves, let the deluge come." We need not here repeat historical facts; they are too well known. This view of things induced the classes in power to give themselves up exclusively to the enjoyment of life, and to oppress their fellow-citizens in order to attain the means for their wasteful pleasures. The deluge came indeed as a natural consequence and swept away with merciless justice the guilty, the frivolous, and the foolish, and together with the guilty the innocent also.

We shall not dwell here on the mistakes that practical materialism makes when as an ethical theory its doctrines are applied to real life. We shall limit ourselves to a consideration of its theoretical mistakes only. There are plenty honest materialists who do not see at all the consequences to which their doctrines naturally lead, and it would be unfair to make them personally answerable for results, and to charge them with having wilfully poisoned the public mind. There are very few materialistic philosophers who are to be stigmatized as frivolous or immoral; on the contrary, most of them are indubitably honest men, who have devoted their lives to the search for truth and who speak out boldly that which they regard as truth. They should not be blamed for that; in that they should be encouraged, for it is only by boldly speaking out that which we believe to be the truth, that truth can be discovered. Nor should other thinkers who are of a contrary opinion doubt their honesty or ever make insinuations respecting their personal character, simply on the ground that their doctrines might in their application lead in the end to immoral practices and thus undermine public welfare. The only remedy against errors is to point out errors without personal malice or imputation, and it is this that we shall try to do in the case of materialism.

Matter is an abstract, made in the same way as all other abstracts. Abstraction is a mental process. We abstract (we take away) in our thoughts from a number of things certain properties which perhaps in reality are inseparably connected with other properties; but in our thoughts we exclude all the other properties. We need not explain here the advantage of this method, which is undeniable, for abstract thought is the condition of all exact discriminations, and science would be impossible without it. Matter is generally defined as "anything which can affect one or more of our five senses."

It is understood that all other properties, such as spirit, are excluded from the term matter. There are two properties which in reality are always inseparably connected with material things, yet in the term "matter" they are not included; viz., (1) motion, and (2) form. If I speak of the matter of an object, I limit my attention to the bodily particles of which it consists and take no notice of their forms or of the relations that obtain among the particles, or of their motions. It is their quantity in mass, without reference to any one of their many other qualities. I cannot in reality separate matter from all form or from all motion. I can perhaps impart to a piece of matter more or less motion, I can destroy its present form. But it is impossible to take away every motion and every form. There is no such a thing in reality that would be matter *alone :* abstract matter, matter void of all motion and without any shape or form. A stone may be in a state of relative rest ; for instance, it lies quietly on the ground. Yet it moves with the earth through the space of the solar system with an average speed of nineteen miles per second. There is relative rest, yet there is no absolute rest, and there is matter without regular form, yet there is no matter without any form whatever.

Materialism contains one great truth ; and it is this truth that gave materialism its strength and its prominence. Materialism rose in opposition to supernaturalism. Certainly, materialism went too far when it tried to explain everything from matter, when it identified matter with reality ; yet it stands on solid ground when it maintains that every reality is material. There are no pure forms : the forms of reality are forms of matter. There are no mere motions : real motions are changes of place among material particles. Yet matter is only one aspect of reality; matter does not cover all and the whole of reality. Besides the material there is the formal, and there is the life displayed in the spontaneous motion of all things. Materialism is right as opposed to idealism, when idealism claims that abstract forms are entities by themselves. Plato proposed the theory that ideas, or abstract forms, are the only true realities, and that the things from which we have abstracted these forms are mere shams, mere transient appearances. Materialism is right also as opposed to spiritualism, when spiritualism claims that spirits exist or can exist apart from material bodies, that the spiritual has an empire of its own in abstract independence, and that ghosts can walk about in bodiless nudity.

The reaction which, as we can everywhere observe, is taking place against the errors of materialism is based upon a great truth, and it is this truth that will survive the crudities of the movement. There can be no doubt about the fact that this world is spiritual in its inmost nature. The spiritual animates every particle of matter and appears in its most beautiful and grandest development in the human soul. The spiritual is no incidental feature of reality, but an intrinsic quality of its existence, which will surely blaze out in the course of the evolution of worlds. It is, as it were, the revelation of the secret concealed in the potentialities of the elementary conditions of the universe.

We do not maintain that a spirit resides in every atom, but we maintain that the elements of feeling are a property that is inseparably connected with matter. Feeling originates when a certain configuration of molecules produces a definite interaction among the particles of organized substance. The motions of every particle take place according to the laws of mechanics, and are accompanied not with feeling but with elements of feeling. The feeling that takes place in organized substance during its activity is not a product of its mechanical motion (i. e., motion is not changed into feeling), but it is a phenomenon that accompanies its mechanical motions. Mechanical motions and the elements of feeling are not interchangeable, but run parallel to each other; and special combinations of these elements form the phenomena we call feelings. Thus together with the evolution of the mechanism progresses the development of feeling which reaches in man the height of conscious thought.

The elements of the spiritual we consider accordingly, as a universal property of matter. Nature is not dead, it is alive ; it bears in its bosom the germs of life and will develop them in the course of the natural process of evolution. Spirit is a special combination, a certain form, the mechanical parallelism of which is found in the activity of living substance ; and the growth of the spiritual depends upon and accompanies the perfectionment of organism.

Materialism overlooks the importance of form. Materialists by identifying the material with the real, imagine that they have exhausted the reality of objects when they consider their material existence alone. Without the material, of which it consists, a thing would disappear ; the material element in it, it is true, makes the thing real, in so far as it gives substantiality to it. Yet the form is no mere nothing, as materialists are too apt to say. The form is exactly that which makes the thing such as it is. Without its present form a watch might be anything ; it might be a lump of metal, or any other thing, but it would be no watch. The form of things, therefore, is the most important part of reality. It is the form only, be it in motion or in matter, that excites the interest of the scientist ; form arouses the imagination of the artist and the industry of the inventor.

Spiritualists, in a certain sense, ought to be called materialists, for they have one error in common with materialists. They cannot see that the formal and the relational, although real, are non-material. But while materialists consider forms as mere nothings, spiritualists are prone to look upon forms as if they were substances, and thus materialize spirit. They conceive spirit as a substance like matter, only much more subtile, and not perceptible by our senses. Thus they lack in the properly spiritual conception of form, and become blind to the irrefragibility of the mechanical law. They dream of a realm of life in which a different and a higher kind of mechanics, a hypermechanics, will supersède the usual mechanical laws that prevail in the realm of material existences.

Science traces the laws of form everywhere. The laws of form are our guides and the instruments of research. No scientific problem, whether it concerns matter or motion, is fully solved until it is shown to be a problem of form. Thus the motions of the celestial bodies are reduced to simple arithmetical formulas, being mere applications of purely formal laws, and in this astronomy has reached a certain stage of perfection. Similarly, the problem of the chemical elements would be solved, if chemistry could demonstrate that the different kinds of matter, as oxygen, carbon, iron, etc., are special forms of one and the same substance only, and that their different properties are natural consequences of their difference in configuration as well as density.

There is no absolutely dead matter. But every atom is freighted with the potentialities of life. The living spontaneity of the world is the condition of the spiritual; but it is not as yet the spiritual in its development, and in its full importance. The spiritual grows in and with the forms of life; it would be nothing without the forms of organization. The spiritual, therefore, appears in its glory in organized life, and has reached upon earth the highest stage of its evolution in the intelligence of the spirit of man.

REAL AND REALITY.

[EXPLANATORY NOTE.]

THE following sentence of the preceding article, "The Reaction against Materialism," seemed to some of my readers to contain a contradiction :

"Materialism went too far when it tried to explain everything from matter, when it identified matter with reality. Yet it stands on solid ground when it maintains that every reality is material."

The contradiction is only apparent, as will be learned from the following consideration :

Every reality has three elements. First, it consists of matter ; secondly, its material particles have a special form ; and thirdly, they are endowed with a certain motion. Matter, form, and motion are abstracts representing certain qualities that are real ; we call them "real" because they are qualities of reality. Matter is real, form is real, motion is real. Yet matter is not all of reality, nor is form, nor is motion ; for every reality, besides being material, possesses at the same time a special form, and is also endowed with some kind of motion.

It is apparent that adjectives have often a wider application than their nouns. The adjective "real" covers a larger field than the noun "reality." Thus every fool is foolish, but every thing that is foolish need not exactly be a fool. I may say, without falling into a contradiction, this : Space is real ; yet space is not a reality. This, in other words, means : Space is a certain quality of reality ; the relations among things, the qualities of things, are objective properties and not mere subjective illusions ; yet is space no thingish entity, no tangible object, as concrete bodies are, e. g., stones, plants, and animals. Space is non-material, and yet space is real. If I have the following two premises :

> Every reality is material.
> Space is real.

I cannot conclude the syllogism with the statement :

> Therefore space is material.

And there is no contradiction involved if I add the sentence :

> And yet space is non-material.

FREEDOM OF WILL AND RESPONSIBILITY.

THE question has often been asked : "Is a man responsible for his actions, or is he the slave of conditions?" The standpoint of science and that of ethics
does not appear to agree. Science rests upon, it presupposes, and, indeed, it proves by its very existence
the rigidity of law. All natural processes are pervaded
by an irrefragable necessity, and psychical acts are
no exception to the universal order of things. But
the clergyman, the teacher, the ethical instructor
step in, proclaiming the moral law : Thou shalt and
thou shalt not. What is the use of moral behests, if
the formation of future events is unalterably fixed, if
we are unable to make or to mar? If this be the case,
does not the *must* of science collide with the *ought* of
morals?

It does not collide, unless the one or the other or
both are misunderstood. The *must* and the *ought* do
not contradict each other ; on the contrary, they condition and they explain one another. The *ought* of
morality has sense only on the supposition of the *must*
of science.

Theologians made the mistake of defining freedom
of will as something that breaks through all natural
laws ; and they were thus obliged to look upon it as a
mystery beyond the grasp of the philosopher. On
the other hand, the philosopher was obliged to deny

the possibility of a freedom of will that infringes
upon natural laws.   Freedom of will was defined
as a contradiction of scientific necessity, as an annihilation of physical laws, and as an exception to the
natural order of things.

What is freedom of will ?   Freedom of will means
that a man is free to do that which he wills.   A prisoner is not free ; his liberty is curtailed : he cannot do
what he wills.   A vanquished man who lies at the feet
of his conqueror, is not free in his action ; he depends
upon the mercy of his adversary.   Yet in a certain
sense even the fettered man, the slave and bondsman
remain, or at least can remain, free.   Their actions
do not, and need not, entirely depend upon circumstances outside of them.

Hagen in the Teutonic Saga stands locked in iron
chains before Chriemhild; he is asked where he had
hidden the treasure of the Nibelungs.   Yet he answers
proudly :

> Den schaz weiz nu nieman wan got unde mîn,
> Der sol dich valantinne immer gar verholn sîn.
>
> [The treasure is known to no one except to God and me,
> Forever, fiendish woman, be it concealed from thee.]

Hagen proves to the Queen of the Huns his freedom of will ; and his will is stronger than the fear of
death, which thereupon he suffers at the hand of the
revengeful woman.

* If the decision of a man is determined by surrounding conditions solely, he feels himself to be, and
indeed he is, a slave of the situation.   But if his decision is determined solely by his character, by the
thoughts and principles that move his mind ; if he remains unbiased by surrounding conditions ; if on the
one hand dangers, calamities, and the prospect of

death cannot frighten, and on the other hand allurements and pleasures cannot decoy: then does his decision depend in all situations upon himself, then is he independent of the influences of surrounding conditions; he is a free man, even if he were laden with chains, even if he were a slave as was Epiktetus.

The motives that set the psychical mechanism of a human soul in motion have two phases—an objective and a subjective phase. They represent, (1) certain facts of the outside world, and, (2) certain principles or maxims in the mind indicating how to deal with the facts of one's surroundings. The objective fact is the one phase and the subjective attitude is the other phase. A man, in whom the objective fact constitutes the overwhelming part of a motive, cannot be said to be free ; but if the subjective attitude remains the decisive element in a motive, he is free, and his actions will be the true expression of his character. He will preserve his freedom even under conditions where weaker souls would yield to a compulsion of circumstances.

The consciousness of man's moral freedom and of the dignity that rises from this freedom should never be lost by any one of us. For the idea that we can be free, if we dare to, that we are free if we do not allow ourselves to be enthralled, will afford us an incalculable power of self-possession. It will give us stability and quietude in the turmoil of exciting events which threaten to carry us away ; whatever be our fate, we can be, and can remain, faithful to ourselves and to our principles.

Freedom of will is man's mark of dignity over brute creation, and Schiller, the poet of liberty, proudly sings:

Man is free, e'en were he born in chains !

•   ˜

In answer to this view, some theologians of a mystical cast of mind declare, that freedom of will does not denote the freedom of man's will to do a thing, but it means the freedom of a man's will to will another thing than he wills. It is plain that the freedom of a man to do what he wills as explained above, does not stand in contradiction to natural laws, it forms no exception to the universal and necessary course of nature. For whatever a man wills, he must will of necessity. The decision of a scoundrel if his freedom of will is not curtailed, if he can act as he pleases, will of necessity be that of a scoundrel ; his actions cannot but show his character: That is his prerogative, flowing from the freedom of will that nature allotted to man. The decisions of an honest man will of necessity be honest and will prove the honesty of his character. If freedom of will means that the decision of the one or the other—granted their characters are as they are—might be different from what it is, this would indeed be a reversion of the order of nature, it would be an annihilation of the law of cause and effect, and it would make ethics impossible, —not only science in general, but among the sciences the science of the moral *ought* also.

We reject any conception of the freedom of will which implies the nonsensical statement that a man could will one thing and the contrary of that thing at the same time. Certainly a man can *wish* two things of which the one excludes the other ; but he can *will* the one only. So long as he wishes to do at the same time two contradictory things, he will do neither the one nor the other, and unless the motive of the one is stronger than the other, he will be like Buridan's donkey, who starves between the two bundles of hay.

Will is the decision to let some of our wishes pass into act. The decision of a fully conscious and responsible man is the end and outcome of a deliberation. It is the plan of action sanctioned by the verdict of a consensus of the principles, the wishes, and the hopes—in one word, of all the ideas of a man. The decision is arrived at by a struggle of the conflicting wishes and it is natural that the strongest wish will of necessity gain the upper hand.

Let us for instance imagine, that a young man is led into temptation. An occasion offers itself to commit a defalcation. The hope of gain is the motive to commit a wrong ; there is the chance of not being discovered ; the stronger that chance is, the more will it strengthen the motive of the deed. On the other hand, there is the remembrance of the eighth commandment '' Thou shalt not steal." There is the shame of becoming a thief, and then perhaps the exhortations of mother and father are remembered. Their shadows may be too dim and their voices may be too faint. Perhaps they grow clearer and stronger, the more the unhappy youth hesitates ; they at last eclipse all other motives and he exclaims '' Never ! I shall never disgrace the name of my family ; I shall keep holy the remembrance of father and mother, and remain as honest as were my parents."

The decision of a deliberation will always turn out as it does, with necessity. The decision, however, does not depend on the circumstances of the surrounding world alone, not solely on conditions outside of us, but also and chiefly on our character, on the conditions inside of us. If our moral principles, if the remembrances of dear parents and instructors are strong in a man, if he is clear-minded and far-sighted enough to see the evil consequences that, perhaps not at once but after a while, will be sure to fall upon him, he will not be in danger .of falling an easy prey to every temptation. And it is for this reason that an ethical instruction of the young is necessary, that we build churches and have preachers to tell us again and again, how necessary is the moral ought. Noble ideals and virtuous principles must be implanted into the minds of men. They must become parts of their souls and truly the dominant parts, so that they will never be overruled in temptation by evil motives and low desires.

Could we preach morals, if after all an honest man might will the contrary of what he wills, if his decision did not result from his character with necessity, but might perchance be different from what it is? Or again, would it be worth while to trouble about preaching morals, if a bad character, into whose soul never entered any idea of obeying another command than the impulses of egotism, might after all act right as if he were a good and honest and well conducted man ?

The *ought* of ethics would have no sense, if there were no *must* in the course of nature, such as science can prove. The *must* in natural events and in history is not such as is taught by Fatalism, that man is unable to change its course. The fates of individuals and of nations do not depend upon the circumstances of environment only. The most important factor of our personal development and of the future of a nation lies within—within the minds and the hearts of people. *Jeder ist seines Glückes Schmied,* ("Every one forges his own fate,") says a German proverb, almost too trite to be quoted. And yet it is so very true ! The result of our development depends not only upon the circumstances under which we are born and live, but necessarily and naturally also, and chiefly, upon the manner in which we use these circumstances.

Therefore it is not true—although it is often contended—that science when recognizing the necessity with which decisions of the will take place, destroys the responsibility of man. What is responsibility but the consciousness that a man has to bear the consequences of his actions, be it for good or for evil? The experience of common sense teaches and science proves that every action always has definite consequences, which upon the whole can be calculated and ascertained before the execution of the action ; and the person who does an action must accordingly be looked upon as the author not only of the action, but also of the consequences contingent upon that action.

A man in whose mind this idea is always present, i. e., a man who feels himself responsible for his actions, has a great advantage over persons in whom it is lacking. Those in whom it is lacking are, properly speaking, not men ; they are children. They are liable to commit indeliberate actions which must in the end lead them into trouble ; and if their own misfortunes do not educate them to become responsible men, they will ultimately go to the wall.

A man in whose soul the idea that he is responsible for his actions is a controlling power, is called a character. In whatever he does he will prove a consistency with himself and will never have occasion for regret. This idea so long as it is present in his mind, will exercise in difficulties a decisive, and in temptations a wholesome, influence upon all his decisions.

*   *   *

A criticism by Mr. John Maddock on this article, "Freedom of Will and Responsibility," appeared in No. 142 of *The Open Court,* in reply to which the following remarks were made :

Mr. John Maddock apparently misunderstands the position taken in the article "Freedom of Will and Responsibility." Freedom of will is defined, not in a theological or metaphysical sense, but in the physical or natural sense, as the power to do that which one wills. A slave who works because he is compelled to work is not free : he acts under compulsion ; but a man who works because he is eager to perform a certain work, is free : he acts of his own free will.

The old theological or metaphysical conception defines Freedom of Will as the freedom of a man to will whatever he wills. This definition is widely different from our definition "to do that which one wills." According to this wrong view of the Freedom of Will, generally called indeterminism, the decision of a man is not bound, not determined by any law ; he may will as he does, but he might under the very same circumstances will differently.

Indeterminism is based upon error ; it attributes to man an exceptional place in the universe ; he is supposed to be exempt from natural laws, and the rigid law of cause and effect, it is maintained, does not apply to his will.

Mr. Maddock's objections are all valid and sound against Freedom of Will in the metaphysical sense, viz., against indeterminism, that a man can will whatever he wills. Indeterminism admits law in the environment in nature, but denies it in the organism, in the will of man. Indeterminism declares that there is a cause for every natural phenomenon, but there is no cause for human action ; man is supposed to act without a cause. This view is the very basis of dualism, and we have repeatedly called attention to the untenableness of its position.

Matters are very different, if our definition of Freewill is accepted. The decision of a free man depends upon his character. He will not yield to compulsion, but act as he sees fit. And a free man must of necessity will and act as he does. This theory of free will is not indeterminism ; on the contrary, it is in accord with determinism.

We are wont to call a man who is easily carried away to inconsiderate actions, a slave of his passion. The action of a rash man may be called free, because he acts without compulsion ; yet he is not free in so far as his decision is made without proper deliberation. One part of his soul alone decides his will, and this part, at the time unduly strong, suppresses all other thoughts, all nobler ideals, and worthier considerations. His better self is not allowed to be heard on this occasion and does not speak until it is too late. The result of such action is called regret, or if it be very strong, remorse.

A man who either from ignorance or malevolence does not care to have his decisions governed by justice and rectitude, will commit actions which he would have to regret if he were a moral man. Such a man society forces by its judicial and police institutions to do right. Such a man is not free ; society makes him a slave of the laws of society ; "he needs a policeman," as Mr. Maddock says. And I believe every one of us possesses a tendency to overstep the limits of our rights and infringe upon our neighbors'. Yet at the same time, every one of us is animated (if it were not from natural kindliness it would be from mere egotism) by a spirit of benevolence toward our fellow-beings and the good intention to be a useful and worthy member of society. In that case, however, the law would become part of our soul ; "the policeman," to use Mr. Maddock's expression, would be within us ; and in that case our decisions, being regulated by ourselves, would be the expression of our own character. We would not be slaves of the policeman ; we would be policeman and subject in one person ; and accordingly would be our own commanders : we would be free.".

IS DEATH A FINALITY?

It is a well-known fact to which scientists and thinkers have more than once called our attention, that there is no natural death among the lowly organized animals that stand at the bottom of the ladder of evolution. Moners and amœbas grow and divide; and if they are not starved or crushed to death, they will live and multiply into eternity. The moner which we fish out of a pond of stagnant water for observation to-day, is the same individual or part of the same individual that lived æons ago, long long before man appeared upon earth.

Is not man a part of animal life, and indeed the highest part? How is it that he must die? If immortality is the natural state of those creatures of which all higher animate beings are but complex and differentiated forms, how did it happen that death came into this world of life?

DEATH AND BIRTH.

Death is the twin of birth. It seems natural to say that all that lives must die. This, however, is a wrong statement of facts. It is more correct to say that every creature that is born will die. Birth is the beginning of a new being and death is its end. Yet we shall easily recognize the truth that neither birth is an absolutely new beginning nor death an absolute finality. Beginning and end of individual life are relative.

When we investigate the problem of the origin of death, we must at the same time answer the question, " How did birth come into the world? "

The moner knows of no birth; it grows and divides, thus passing beyond the limits of its individual existence. There is not a mother-moner, and its child; there are only the results of a division. The same moner is before us, not in one coherent lump, but in two parts.

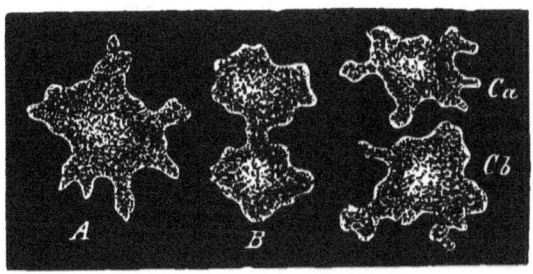

PROPAGATION OF A MONER.

The propagation of moners, the lowliest organized of beings, occurs by spontaneous division. *A*, The complete moner—a Protamœba. *B*, Splitting up of the same by a median contraction, into two halves. *C*, Each of the two halves has separated from its companion and makes up an independent individual. (After Haeckel.)

The process is a little more complicated in such unicellular organisms as the *amœba sphaerococcus* for instance. This amœba contains a nucleus (*A*, *b*), with a nucleolus (*A*, *a*); and its plasma (*A*, *c*) is encased in a membrane (*A*, *d*). When the amœba grows the nucleolus doubles, and the plasma bursts its membrane (as seen in *B*). Each nucleolus forms its own nucleus, and the plasma gathering round each nucleus begins to separate into two parts, until the division is perfect.

PROPAGATION OF AMŒBA SPHAEROCOCCUS.

The propagation of this unicellular organism takes place by spontaneous division. *A.* Encased amœba, a simple spherical cell, consisting of a lump of protoplasm (*c*), which contains a nucleus (*b*) and a nucleolus (*a*), and is enclosed in a membrane. *B.* The released amœba that has burst its cyst or membranous pouch and left it. Its nucleus contains two nucleoli. *C.* The amœba begins to divide, its nucleus splitting up into two nuclei and the plasma between the two contracting. *D.* The division is completed, the plasma also having been completely divided into two parts (*Da* and *Db*). (After Haeckel, *Natürliche Schöpfungsgeschichte.*)

The next step in the evolution of a 'growth beyond the limits of individual existence' is gemmation. Gemmation is a process that can be observed in spring in all trees and flowers. A bud appears, and grows rapidly to maturity. Many worms, some medusas, and some corals multiply by gemmation. In gemmation the parts are not equal at the start. There is a mother, and a child; for the division is only partial, and the child begins as a germ.

Sporogony is not much different from gemmation; it is the secretion of germinal cells, called spores. The spores possess the faculty of developing the same structures of which its mother organism consists.

Sporogony is the connecting link leading to sexual generation, which for all higher stages of life is destined to become the sole method of procreation. Among that order of beings whose nature is not yet

so defined that they can be classed either with animals
or with plants, and which Professor Haeckel calls
protists, many instances are to be found where the
procreation of spores results from a union of two individual cells. These cells may, in many cases, yet
not always, be of a homogeneous nature. And in the
course of further advancement the two cells become
distinct ; they commence to disintegrate into two different and complementary elements, which show an
affinity for one another, similar to that between chemical alkalis and bases which tend to unite into salts.
As soon as this differentiation takes place we have examples of sexual generation.

Multiplication by division is not entirely limited
to the very lowest creatures ; we find it also among
animals that stand comparatively high in the scale
of evolution, much higher at least than the moner.
Some polyps, and among them corals, multiply by division. Their mouths, having the appearance of a
flower, grow broader in size ; the opposite edges approach each other at the median line, until they unite.
Thus the two corners of the mouth are separated for
good and form two corals upon one stalk.

There is, for the individual animals that come into
existence, a great advantage in the process of multiplication by division. Every moner, every polyp thus
produced starts in life as a full-fledged creature.
There is no state of infancy with all its troubles and
dangers to be passed through, for these creatures make
their first appearance in a state of maturity. It is
natural that the form and soul of the original organism
should thus be preserved in all the details of their
parts. The heredity of these animals is no similarity,
but absolute identity.

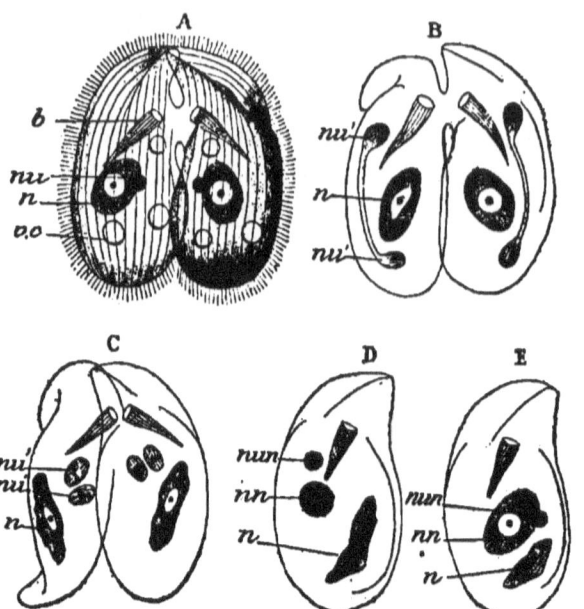

CONJUGATION OF CHILODON CUCULLULUS.

A shows the two individuals in immediate contact; *b*, mouth; *v. c.*, contractile vesicle; *n*, nucleus; *nu*, nucleolus or attendant nucleus, i. e., new formation of a smaller nucleus.

B. The attendant nucleus divides into two segments, *nu'* and *nu'*. The old nucleus *n* shows signs of regression.

C. After the division of the segments has been completely effected, one segment of each individual is exchanged for one of the other individual, when a union of both as thus exchanged takes place.

D shows an unequal breaking up of the newly formed mixed nucleus into a larger (*nn*) and a smaller (*nun*) segment.

E. The old nucleus dries up, and the larger segment of the new-formed nucleus assumes its function in the individual; the smaller segment forms the new attendant nucleus.

Many details of this process, the investigations regarding which have been carried on particularly by Bütschli, Maupas, and Balbiani, have not as yet been satisfactorily established. Whether the exchange of the differentiated parts takes place through the mouth or through a special orifice, could not, owing to the small size of the creatures, be determined. Still, whatever obscurity may prevail in matters of particular process, it is firmly settled that we have to deal in such cases with a fertilization constituting the beginning of sexual generation.

These advantages are lost in the measure that the procreation of new individuals approaches the system of sexual generation. Buds are at first very tender and may easily be injured before they are as strong as their mother organism. Spores are helpless and may be devoured as food by the many hungry animals that swarm about them. And the higher we rise in the scale of evolution the greater become the difficulties of a germ to reach maturity. These disadvantages to the individual, however, are richly overbalanced by the higher advantages afforded through greater possibilities of development and progress. The struggle for life grows fiercer, yet in and through the struggle the organisms grow stronger ; they adapt themselves to conditions, first unconsciously, then consciously, and in man they acquire that foresight and circumspection which make him the lord of creation.

Those animals that survive can upon the whole survive only by great efforts ; they were not strong at the start, so they had to learn to be strong ; they were unmindful in the presence of dangers, so they had to learn to be on their guard in perilous situations. In every respect they had to pass through a severe school and every single virtue that can lead them onwards, they had to acquire themselves.

Innumerable individuals, it is true, are sacrificed in the struggle for existence ; yet their lives are not mere waste in the household of nature : they are the martyrs of progress ; and the generation of to-day lives upon the fruits of their sacrifice.

In sexual generation there is a blending of two individuals which affords greater possibilities for improvement. The conditions under which the complementary germs unite, and the proportions of their

mixture may be different. Thus a variety is produced
which admits of a selection of the best, the strongest,
and the most adapted for survival. The original conservatism of life that tended to reproduce itself exactly, down to the minutest details, is in this way not
abolished, but modified or checked by the possibility
of changes. Life becomes more plastic ; and the severe teacher of life, nature, takes care that bad qualities unfit for preservation will soon discontinue.

WHENCE CAME DEATH ?

There is a moral in the victory of sexual generation over the multiplication by division. Sexual or
amphigonous generation is less egotistical than non-
sexual or monogonous generation. It is no mere reproduction of self, but the reproduction of a unison of
two selves. Sexual generation, propagation by birth,
and the helplessness of offspring in infancy impose
heavy duties, as of nursing and education, upon parent-
individuals ; yet the performance of these duties is
richly rewarded in the progress of the race. These
duties teach even creatures of lower rank to care
for the preservation of their kind more in their children than in their individual selves. The rise to
higher planes in evolution is conditioned by the development of moral faculties.

The sacrifice that creatures have to bring for the
amelioration of their offspring is greater still : they
have to sacrifice their individual immortality. It appears that the regenerative faculty of an amœba depends upon the function of its nucleus, perhaps even
of the nucleolus. The ingenious experiments of Gruber,
Nussbaum, and Ehrenberg, prove, that if we cut out
the nucleus from one of the lowly organisms the

animal will continue to live, but that it has lost the power of renewing its form.* Balbiani, who repeated the experiments of Gruber upon *Stentor cœruleus*, shows in the adjoined diagram the renewal of the whole individual from any part if but one nucleus be preserved.

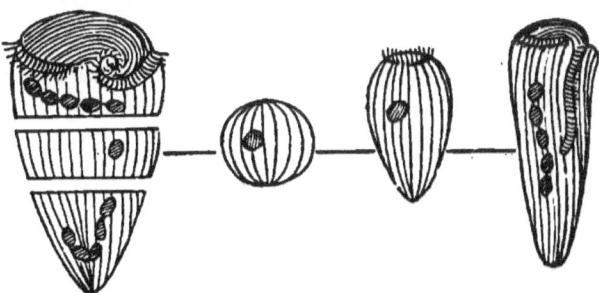

ARTIFICIAL DIVISION OF STENTOR CŒRULEUS.

The nucleus of *Stentor cœruleus* consists of a chain of nuclear beads. The prefixed figure shows the restoration of the middle section which contains only a single nucleus. After M. Balbiani.†

It is the nucleus that in lower animals represents the inner organs of reproduction, which, as we have seen, in the two sexes are differentiated into two com-- plementary parts. In a child the differentiation of the nucleus into either a male or a female germ has begun but is not yet perfect. The child, still possessing a re-formative nucleus, thus grows; and in many respects its tender system possesses more vitality than an adult person. But as soon as the child has reached the state of maturity, when the differentiation of the nucleus has become perfect, its growth ceases. The nucleus in each individual of the two sexes no longer being complete loses its re-form-

* *Biologisches Centralblatt*, 1885, p. 73; *Encyclopedia Britannica*, Protozoa.

† From Alfred Binet's monograph, *The Psychic Life of Micro-Organisms.* Open Court Pub. Co., Chicago, Ill.

§

ative power with regard to the individual and can
temporarily regain it only through fecundation. Properly speaking neither man nor woman is a perfect and
independent being. Separately they are mortals, they
are doomed to die. They will live for a while like a
micro-organism whose nucleus is imperfect. Yet in
their unison, man and woman together, are as immortal as the moner.

Upon this fact is based the holiness of matrimony.
Matrimony is a union not for this life only, but for our
life after death in the coming generations. This makes
of wedlock an act of religious sanctity ; and it is apparent that it should not be entered upon merely from
personal considerations, for the benefit, the pleasure,
or happiness of either or both parties. The future
of humanity depends upon the sacredness of matrimony.

Birth, we have learned, is a special kind of multiplication ; and, as such, it is a growth beyond the limits
of individual existence. Before the life of a child
commenced, it was a part of its parents ; and its existence is nothing but an outgrowth and a continuation of their lives. Thus the immortality of the
moner is not lost in the higher stages of organized
life, it only becomes more spiritual. It ceases more
and more to be an identity of the body, and becomes
a preservation of the soul. The soul of an animal,
however, is not its mere shape, not its present form
alone, but its formative principle also : the form of
special motions, and the form to which these motions
in a further evolution will lead. The soul of an as-
piring man is not only the faculties he possesses at
present, but the ideals also which he aspires to ; it is
the direction of his energy and the goal of his en-

deavors. This preservation of human souls, admitting of development, is therefore greatly superior to the conservatism of the soul-life in moners ; it is the preservation, not of the present form, but of an upward movement, of the soul of soul, and this leads to a realization of ever higher possibilities.

Is the immortality of soul-life not more valuable than individual existence? If the death of ourselves, as individuals, is the price thereof, let Death have his prey, and let him teach us the earnestness of life, so that we may regulate our conduct, not from the standpoint of narrow egotism, not according to the view that death is a finality, but from the ethical standpoint of immortality.

THE ETHICS OF IMMORTALITY.

Death is no finality, and we must not form our rules of conduct to accord with the idea that the exit of our individual life is the end of all. People who have no interests, no hopes or fears, no cares or ideals that reach beyond the grave, may enjoy themselves better than others who live their lives with a constant prospect of immortality ; yet, in the long run of many generations they will go to the wall. Nature does not preserve the individual that cares for itself alone. But nature preserves those individual features of great men who conquer egotism, and lead moral lives of self-discipline and ideal aspirations.

The immortality of the soul was instinctively felt even before man could have a distinct and clear idea about its possibility. The moral teachers of mankind found it necessary to build their ethics upon this truth, and it is not at all to be wondered at that the opinions of the churches survived in the struggle for

•

existence against those people who looked upon death
as an absolute finality. The belief in the immortality of soul·life is a marvelous preservative among
the many dangers and temptations of the world, and
the ethics that are derived therefrom are innervating
and refreshing and strengthening.

The immortality of the soul was taught to be
the migration of a disembodied ghost, who was supposed to wander through unknown haunts, or to soar
upward to some distant star. We now know that this
view is, upon scientific grounds, untenable. But this
erroneous conception was, after all, truer than the
flat denial of any immortality. The truth that lives
in the error keeps it alive, to the great astonishment
of those who look upon the immortality of the soul as
a mere superstition.

The ethics that Sophocles taught in his time was a
rule of conduct dictated by a regard for our state after
death. There was nothing higher, nothing greater
to a Greek citizen than obedience to the laws of his
country. Yet the regard for our state after death,
the poet declared, is holier still ; it is an unwritten
law graven in our hearts, and it rules supreme over
all the written laws of states. The ruler of a city
may impiously deny the rite of burial to his enemy ;
he may, by the written law of state authority, inflict
capital punishment upon the transgressor. But a
woman like Antigone will disobey the royal authority,
because of the higher authority of the unwritten law
in her heart. An offence like that is a righteous offence.   •

Sophocles makes her declare to Creon the motive
of her deed in the following lines :

"Thus have I righteously offended here.
For longer time, methinks, have I to please
The dwellers in that world than those in this;
For I shall rest forever there ; but thou
Dishonor, if thou wilt, the laws divine."

The whole gist of ethics—if it be real ethics, and not mere worldly prudence—is the regulation of life from the standpoint of eternity. The attempt has been made by philosophers who look upon death as a finality, to construct a new kind of ethics which should have nothing to do with any aspirations that reach beyond the grave. They succeeded to a certain extent ; they succeeded in so far as they showed that all egotism will necessarily fail to accomplish its ends, and that those who yearn for happiness will be sure never to gain it. Therefore, they said, if you want happiness, do not seek it, do not long for it, for if you do, you will miss it. * This is the negative result of an attempt to base ethics on man's yearning for happiness ; and this result is most valuable, in so far as it proves that our yearning for happiness is just that instinct which must be checked by the behests of ethics.

Ethics must be based on facts, and must be applied to facts. The facts of soul-life and its relations to the surrounding world, do not make it likely that living creatures exist for the mere enjoyment of life. Happiness is one important component of life. But so is work, so is recreation, so is the endeavor to progress, and so is the satisfaction of having accomplished something useful for humanity. Happiness is

* Mr. Herbert Spencer in the *Popular Science Monthly* for August, 1888, compares happiness to the bull's eye of a target which must not be directly aimed at. "If you do," the instructor in archery says, "you will inevitably miss it.' Happiness, we agree with Mr. Spencer, is generally desired ; but says Mr. Spencer, "happiness will not be found if it is directly sought."

not the end and purpose of life. If it were, the great pessimist, Schopenhauer, would be right, that life is not worth its own troubles. Life is the dénouement, the development, the evolution of the cosmos. If life can be said, at all, to have a purpose, it is its own evolution. And the evolution of life is no mere blind struggle for existence, but a race in an arena for ethical aspirations.

There are dreamers who think that competition is the root of all evil ; they picture a state of society in which happiness will rule because competition has disappeared. It is the dream of a Schlaraffia, of an Utopian country, where *dolce far niente* makes a paradise in which men live without backbones, because no backbone is needed in a heaven where the struggle for existence is abolished. Let them beware lest their dreams make them unfit for real life.

There is another class of men who like such dreamers hanker after a state of peaceful enjoyment. Being in possession of some worldly goods, they wish to preserve them without being exposed to the constant struggle for life, which forces them to be always alert to keep abreast with competitors, and to progress with the spirit of the time. These men clamor for protection of national industry, they favor combinations, trusts, and pools. A high tariff and strong trusts may certainly for a time make business life easy in our manufacturing-world, but in the long run it will weaken it. Indeed, high tariffs and "combines" are (so I am told, the greatest iron manufacturer of America said) certain signs of weakness. I do not intend to discuss politics here. A tariff may or may not be justified in special cases for some reason or another. We might indeed be obliged to wage a commercial war against

England, or against Europe generally. Yet we must
bear in mind that if a country introduces tariffs for
protection, it must be considered as a time of education; it is the raising a child and bringing it up to
maturity. The purpose of each war is an honorable
peace, the purpose of school is practical life. The
purpose of a tariff for protection must be its abolition
in not too distant a time.

Let us not look for ease in this world unless it be
on the eve of a life that has been full of aspirations
and labor. There is no ease for those who wish to progress. And let us find satisfaction not in the pleasures
of life, but in the noble struggle for advancement and
amelioration.

Facts being as they are, we must adapt ourselves
to facts. If we do, we shall master them and govern
the course of nature. But our adaptation to facts must
not be from to-day to to-morrow, but so far as we can
see. It must be made from the standpoint of immortality, and with due regard for the unity of all life upon
earth and in consideration of the grand possibilities
and noble ideals of mankind. Here lies the basis of
ethical aspirations.

THE COMMUNISM OF SOUL-LIFE.

THE nature of all soul-life, intellectual as well as emotional, is founded upon communism. No growth of ideas for any length of time is possible without communication. It is the exchange of thought and mutual criticism that produces intellectual progress. And it is the warmth of a sympathetic heart which kindles similar feelings in others.

With every sentence that you speak to others, a part of your soul is transferred to them. And in their souls your words may fall like seeds. Some may fall by the wayside where the fowls come and devour them up. Others may fall upon a rock where they have not much earth. Some may fall among thorns which will choke them. Yet some of them will fall upon good ground : and the words will take root and grow and bring forth fruit, some a hundred-fold, some sixty-fold, some thirty-fold.

We may compare humanity to a coral plant. The single corals are connected among themselves through the canals in the branches from which they grow. No one of them can prosper without supplying its neighbors with the superabundance of its prosperity. The main difference is that the communism of soul·life is much closer and more intimate, and the thinker who freely gives away his spiritual treasures, unlike the giver of material gifts, does not lose : he is rather the gainer, for spiritual possessions grow in importance the more profusely they are imparted. The commoner they are, the more powerful they become.

Every spiritual giving is a gaining ; it is a taking possession of other peoples' minds. It is an expansion, a transplantation of our thoughts, a psychic growth beyond the narrow limits of our individual existence into other souls ; it is a rebuilding, a reconstruction of our own souls or of parts of our own souls, in other souls. It is a transference of mind. Every conversation is an exchange of souls. Those whose souls are 'flat, stale, and unprofitable,' cannot be expected to overflow with deep thought. But those who are rich in spiritual treasures will not, as misers, keep them for themselves. For out of the abundance of the heart the mouth speaketh, and spiritual treasures are not wasted when imparted ; they are not lost, but put out on usury, and will multiply and thus bring great reward, although the reward be not personal profit to ourselves.

Good and noble ideas, instructive truths, warm words of good-will and sympathy will accomplish great things. But evil words possess a similar power. Strong characters will hear and reject evil words, but weak minds will be poisoned by them. It is the great consequence that speech draws with it, which demands that before uttering it we should weigh every word. Every idle word that men speak, says Christ, they shall give account thereof in the day of judgment. And the day of judgment takes place now and here. The day of judgment is the time when every action produces its natural results. Schiller says :

" Die Weltgeschichte,
Ist das Weltgerichte."

"History is the judgment of nations," and the history of every person is his life and future fate. And in addition to this fate during life-time, the day of judgment is the blessing that later on will attend every good deed and the curses that will inevitably follow upon every bad action.

Who is so vile as to be indifferent to the effects of his life after he has passed away? Who is so base as not to care whether the effects of his actions shall or shall not prove a curse to humanity? We ought to consider how posterity will judge of our actions after we are gone and what we would think of ourselves when, in the peaceful rest of the grave, we hope for neither personal advantages nor disadvantages.

We ought to reason from the standpoint of the progressive spirit in a future humanity. These considerations should be among the strongest of the motives that determine our actions.

The communism of soul-life is not limited to the present generation; it extends to the past as well as to the future. The present generation of humanity is like the present generation of live corals who have grown from, and rest upon, the work of former generations. The ancestors of the corals now on the surface lived in the shallow places of the ocean, where the sun made the waters warm and the surf afforded them sufficient food; and when in the lapse of time through terrestrial changes the bottom on which they had settled, sank slowly deeper and deeper, they built higher and higher, and in this way they managed to keep near the surface. The branches in the cold deep waters are now dead; yet they furnish a solid basis to the coral life above, where the sun shines and the currents of the surf pass to and fro.

If the corals could think and speak, I wonder whether the living generation on the surface would not rail at the corals in the cold deep below! At least the present human generation very often does. Those who feel the necessity of progress, who wish humanity to remain uppermost and to rise higher, are apt to overlook the merits of their ancestors; they observe that the ideas of former generations are antiquated and do no longer fit into the present time. Thus they brand the old views as superstitions and forget that the views of the present generation have developed from the old, and that they stand upon their ancestors' work. It would seem as if the dead corals in the cold dreary deep must have been always unfit for life; yet there was a time when their coral homes thrilled with life; and so there was a time when the superstitions of to-day were true science and true religion although they are now dreary and cold.

Where is the coral life of the past? Has it disappeared? It has not disappeared; but continued, and its continuation is the coral life of to-day. So the humanity of former generations has not disappeared. The life of humanity continued, and lo! it is present in every one of us. We may reproach our ancestors for mistakes, but whenever we reproach them, we reproach ourselves.

We wish to be individuals, and flatter ourselves that we are quite original. Goethe explains in a little poem that the different features of his character are derived from his parents and grandparents. All together make up his character. He concludes:

> " Since from the complex you cannot
> The elements extract.

What is in man, that will remain
Original in fact."*

It is vanity to think that we are something by ourselves. By vanity we understand a conceit which at-
taches a special value to Self. It is an inflation of the
ego, of a something which is erroneously supposed to
be quite individual and original. This pride is always
ridiculous, because Self by itself is a mere nothing : it
is a hollow bubble ; and pride of Self is therefore correctly called vanity, which means emptiness. Our
spiritual existence is an inheritance. We are a "tradition," as Goethe says in another little poem, in
which he depicts the vanity of the boast to rid oneself of tradition. He says :

> " Would from tradition free myself,
> Original I'd be !
> Yet great the undertaking is
> And trouble it heaps on me.

> " Were I indigenous, I should
> Consider the honor high,
> But strange enough ! it is the truth,
> Tradition myself am I."

> [" Gern wär ich Ueberliefrung los
> Und ganz original ;
> Doch ist das Unternehmen gross
> Und führt zu mancher Qual.

---

* Of this poem the beginning is better known than its conclusion. It reads
in the original :

> "Vom Vater hab' ich die Statur,
> Des Lebens ernstes Führen,
> Von Mütterchen die Frohnatur
> Und Lust zu fabuliren.

> Urahnherr war der Schönsten hold,
> Das spukt so hin und wieder,
> Urahnfrau liebte Schmuck und Gold,
> Das zuckt wohl durch die Glieder.

> Sind nun die Elemente nicht
> Aus dem Complex zu trennen,
> Was ist denn an dem ganzen Wicht
> Original zu nennen ?

Als Autochthone rechnet' ich
Es mir zur höchsten Ehre,
Wenn ich nicht gar zu wunderlich
Selbst Ueberliefrung wäre."]

There is nothing in us, but we owe it to humanity ;
for all soul-life is based upon communism. We cannot entirely escape its evil consequences, but neither
can we entirely forfeit its blessings, and the blessings
are greater than its curses.

SOUL-LIFE AND THE PRESERVATION OF FORM.

MAN is not the sum of the material particles of which at any given moment he consists. Every man is a special form that has taken shape in matter; and the material particles are not the really essential elements that make him what he is. A man might have eaten the meat intended for his dog, and the dog might have gotten the piece that his master ate. And so, too, the dog might have breathed the air that the man breathed, and *vice versa*. But that would have made no difference in the assimilation by each of the material particles in question. In man's stomach they go through the process of being changed into human flesh and blood, while that nutriment on which an animal has fed will become part of the animal.

This appears wonderful, and yet the principle obviously accords with the simple law of mechanics. Materials can be shaped, mechanically, into certain forms. The shape of a bronze figure depends upon the mould into which the metal is poured, and the products of a machine, be they nails, or pins, or needles, or books, or newspapers, or hardware, depend upon the mechanism of the machine. The form of the machine produces a special form of movement, for the movement of the cogs and wheels will follow the grooves and other mechanical contrivances; and upon the form of the movements necessarily the form of the product depends.

The process of changing food into flesh and blood is immeasurably more complicated than the work of a machine, yet the basis of mechanical law is the same in both. The difference of form in the product can depend solely upon the difference of the mechanisms. In the living mechanisms of organized substances, in plants, in animals and in man, we can, with the microscopical methods at our disposal, recognize the rudest and roughest features only of the mechanical differences in the innumerable parts which contribute to shape the sap of trees and the blood of animals. And these differences of form are the problems of scientific investigation. We can appreciate the differences in the result, (say for instance between an animal brain and a human brain,) we know also much about the conditions which produced these different results, yet we know little about the mechanical details of organisms, i. e., *how* the living machines of animals and plants assimilate food. But we have sufficient evidence to believe, that the process is in full agreement with mechanical laws, and that the problem is merely a problem of form.

Man's soul does not consist of matter; nor can it be a substance like matter, such as are fluids or gaseous and ether-like substances. Conceptions, that materialize the soul, are the materialistic views of spiritists. It is not matter which makes of us that which we are, it is not substance, but form; and the formation of a man's life does not commence with his birth, nor does it end with his death.

Our material existence is constantly changing, and yet we remain the same persons to-day that we were yesterday. How is this? It is because man's life consists not of his material presence alone, but of his formal being, and his formal being shows relatively more continuity than his material existence. There is a law of the conservation of matter and energy, but there is another law of no less importance, which I will call the law of the preservation of form.

We call it preservation and not conservation, in order to mark the difference between the two laws. Matter and energy are indestructible, but all special forms are destructible, they are not conserved in their kind or amount. Yet they are preserved; they remain as they are according to the law of inertia until changes take place which do not destroy the present forms, but which alter them in the measure that special causes affect them. The old form is in a certain sense fully preserved even in a most radical change, for the old form is one of the elements in the change. It may be destroyed in all that gives value to it; its trace can become infinitesimal; yet being one of the factors in causation it can never be blotted out entirely.

The changeability of form constitutes what we call evolution. Evolution indeed means 'change of form according to certain laws.' Laws of form are geometrically demonstrable, and laws of the changes of form can be ultimately accounted for with mathematical precision.

In Dr. Johannes Ranke's most excellent work on anthropology* man and mankind are compared to a wave. A wave appears to the eye as a material unit. Its form travels along on the surface of the water, ever one and the same; but its substance is constantly changing. It is the mere expression of a number of

* Dr. Johannes Ranke: *Der Mensch*, p. 1.

rhythmical motions, and there are not two consecutive moments in which the constituent particles are the same. The drops which one moment are seized by the approaching wave, rise in the next to its crest and then glide gently back on the other side of the billow to the quiet surface of the ocean.

The body of the wave is formed by the particles of water which enter into and pass through the wave. Similarly the human body, like a wave of water, is a certain form of rhythmical motions. Material elements, the air we breathe, the food we take, are seized upon, only to pass through and leave the body, whose form continues and appears to the uninitiated as the same material unit.

The same simile is true of mankind as a whole. The activity of the human race, as we observe it in history, rolls onward like a huge wave over the surface of the habitable globe. It incorporates and transforms the organic materials in its way only to give them back to the ocean of unorganized material existence from which they were taken. In the onward course of human evolution, the generations of which it consists rise into existence and sink back as the wave of humanity rolls on. The generation of to-day is different from the generations of former centuries, but humanity is one continuous whole throughout all of them. It began with the origin of life on our planet, and its onward movement will continue as long as the organic substance of the earth can afford sufficient material to renew its form.

In all the material changes that organized bodies undergo, there is a preservation of their forms. An impression once made will remain, as a wound once received will preserve the scar. The new formation of the ever changing tissues will be made in the shape which they possess. Scars will in time become invisible, but they will never be effaced entirely. A sensation that has been once perceived will leave some trace in the tissues of the living brain, and the form of this trace will not be effaced amid the change of matter that the nervous substance constantly undergoes. It will be preserved; and as soon as, through the stimulus of nervous action, it is again excited, the sensation will be revived, although it will be weaker than it was when it first impressed itself. If the sensation be strong enough it will be felt again, and may be accompanied more or less intensely with consciousness. Thus the preservation of form accounts for the continuity of memory.

The identity of memory-structures does not depend upon an identity of the very same material particles, but upon an identity of form in tissues of the same kind. Nervous substance is the most unstable, and its material changes are the most rapid of all. It is therefore all but impossible that in the constant flux of matter, the continuance of memory should be attached to the material particles. It is a continuance of form only, just as a fountain preserves its form during the uninterrupted change of the water. The fountain-jet remains the same and we consider it in different moments as the same not otherwise than ourselves, because in the flux of its material constituents, its form remains constant.

The solution of the problem of memory, accordingly, solves the problem of the personality of man also. The personality of man and the continuity of his soul-life, can find their explanation only in the preservation of all the living forms of his organism.

Supposing that all motions of material elements are accompanied by elements of feeling, we then understand how feeling, as a special combination of its elements under special circumstances can originate in organized substance. Further, we understand how from simple and dim feelings specialized sensations evolve as a kind of articulated feeling, and these sensations naturally become representatives of the objects which occasion them. When we notice in a number of sensations their common features, and observe their differences, we begin to think, and we learn to classify things around us under abstract terms. Thus we understand how the soul of man with its wonderful structures rises into existence, building one tier above the other, and culminating in an organ of co-ordination which makes a comparison and unification of all the elements of soul-life possible.

Man's soul was formed in the course of the evolution of the human race, by the reactions upon the external influences of the surrounding world, and the present man is the outcome of the entire activity of his ancestors. Thus every one of us can say with Christ : "Before Abraham was, I am." Every one of us began his life with the beginning of all life upon earth. We are the generation in which the huge billow of human life now culminates. We, ourselves, are that ·billow, our real self, our spiritual existence will continue to progress in that great wave.

Our existence after death will not merely be a dissolution into the All, where all individual features of our spiritual existence are destroyed. Our existence after death will be a continuance of our individual spirituality, a continuance of our thoughts and ideals. As sure as the law of cause and effect is true, so sure is the continuance of soul-life even after the death of the individual according to the law of the preservation of form.

THE OLD AND NEW PSYCHOLOGY.

WHEN the wonderful workings of electricity were first discovered, electricity was considered as a substance, as a kind of an ethereal fluid that permeated bodies. And the very terms used by our scientists to-day still show traces of this error. We now conceive electricity to be a certain mode of motion rapidly transmitted from atom to atom, we no longer believe in a special electrical substance that flows through bodies ; and yet we retain the expression "electrical current."

The scientists of former ages were wrong with regard to the scientific understanding of the nature of electricity ; but in spite of their errors they formulated various laws that held good even after the error was corrected. The idea that electricity is a current served as a simile, which in many respects is so appropriate that even now our professors have to fall back on it in their explanations and probably always will, although they have to add the special warning not to take the simile for more than it is worth.

Suppose that in former centuries you had come upon two opposed views, the one of a scientist who declared that electricity existed as a substance, and the other of a man who maintained that electricity could not possibly be a substance, and that it did not

•

exist at all. On which side would there have been more truth? Unquestionably on the former.

Now the old psychology of former centuries considered the soul as consisting of a special substance, a kind of ethereal fluid endowed with several mystical qualities. Modern psychology, not unlike modern science in other fields, now comes to the conclusion that there is no special soul-substance; the soul is but a special form of life. The old psychologists, however, were not entirely wrong, for they committed an error that was natural in the evolution of psychological truths. Their views were after all more correct than the views of their adversaries, who, objecting to the existence of a soul substance, denied the existence of the soul altogether. The old psychologists discovered some of the laws of soul-life, and also derived from them certain principles which they laid down as rules of moral conduct and which will remain true forever.

There is a strange objection made to the new view of modern psychology. " If the soul," it is said, " is no entity, but the form of living and feeling substance, how can you speak of the importance of soul-life? The declaration that the soul is not a substance is equivalent to the statement that the soul does not exist."

Are we to say of a flame that it does not exist because we have ceased to believe in a special fire-stuff, the *phlogiston*, which some time ago was supposed to be a substance endowed with certain mysterious qualities that manifested themselves in the phenomenon of a flame? Is a flame not a reality also to us who know that fire is a special form of motion.

The old psychologists who to-day still form the

majority and of whom many will survive for a long time to come, look upon the new view with suspicion and say that it is a psychology without a soul, that is to say, without a soul consisting of soul-stuff. So the old physicists with the same plausibility might have objected to modern physicists that according to their conception, flames are fire without fire-stuff. And is it not strange that the old psychologists arraign the modern view as materialistic? Is not rather the old view materialistic, which conceives the spiritual as a substance—a kind of ethereal and purified matter? We however regard the new view as a redemption from the cruder and materialistic conception of soul-life.

The physicians of the soul are the ethical teachers of mankind. The task of a Confucius, of a Buddha, of a Christ, was the practical psychology of soul-preservation, and it is natural that experience should have taught them many important truths, which, as represented by every one of the great moral teachers, agree among themselves almost as much as arithmetic in English agrees with arithmetic in French and German. There can be no doubt that in many respects these ethical teachers, and more so their disciples, were greatly mistaken as to the nature of the soul. Nevertheless we inherited from them spiritual treasures more valuable than material wealth. By these spiritual treasures we mean chiefly the ethical truths which in the change of position caused by a progress of the science of the soul, remain intact and will find corrections in unessential points only.

The progress of psychology however is marked by the fact, that while the moral truths had to be looked upon in former times as unexplainable, and thus were

•

supposed to be of supernatural origin, we now can show their natural growth and base them upon a strictly scientific foundation.

Modern psychology must recognize the truth that it is developed from the old psychology. Although the new view stands in one essential point in vivid contrast with the old view, the new is the legitimate outcome from the old, not otherwise than modern chemistry is from the old phlogistum chemistry; and modern psychology has accordingly the right and the duty to enter upon the inheritance of the spiritual treasures gathered by its ancestors.

THE PSYCHOLOGICAL PROBLEM AND RELIGION.

By religion must be understood a conception of the universe that shall serve as a guide through life, as a regulative principle of conduct, as a basis of ethics. There are, accordingly, two elements in religion : the one of knowledge, the other of action. It is necessary that we have a knowledge of what the world is in which we live, and of what the laws are that consti- tute its cosmic order. This knowledge must find a practical application. It must encourage us to submit willingly to that which is necessary, however hard it may be, and to comply cheerfully with the demands that are founded in the nature of things.

Our view of the world for religious purposes need not be the accurate science of the naturalist ; a concep- tion of the universe in most general outlines is suffi- cient. Yet we must not forget that a clear and definite idea of the sociological law that regulates the relations between man and man and thus produces human society, is the most important and indispensable part of it. The laws of nature, in this sense, include the laws of spiritual, emotional, and intellectual soul-life.

Since natural laws remain the same, from eternity to eternity, it is thus apparent that religion has in it an element of immutability which makes it impossible that there can be more than one true religion. Yet

•

since man's knowledge of natural laws has to undergo a constant evolution, his religious ideals, consequently, also grow and expand step by step with his scientific progress. And religious progress has always lagged and still lags a little behind scientific progress ; for moral instructors are necessarily of a conservative turn of mind and slow to accept new truths which have not as yet passed through all the crucial tests of a critical examination.

Luther certainly was a progressive spirit, a bold and courageous man, who for the sake of truth feared neither the fagot of the inquisition nor the ban of the Pope. And yet how narrow-minded was Luther's opinion of his great countryman and contemporary, Copernicus. We read in Luther's *Table Talk:*

" Mention was made of a contemporary *astrologus* who wanted to prove that the earth moved and turned about, but not the Heavens, nor the Firmament, nor Sun, nor Moon ; just as when a person is seated in a wagon or on a boat and is in motion, and fancies he is sitting still and at rest while the earth and trees do seem to pass along and be in motion. But the whole matter is just this : whensoever a person means to be clever, he must perforce make up something of his own, which has to be the best that is, just as he makes it. This fool will upset the whole Science *Astronomia*. But the holy Scriptures tell us, Joshua bade the *Sun* stand still and not the Earth."

It is perhaps natural that every new discovery in science should apparently threaten to destroy the very basis of religion. But it turns out quite different as soon as men's minds get accustomed to the new conception of things. What has been destroyed by science, it then appears, was after all a childish error only. The world becomes greater and grander through an expansion of our conception of the world, and religion reaps the fruit of the scientist's work; religion is purified, spiritualized, and meliorated.

At the present time a new problem is again presented to religion—a problem which ought not and cannot be blinked by the clergy. This problem shakes our religious conceptions to their foundation, for it concerns the object and purpose of all religious work—the human soul. Religion being a guide through life and a regulative principle of conduct, what is it but a means devised for the salvation of souls?

Modern psychology throws a new light upon the nature of the soul. The soul was in former times and is still by many people conceived to be a mysterious being that is in possession of a certain stock of ideas. This mysterious being, the centre of man's spiritual existence, is called the Ego or the Me; it is the subject in the "I think," the agent that does the thinking; and the assumption of this ego has constituted the corner-stone of the most prominent philosophies since Descartes. Descartes pronounced the famous dictum *Cogito ergo sum*—"I think, therefore I am"; and this sentence has for two centuries been considered as the axiom of philosophy. Yet Kant objected to its so-called self-evidence. He denounced it as a fallacy. The existence cf the I or Ego, which is to be proved in the conclusion *ergo ego sum*, says Kant, has been assumed in the premise *ego cogito*.

Kant who owes so much to David Hume most likely followed a hint of the great Scottish thinker who said:

"As for me, whenever I contemplate what is inmost in what I call my own self, I always come in contact with such or such special perception as of cold, heat, light or shadow, love or hate, pleasure or pain. I never come unawares upon my mind existing

•

in a state void of perceptions : I never observe aught save perception. . . . . If any one, after serious reflection and without prejudices, thinks he has any other idea of himself, I confess that I can
reason no longer with him. The best I can say for him is that perhaps he is right no less than I, and that on this point our natures
are essentially different. It is possible that he may perceive something simple and permanent which he calls himself, but as for me
I am quite sure I possess no such principle."

Hume's view is a negation of the ego as a constant
and immutable centre of the soul. The soul is recognized as a combination of many ideas, and the ultimate
elements of soul-life are the simple feelings of nervous
irritations with the reflex-actions resulting therefrom.
The centre of our soul-life, the present state of consciousness or the subject of the act of thinking, is not at
all a mysterious agent distinct from the different ideas
that are thought, but it is the very idea itself that is
thought. The ego is not a constant and immutable centre, but it shifts about and brings into active play,
now this and now that concept or wish ; so that now
this and now another feeling, or thought, or desire is
awakened and stirred into prominence.

We distinguish between the ego, or the present
state of consciousness, in its continuity with former as
well as future states of consciousness, and the concept of our own personality. The idea of our own
personality is a complex conception of our bodily form,
of our past experiences, and of all our future intentions. It is comprised under the little pronoun " I ".
The idea of one's own personality is among all the
ideas of a man perhaps the most important one,
because of its constant recurrence. Yet we must
bear in mind that as an idéa it is not different from
any other idea, representing other personalities or
objects in the surrounding universe. If this con-

cept of one's own personality is stirred in a man in combination with the idea of a certain work which is carried out by his hands, the thought rises in his brain, "I am doing this," or "I am thinking this," "I am planning this." In such a case, accordingly, the ego of a man happens to coincide at the moment with the idea of his personality. At the next moment, however, he may have forgotten all about himself, i. e., about his personality; and his ego, i. e., the present state of his consciousness, may be wholly absorbed in his work. For instance, he is felling a tree and thinks, Will it fall to the right or to the left? His ego, in that case, resides in the contemplation of the tree before him which is combined with the consideration as to where it is likely to break down. There is not an ego which thinks of the tree in its special predicament, but the idea of the tree *is* the ego at that moment.

Lichtenberg very wittily remarked: "We should say, 'It thinks,' just as well as we say 'It lightens,' or 'It rains.' In saying *cogito* the philosopher goes too far if he translates it 'I think.'"

This conception of the nature of man's ego has been generally accepted by psychologists. The recent investigations of experimental psychology carried on in France by Charcot, Th. Ribot, Alfred Binet, and others, and of physiological psychology in Germany, inaugurated by Fechner, and perfected by Wundt and his school, have only served to corroborate the fundamental truth of the fact that there is no independent ego aside from the various thoughts of a man. Man's mind is a society of ideas, of which now the one and now the other constitutes his ego.

This discovery appears at first sight appalling. It

destroys, it would seem, the human soul itself, and it is not at all astonishing that the clergy are shocked, that they abhor the outcome of psychical researches and speak of the new psychology as "a psychology without a soul."

.It is not at all astonishing that people and especially the clergy are shocked; for the situation in our scientific conception of the soul is as thoroughly altered as our conception of the universe was in the times of Copernicus when the geocentric standpoint had to be abandoned. It took some time ere people could accustom themselves to the idea that they whirled through space with a rotatory motion of nineteen miles a second. When trying to think of it they became dizzy; Nature appeared to be deprived of her dignity, for if matters were as Copernicus said, all fixedness, all solidity and stability seemed lost forever in the material as well as in the moral world.

*   *   *

Modern psychology will influence the religious development of humanity in no less a degree than did modern astronomy. At first sight the new truth seems to destroy the soul itself; but it does not. It destroys a false view only of the ego.

To those who have not as yet fully grasped the new conception it appears difficult to renounce the ego-centric standpoint. However, a closer acquaintance with the modern solution of the problems of soul-life shows that instead of destroying religion they place it upon a firmer foundation than it ever before possessed.

The new psychology destroys the dualistic view of the soul. The soul has ceased to be something independent of and distinct from psychical activity.

The new view is monistic : it regards the soul as identical with its activity ; the human soul consists of man's feelings and thoughts, his fears and hopes, his wishes and ideals.

With the psychology of dualism an individualistic error is destroyed. The soul ceases to be identical with the ego, and the individual can no longer be considered as 'the little God upon earth ' for whom all things are created, who from the moment of birth will remain unchanged into eternity. He is no longer the mysterious agent behind the many different phenomena of psychic growth and soul-life. But while destroying this metaphysical superstition, modern psychology does not at all deprive the human soul of its worth, its dignity, and its nobility. The human soul remains as great and noble, as precious and holy, as it ever was. This wonderful organism of innumerable ideas, of sentiments, longings, hopes and fears, wishes, desires, aspirations, and ideals that reside within man's brain, is the highest and grandest phenomenon of nature upon earth ; and the moral aim of constantly improving and elevating the soul of man is rather helped than hindered by the new insight gained through psychological investigation.

Science never comes to destroy. On the contrary, it comes to purify. Thus the new psychology frees our conception of the human soul from an error which was the root of the belief in witchcraft and of many other evils. We must expect that a better understanding of the facts of psychology will be beneficial in all other fields of human activity and thought. The solution of the most important psychological problem will help us to solve other problems of a properly religious, social and socialistic, philosophical and scientific nature. It will advance humanity along the whole line of its brave army of progressive aspirers.

Truth seems to injure morality so long only as we have not as yet fully grasped the truth. Half truths may be dangerous, but the whole truth will ever serve to purify and to ameliorate. The psychical problem is a new crisis through which religion has to pass, and it is to be hoped that in the struggle between the old view and the modern view, between the popular and dualistic conception on the one side, and the scientific and monistic conception on the other side, religion will come out not only unbruised and unimpaired, but even greater and nobler and truer than it ever has been before. Religion, in so far as it will progress with the general progress of science, must lose all sectarianism, all anti-scientific narrowmindedness, and broaden into a cosmic religion. This cosmic religion will be a natural religion, because it is founded upon the laws of nature. It will be the Religion of Science, because its truth rests upon scientific evidence. It will be the only orthodox religion destined to become catholic among all thinking mankind—orthodox and catholic in the etymological and proper meaning of those words.

The time of this religion is not as yet come ; but come it must. At present we can only give encouragement not to shrink from investigation, but to inquire boldly into the basic problem of human existence, of moral ideals, and of religious aspirations.

Never fear truth, be it at first sight ever so alarming ; truth will always lead to higher planes, to grander views, to nobler deeds.

THE SOUL OF THE UNIVERSE.

IF we understand by the "soul of a thing" the formative principle which gave and still gives shape to it so as to make it the thing it is, we use the word soul in quite a legitimate yet in a broader sense than is usual.* The laws that rule the changes and formations in the world, are not material things, yet they are realities nevertheless. When we call them realities, we do not mean that they are entities which exist of themselves, nor are they mysterious powers outside of or behind things. They are in the things and are part of the things ; and it is through the mental process of abstraction that we acquire an insight into them.

The universe does not consist of matter alone, but of the relations among things, the forms of things, and their changes, also. The so-called laws are formulas only, abstracted from many instances and summing up their common features, so as to enable us to recognize in a general survey the regularity that prevails in the innumerable variations of all the particular and special cases. Although the relations among things and their forms are not palpable concrete objects, they are of greatest concern, for it is the form that makes a thing what it is. The form is the soul of the thing, and the possibility of all higher life, all intellectual existence, and all ethical aspirations depends upon the evolutions of forms. The practicability of ideals rests upon the

* As a rule we understand by "Soul" the form of action in feeling substance.

feasibility of a new arrangement of things, upon the possibility of a re-formation of ourselves as well as the world around us.

Taking this view of the importance of form and using the word soul to signify the formative factors of the various forms and their relations that have been evolved and constantly are evolving and re-evolving; we are naturally led to the conception of a soul of the universe. The soul of the universe we call God.

God, accordingly, is to be conceived as the law that shaped and is still shaping the world, that is forming and ever re-forming, evolving and ever re-evolving the universe. God is the factor that produced the solar system out of the concourse and whirl of the nebula. God is the factor that created vegetable and animal life upon earth. He is the light of mentality that flashes up in consciousness and finds its divinest expression in the clear thought of articulate speech. God is the moral law that binds human society and leads it to ever grander ideals, to always higher goals and aspirations. God in one word is the *sursum* that everywhere animates nature, the upward and forward tendency that manifests itself in the natural growth of things and in the progress of evolution.

If after millions of millenniums—long after the time when humanity, tired of life, has disappeared from the earth—the solar-system should break to pieces and be scattered as cosmic dust among the other solar systems of the universe, our present world would be destroyed, but its life would not be extinct. The scattered parts would roam about through cosmic space as comets. Some of such comets, rushing, the one upon the other, according to the law of gravitation, would blaze out in a gorgeous conflagration and produce a new centre of attraction for the cosmic dust that is to be gathered in the new-forming nebula. God does not die with the break-up of a solar system. The formative power of the universe will prove itself active again and again. It is a living presence indestructible and eternal. The formative law of the world is as eternal as are matter and energy.

In approaching the idea of God from this side we gain more than one advantage over all the methods employed by other philosophers and theologians. The greatest advantage I deem to be, that we need not give up the principle of Positivism (as explained in a former article of this book); we need not leave the secure and firm ground of positive facts. God as defined by us is no mere fancy of our mind, no creature of our imagination. He is a reality of actual life, a reality whose presence in the universe is as undeniable as the quality of gravity in matter, and whose manifestation is as demonstrable as the correctness of the rule $(a + b)^2 = a^2 + 2\,ab + b^2$ in mathematics.

We may mention points of secondary advantage also. By conceiving God as we do, we enter the domain of science and can state, according to scientific methods, what God is like, and what he is not like. We propose positive issues which can be investigated and discussed impartially *sine ira ac studio*. We can arrive at results based upon scientific inquiry, results that are beyond the trivial impositions of private opinions and personal authorities. Private opinions, suggestive thoughts, sermons full of sentiment, be they ever so ingenious and beautiful, are after all empty talk and vain repetitions.

Thus we get rid of the useless controversies with atheists as well as with dogmatists; the latter stating a-priori that by an act of special revelation they are in possession of the only true idea of God, and the former stating a-priori that there is no God, because they do not believe in the God of the dogmatists.

The objection may be made that God as here defined is no God, but a natural law ; that he is a principle of all-importance, but not necessarily a deity, as are the gods worshiped by Heathens and Mohammedans and Christians. To this objection we answer, that whether we name the creative, i. e., the formative, factor of the world God or not, whether we call it the soul of the universe or anything else, it remains as it is, and indeed it remains of equal all-importance. For it is that formative power, that creative principle, that life-giving law, in which, as St. Paul beautifully says, we live and move and have our being.

The words "God" and "Nature," as I use the terms, are not identical, yet I would say that God and Nature are inseparable, they are one indivisible whole.

When we speak of "Nature," we think of the world with reference to its physical laws chiefly. We see before our mental eye mountains and forests, minerals and plants, animals and men, and human institutions, from which the word Nature has been abstracted and which embraces them all. But if we speak of "God," we think chiefly of those facts of nature's life that are at the bottom of its evolution, of those facts that have produced all that is great and noble and good, for they are the conditions still of our ideal aspirations and make their realization possible.

God and Nature were formerly considered as two separate beings. We now look upon them as being one. God, accordingly, means Nature, or the Cosmos, or the All, or the Universe considered in its ethical importance, considered as that power which works out our future and as a matter of fact, constantly elevates, enhances, and ennobles life. This power is no unknown or unknowable thing ; the laws of its manifestation are perfectly ascertainable, and a society in which these laws are not obeyed, will hopelessly rot away and perish.

Nature and God, as we conceive them, are ideas equal in their circumscription. They cover the same field of facts ; yet they are different in so far as each of the two expressions makes different features more prominent.

The words "my house," "my residence," " my home," are three expressions, it may be, for the very same thing to a man who owns the building in which he lives. Yet each of these words makes a different feature more prominent without positively excluding the others. He says "My house" when thinking of it as the building he owns ; he says " My residence " when thinking of it as the rooms in which he resides, and he says "My home" when thinking of the seat of his family-relations and all the pleasant remembrances connected therewith. For different purposes we would employ different expressions, and yet in reality they may signify one and the same thing.

Thus also, God and Nature are one, and yet they are different. God is nature, and nature is God. Yet by nature we understand God's life and manifestations in their roughest outline only, in so far as they are palpable to every living being. By God, however, we mean more than the word Nature conveys ; we mean chiefly the still and grand and powerful workings of nature, almost invisible to mortal eye, yet plainly perceptible to the knowing, in their awful majesty and holiness.

*   *   *

We have after a long consideration adopted, or rather re-adopted, the word God as a signification of this highest reality in the world, for there is no conception of God, be it ever so pagan and anthropomorphic, that does not contain a noticeable endeavor to express this our idea of the world-soul, of the creative principle of the cosmos and the life of the cosmos. The idea of God signifies at the same time in every religion the standard of morality and the highest authority, which must be obeyed. God is that law in life which visits the iniquity of the evil-doer unto the third and fourth generation, and which blesses the righteous unto the thousandth generation. And in this respect our conception of God is not at all different from that of former times. Those among freethinkers who are pleased to call themselves atheists, lack a proper word and often they do not even feel the need of one for expressing the authority or norm according to which they regulate their rules of conduct. If there is a difference of importance between our view and that of dogmatic orthodoxy, it is this, that the conception of God as proposed by us from the standpoint of a positive philosophy, is free from all anthropomorphism.

Theologians claim that this highest reality of the world, the soul of the universe, its formative law, must be supposed to have been fashioned by a great personal being, by an omnipotent God. But in this they show their misapprehension of the independence and inherent necessity of natural and of formal laws. They are like children that look upon their teacher as the author of the multiplication-table. Some one, they think, must have arranged and fixed these tables, that such order and harmony and proportion could be in them. Theologians think there is a God above the God of the Universe who created the divinity of the Cosmos. But the divinity of the Cosmos, its order and harmony, is a God so divine that he cannot have been created or produced.

We are in no need of such an hypothesis. We can better do without the assumption of a supernatural arithmetician, who so arranged the formal laws and dictated them to the atoms that they would obey them. For we know that the formal laws are necessary in themselves. They could not be otherwise than they are. Their harmony is intrinsic and immanent. The order which they naturally produce cannot have been imposed upon them by the ukase of a personal master, be he ever so great. There is no way out of this, and therefore the idea of a personal God, of an extramundane author of the immanent God as the soul of the universe, is untenable.

*   *   *

What is a person but a human individual? And what is an individual but a thing which, if broken or divided, ceases to be that which it is? A quartz-crystal is an individual; if you crush it, it ceases to be a crystal, and is mere grains of sand. A plant may, but need not, be an individual. There are plants that you can cut in twain, and each part represents all the characteristic features of that plant. Some plants are individuals, and if divided, will grow into individuals again; each part will continue to grow and perfect itself. Most animals are individuals, but there are some that are not individuals, some that can be divided and will continue to live. Amœbas, properly speaking, are not individuals; they are lumps of living matter—mere specimens of animal life.

A person is the highest type of an individual; it is an individual that in its activity does not depend upon simple reflex-motions only, but can regulate its actions with the assistance of former experiences and under consideration of probable results. Thus a person is an individual that should not and need not follow the impulse of the moment, but can look freely around into the past as well as the future. We can, accordingly, make a person responsible for his actions, we can expect him to use the advantages which he enjoys. In short, a person is an individual endowed with freedom of action and moral responsibility.

Every individual, and more so every person, possesses a special idiosyncrasy; an individual is of a particular form and limited in space and time. Every individual at the same time possesses a soul of its own; its formative principle makes a unit of it, it organizes it into a microcosm. The microcosm of individual existence, it is true, represents the order of the macrocosm upon a smaller scale. And it could not be different, for every individual has grown out of the cosmic universe. How can it be otherwise than created in the image of the whole cosmos? Man, being a microcosm, has a right to shape his idea of God, of the soul of the macrocosm, after his own likeness, for the human soul cannot but be a part, an exponent, a revelation of the soul that pervades the All. Yet in fashioning our idea of God after the pattern of our own soul, we must be careful not to select those characteristic features which are individual and belong to the limitedness of our existence. We must select those which are not limited, those which show the

universality of God; we must not select the properly
human, but the divine, not the transient, but the eternal, not the fleeting and unstable, but the immutable,
the permanent and the everlasting. The blossom is a
revelation of the whole tree, so is every leaf; but the
blossom is a more perfect revelation. Says the blossom : "I am made in the image of the tree. Accordingly the tree is one huge blossom. He is just like
me and not like the leaves." Let us beware of such
narrowness.

God, as I conceive him to be, is not less than a
person, but more than a person. The frailty of personality does not apply to him; there is no limitation,
no individuality, no distinct idiosyncrasy about him.

He is not (as according to my conception every
person is) one special form and combination, yet he is
the universality of law, inflexible, immutable, eternal.
You can adapt yourself to him, but you can never
adapt him to yourself. The heathenish custom to
attempt an adaptation of God to ourselves is not yet
extinct in Christianity.

Certainly, the Universe is not mere force, but is
force ruled by law. I find that "Law" and "Force"
are often called blind by naturalists. Natural laws are
called blind, I suppose, because they allow of no exception whatever; because they do not adapt themselves to circumstances, as persons might do. But is
not the expression "the blind laws of nature" nevertheless a contradiction, or at least an inadequateness
of simile? If natural laws do not adapt themselves to
us, we must in our turn adapt ourselves to them. But
is that any reasonable pretence for calling them blind?
Certainly not; for they make it possible that we need
not grope blindly about; being irrefragable, they throw

light upon natural phenomena and thus become our
guides and teach us, how we can adapt ourselves to
nature.

We welcome the idea that God is no person, but a
law; not a being adaptable to circumstances, but an
irrefragable authority ; no deified egotism but the omnipotent power of All-existence! This idea is the
republican conception of theology which can conceive
of order and of law without a Prince, and of religion
without the fetish of anthropomorphism.

We have no objection to representing the moral
law of the Universe to which we have to conform, as
a person.   We may compare it to a father, and with
Christ call it "Our Father," just as we like to speak
of Mother Nature.   But we wish to have it understood
that this expression is a simile only—a simile which,
if carried out, will lead to serious misconceptions.

INDEX.

SUPPLEMENTARY NOTE.

An excellent help for the study of Physiological Psychology are the Brain Models of Dr. Auzoux, Rue de Vaugirard 56. Price of the large one (in Paris) 300 Francs. I have found Dr. Auzoux's models of clastic Anatomy far superior to those of any other manufacture.

PUBLICATIONS OF THE OPEN COURT PUBLISHING CO.

169-175 LA SALLE STREET, CHICAGO, ILLINOIS.

THREE LECTURES ON THE SCIENCE OF

LANGUAGE. By PROF. F. MAX MÜLLER.
With a Supplement "MY PREDECESSORS." Cloth, 75 Cents.

THREE INTRODUCTORY LECTURES ON

THE SCIENCE OF THOUGHT. By F.
MAX MÜLLER. (London Publishers: Longmans,
Green, & Co.)

1. The Simplicity of Language; 2. The Identity of Language and Thought;
and 3. The Simplicity of Thought. Cloth, 75 Cents.

EPITOMES OF THREE SCIENCES.

1. COMPARATIVE PHILOLOGY. By PROF. H. OLDENBERG.
2. COMPARATIVE PSYCHOLOGY. By PROF. J. JASTROW.
3. OLD TESTAMENT HISTORY. By PROF. C. H. CORNILL. Cloth,
75 Cents.

THE PSYCHIC LIFE OF MICRO-ORGAN-

ISMS. By ALFRED BINET. (London Publishers: Longmans, Green, & Co.) Authorised Translation. Cloth, 75 Cents.

ON DOUBLE CONSCIOUSNESS. New Studies

in Experimental Psychology. By ALFRED BINET.
Price, 50 Cents.

THE PSYCHOLOGY OF ATTENTION. By TH.

RIBOT. (London Publishers: Longmans, Green,
· & Co.) Authorised Translation. Cloth, 75 Cents.

THE DISEASES OF PERSONALITY. By TH.

RIBOT. Authorised translation. Cloth, 75 Cents. (Ready about
April 15th, 1891.)

WHEELBARROW. ARTICLES AND DISCUS-

SIONS ON THE LABOR QUESTION.
C'oth, $1.00

FUNDAMENTAL PROBLEMS. By DR. PAUL

CARUS. (London Publishers: Longmans, Green,
& Co.) Cloth, $1.00.

THE ETHICAL PROBLEM. By DR. PAUL CARUS.

Three Lectures Delivered at the Invitation of the Board of Trustees before the Society for Ethical Culture of Chicago, in June, 1890. Cloth, 50 Cents.

THE IDEA OF GOD. By DR. PAUL CARUS.

A disquisition upon the development of the idea of God. Paper, 15 Cents.

THE LOST MANUSCRIPT. A Novel. By GUSTAV

FREYTAG. Authorized translation. Elegantly bound, $4.00.

THE OPEN COURT.

A WEEKLY MAGAZINE

—OF—

SCIENCE AND PHILOSOPHY.

——PUBLISHED BY——

THE OPEN COURT PUB. CO.

CONTAINS CONTRIBUTIONS AND ESSAYS BY

PROF. MAX MÜLLER.	GEN. M. M. TRUMBULL.
GEO. J. ROMANES.	PROF. ERNST MACH.
PROF E. D. COPE.	MONCURE D. CONWAY.
ERNST HAECKEL.	DR. FELIX L. OSWALD.
ALFRED BINET.	PROF. AUGUST WEISMANN.
TH. RIBOT.	PROF. JOSEPH JASTROW
PROF. EWALD HERING.	CARUS STERNE.
LUCIEN ARREAT.	CARL HEINRICH CORNILL.
PROF. GEO. VON GIZYCKI.	PROF. H. OLDENBERG.
PROF. W. PREYER.	LUDWIG NOIRE.
WM. M. SALTER.	AND OTHERS.

The current numbers of *The Open Court* contain valuable original articles from the pens of distinguished investigators and *littérateurs*. Accurate and authorised translations are made in Philosophy, Science, and Criticism from the periodical literature of Continental Europe, and reviews of all noteworthy recent investigations are presented. It is the pronounced object of *The Open Court* to HARMONISE RELIGION WITH SCIENCE; and the philosophical problems that bear upon this important question are editorially treated in its columns. A wide range of discussion is allowed all who will participate.

The Open Court is neither exclusive nor sectarian, but liberal : it seeks to aid the efforts of all scientific and progressive people in the churches and out of them, toward greater knowledge of the world in which we live, and the moral and practical duties it requires.

The Open Court does not understand by religion any creed or dogmatic belief, but man's world-conception in so far as it serves him for a regulatio n of his conduct. Although opposed to irrational orthodoxy and narrow bigotry, it does not attack the properly religious element of our various religions. The religion of *The Open Court* is the Religion of Science, that is the Religion of verified and verifiable truth ; and there being but one truth, not two or several contradictory truths, *The Open Court* stands on the ground of Monism— namely, a unitary conception of the world.

TERMS:

Two dollars a year throughout the Postal Union ; Australia, New Zealand, and Tasmania, $2.50. Single Copies, 5 Cents.

A NUMBER OF ARTICLES

—— ON ——

BIOLOGY, PSYCHOLOGY, PHILOLOGY, ETC.,

that have appeared in

THE OPEN COURT.

——— ——

MEMORY AS A GENERAL FUNCTION OF ORGANIZED MATTER. Prof. EWALD HERING, of the University of Prague. A Series.

WHAT MIND IS. Prof. E. D. COPE.

THE PSYCHIC LIFE OF MICRO-ORGANISMS. A Controversy. G. J. ROMANES, LL. D., F. R. S., and ALFRED BINET.

ON RETROGRESSION IN ANIMAL AND VEGETABLE LIFE. A Series. Prof. AUGUST WEISMANN, of Freiburg.

HYPNOTISM AND MODERN PSYCHOLOGY. By Dr. J. LUYS, Physician at the Charity Hospital, Paris.

MAN AS A MICROCOSM. By CARUS STERNE, of Berlin.

SEXUAL CHARACTERISTICS. By FELIX L. OSWALD, M. D. A Series.

THE DOUBLE PERSONALITY AND DOUBLE CONSCIOUSNESS OF HYSTERICAL INDIVIDUALS. Original Psychological Studies. ALFRED BINET, of Paris. A Series.

THE PSYCHOLOGY OF ATTENTION. By TH. RIBOT. A. Series.

THE STUDY OF SANSKRIT. Prof. II. OLDENBERG, of Berlin. A Series.

ASPECTS OF MODERN PSYCHOLOGY. By JOSEPH JASTROW, Ph. D. A series, including "Psychology in Germany," "Psychology in France, Italy, Belgium, and Switzerland," and "Psychology in England and the United States.

THE SPECIFIC ENERGIES OF THE NERVOUS SYSTEM. By Prof. EWALD HERING, of the University of Prague. A Series.

GOETHE ON EVOLUTION. Prof. ERNST HAECKEL.

REPORTS OF THE GIFFORD LECTURES (1890). Prof. MAX MÜLLER.

THE ORIGIN OF LANGUAGE. LUDWIG NOIRÉ. A Series.

THE ORIGIN OF REASON. T. BAILEY SAUNDERS. A Series.

THE DISEASES OF PERSONALITY. TH. RIBOT. A Series.

●

THE MONIST.

A NEW QUARTERLY MAGAZINE

OF

PHILOSOPHY, SCIENCE, RELIGION, AND SOCIOLOGY.

The first three numbers contained the following articles :

CHICAGO :

THE OPEN COURT PUBLISHING CO.

Per Copy, 50 Cents. Yearly, $2.00. ,
In Cloth, 75 Cents. In Cloth, $3.00.

LONDON :

Per Copy, 2s. 6d. MESSRS. WATTS & CO., Yearly, 9s. 6d.
In Cloth, 3s. 6d. In Cloth, 13s. 8d.
17 Johnson's Court, Fleet Street, E. C.